J.A. JANCE

DEAD TO RIGHTS

A Joanna Brady Mystery

AVON BOOKS ◆ NEW YORK

VISIT OUR WEBSITE AT
http://AvonBooks.com

AVON BOOKS
A division of
The Hearst Corporation
1350 Avenue of the Americas
New York, New York 10019

Copyright © 1996 by J. A. Jance
Interior design by Kellan Peck
Library of Congress Catalog Card Number: 96-24634
ISBN: 0-380-97394-4

Library of Congress Cataloging in Publication Data:

Jance, Judith A.
Dead to rights / by J.A. Jance.
p. cm.
I. Title.
PS3560.A44D4   1996   96-24634
813'.54—dc20   CIP

First Avon Books Hardcover Printing: October 1996

AVON TRADEMARK REG. U.S. PAT. OFF. AND IN OTHER COUNTRIES, MARCA REGISTRADA,
HECHO EN U.S.A.

Printed in the U.S.A.

FIRST EDITION

QM   10 9 8 7 6 5 4 3 2 1

This book is dedicated to M.A.D.D., Mothers Against Drunk Driving, for making possible the constructive use of pain and anger. It is also dedicated to W.I.C.S., Widowed Information Consultation Services of King County, for providing a place for the mending of broken hearts.

DEAD TO RIGHTS

Prologue

HAL and Bonnie Morgan wended their way through the crowded, overheated movie-theater lobby into the cool air of a midwinter Phoenix night. Once outside the theater doors, the aroma of popcorn quickly gave way to a haze of smoke from a dozen hastily lit cigarettes. As they moved across the open-air patio, Bonnie reached out, took her husband's hand, and squeezed it.

In response, Hal leaned toward her. "The name's Bond," he whispered, "James Bond." Bonnie and Hal had just finished seeing *Golden Eye* for the third time. Hal's imitation of Pierce Brosnan's accent and delivery was so dead-on that Bonnie giggled aloud.

"You're good enough that they should have made you the new James Bond," she told him.

A passion for James Bond movies was something the two of them had shared in common when they met twenty years earlier. And now, after a celebratory dinner in honor of their nineteenth wedding anniversary, they were on their way back to the Hyatt Regency two blocks away. They came to

Phoenix each February to celebrate both Saint Valentine's Day and their wedding anniversary. Once a year, they would splurge and pretend, for that one evening at least, that they, too, were a pair of carefree snowbirds.

On their anniversary trips they made a conscious effort to put aside all day-to-day concerns. Hal would do his best to forget whatever crisis might be brewing in the small trailer park he managed up in Wickenburg while Bonnie turned her back on the petty small-town grievances simmering in the Wickenburg Post Office where she worked as a part-time clerk. For that single day, they concentrated on each other and on the miracle that had brought them together in the first place, one that had given them the blessing of nineteen wonderful years.

Riding down on the outdoor escalator, Bonnie breathed deeply. As the pall of cigarette smoke dissipated, a sweet, delicate scent permeated the air. "Smell those orange blossoms," she said. "It's like every year God gives us my wedding bouquet all over again, except now it's free. We don't even have to pay for it."

Bonnie had carried a bouquet of orange blossoms to their Valentine's Day wedding ceremony in front of a curmudgeonly Justice of the Peace in Palm Springs. They had gone to Palm Springs to marry in hopes Bonnie's recently divorced ex-husband wouldn't get wind of the ceremony and try to screw things up.

"You were a very beautiful bride," Hal said with a sudden catch in his throat. He was still as smitten with his wife as he had been the first day he laid eyes on her, as she had walked along the beach with her little niece and nephew in tow.

Before meeting Bonnie, Hal Morgan had already had a

disastrous first marriage blow up in his face. In the lonely aftermath of his divorce, he had thrown himself into his work as a police officer with single-minded dedication. He had been the one who always volunteered to take those unpopular Sunday-afternoon and holiday shifts. What little spare time was left to him he had spent prowling around dusty used-book stores.

From the moment he and Bonnie had struck up a casual conversation outside a snow-cone stand, all that had changed. Bonnie had come into his life bringing both her radiant smile and her sunny disposition, either of which would have been enough to melt Hal Morgan's heart. Her spontaneous joy of living had caught him up and carried him along like the current in a swiftly moving babbling brook. Even now he sometimes couldn't help but marvel at his great good fortune.

"You were beautiful then," he added, almost as an afterthought. "And nineteen years later, you still are."

Bonnie looked up at him and smiled. As usual, Hal Morgan's heart seemed to skip a beat.

They reached the intersection of Third and Van Buren just as the light changed from red to green. At nine o'clock at night, downtown traffic was almost nonexistent. Still, Hal checked in both directions before they stepped off the curb.

There were a few headlights coming toward them in the right-hand, west-bound lanes, but they were a block away, stopped at the next light as Hal led Bonnie into the marked crosswalk. They were in the middle of the street when Hal heard the squeal of rubber as a car came careening around the corner, coming the wrong way on Third and then skidding into a wrenching right-hand turn onto Van Buren. The speeding vehicle, a late-model full-sized Chevy pickup of some kind, bounced over the edge of the sidewalk and then slid, spinning out of control, into the intersection.

Hal jumped back out of the way and tried to pull Bonnie with him, but he was too late. One moment Hal was holding Bonnie's hand; the next she was yanked from his grasp. He stood there frozen in stunned silence as she flew away from him, up into the air, seeming to float above him like a rag doll someone had tossed out of the window of a moving vehicle. The pickup was still doing a 180 when Bonnie Morgan started back to earth. She crashed to the pavement just to the left of the spinning truck, hitting the ground back-first with an awful, bone-crushing impact and then disappearing completely beneath the body of the truck as it finally came to rest, landing on its side.

Almost at once there were horns honking. Within seconds a crowd gathered out of nowhere, but Hal Morgan heard nothing, saw no one. He vaulted forward, reaching the truck at almost the same time it stopped moving. Several passersby, most of them fellow moviegoers who had followed Hal and Bonnie down the escalator, joined him an instant later.

The engine was still running.

"Turn the damned thing off before it catches fire," someone shouted. "For God's sake, turn it off!"

Knowing the danger, Hal did what years of police training had taught him. He scrambled in through the smashed passenger side window, into a fog of spilled booze and across a seat slick with whiskey-laced vomit. The driver, cushioned by the now deflated air bag, was still strapped inside.

"Whazza matter?" he was asking. "What the hell happened?"

Ignoring him, Hal managed to reach across the seat far enough to turn the key in the switch. Then he clambered back outside.

The swelling crowd stood together in stricken silence. All that was visible of Bonnie Morgan were the graceful fingers of a single hand protruding from underneath the pickup's crushed driver's side. On one of those fingers the gold from Bonnie's wedding band glinted in the glow of a streetlight.

It was then Hal noticed there was someone standing next to him—a young black man in torn jeans and a ragged shirt with a baseball cap perched on a thicket of dreadlocks.

"Help me," Hal choked. "Maybe we can lift it off her."

"Sure thing, man," the kid said. "No problem."

As the two of them set to work, several of the passersby joined in. They knelt together alongside the fallen pickup. Then, on the count of three, they lifted it, rolling it back upright, pushing it onto its wheels. Uncovered, Bonnie Morgan lay inert. In the lamp-lit dusk, a thin dribble of blood, tinted purple by the mercury vapor lights, leaked out of the corner of her mouth and ran downward into her ear and hair.

Hal rushed to his wife's side and threw himself down on the pavement beside her. As he took her wrist to check for a pulse, a hushed silence once again drifted over the crowd of onlookers. That was broken suddenly by a frantic pounding from inside the truck.

"Hey, somebody!" the trapped driver yelled. "Lemme out! The door's stuck. I can't get it open. Get me out of here."

Gently, as if the bone might shatter, Hal Morgan placed his wife's still wrist back where he had found it. Then, with a groan that was more rage than anything else, he sprang to his feet and headed for the truck once more. Of all the people gathered around at that moment, only the kid in the torn jeans read the murderous look on the other man's face.

"Leave him be, man," the kid said, taking hold of Hal's

shoulder, forcibly restraining him. "Let the cops take care of the stupid jerk."

Seemingly on command, the cops showed up just then, arriving in a cacophony of sirens and a blinding flash of lights. Hal barely noticed. His whole being remained fixed on his wife's crushed body and on the spot of pavement where the trickle of blood had become a puddle.

Burying his face in his hands, Hal subsided once again next to his wife's body. The ambulance and fire trucks might be coming, but he knew that whatever aid they brought would be too little, too late. Bonnie Genevieve Morgan—Hal's beloved Bonnie Jean—was dead at the age of fifty-two.

A uniformed police officer burst through the crowd. "What's going on here?" he demanded. "What happened?"

"He killed her," Hal Morgan murmured brokenly into his cupped hands. "That rotten, drunken son of a bitch murdered her."

"Are you okay?" the cop asked. "Were you hit too?"

"I'm fine," Hal insisted. "He hit *her*, not me."

Reassured, the cop turned away and fixed his attention on Bonnie. As he did so, Hal tried to rise to his feet, but there was something holding him down, some unfamiliar weight on his shoulder that made it almost impossible to stand. Grunting with effort, he managed to struggle himself upright. Only then did he realize that the extra weight came from a hand gripping his shoulder—a hand that belonged to the kid with the torn jeans and dreadlocks. Tears streamed down the young man's face. He seemed incapable of letting Hal go.

"I'm sorry about your wife, man," he managed to say. "I'm really sorry."

Hal nodded. "Thanks," he said. "Thanks for everything."

When he said thanks, he meant it, because he knew in his

soul that had it not been for the restraining weight of that powerful grip, Hal Morgan, too, might have killed someone that night. If the kid hadn't held him back when Hal started for the truck, the son of a bitch of a driver would have been dead, too. Right then and there. Of injuries inflicted after the incident itself.

Feeling suddenly weak and shaky, Hal limped back over to the edge of the street and sank down on the cold concrete curb. He sat there quietly, knowing all too well what would come next. There would be a world of inquiry—of investigators and paperwork, of questions and answers. In the long run, none of it would make a single whit of difference. Whatever the cops decided in determining how to fix the blame, it wouldn't bring Bonnie back. She was dead. Gone forever. Nothing any well-meaning cop could do would restore her to him.

As Hal sat there with unnoticed tears streaming down his face, an uncontrollable tremor assailed his whole body. Another concerned police officer hurried over to him. Kneeling beside him, the cop shone a flashlight into Hal Morgan's eyes.

"How did it happen?" the officer asked.

"The guy creamed us," Hal answered through chattering teeth. "The bastard in the pickup was driving the wrong way up Third. He came screaming around the corner on two wheels and smashed into us right in the middle of the crosswalk."

"Officer Stephens told me you weren't hurt, but are you sure you're okay?"

Hal Morgan shook his head. Already the finality of it was soaking in. "No," he groaned. "I'm not okay. Bonnie's dead. I don't think I'll ever be okay again."

1

"MOM," Jenny Brady shouted, pounding on the bathroom door. "Come quick."

Joanna Brady, half-dressed in her slip, bra, and panty hose, stood in front of the steamy bathroom mirror. A mascara brush was poised in her hand. Jenny's frantic pounding startled her enough that she left a smudge of mascara under her green eyes as she hurried to throw open the door. "What is it?"

"Tigger did it again."

"Did what?"

"Got into another porcupine. Look," Jenny said, kneeling next to the panting dog. "He's got quills all over his face, even in his tongue this time."

Joanna knelt beside her nine-year-old daughter to examine the injured dog. Tigger's mixed bloodlines, half golden retriever/half pit bull—had left him looking more comical than fierce. He had the blunt nose and the white eye patch of a pit bull combined with a lush, flowing golden-retriever coat. Now he stood there, patient and dejected, letting Joanna study him. His head resembled a pincushion, only the pins in question were three-to-four inches long and a quarter of an inch wide. Threads of bloody drool dangled from his mouth and dripped onto the tile floor.

"What about Sadie?" Joanna asked, referring to their other dog, a female bluetick hound.

"Sadie's fine." Jenny struggled to hold back her tears. "She's eating and Tigger can't, so I brought him inside."

Joanna Brady, sheriff of Cochise County in the far-southeastern corner of the state of Arizona, glanced at her watch and then back into her daughter's blue eyes. There wasn't much time. The last thing she needed was some new crisis on the home front as she set off to fight her department's budget wars. Still, the seriousness of the quills embedded in Tigger's nose precluded any delay.

"That was good thinking," Joanna said, touching Jenny's shoulder and trying to reassure her troubled child that she had done the right thing. "If we hurry, I'll have time to drop him off at Doc Buckwalter's on my way to the board of supervisors meeting. Do you think you can load him into the Blazer while I finish getting dressed?"

Jenny nodded wordlessly and started toward the kitchen, with the dog trailing obediently at her heels. "And, Jenny?"

Jenny stopped and turned back to her mother. The tears were flowing now, sliding down her cheeks, dripping onto her blouse. It wounded Joanna, made her heart hurt, that Jenny had tried so hard to keep her tears from showing.

"What?" Jenny asked.

"Make a bed for him in the backseat with some of those old clean blankets from the laundry room," Joanna cautioned. "Otherwise he's likely to drip all over the carpet."

Nodding again, Jenny set off.

The new Blazer Joanna drove was, after all, a county-owned vehicle. She wasn't eager to explain to the guys in Motor Pool how bloodstains found in the back of her vehicle came from a dog so terminally dumb as to go after a porcupine—most likely the same one—for the third time in as many months.

Back in the bathroom, Joanna repaired the mascara damage and ran a brush through her red hair. It was getting too long, she noticed. She'd have to have it cut soon, although she had delayed going back to the beauty shop because she was still irked about Jenny's awful and unauthorized permanent.

While Joanna had been off in Phoenix attending a police officer training school, her mother, Eleanor Lathrop, had engineered a trip to Helene's Salon of Hair and Beauty for her granddaughter as a "surprise" for Joanna—with disastrous results. Jenny's fine blond hair had been chemically fried to a crisp in the process. Two months later, she still looked as though she had put her finger in an electrical socket. And although Joanna held her mother primarily responsible, she was still peeved at Helen Barco, the beautician, as well.

Hurrying into the bedroom, Joanna grabbed clothes from the closet. Since most of the day would be taken up with meetings with the Cochise County Board of Supervisors, she was tempted to leave her body armor at home. Supervisor meetings were held in an overheated conference room, and the soft body armor always made the heat that much worse. But Joanna was a sheriff who was determined to lead by example. Since she was trying to convince her officers of the advisability of wearing bullet-resistant vests whenever they were on duty, she put hers on as well. Besides, considering the fact that the new sheriff's honeymoon period with the board was already over, maybe wearing body armor to the meeting wasn't all that bad an idea.

Jenny came back into the bedroom and dropped onto the bed. Her eyes were still red, but she was no longer crying. "Can I go with you to drop Tigger off?" she asked.

Joanna shook her head. "I don't think so, sweetie. Look at the time. If I take you by the clinic and then to school, we'll both end up being late. If you want to, though, you can ride with me as far as the bus stop."

Joanna thought her reply was perfectly reasonable. Jenny's response was not. "I hate school!" she lashed out with an unexpected vehemence that took Joanna by surprise. "And I hate meetings, too! You always have to go to meetings. You're always in a hurry!"

With that, Jenny turned and stormed out of the room, slamming the door behind her. Joanna hurried after her. "Jenny . . ."

"I don't want to ride with you!" Jenny yelled angrily from the laundry-room door. "I'll ride my bike to the bus stop, and I don't care if you take Tigger to the vet or not. Just leave him here if you want to. That way you won't be late."

Stunned by her daughter's angry outburst, Joanna started with a conciliatory "Jenny," but by then the child was beyond hearing. She had slammed the outside door as well, rattling the window, and was already halfway across the yard on her way to the old farm equipment shed that served as a garage.

Fighting back tears herself, Joanna followed Jenny as far as the door, but she didn't open it. Through the windowpane she watched her daughter push her bike out of the garage, mount it at a run, and then go charging up the road, disappearing finally as the road meandered off through a forest of bleak, winter-weary mesquite. Watching the speeding bike, it seemed to Joanna as though all of Jenny's pent-up anger and grief were localized in those stiffly set shoulders and in the furiously pumping little legs.

No doubt, Jennifer Ann Brady had every right to be angry. Her father was dead. Andrew Roy Brady had fallen victim to a drug lord's hit man some four months earlier. For a nine-year-old, this was a heavy burden to bear. In the past few months, Joanna had done some serious reading on the subject of children and the grief process. The experts had all warned that children often coped with their pain by doing a certain amount of "acting out." The problem was that Joanna felt as though she was always the target of that acting out. She had searched the reading material for possible suggestions in dealing with her troubled daughter. The difficulty lay in the fact that helpful suggestions from experts seldom took into consideration the fact that the parents were grieving too. Had Joanna been at the top of her own form, Jenny's periodic outbursts might not have been that bad. As things stood, Joanna's own grieving process was far from over.

"Damn you anyway, Andy," Joanna mumbled as she hurried back to the bedroom to stuff her feet into a pair of shoes that had somehow migrated under the bed. "Why did you have to go and die and leave me holding the bag?"

Joanna was glad there was no one to hear when she talked aloud to Andy that way. He had been a Cochise County deputy and a candidate for sheriff at the time of his death back in September. After his death, Joanna had been persuaded to run for the office of sheriff in his stead. The campaign and the election had happened while she was still in such a fog of grief that Joanna barely remembered them. Now, though, as she tried to cope with both the complexities of her new job and the difficulties of being a newly single parent, there were times when she found herself taking Andy to task for leaving her to manage alone in the face of such daunting responsibilities.

Outside, the late-January chill of Arizona's high desert country had put a thin layer of frost over the Blazer's windshield. It scraped off easily enough with one or two swipes of the wipers. A steady wind was blowing up out of the Gulf of Mexico, with the wind-chill factor making it seem far colder than the forty-five degrees the thermometer indicated. The sky up over the Mule Mountains behind High Lonesome Ranch was a deep, cloudless blue.

As the Blazer started down the rutted dirt road, Sadie was coming back from accompanying Jenny on the ride down to the end of the road, where a school bus would pick her up sometime within the next ten minutes. Without the challenge of a race with Tigger, Sadie made only a halfhearted attempt to follow the Blazer, giving up the chase long before Joanna reached High Lonesome Road. Usually Joanna would stop half a mile down the road and order the dogs back into the yard, but for Sadie, alone that morning, all joy seemed to have gone out of the game.

Even the dogs are having a bad day, Joanna thought with a grim smile.

At the intersection where High Lonesome Ranch's mile-long private road met up with the county-maintained High Lonesome Road, Joanna spotted Jenny. She had chained her bike to one of the uprights on the cattle guard and was standing, with her arms crossed tightly across her chest, facing into the blowing wind.

She looked so small, lost, and lonely standing there all by herself that Joanna's arms ached with the need to comfort her, to heal the hurt somehow. Tigger seemed to have the same inclination. As they drove up to where Jenny stood, the dog sat up in the backseat and whined forlornly.

Joanna pulled over next to the child and rolled down the window. Jenny stared down at her feet and began kicking rocks.

"Don't forget, you're supposed to go to Grandma Brady's after Brownies this afternoon," Joanna said. "I'll pick you up from there as soon as I get off work."

"Okay," Jenny acknowledged without looking up.

"Aren't you going to come kiss me good-bye?" Joanna asked.

Jenny shook her head and continued to kick pebbles.

"I'm sorry we had a disagreement," Joanna ventured, hoping an apology would put things right for both of them. Jenny relented, but only a little.

"It's okay," she mumbled. "You'd better go. You'll be late."

"I love you," Joanna said.

But Jenny wasn't ready to unbend enough to respond in kind. "Here comes the bus," she said. "I'd better go, too. Take good care of Tigger." With that she was gone, turning from her mother with her frizzy disaster of a permanent standing almost straight up in the stiff breeze.

"Have a nice day," Joanna murmured behind her out the open window of the truck. It seemed to her that the rocks and windblown ocotillo paid more attention to her words than Jenny did. Joanna waited long enough to see Jenny safely on the school bus before she drove off.

As Joanna put the Blazer back in gear and started down the road in a moving cloud of red dust kicked up by the big yellow school bus, she had a prickly sense of déjà vu, although it wasn't exactly the same. Joanna had been far older than Jenny when her own father died—fifteen to Jenny's nine, but the situation had been eerily similar. It had been a chill winter evening and she had been walking home from the ballpark along Arizona Street in a driving rainstorm. Her mother, Eleanor, had come looking for her. Eleanor had driven along beside Joanna, pleading with her to get in the car.

For the first time, Joanna remembered that Eleanor had been crying as she begged her daughter to please just get in the car.

Fourteen years later, Joanna had no idea what the exact origins of the quarrel had been that night or what had driven Joanna out into the awful weather. She was sure, though, that it had happened within a few months of Big Hank Lathrop's death. Now she found herself wondering if she and her mother hadn't been locked in the same kind of battle she and Jenny were dealing with now. Maybe part of the wedge between Eleanor and Joanna, the thing that had kept them at loggerheads for years, was the sudden violent death of a husband and father. D.H. Lathrop and Andy Brady had both been wiped out of existence without a moment's warning, leaving behind an awful void, to be filled by years of shed tears and hurt feelings.

For the first time in all those years, Joanna Brady felt a twinge of guilt as she wondered if it was possible that she had been as hard on Eleanor as Jenny was being on her.

As the school bus turned left and started down Double Adobe Road, Tigger whined and began pacing back and forth in the seat, wanting to follow the bus. The sound of his whine burst through Joanna's bubble of introspection and brought her abruptly back to the present.

"Sit," Joanna ordered. Obediently, the dog sat and then,

with a sigh, finally settled back down on the blanket.

Off High Lonesome and heading west on Highway 80, Joanna drove straight past the sheriff's office in the Cochise County Justice Complex and on toward town. The Buckwalter Animal Clinic, located in a converted gas station/garage, sat just outside of town, across Highway 80 from the 350-foot-high tailings dump that contained most of the waste left over when Phelps Dodge removed a mountain and turned it into an open-pit mine called Lavender Pit.

When Bisbee native Dr. Amos Buckwalter returned to Bisbee as a newly minted vet with a teenaged bride some twenty years after the beginnings of Lavender Pit, he had established his clinic facility on property that had been developed as an indirect outgrowth of that early-fifty's era of expanding mining operations. In order to connect Lavender Pit with the original Copper Queen, it had been necessary to take out some of the neighborhoods that had grown up in nearby canyons. Johnson's Addition, Upper Lowell, and Jiggerville all had gone the way of the dodo bird. The existing turn of the century buildings in those neighborhoods, many of them framed Victorian wanna-bes with modest gingerbreading and tin roofs, were loaded onto wheeled axles and then relocated. Company-paid movers trucked them three or four miles south and east of their original locations, where they were reinstalled on company land in newly created neighborhoods called Bakerville and Saginaw.

All her life Joanna had heard stories about one of the Jiggerville old-timers, Melvin Kitteridge. Local legend had it that Kitteridge, a mean-spirited, wily old codger, had nursed a long-standing grudge against the then duly-elected mayor of Bisbee. Offended by the idea of having his residence transplanted inside the city limits, Kitteridge had raised such a furor that the company had finally agreed to place his house on company property just outside the city limits. To this day, some forty years later, that property remained under the county's jurisdiction.

According to local gossip, Kitteridge had gone on to devil the city fathers by having the remains of both a gas station and another garage transported to the same site. For years the two not-quite-connected buildings functioned as a low-brow antique store, with Kitteridge living in his relocated house which, although on the same property, faced another street farther off the highway.

When Melvin Kitteridge died at age ninety-one, his heirs had been only too happy to unload the whole shebang at bargain-basement prices. Dr. Amos Buckwalter was the purchaser. Bucky Buckwalter had worked construction for years before earning enough money to attend college. He and his energetic but exceedingly young wife, Terry, had hauled out four truckloads of junk and then remodeled what was left, transforming the separate shells of garage and service station into a single building to serve as a clinic for small animals. Thirty yards away, across an expanse of red-graveled parking lot, they added a barn and corral for use with some of their larger patients.

Joanna remembered Bucky telling her once that if he'd had any inkling the mines would close down for good in the early seventies, he would have chosen somewhere else to set up his fledgling practice rather than coming back home. By the time the shutdown ax fell, however, Bucky and Terry Buckwalter were already committed, and they stayed on.

As Joanna approached the Buckwalter Animal Clinic, she saw several cars parked along the shoulder on either side of the road, including one of her department's newly acquired

Crown Victorias. Switching on the flashers on her Blazer, Joanna pulled in behind the other vehicles. Once parked, she noticed someone—a man—carrying a protest sign of some kind and marching back and forth in front of the cattle guard that led to the clinic's grounds. One of the cars parked across the highway carried a magnetic sign that said "*Bisbee Bee.*" Kevin Dawson, a journalism-school dropout who happened to be the son of the publisher and who doubled as both reporter and photographer, was down on one knee in the gravel busily snapping one picture after another through the lens of an automatic camera.

Kevin's presence meant that whatever was happening in front of the Buckwalter Animal Clinic had been deemed newsworthy. That was worrisome to Joanna Brady, since one of her younger and most inexperienced deputies, Lance Pakin, was standing in the center of the camera's range, along with the unidentified protester. Unfortunately, Frank Montoya, Chief Deputy for Administration—the guy who doubled as Joanna's official public information officer—was nowhere in sight.

Stepping out of the stopped Blazer, Joanna walked toward the action just in time to see Dr. Bucky Buckwalter himself erupt out the door to the clinic and storm across the parking lot. His face was livid with anger.

"I want this man off my property," he shouted, waving a fist in the protester's direction. "He's been here two days in a row now, and I want him gone."

All the while Kevin Dawson's camera finger continued to click away.

Still unable to see the sign the unidentified man held over his shoulder, Joanna's first thought was that he was most likely one of those radical vegetarian/animal rights activists, some of whom found Dr. Buckwalter's involvement in the beef industry offensive. In the past few years, Bucky's modestly lucrative specialization in performing artificial insemination procedures on beef cattle had been the subject of more than one "cows-are-people-too" type of protest.

Bucky didn't stop his advance until he and the other man were almost face-to-face, although the guy with the sign stood a good head taller than the diminutive vet. To compensate for his size, Doc Buckwalter customarily wore a pair of Tony Lama boots complete with two-inch heels, but even they didn't help very much in this instance. Had the two men squared off physically right then, Joanna doubted it would have been much of a contest. Dr. Buckwalter, however, appeared not to notice the disparity in their relative sizes. Or, if he did, it had no muting impact on his seething anger.

"This is private property," he raged. "Like I said on the phone," he added, turning to Deputy Pakin. "Either get him out of here or arrest him for trespassing."

"I'm on the right-of-way side of the fence," the other man returned calmly, gesturing with his sign in a way that, depending on your point of view, might have been considered brandishing. "I'm here exercising my right of free speech and passing out some literature, Dr. Buckwalter. You can't stop me from doing that."

"I'm afraid that's true, Doc," Deputy Pakin said, speaking respectfully and sounding genuinely conciliatory toward both sides. "As long as Mr. Morgan here stays on this side of the cattle guard and fence, he's on public property. Since he isn't disrupting traffic, there's not much we can do. Why don't you just go on inside and let him be?"

"He may not be disrupting traffic, but he's certainly disrupting my business," Amos Buckwalter complained. "He was here half the night with his damned candlelight vigil. Now he's interfering with my customers."

"I haven't done anything to your customers," the other man returned. "All I've done is offer them one of my brochures."

"Like hell," Bucky replied.

Not wanting the potentially volatile situation to deteriorate any further, Joanna chose that moment to step into the fray. "Good morning, gentlemen," she said calmly. "What seems to be the problem here?"

"Sheriff Brady." Deputy Pakin's face brightened considerably with the arrival of some backup. "Mr. Morgan, here, and Doc Buckwalter seem to be having a little disagreement . . . "

"It's hardly a little disagreement," the man with the sign interrupted. "Dr. Amos Buckwalter killed my wife. He could just as well have murdered her in cold blood. Now he's back home with his life and his business intact, while Bonnie's life is over. Mine, too, for that matter."

That was when Joanna finally caught sight of the sign. "Point 28," it said. "A license to kill." From there it took only a second to realize what was going on. Joanna wasn't entirely sure of the date, but she did remember the incident.

Early the previous year—maybe as far back as January or February—Bucky Buckwalter had gone off to an annual veterinarians' gathering being held at the convention center in downtown Phoenix. Smashed to the gills after partying too much, he had smashed his pickup into a woman crossing a street at an intersection. She had been killed on impact. Point two-eight was what he'd blown into the Breathalyzer two hours after the incident. That long after the incident, his blood alcohol level had still been almost three times the .10 that Arizona law deems legally drunk.

"Look, Morgan," Bucky said. "I'm sorry as hell about your wife. But I've paid my debt to society—spent my two months baking in an unairconditioned tent at the Maricopa County Jail. I went through six weeks of court-ordered in-patient treatment. Now I'm attending court-ordered AA meetings and doing my community service. My new truck had to go back and I've had to mortgage my clinic just to pay the fine, the lawyers, and the treatment. What else do you want from me?"

"Bucky," Terry Buckwalter called from the door to the clinic. "What's going on out there?"

If Doc Buckwalter heard his wife call to him, he didn't acknowledge it. He and the other man had eyes and ears solely for one another.

"I'll tell you what I want," Morgan returned. "You may have paid the state, but you haven't paid me. Bonnie's gone. What about her? What about me? What about our life to-gether?"

"The court ordered me to pay a fine and to get treatment. I've done that," Bucky Buckwalter replied stiffly. "If you want to take me to civil court, fine. Go ahead. That's up to you. In the meantime, I've got a business to run, Mr. Morgan, so why don't you get the hell out of here and let me do it? And if you so much as set one foot on my property, I swear I'll have you arrested."

With that, Dr. Amos Buckwalter turned his back on the group and stalked off toward the building's entrance where his wife still stood waiting for him. When the man with the sign made as if to follow, Joanna stepped in and stopped him. "Excuse me, Mr. Morgan. Maybe we should talk about this."

Morgan spun around and turned on her. His dark brown eyes flashed with barely suppressed fury. "What's there to talk about?" he demanded. "And who the hell are you?"

Obviously Morgan hadn't been paying much attention to Deputy Pakin. "I'm Joanna Brady," she answered coolly. "Sheriff Joanna Brady."

"How many cops did that jerk call? I'm surprised he didn't have someone issue an all-points bulletin."

"Nobody called me," Joanna replied, matching the severity of her tone to his. "And there's no APB, either. My dog got into a porcupine last night. I came by to drop him off so Dr. Buckwalter can pull out the quills. What are you doing here, Mr. Morgan?"

"Picketing," he replied more evenly, making a visible effort to calm himself. His troubled eyes met and held Joanna's questioning gaze. "This is the first time I've had a whole week off since he got out of jail and treatment. And if this is what I want to do with my spare time, no one's going to stop me."

In that tense atmosphere, when Morgan's hand disappeared into a jacket pocket, Deputy Pakin made as if to reach for his own holstered weapon. Instead of a gun, however, Morgan's hand emerged from his pocket holding a fanfold of brochures. While the deputy breathed a sigh of relief, Morgan handed one of the brochures to Joanna.

"It's informational picketing only," he added. "I'm passing out literature for Mothers Against Drunk Drivers. There's no law against that, is there?"

Joanna looked down at the brochure. On the cover was the cap-and-gown high school graduation portrait of a sweet-faced young woman. "Danielle Leslie Mitchell," the caption read. "Born June 17, 1976. Died June 18, 1994." That was all it said, but it was enough. For Danielle Leslie Mitchell, eighteen years had been an entire lifetime.

Joanna raised her eyes once more and met Morgan's challenging stare. "There's a law against this," she said, nodding toward the picture. "But not against picketing, as long as you do as the deputy said and don't disrupt traffic or trespass on private property. Understood?"

Morgan said nothing, but he nodded. She turned to the photographer. "I think you can stop now, Kevin. The incident's over. And Deputy Pakin, since it looks as though everything's under control, you might as well go on to your next call while I take my dog into the clinic."

"Right, Sheriff Brady," Lance Pakin said. "Thanks for the assist."

Joanna returned to her Blazer, turned off the flashing lights, and drove across the cattle guard. As she passed the man with his sign, she paused and rolled down her window. "Please accept my condolences about your wife, Mr. Morgan," she said. "You must have loved her very much."

For the space of a second or two, the mask of anger dropped away from the man's face, leaving behind nothing but an expression of naked, unaffected grief. That painful look was one Joanna Brady recognized all too well. Something very much like it reflected back at her every time she gazed into a mirror. However long Mr. Morgan's wife had been dead, the man's overwhelming grief was still close enough to the surface to be noticed by even the most casual observer.

"Thank you," he murmured and then turned away, wiping at his eyes with the back of his sleeve. It was possible that a sudden gust of wind had blown some dust or grit into his eye, causing it to tear, but Joanna didn't think so. Anger was all that had held Morgan together during his heated confrontation with Doc Buckwalter. With that gone, the slightest kindness—even something so small as an expression of condolence—made him fall apart. That was something else Joanna recognized. That, too, had happened to her—more than once.

Shaking her head, Joanna drove on through the gate and into the clinic parking lot. *Poor guy,* she thought. *There's somebody who's in worse shape than I am.*

2

"**NOT** Tigger and the porcupine again," Terry Buckwalter said, peering over the reception desk as soon as Joanna led the quill-sprouting dog into the animal clinic's waiting room.

Joanna leaned down and rubbed the dog's ears. "I'm sure it hurts, but he doesn't seem to mind the quills as much as we do. Still, you'd think he'd wise up after a while."

"Some dogs can be pretty hardheaded," Terry said.

Joanna laughed. "To say nothing of expensive. For what we've spent on porcupine quills, we probably could have ended up with a purebred puppy, as opposed to this ugly mutt. But Jenny loves him to pieces, and he's great at catching Frisbees."

"And porcupine quills," Terry added with a smile. She came around the counter and took Tigger's lead. "We already have several surgeries scheduled for this morning," she said. "Bucky probably won't be able to get around to doing this until mid-afternoon. If it looks like Tigger's starting to get dehydrated, we'll start him on an IV."

Joanna nodded. "What time do you think he'll be ready to pick up? I won't be off work before five."

"He should be ready to go by then," Terry said. "If not, we may have to keep him until tomorrow morning."

"That's all right with me," Joanna said, "but Jenny isn't going to like it."

Terry Buckwalter led a subdued and unprotesting dog through a swinging door into a kennel area at the back of the clinic. The new arrival was greeted by frantic barking from the several dogs already in residence.

"Sounds like you have quite a crowd back there," Joanna commented when Terry returned to the waiting room.

She nodded. "Some are patients and some are being boarded," she said. "We also have three reject Christmas puppies that we're hoping to find other homes for. You don't happen to need another dog, do you?"

Joanna shook her head. "Two are more than enough. What do you mean, 'reject puppies'?"

"It only takes a couple of weeks after Christmas for some people to figure out that owning a puppy isn't all it's cracked up to be. The reality turns out to be a whole lot different from those red-ribboned golden-retriever pups in all those cute Kodak photo ads."

"You're right." Joanna grimaced. "Now that you mention it, I don't think I've ever seen an ad showing a dog with his nose full of porcupine quills."

Terry went back behind the counter, searched through a file drawer, and pulled out a folder that was evidently Tigger's treatment record, which she perused for a few moments. "Tigger's due for his rabies shot next month. Do you want us to go ahead and handle that while he's here? It'll save you an extra trip later on."

"Sure," Joanna replied. "That'll be fine."

Terry Buckwalter added the file folder to several others that were already stacked on the counter. "I'm sorry you got stuck in all that mess outside," she said. It was the first time either woman had referred to the earlier confrontation by the clinic's entrance.

Joanna tried to pass it off. "It wasn't any big deal," she said reassuringly. "Don't worry about it."

But Terry Buckwalter didn't seem ready to let it go. "It just goes on and on," she said, shaking her head. "This whole year has been a nightmare. Ever since Bucky's accident . . ."

She broke off suddenly, as if concerned that she had said too much.

Terry Buckwalter was a slight, potentially attractive woman in her mid-thirties. She might have been better-looking if she had made the effort. She was tanned and solidly built, but whatever figure she had was perpetually concealed beneath the flowing folds of a man-sized, knee-length lab coat. Her shoulder-length, naturally streaked blond hair was pulled back into an unbecoming bun. And her tanned, sun-lined face showed not the barest hint of makeup. There were dark circles under her eyes, and a grim set to her mouth.

Looking at her, Joanna was struck by the thought that Terry Buckwalter was living under the weight of some heavy emotional burden. Although Terry herself had been at home in Bisbee, some two hundred miles away from her husband's fatal car accident, no doubt she had been dealing with fallout from that event ever since. Clearly, Hal Morgan wasn't the only innocent victim suffering in the aftermath of Bonnie Morgan's death.

"I'm sure it's been difficult for you," Joanna said sympathetically. "Situations like that are tough on everyone connected to them."

Terry nodded, biting her lip in agreement, although she said nothing more, and neither did Joanna. A few empty-sounding platitudes came to mind—"This too will pass," for instance, and "Time heals all wounds." The problem was, those were the very same supposedly comforting words that had been passed along to Joanna in the emotional devastation following Andy's death. They hadn't helped her much, and she cringed at the idea of inflicting them on someone else.

Glancing at the time, Joanna was ready to start for the door when Bucky Buckwalter's voice burst in on them from another room, from somewhere beyond the swinging door.

"Is that son of a bitch still out there, or did he finally leave?"

Terry flushed with embarrassment. "Bucky," she cautioned. "Sheriff Brady's . . ."

If Bucky heard Terry's warning tone, he disregarded it completely. "Just tell me whether or not he's gone."

"He's still here," Terry answered, "but—"

"That media-courting asshole!" Amos Buckwalter snorted. "Maybe I should take the hose out and water down the parking lot . . ." He charged through the swinging door, stopping abruptly when he finally realized that his wife wasn't alone in the outer office.

He turned on Terry. "Why didn't you tell me someone was here?" he fumed. "The least you could have done was let me know."

Over the years, Bucky Buckwalter had established the reputation of having a great bedside manner where animals were concerned. His people-handling skills, however, were something less than wonderful.

She tried to, you arrogant jerk, but you weren't listening, Joanna wanted to say.

Meantime, Bucky stopped in mid-tirade. Leaving off the harangue, he turned to Joanna with an instantly manufactured smile that oozed public charm. Joanna's mother-in-law, Eva Lou Brady, would have called it turning on his company manners. The telling difference between Bucky Buckwalter's public persona and his private one wasn't lost on Joanna.

"Why, Sheriff Brady," he said smoothly. "I had no idea you were still here. Hal Morgan isn't filing some kind of complaint against me, is he?"

Joanna shook her head. "Not that I know of," she said. "I'm here because Tigger has another faceful of porcupine quills."

The vet frowned and looked at Terry. "Another?" he asked. "Have we removed quills from him before? I don't remember doing it."

"It happened while . . ." Terry paused, as if struggling to find the right thing to say. ". . . while you were away," she finished lamely. "Twice. Dr. Wade took care of it both times."

"Oh, I see," the vet said, nodding and rushing on in a way that was calculated to smooth out any awkwardness. "Well, I'm sure we'll be able to handle it just fine. Maybe we can juggle the schedule enough to work Tigger in sometime this morning."

"I'd appreciate it if you could," Joanna told him. "And I'm sure Tigger would be more than happy to second that motion. I'll be back to pick him up right after work. Right now, though, I have to run or I'll be late for the board of supervisors meeting."

Joanna made it as far as the door before she paused and looked back. Terry and Bucky Buckwalter were standing on either side of the counter. There was an almost palpable tension between them. Joanna sensed that they were holding off the beginning or, more likely, the continuation, of a serious family argument. No doubt, hostilities would resume the moment Joanna stepped outside. In the meantime, Bucky—with almost casual nonchalance—picked up the pile of folders and began thumbing through them.

"Dr. Buckwalter?" Joanna said.

He glanced up at her. "Yes. What is it?"

"Don't worry about Mr. Morgan," Joanna said, looking Dr. Amos Buckwalter straight in the eye. "He's doing what he feels he has to do—what he has a constitutional right to do. If you just leave him alone, I doubt he'll cause you any trouble."

The practiced but phony smile dimmed. "You're saying I have to let him stand out there and harass my customers without doing anything about it?" Bucky returned irritably.

Instead of being irate that Hal Morgan was outside the clinic gates of Buckwalter Animal Clinic protesting Bonnie's death, Bucky might have shown a little contrition, acted as though he were sorry, even if he was only going through the motions. As far as Joanna was concerned, spending two months in jail, paying a hefty fine into the coffers of the Maricopa County Superior Court, and going through a drug-and-alcohol treatment didn't seem like much of a punishment for the taking of a human life.

Joanna had known Bucky Buckwalter for years, not only as the family vet but also as an insurance client at the Davis Insurance Agency, where she had worked for years, both as office manager and as saleswoman, prior to her election to the office of sheriff. Bucky had always struck her as an egotistical, overbearing blowhard. As an employee of the Davis

Insurance Agency, Joanna Brady had endured his tantrums because it was in the company's best interests for her to do so. Now, though, she was out of the insurance business. Glossing over Bucky's bad behavior was no longer necessary. Amos Buckwalter was accustomed to pushing people around. Sheriff Brady decided it was high time someone pushed back.

"That's right," she replied firmly. "You're to do nothing at all. Leave Hal Morgan alone. And just to be on the safe side, don't water down your parking lot as long as he's out there, either. Some of that icy spray just might make it over the fence into the public right-of-way. That would be unfortunate. Don't forget, Dr. Buckwalter, harassment is a two-way street."

Before Bucky could respond and before Joanna could complete her exit, the clinic's front door slammed open. A disheveled woman darted inside. Joanna recognized her as Irene Collins, a retired schoolteacher who lived up Tombstone Canyon in Old Bisbee. One arm cradled a huge calico cat. The other hand clutched one of Hal Morgan's M.A.D.D. brochures.

"Oh, Dr. Buckwalter!" Irene exclaimed. "I'm so glad you're here. Murphy Brown has some kind of bone stuck in her throat. I've been trying for almost an hour to get it out with a pair of tweezers, but I can't do it myself. She just won't hold still long enough so I can grab it."

"Come on," Bucky said at once, holding open the door to one of the examining rooms. "Bring Murphy right on in here. I'll see what I can do for her."

Irene Collins dropped both her purse and the brochure on the counter as she hurried toward the examining room. Terry Buckwalter left the purse where it was, but with a

glance in her husband's direction, she snatched up the brochure and tossed it into the trash. She wasn't quite fast
enough at removing the offending piece of paper. Bucky had
already seen it. They all had.

Irene and the ailing Murphy Brown disappeared into the
examining room. Shaking his head, the vet stalked after them.
Joanna turned back to the door.

"I'm sorry about all this," Terry Buckwalter called after
her. "It's so embarrassing."

Terry was clearly stuck in a no-win situation. Maybe
Bucky Buckwalter didn't feel any regret over the death of Hal
Morgan's wife, but Joanna was convinced that his wife did.
"Don't worry about it, Terry," Joanna said. "It's no big deal.
Besides, you've got nothing to apologize for. It's Bucky's
problem."

Terry Buckwalter's eyes filled with tears. "That's where
you're wrong," she mumbled. "It's a problem for both of us."

Joanna left the clinic then. As she drove through the gate,
she gave Hal Morgan a passing wave, but she didn't stop to
talk. Instead, she headed straight for the county administration building on Melody Lane, where the board of supervisors meeting was already in session. Frank Montoya, Chief
Deputy for Administration, had saved a seat next to him in
the far back row.

"How's it going?" she whispered.

"It's a good thing you got here when you did," he said.
"You're up next. From the treasurer's report of another
downturn in expected tax revenues, it isn't going to be any
kind of picnic."

And it wasn't, either. Joanna spent the better part of the
next three hours in the hot seat being grilled about exactly
how she intended to reduce her departmental budget by the

required seven and a half percent across-the-board cuts that were being demanded of all of Cochise County's department heads. When twelve o'clock rolled around, she was relieved to head for Daisy's Café in Bakerville for a quiet lunch with the Reverend Marianne Maculyea, her pastor and also her best friend.

Their friendship had started with their first day in seventh grade at Lowell School. During lunch recess, one of the boys had made the mistake of calling Marianne Maculyea a half-breed. Marianne's Hispanic mother and Irish father had met and married in Bisbee at a time when such unions were regarded with a good deal of disapproval. Marianne's two younger brothers had inherited both their mother's lustrous dark hair and brown eyes. Like her brothers, Marianne had come away with Evangeline Maculyea's hair, but that was combined with Timothy Maculyea's arresting gray eyes as well as his volatile temper.

The half-breed comment had been a typical grade school taunt, delivered with casual indifference and with zero expectation of consequence. What Marianne's hit-and-run tormentor failed to realize was that Marianne Maculyea was a confirmed tomboy and the fastest sprinter ever to come out of Horace Mann Grade School up the canyon in Old Bisbee. The boy—a year older and half a head taller than his victim—never anticipated that she would turn on him in pint-sized fury, chase him to the far end of the playground, capture him by his flapping shirttail, and then proceed to beat the crap out of him. Joanna Lathrop, a fellow seventh grader and also a confirmed tomboy, witnessed the whole drama, cheering for Marianne at the top of her lungs. Once Marianne escaped her sentence of detention in the principal's office, Joanna had been the first to offer her congratulations. They had been best friends ever since.

The Maculyeas had moved to Safford by the time Marianne announced her intention of leaving the Catholic Church to become a Methodist minister. Eventually, Marianne had been appointed pastor of Canyon Methodist Church. When she returned to town, bringing along her easygoing husband, Jeff Daniels, the two women had resumed their long-term friendship as though the ten intervening years of separation had never existed.

"You look like you've been through a meat grinder," Marianne said as Joanna sat down across from her and slid wearily across the booth's sagging orange bench seat.

"I'm sorry it shows that much," Joanna said with a rueful shake of her head. "But meat grinder just about covers it. Actually, slaughter of the Christians might be more apt."

Joanna paused long enough to study Marianne's face. Usually, Marianne Maculyea's whole being radiated a kind of glowing confidence. Today the glow was missing completely. Marianne's tan skin had a sallow look to it. The sparkle had disappeared from her eyes.

"Besides," Joanna added. "Who's calling the kettle black? You don't look all that chipper yourself."

"You've got me," Marianne said with a grin.

Daisy Maxwell, the café's rail-thin, seventy-year-old owner, plunked an empty cup and saucer down in front of Joanna. Knowing her regular clientele's habits and preferences, Daisy poured two cups of coffee from the regular pot without having to ask if coffee was what they both wanted.

"It's Tuesday," she announced, setting the pot down on the table and pulling a pencil from her towering beehive hairdo and a tablet of tickets from the pocket of her uniform.

"The lunch special today is two tacos with a side of beans. That, or meat loaf and gravy."

Joanna and Marianne both ordered tacos.

"You go first," Marianne said, once Daisy had taken the pot and their order and headed back to the kitchen. "What's going on?"

"If the board of supervisors wanted me to do a seven-and-a-half percent across-the-board budget cut," Joanna groused, "why didn't they tell me that *before* I took delivery on all those new Crown Victorias? They were all contracted for last year by Walter McFadden's administration. It seems to me it would have been easier to renege on the purchase of several vehicles than it's going to be to cut head count in either patrol or jail personnel. I've got a fifteen percent increase in caseload and an eighteen-percent increase in jail population, but I'm supposed to handle all of it with seven and a half percent less money than we originally budgeted. And that, I might add, was far less than the department should have had to begin with."

Marianne smiled at Joanna over the top of her coffee cup. "Sounds like loaves and fishes time. You'll just have to take what you have and make it stretch."

"Right," Joanna said. "But how? They won't let me move any of the money from one category to another. According to Melanie Hastings, the funds used to pay for the cars came out of the capital-improvement budget. That money had to be spent for the vehicles or we would have lost it entirely. According to her, those figures were frozen. So here I sit with ten brand new cars in a department where I'm expected to get by with two fewer deputies to drive them. It doesn't make sense."

"Since when do bureaucracies have to make sense, Joanna?" Marianne asked.

Joanna sat back in the booth. "All right now," she said. "Your turn."

Marianne shrugged. "Same song, second verse. Bureaucracies are the same all over."

"The adoption people?" Joanna asked.

Marianne nodded. "That's right," she said.

Jeff Daniels, Marianne's career homemaker husband, had left for China the day after Christmas on what was supposed to be a two-week expedition to bring home an orphaned baby girl. Those two weeks had stretched into three and now almost four, with no end in sight.

"What do you hear from Jeff?" Joanna asked.

"Not much," Marianne replied. "I talked to him last night. He said there's lots of coal dust in the air. I'm worried sick."

Joanna frowned. "How come? Is Jeff allergic to it or something?"

"It's code," Marianne explained. "We talked to some of the other parents who've gone through this same agency. They warned us that the Chinese authorities sometimes monitor phone calls, so before we left, Jeff and I established a code. The orphanage is located in Chengdu. People there mostly burn coal for heat, so in the winter especially the whole city is hazy with smoke and soot. The coal dust gets into everything.

"Since visiting Americans always complain about the coal dust, Jeff's talking about it on the phone shouldn't worry the authorities, but it does me. It means trouble."

"What kind of trouble?"

"That's just it. I don't know, but he did tell me that he's

got to have more money. I spent the rest of the night worrying about where I'm going to get it."

"How much more money does he think he'll need?" Joanna asked.

Marianne sighed. "Five thousand dollars."

Joanna whistled. "That sounds like a lot."

"It is," Marianne told her. "It's exactly double what we'd been told to expect. What I'm afraid is that the authorities have changed their minds. Maybe the baby is sick and they don't want to release her. From what Jeff said, it sounds as though, if we don't come up with the extra money, they won't let us have her."

"What are you going to do?" Joanna asked.

"There's a special board of directors meeting going on up at the church right now. I've asked them to advance me the money. Jeff told me last night that he needs it right away. Today, if possible. I didn't know what else to do."

Jeff and Marianne, almost thirty and childless not by choice, had been on several potential adoption lists for years. Andy Brady's sudden death the previous fall had infused a whole new urgency into the process. When the possibility of adopting a little girl from China had presented itself, they had jumped at the chance.

Having both of them fly across the Pacific to pick up the baby had turned out to be prohibitively expensive, so they had opted for Jeff to go on his own. That somewhat unorthodox behavior—the idea of having an adoptive father show up to collect the baby rather than an adoptive mother—had proved to be a real stumbling block. What had seemed like a perfectly sensible idea to Jeff and Marianne—having the primary caregiver pick up the baby—seemed somehow suspect in the eyes of officials in the Chinese orphanage. For weeks now, they had been throwing up one obstacle after another.

"Do you think it would help if you were there?" Joanna asked.

Marianne shrugged. "Probably not," she said. "Besides, having me there would make it far more expensive. It would only complicate things that much more. We'd be having to worry about my schedule and about finding someone to substitute for me while I was gone. At least this way, Jeff's time is totally his own."

With a disconsolate Marianne staring into her almost empty coffee cup, Joanna tried to offer some words of encouragement.

"Come on," she said. "Jeff Daniels may seem like the most mild-mannered guy on earth, but that's only on the surface. Once he gets his back up, you know as well as I do that he'll shrivel up into a little old man before he'll come back home empty-handed."

Acknowledging Joanna's support with a wan smile, Marianne changed the subject. "Speaking of world travelers," she said, "what do you hear from your mother?"

Joanna glanced at her watch. "Her plane's due into Tucson International around four. She was bound and determined to be back in time for the women's club luncheon tomorrow. That's when the Historical Committee presents the framed picture of me to hang in the lobby out at the department."

Marianne smiled. "I know," she said. "I'm on the committee."

Joanna continued. "Since today is a workday, I told Eleanor I wouldn't be able to come pick her up. Jim Bob and Eva Lou offered to go get her, but Mother insisted on having her friend, Margaret Turnbull, meet her instead. They'll have an early dinner in Tucson and then be home around nine or so."

"Has she had fun?" Marianne asked.

Joanna nodded. "It sounds like it. Marcie and Bob must have seen to it that they've hit every tourist attraction and museum for miles around. I'm sure my mother has been in seventh heaven."

The previous Thanksgiving, Joanna's long-lost brother had resurfaced. As a baby, he had been given up for adoption prior to Joanna's parents' wedding. Joanna had grown up without ever knowing that her mother and father, Eleanor and Big Hank Lathrop, had an out-of-wedlock child that Eleanor's parents had insisted they not keep. After the death of both his adoptive parents, forty-four-year-old Bob Brundage had come searching for his biological mother. Eleanor Lathrop had welcomed him with open arms. The feeling was evidently mutual. For Christmas, Bob and his wife, Marcie, had invited Eleanor to come visit them in Washington, D.C., for two weeks.

"She's never had a chance to do anything like that before, has she?" Marianne asked.

"Never," Joanna said. "She was widowed young and had a snotty teenager to deal with, sort of like yours truly and a certain hot-tempered nine-year-old."

"Well then," Marianne said, "I'd say she's earned the right to have some fun."

Joanna nodded. "Me, too," she admitted.

The very fact that Joanna was finally able to concede that maybe the difficulties between her and her mother weren't all Eleanor's fault was in itself a gigantic first step. Eleanor was tough to live with, but perhaps Joanna hadn't been all sweetness and light, either. Still, it was difficult for Joanna to forget or forgive Eleanor all the years she had spent carping about Joanna's shotgun wedding when she herself had been guilty of a very similar transgression.

Maybe, Joanna thought, *it's time for me to stop acting like a big, overgrown kid. Maybe I should just shut up, and get in the damned car.*

"Where did you go?" Marianne asked.

"I was thinking," Joanna said. "Maybe I've been too hard on my mother."

Marianne Maculyea laughed. "It's possible," she said. "But then, haven't we all?"

Daisy Maxwell brought their lunches right then. That was pretty much the last chance the two women had to talk. During the course of the meal, several people stopped by to visit with one or the other of them—parishioners from Canyon Methodist Church who were worried about how the organ repairs were going, or someone trying to sign them up to bake cakes to be sold at a local charity auction.

Joanna and Marianne had finished up the last of their coffee and were standing in line at the cash register when a fire truck, siren blaring, roared past the outside door. The truck was headed north on Bisbee Road.

"Somebody's probably trying to burn down Brewery Gulch again," Daisy Maxwell quipped as she took Joanna's money and handed back a fistful of change. In the past few months there had been a series of arson fires up in Old Bisbee, where a combination of steep terrain and tinder-dry conditions had made fire fighting difficult.

"Let's hope not," Joanna answered. "If the wind happens to be blowing in the wrong direction, we could end up with a disaster on our hands."

Out in her vehicle, Joanna turned the Blazer in the direction of the department, heading north on Bisbee Road, following the same route the fire truck had taken. When she came through the underpass that had been used to carry mine waste out to the tailings dump, she could see smoke just off to the right over the crest of the hill.

Beyond the underpass, a traffic circle had been installed to facilitate movement of traffic on Highway 80 and in-town vehicles moving from one area of Bisbee to another. Half a mile east of the traffic circle, Joanna could see a flock of emergency vehicles gathered on either side of the roadway at a spot she knew had to be right by the entrance to the Buckwalter Animal Clinic. Not only was there a clot of emergency vehicles, there was also a cloud of smoke billowing up into a deep-blue sky.

Joanna's heart fell. If the clinic had somehow caught fire, what did that mean for the animal patients there awaiting treatment? What about Tigger? What if he was dead? Jenny was already an emotional powder keg. After everything else that had happened to her, would she be strong enough to withstand the loss of a beloved pet?

Traffic had come to a halt, backing up for the better part of a mile, almost as far as the traffic circle itself. Turning on both flashers and siren, Joanna made her way into the left-hand lane, but even there she had to swerve around vehicles that had simply stopped in the middle of the road. As she picked her way forward, she pulled the Blazer's two-way radio microphone out of its holder and thumbed the push-to-talk button.

"Dispatch," she said. "This is Sheriff Brady. I'm just east of the traffic circle on Highway 80. What's going on?"

"We've got a fire at the Buckwalter Animal Clinic," dispatcher Larry Kendrick answered.

"I can *see* that from here," she returned. "What kind of fire?"

"It's confined to the barn."

"Not the clinic?"

"No, the clinic is fine."

Joanna allowed herself the smallest sigh of relief. Tigger wouldn't have been anywhere near the barn, so he was obviously fine. "As many emergency vehicles as they have out here, it must be some fire."

"That's because of the body," Kendrick answered. "One of the deputies on the scene just radioed in asking me to locate Ernie."

Veteran Detective Ernie Carpenter was the Cochise County Sheriff Department's lead homicide investigator.

"What body?" Joanna demanded. "My pager's been on. Nobody's tried to contact me."

"There hasn't been time. The deputy on the scene only called a few minutes ago."

Just as he said that, an ambulance pulled out from the clinic grounds and came shooting west along the highway, leaving Joanna no choice but to cut back in between two of the stopped cars lining the right-hand side of the road.

Sitting there waiting for the ambulance to drive past, Joanna couldn't help thinking about the confrontation at that same entrance several hours earlier. She had assured Deputy Pakin that everything was fine—under control were the words she remembered using. But if a body had turned up there, Joanna must have been dead wrong about that. She had mistaken grievances under wraps for grievances under control. Now someone had paid for that mistake with his or her life.

It didn't take much imagination to figure out that whoever was dead was most likely Bucky Buckwalter. If that was the case, it followed naturally enough that his killer would turn out to be none other than Hal Morgan, the bereaved, sign-wielding protester.

Joanna's two-taco lunch staged a sudden rebellion in her gut. If that was true, how much of the responsibility for what had happened would rest squarely on the all too inexperienced shoulders of Sheriff Joanna Brady?

Too much, she thought grimly, clutching the steering wheel. *Too damned much!*

3

B Y the time Joanna bounced over the cattle guard and into the grounds of the Buckwalter Animal Clinic, Richard Voland, the Cochise County Sheriff Department's Chief Deputy for Operations, was already there. He was standing outside his Ford Bronco, conferring with Captain Ben Lowrey of the Bisbee Fire Department. In the background, thirty yards from the clinic itself, stood the sagging remains of Bucky Buckwalter's metal Bild-a-Barn shed.

The some-assembly-required shed was a mini replica of an old-fashioned barn slapped together over a concrete slab. Beyond that was a corral. At the far end of the corral, tethered to the fence by a halter but dancing nervously from side to side, was Bucky's winter-coated, eight-year-old quarter horse, Kiddo. A young woman Joanna recognized as Bucky's veterinary assistant, Bebe Noonan, was with the distressed animal, petting it and trying to calm it. The horse seemed unconvinced.

"How bad is it?" Joanna asked as she came within speaking distance of Dick Voland and Ben Lowrey.

A long-time sheriff's department officer, Voland had served as chief deputy in the previous administration, and he had actively opposed Joanna's election. Once elected, Joanna's first impulse had been to dump him. It had taken her only a matter of days, however, to realize that his experience was a vital asset—one her fledgling administration couldn't afford to ignore. As a result, she had kept Voland on even though their day-to-day working relationship continued to be prickly at best.

Balding and massive at six-four, Dick Voland shook his head. "Bad," he said. "We've got at least one dead body inside. There could be more."

Joanna felt sick. "Bucky Buckwalter?" she asked, dreading the answer.

Voland shook his head. "Can't say for sure. Right off the bat, though, the doc would be my first guess."

"Who left in the ambulance, then?"

"The perpetrator," Voland growled. "I understand the guy's an acquaintance of yours, Sheriff Brady. Somebody named Hal Morgan. According to Deputy Pakin, a few hours ago you seemed to be of the opinion that Morgan didn't pose any kind of threat to the Buckwalters. Looks to me as though you were wrong about that."

Joanna nodded. She had already reached the same conclusion, but it was far worse to hear confirmation of her own worst fears coming from someone else, especially from her second-in-command.

"What happened?" she asked.

"It's too soon to tell. The fire crew is mopping up inside. One of the firemen discovered the body. Bebe Noonan . . ." Voland paused long enough to consult a notebook. "Full name's Bianca Noonan—the young woman over there with the horse—is the one who reported the fire. If you're looking for heroes, she's it. She found Morgan lying just inside the door to the barn and dragged him outside. She also rescued the horse."

Following Voland's glance, Joanna saw that Bebe Noonan had untied the skittish gelding and was leading him to the far end of the parking lot, where she tethered him to the chain-link fence that marked the westernmost boundary of the animal clinic property. Even there, she remained with the animal, alternately petting him and clinging to his neck.

Joanna turned to the fire chief. "How soon do you think we'll be able to get inside?" she asked.

"The fire's out, except for a couple hot spots, but we'll have to check for structural damage before we can let anyone else go inside. I'll let you know."

Lowrey walked away, leaving Joanna and Dick Voland alone. The chief deputy waited until the other man was out of earshot before he attacked. "You never should have ordered Pakin off the case," he said. "Obviously the incident was far from over . . ."

Joanna knew full well that the only way to survive with Dick Voland was to push back. "No Monday-morning quarterbacking, Dick," she snapped. "That particular incident *was* over. You know as well as I do that we don't have the manpower to have one deputy spend his whole shift waiting to see if something *might* happen."

"Well," Voland said derisively, motioning toward the still smoldering hulk of a barn. "If you call this over, I'd hate to see what you call an ongoing."

Joanna had to struggle to maintain her composure. "Look, Dick," she said, "you've made your point. Now how about getting down to business and telling me precisely what went on."

"Bebe came to work at noon," he said. "She evidently works afternoons and most weekends. That's her little brown Honda parked over there by Doc Buckwalter's van. She said she parked her car, went inside the clinic, and was getting things lined up for the afternoon appointments. Bucky wasn't here, and neither was Terry, but she didn't think anything about it.

"About a quarter to one or so," Voland continued, "she looked out the window and saw smoke pouring out the door to the barn. She called nine-one-one right away to report the fire and then came running out here to make sure the doc's horse was all right. She went in to let the horse out of his stall. That's when she stumbled over Morgan. He was lying on the floor just inside the door. If she hadn't dragged him outside, he'd probably be a goner now, too, instead of just on his way to the hospital."

"Smoke inhalation?" Joanna asked.

Voland nodded. "That and an egg-sized knot on the back of his head."

"Somebody hit him then?" Joanna asked, thinking that someone else, a third party, must have been in the barn with the other two men.

Voland scowled and shook his head. "Most likely he cracked the back of his head on the cement floor when he fell. Anyway, according to Ben, the fire was mostly confined to the tack room and to the hay and grain stored at the far end of the barn. It made for lots of smoke, although, as you can see, there's not much damage to the front of the building."

Joanna swallowed hard before she asked the next question. "What about Terry? Is there a chance she's in there as well?"

"Maybe, maybe not," Voland replied. "According to Bebe, she drives an old T-Bird. Since it's not in the parking lot, we're hoping she went somewhere. I've got people looking for her right now."

Joanna found herself praying that Terry Buckwalter was safe, that her body wouldn't be found among the ruins. It was bad enough that one person was dead. If there were two . . .

Unable to speak, Joanna studied the roofline of the building, especially the noticeably sagging far end. She had been inside this particular barn only once, several years earlier, shortly after it was completed.

Bild-a-Barns were the construction equivalent of fast food. They came from the modular school of design and were shipped in lots made up of prefabbed numbered pieces. Once at a site, they came together like a giant Erector set, clipped together over concrete slabs and preassembled metal frames.

Bild-a-Barns came in several different styles and configurations. They could be as small as one stall and one storage room or as large as ten stalls, depending on how many sections the owner was willing to fasten together. This one was a five-stall/tack room version, giving Bucky Buckwalter enough room for Kiddo along with space left over to board four additional animals.

Joanna remembered the barn dance the local Rotary Club had thrown in conjunction with the completion of the building. They had staged an old-fashioned square dance complete with a live band and a traveling barbecue outfit that had been trucked in from Tucson. The proceeds had been used to benefit the local Little League.

On that happy occasion, Bucky Buckwalter had been ex-traordinarily proud of the latest addition to his clinic. At the time, no one could possibly have predicted that three or four years down the road, that same barn would be the site of its owner's death. *And not just death, either,* Joanna corrected her-self. *The site of Bucky's murder.*

Joanna was so lost in contemplation of both the damaged building and her own thoughts that she almost didn't hear Dick Voland's question. "Are you all right?"

His sudden show of concern caught Joanna totally off bal-ance. "I'm okay," she answered quickly. "But you're right, you know. All this is my fault."

"No, it's not," Voland returned quickly, with almost no trace of his customary gruffness. "Forget what I said earlier. Sure, it's easy as hell to have twenty-twenty hindsight in sit-uations like this. Our manpower's spread way too thin to have a deputy stand around all day holding some damn pro-tester's hand. What's important, though, is that we've got the perpetrator. It'll save Ernie the time and trouble of going looking for him."

Trying not to betray how much Voland's unexpected kindness had affected her, Joanna turned away and glanced around the parking lot. "Where is Detective Carpenter, by the way?" she asked.

Ernest W. Carpenter—Ernie for short—was Cochise County's sole homicide investigator. "He and Deputy Car-bajal are on their way back from working that natural-causes stiff up in Sunizona," Voland answered. "According to Dispatch, they should be here within a matter of minutes. The last I heard, they were still fifteen miles out."

At the far end of the parking lot, Bebe Noonan continued to work at calming the panicky horse. The two of them, woman and horse, were just beyond Bucky's Ford Econoline van.

Joanna started across the parking lot, heading for Bebe. "Come get me as soon as Lowrey clears it for us to go inside."

"*Us?*" Voland asked after her.

"Us," Joanna repeated wearily.

She knew full well the need of keeping the number of crime-scene visitors to a minimum. Unfortunately, she also understood the need for people in her department and in the community at large to see her as a "real" police officer—as an active player and investigator rather than as a mere figurehead.

"If you say so," Voland replied. Joanna could tell by the change in the tenor of his voice that he didn't approve, but he accepted her decision without argument. "Where are you going to be?" he asked.

"Right now I'm going to go talk to Bebe," Joanna said.

Leaving Voland alone, Joanna picked her way across the parking lot. The high heels she had worn for the board of supervisors meeting proved hazardous in the loose gravel and ankle-twisting potholes. By the time she reached the chain-link fence, Bebe had finally succeeded in calming the skittish horse. He was standing still while Bebe rested her head against his chestnut-colored neck.

Bianca Noonan was a slight, painfully thin young woman in her early twenties. Mousy hair, a slight overbite, and close-set eyes all combined to make her less than beautiful. She was crying. Her narrow, tear-stained face was smudged by smoke, with rivulets of tears cutting through the grime.

"Bebe?" Joanna said tentatively.

The young woman straightened up and shot Joanna a despairing look. "Dr. Buckwalter's in there dead, isn't he," she said.

"Someone's dead," Joanna replied carefully. "We still don't know for sure who it is."

"But it has to be him," Bebe insisted. "I mean, who else could it be? Dr. Buckwalter's van is here and he's not. I already looked through the whole clinic. He's not in there. Not anywhere."

"We won't be able to find out for sure until the fire chief lets us go inside the building to check. Until we make a positive identification of the victim, it's best not to speculate. Meanwhile, we're going to need your help."

Bebe nodded mutely.

"Chief Deputy Voland said you were the one who discovered the fire. Is that true?"

Bianca Noonan nodded again. "I also found the other man. When I went into the barn to get Kiddo, I stumbled over him. There was so much smoke that I couldn't see. I fell right on top of him. At first I was afraid he was dead. The only thing I could do was grab him by one arm and drag him outside. Then I went back in for Kiddo. I saw the ambulance leave. Is the man all right?"

Joanna shook her head. "We don't know that, either," she said. "As soon as we hear something, I'll let you know."

For several seconds, Joanna and Bianca stood there in silence. "What about the clinic?" Joanna asked finally. "When you went in there, was there anything amiss—anything out of place, or else anything in there that didn't belong?"

Bebe shook her head. "Nothing," she answered. "As far as I could tell, everything seemed fine."

The young woman shuddered and took a ragged breath. "I guess you could go inside and look for yourself, Sheriff

Brady," she offered. "I have the keys right here."

"No, that's not necessary," Joanna said hurriedly. "We shouldn't do that. We might inadvertently disturb some important piece of evidence. Detective Carpenter will be here in a few minutes. He'll need to go through it, of course. Until then, however, the fewer people inside, the better. The detective will probably want to talk to you as well."

The horse stirred restlessly. "It's okay, Kiddo," Bebe said, stroking the horse's long, smooth neck. That action seemed to have as much of a soothing effect on the tearful young woman as it did on the horse.

"But I already told Deputy Voland everything I know," Bebe objected.

"What about Mrs. Buckwalter?" Joanna asked. "Her car isn't here in the lot. Where's she?"

Bebe sniffed and brushed away tears. "Like I told Mr. Voland, it's Tuesday," she said. "Terry's pro'ly off playing golf. That's what she does most afternoons."

"Where?"

"At that new place out by Palominas—the Rob Roy. She plays there three or four times a week—for sure on Tuesdays, Thursdays, and Fridays."

Several years earlier, a wealthy and decidedly gay couple—motorcycle-riding California transplants with more money than good sense—had shown up in Cochise County prepared to buy a golf course. When their initial plan to buy one course was derailed at the last minute, they bought themselves a chunk of cow pasture along the San Pedro River where they built a brand-new state-of-the-art course, starting from the ground up.

Locals who had grumbled and gritched and said it would never work had long since been proved wrong. Rob Roy

Links—named after a gloomy biker-frequented bed-and-breakfast in Folkstone, England—had become a rousing success. Peter Wilkes, the younger of the two, served as the resident golf pro, while his partner of twenty years' standing, Myron Thomas, along with Esther Thomas, Myron's seventy-something mother, ran the food concessions.

The course was so well-maintained and the food so outstanding that the Rob Roy had become the county's destination golf course and a popular watering hole/dining establishment as well. Not only had it attracted a loyal local following, it was also frequented by golf-crazy touring gays who sometimes stayed for weeks at a time in one of the Rob Roy's five stand-alone *casitas.*

Over time even the most recalcitrant local golfers had been won over. Members of the two vastly divergent clienteles—locals and visiting gays—mingled together in tee-time forged foursomes under the same rule that applied to the armed forces: "Don't ask, don't tell." As Peter Wilkes liked to point out on occasion—the rule might be new to the army, but it was one of golf's enduring traditions of etiquette.

"Do you want me to call out there and talk to Terry?" Bebe Noonan offered. "I could pro'ly get Mr. Thomas to go get her off the course to tell her what's happened."

Joanna shook her head. "Not right now," she said. "It's too soon. We should have some kind of positive ID before we do that. Even if the dead man does turn out to be Dr. Buckwalter, we try not to deliver that kind of news over the telephone. It's better if someone talks to her in person."

Bebe nodded dully while a new cloudburst of tears streamed down her cheeks. "I understand," she said.

"Sheriff Brady," a man called from behind them.

Joanna turned in time to see Detective Ernie Carpenter

come trudging across the graveled parking lot. Dressed in his characteristic suit and tie, he carried a small battered suitcase.

"Detective Carpenter," Joanna said. "This is Bebe Noonan, Dr. Buckwalter's assistant."

"The one who discovered the fire?" Carpenter asked, giving Bebe a quick appraising once-over.

When Bebe didn't reply, Joanna answered for her. "She's the one."

Briskly businesslike, Carpenter looked around. "Is there a place where I could change clothes?" he asked.

This time the young woman nodded. "There's a bathroom right inside the door at this end of the building."

"Is it locked?"

"Most likely. I can let you in, though. I have a key."

Leaving the tethered Kiddo on his own, Bebe led Ernie around the side of the building. Moments later she returned alone. "I still can't believe any of this," she said. "I'm from out in the valley," she added. "Things like this just don't happen out there."

Joanna felt like telling her that in this day and age no one was immune to crime. The Noonans lived in Double Adobe, just a few miles away from the spot along High Lonesome Road where Andy Brady had been gunned down a few months earlier.

"Is Detective Carpenter the one you were telling me about?" Bebe continued. "The one who'll be asking questions?"

Joanna nodded. "Right," she said. "He'll be in charge of the investigation."

"But why do I have to answer more questions?" Bebe wailed as more tears spilled down her forlorn cheeks. "Like I said, I already told the deputy everything I know."

Joanna tried for a reassuring smile. The realities of a homicide investigation were no doubt a long way from Bebe Noonan's rural experience. Hoping to bolster the young woman's morale, Joanna attempted to give her a little advance warning of what would take place.

"It will probably seem to you as though the detectives do nothing but ask the same questions over and over. It's cumbersome, but that's how the process works. By gathering details from everyone involved, homicide investigators eventually pull together a picture of what really happened."

"I see," Bebe murmured.

"Just as long as you tell the truth," Joanna continued, "you don't have a thing in the world to worry about. All right?"

There was a long pause. "I'll do my best," Bebe replied finally in a strangled whisper. "I promise I will."

Seconds later, Detective Ernie Carpenter came striding back around the corner of the building. Most of the time, Cochise County's lead homicide detective looked as though he had just stepped out of a department-store window. Sometimes called Gentleman Jim Carpenter, he was forever being teased by his fellow officers for conspicuous overdressing. While other plainclothes officers went for a less formal look with sports coats and maybe an occasional bolo tie, Carpenter customarily turned up at the office wearing brightly polished wingtip shoes, white shirt, a spotless tie, and a crisply pressed suit.

What went for office attire, however, didn't work when it came to crime scenes. For those he always carried a little brown suitcase, one he had inherited from his wife, Rose, after her second trip to the Copper Queen Hospital to have a baby. The now battered case went with him everywhere. Called to a crime scene, a dapper Detective Carpenter would

arrive, suitcase in hand. Soon he would disappear into a restroom or behind his vehicle. Minutes later, he would emerge
looking more like a second-rate plumber than a fashion plate.

He reappeared now in a pair of denim coveralls, serviceable high-topped boots, and surgical gloves.

"According to Ben Lowrey, we're about ready to go in,
Sheriff Brady," he said as he walked past. "Dick says you
want to come along, but with all the ashes, soot, and water,
I hope to hell you have something else to wear."

Having wrecked two separate expensive outfits during
her first week in office, Joanna had solved the problem by
ordering a full-length coat from an ad at the back of one of
Eleanor Lathrop's many back issues of *Sunset* magazine. The
fully washable J. Peterman coat—what the ad called a cowboy duster—had arrived with sleeves that hung four inches
beyond Joanna's fingertips and a tail that dragged on the
ground. Joanna's mother-in-law, Eva Lou Brady, had cut the
coat down to size and then fired up her Singer sewing machine to hem it properly. Following Ernie's example, Joanna
kept the remodeled duster, a pair of worn tennis shoes, and
several pairs of thick athletic socks in the back of her Blazer
at all times.

Hurrying back out to her own vehicle, Joanna pulled the
coat on over her two-piece business suit. She exchanged her
heels for socks and sneakers. In less than a minute she was
ready to enter the barn with Ernie Carpenter and the others.

When she rejoined them, Ernie gave her an appreciative
grin. "Whenever I see you in that outfit," he said, "it makes
me think of those old Clint Eastwood spaghetti westerns."

"Thanks," Joanna told him crisply. "I believe I'll take that
as a compliment."

Her reply brought the ghost of a smile to the corners of

Chief Deputy Voland's mouth, but he made no comment about Joanna's change of attire one way or the other.

"If you'll wait just a minute," he said. "I'll pass along some marching orders." Then, raising his voice, he shouted to the parking lot at large. "Okay, folks," he announced, "listen up."

That was one of the reasons Joanna had kept Dick Voland on as chief of operations. His rumbled commands automatically inspired respect and attention. At the sound of his voice, all the people there—assembled deputies and firemen alike—stood still, awaiting direction.

"Until we know otherwise," he told them, "this entire area constitutes the crime scene. That means inside the fence and along the highway outside it as well. I want the whole area searched. As soon as the fire-fighting equipment is out of here, I want the parking lot sealed off. Nobody unauthorized is to come in or out."

Voland paused for a moment before continuing. "Deputy Hollicker."

"Yes, sir."

"You see that Buick parked just outside the fence?"

"Yes, sir."

"That vehicle evidently belongs to the guy the ambulance hauled off to the hospital. I want you to make sure no one goes anywhere near it until we can have it towed away."

Voland paused long enough to let his eyes scan across the several remaining deputies. "Deputy Pakin?" he called.

Lance Pakin separated himself from the others. "Yo," he responded.

"I want you to get on down to the hospital. Whenever this Morgan character comes out of the emergency room, you're to keep an eye on him. Just in case he has some kind of miraculous recovery and they release him, I want you to stick to him like glue. If they admit him and put him in a room, station yourself outside his door and don't leave until you hear from me."

"Got it," Pakin said.

"Deputy Carbajal?"

"Yes, sir."

"I'm putting you in charge of getting a search warrant for the Buick. Talk to Pakin and get the details from him about what went on here this morning. That should be enough to show probable cause. When you finish up with that, I want you to take charge of the evidence search, but the warrant comes first, understood?"

"Yes, sir."

With those details handled, Voland turned to Ben Lowrey. "Ready," he said. "Lead the way."

The four of them—Ben Lowrey, Ernie Carpenter, Dick Voland, and Joanna Brady—walked into the barn in single file. No one said a word about ladies before gentlemen. Joanna was content to bring up the rear.

"The body's all the way in the back," Ben Lowrey explained as they went. "That's where there was combustible fuel in the form of hay, oats, ropes, leather, and so forth. That's also where the fire burned hottest, so be careful. We've still got a few hot spots back there."

Moments later, Joanna understood what he meant. Over what had been the hottest part of the fire, the overheated metal roof had sagged and stretched under the weight of water. Here and there soot-laden water dribbled down from on high. When Dick Voland's crisp khaki uniform took a direct hit on the shoulder, Joanna couldn't help being grateful for the duster. A few steps later, however, a gritty drip from what was most likely the same leak hit Joanna right in the eye.

Slogging along in murky, ash-filled water and breathing smoky air, Joanna was halfway down the barn before she smelled anything other than smoke. When she realized that the vaguely sweetish odor had to be nothing other than baked human flesh, she put one hand to her mouth to suppress a gag. By the time the others stopped walking, she pretty much had herself under control.

When Lowrey and Voland stood aside to let her move closer, she saw Ernie Carpenter crouched on his haunches some four feet from the corpse. The dead man lay face down in another pool of murky water. His clothing had been mostly burned away, but there was enough left for Joanna to see that the body was wearing boots—leather cowboy boots. As many times as Joanna remembered seeing Bucky Buckwalter, either in the clinic or out of it, he had always worn boots. Even without being able to see the dead man's face, Joanna was pretty sure she recognized Bucky's Tony Lamas.

"His arms may have protected his face from the flames," Ernie Carpenter observed, "but we'll have to see about that once we turn him over." The detective glanced at Ben Lowrey. "Nobody moved anything, right?"

"Come on, Ernie, how stupid do you think we are?" Lowrey replied.

"Don't get sore, Ben," Carpenter told him. "Just checking. Everybody stays back while I take a few pictures."

Joanna Brady was more than happy to put some distance between herself and the body while the detective began snapping photos. Standing there quietly with the flash going off periodically, all she could think of was how, mere hours earlier, this lump of charred flesh had been a living, breathing human being, taking care of day-to-day business. Now the man lying face down in the puddle was giving a whole new meaning to the term "ashes to ashes."

"When you finish that, you may want a picture of this, too," Ben Lowrey said.

"What is it?" Carpenter asked, clicking the camera without looking away from the body.

"I'd say it's melted wax. Paraffin," Lowrey answered. "It could be that a candle, or candles, were left burning in loose hay. That could have been what was used to start the fire. The bales would have been slow to start because they're packed so tight, but once they get going, they burn like mad."

"Why would someone use candles to ignite a fire?" Joanna asked. "Why not light a match?"

"To give the arsonist time enough to get the hell out of the way," Dick Voland answered. "That way he could be long gone before the fire was ever discovered. The candles were probably already burning when Bebe Noonan showed up for work, but she didn't see smoke until much later, when the hay actually caught fire."

Ernie Carpenter turned away from the body long enough to look where Ben Lowrey was pointing. After taking a picture of the grayish, soot-covered lump on the floor, he picked it up, stuffed it in a glassine bag, and slid it into the side pocket of his shabby overalls while Joanna found herself wishing that some of her insurance sales experience had included the rudiments of arson investigation.

Meantime, Ernie looked questioningly around the remains of the shed. "But where would the killer get candles out here in the middle of a barn?" he asked finally.

"Maybe they came from Hal Morgan's car," Joanna suggested quietly.

All three men turned at once to look at her. "Why do you say that?" Ernie Carpenter demanded.

"Because I remember Bucky saying something about Hal Morgan holding a candlelight vigil last night out in front of the animal clinic."

"Hot damn!" Carpenter exclaimed. "With any kind of luck, there'll be one or two left so we can do a chemical comparison. Getting a match will go a long way toward helping build our case."

He turned to Lowrey. "Give me a hand here, Ben. Let's turn this guy over and make sure who he is."

With Ben managing the feet and Ernie taking the body by the shoulders, they turned the dead man onto his back. As soon as they did so—as soon as Joanna saw the man's face—she knew that everyone's initial suspicions had been confirmed.

Dr. Amos Buckwalter, also known as Bucky, was as dead as he could be.

4

B Y the time the Cochise County Coroner, Dr. George Win-field, showed up with his two assistants to collect the body, Joanna and Ernie Carpenter were standing beside Ernie's van. Joanna had taken off her wet and filthy duster, shoes, and socks by then, but the socks had left an ugly gray high-water mark partway up her leg. It was possible that washing would dissolve the grime from her No Nonsense panty hose, but Joanna doubted it.

Before handing the body over to the coroner, Ernie had removed Bucky's wallet. Because the wallet had been under the dead man's body, it had been protected from the worst heat of the fire. Even so, Bucky Buckwalter's collection of credit cards had melted together in their equally melted sleeves. Now, prying deformed hunks of plastic apart, Ernie was going through the contents one card and one soggy photo at a time, inventorying the contents and mumbling aloud to himself as he did so.

"I don't understand," Joanna said.

"What don't you understand?" Carpenter asked, never removing his eyes from the task at hand.

"According to what I've read," Joanna mused, "most of the time perpetrators set fires in hopes of concealing evidence of a crime. But this is a metal barn sitting on a concrete slab. There wasn't enough fuel inside the barn to cause the building to collapse or even to burn up the corpse. Morgan must have known that, so what was the point? Why did he bother?"

Ernie stopped what he was doing long enough to fix her with an appraising stare. "Good question," he said. "Damned good question. If you're not careful, we may end up making a reasonably good homicide detective out of you yet."

With that, Ernie returned to checking the contents of the wallet.

"It may be a good question, but you haven't answered it," Joanna insisted.

"And I'm not going to," Detective Carpenter told her. "Remember, this is only the bare beginning of the investigation. Once I know what the answer is, believe me, you'll be the first to know."

"Fair enough," she said.

Moving closer, Joanna observed Ernie's painstaking handling of Bucky Buckwalter's personal effects. Each time the detective removed some item from the wallet, he would examine it carefully and then place it in an evidence bag before making the proper notation on an inventory sheet attached to a clipboard. It was a tedious process, one that required more than two hands.

"Would you like me to help with that?" Joanna offered. "I could either take the stuff out of the wallet and you could list it, or we could do it the other way around."

"Thanks," Ernie said, handing her his pencil and clipboard. "That'll speed things up."

One by one Joanna listed the driver's license as well as the other cards, photos, and pieces of paper. "He was carrying a little bit of cash on him," the detective reported eventually. "I count three twenties, a ten, and six singles. Seventy-six bucks and a package of Trojans."

"Trojans?" Joanna repeated. She heard the shock and surprise in her voice when she uttered the word, and she wondered if Ernie noticed.

"Sure," he said with a short laugh. "As in condoms. These are the nineties, Sheriff Brady. Lots of men pack them around in their wallets these days. What's wrong with that?"

Joanna considered for a long moment before she answered. "Nothing," she said finally. "Except if Bucky Buckwalter had been behaving himself, he wouldn't have needed them."

Rocking back on his heels, Ernie Carpenter regarded Joanna Brady with a puzzled frown. "Do you know something I don't know?" he asked.

Joanna nodded. "The Davis Insurance Agency sold the Buckwalters their health insurance several years ago. With all of Milo Davis's health insurance clients, whenever there was a problem with a claim, I was the designated troubleshooter. It was my job to duke things out with the claims people, to help our clients make their way through the bureaucratic jungle."

"So?" Ernie urged when Joanna paused and seemed disinclined to continue.

"Terry Buckwalter suffered from recurring ovarian cysts," Joanna answered at last. "She finally had a complete hysterectomy up at University Medical Center in Tucson. This was three or four years ago. There was a huge mixup because the insurance company paid the anesthesiologist twice and didn't pay the surgeon anything. It was a mess that took me months to sort out."

That far into the story, Joanna stopped cold.

"Go on," the detective urged.

Joanna shook her head. "That's all. The problem is, that's confidential information. I probably shouldn't even have mentioned it."

Thoughtfully Carpenter dropped the condoms into a glassine bag. "Don't worry about it," he said. "It's interesting information and probably not that important in the long run. If I do end up needing to have official corroboration, though, I can certainly find it out from other sources." Ernie paused. "That's the way it is in small-town law enforcement," he added. "Lots of people know things about other people's business."

Joanna nodded, but still she felt guilty for betraying a confidence, for giving out information without having a proper authorization to do so. Turning away from him, Joanna studied the intensely turquoise sky above the rust-colored man-made mesa of the tailings dump. If she was hoping for guidance in that vast expanse of blue, she found none—only more disturbing questions.

"Does that mean Bucky was having an affair?" she asked.

Carpenter shrugged. "Maybe. Either that, or he was hoping to or seeing professionals. Whichever, it does throw a somewhat different light on the situation. And it opens us up to the idea that things around here might be somewhat more complicated than they look."

Joanna thought about that as Carpenter stowed his collection of glassine bags in a scarred but ample briefcase. In the aftermath of Andy's death, there had been some question about whether or not he had been having an affair, too. Even though those suspicions had eventually proved groundless, Joanna knew from personal experience how much the unwarranted allegations had bothered her—how much additional and needless hurt they had added to her pain. The same thing could happen to Terry Buckwalter if unfounded hints of Bucky's infidelity were tossed around during the investigation into the veterinarian's death.

"What if Terry doesn't know anything about the possibility that her husband was messing around on her?" Joanna asked.

Carpenter seemed unconcerned. "She's bound to find out eventually," he said.

"Not necessarily," Joanna returned. "I'd hate to think that someone in my department was responsible for telling her."

"As in ignorance is bliss?" Ernie asked.

"No," Joanna returned. "Not bliss. It's just that sometimes being allowed to believe a lie is less painful than knowing the truth."

Ernie gave Joanna a searching look. "You don't want me to tell her?"

"Right," Joanna replied. "Not if it isn't necessary. Remember what happened with Andy?"

Ernie Carpenter was one of the homicide detectives who had come to Joanna's house to question her, bringing with him those unfounded and hurtful rumors.

Ernie Carpenter looked down and examined his feet. "A good cop was dead," he said huskily. "In what had been made to look like a suicide. Maybe I was a little overzealous, but it was my job to figure out what had happened. I've been sorry about that ever since."

Joanna nodded. "Me, too," she said. "And if there's any way to keep that kind of ugliness from happening to some other human being, I'd like to. You're a homicide detective, Ernie. I'm not telling you how to do your job. I'm just asking you to go a little easy on Terry Buckwalter. Don't tear her heart up in little pieces and step on them, not if you don't need to. If Hal Morgan turns out to be our killer, then there'll be no need to bring any of this up, will there? No need to mention the condoms at all."

At least Ernie Carpenter did Joanna the courtesy of considering for a moment before he replied. "Like I said before, Sheriff Brady, this is a small town. If Bucky Buckwalter was screwing around behind Terry's back, there'll be plenty of other people besides me who'll be willing to tell her so. The fact is, maybe she already knows."

"That's different from having the information come from you or from someone in my department," Joanna returned. "All I'm saying is if it isn't necessary to the case, don't bring it up. Do I have your word on that?"

Ernie Carpenter shook his grizzled head. "I can't promise it won't come up," he said at last. "But I'll do my best."

"Thanks, Detective Carpenter," Joanna said. "Your best is good enough for me."

By three o'clock, the crime-scene investigation was pretty well complete. Ernie had retreated into the clinic's restroom to change back into his street clothes, and Joanna was about to head back to the department. Just as she was climbing into the Blazer, Terry Buckwalter's mottled white T-Bird bounced over the cattle guard and stopped just inside the clinic compound.

Deputy Dave Hollicker had been stationed at the clinic's entrance all afternoon, telling whoever tried to turn into the parking lot—potential clients and gawkers alike—that they would have to come back some other time.

As soon as Deputy Hollicker waved the T-Bird to a stop, Joanna headed in that direction. Dave wasn't a bad guy, but he had all the subtlety of a baseball bat. Joanna didn't want him to be the one who told Terry Buckwalter that her husband was dead.

As it turned out, she needn't have worried. Dick Voland had issued orders that no information was to be released by anyone other than Frank Montoya, the public information officer. Dave Hollicker was exceptionally good about obeying orders.

When Joanna reached the T-Bird, a frowning Terry Buckwalter peered up at her in frustration. "What the hell is going on here?" she demanded. "This is my property—my business—but your jackass deputy here won't let me in, and he won't tell me what's going on, either."

"It's all right, Deputy Hollicker," Joanna said. "Let her through. I'll take over from here."

They moved forward that way, with Terry Buckwalter driving the T-Bird as Joanna walked alongside. Terry left the driver's window rolled down so they could speak as they went.

Not knowing where to begin, Joanna took a deep, steadying breath. "There's been a fire," she said.

"I *know* that," Terry replied impatiently. "A fire in the barn. Somebody who knows I golf at Rob Roy in the afternoons called out there and spoke to Esther Thomas, the lady who runs the restaurant. Esther sent Tom out on the course to find me and let me know. I can see the barn from here. From the way it sounded, I expected it to be a complete loss, but it doesn't look that bad. So what's the problem? Why all the fuss?"

She glanced off in the direction of the barn. "I've told Bucky a thousand times not to smoke in the barn, but he never listens to me." Parking in the empty space next to Bebe Noonan's Honda, Terry jammed down on the emergency brake and then stepped out of the car, leaving the door open and the keys in the ignition.

"Terry," Joanna said. "The fire had nothing to do with cigarettes. It may have been arson."

"Arson," Terry repeated with a puzzled frown. "Why would anyone want to do that? And what does Bucky think about all this?"

"I'm afraid things are much worse than they look. About Bucky . . ."

"What about him? Where is he?"

Joanna remembered hearing her father, D. H. Lathrop, and her late husband, Andy—both of them police officers— say that the worst part of being a cop was having to deliver death notifications. After little more than two months in office, Sheriff Joanna Brady already knew from personal experience that the same thing applied to her. Delivering that wrenching news was the worst duty possible.

She took a deep breath. "I'm sorry to have to tell you this, Terry, but your husband is dead."

As soon as Joanna uttered the words, Terry Buckwalter's knees seemed to collapse beneath her. Her breath came out in a gasp, and her well-tanned face turned pale and her lips stark-white, as she sank back down into the driver's seat of the car.

Seeing Terry's reaction, Joanna immediately began railing at herself for botching the job. Surely there must have been some better way to deliver the news than simply saying, "Your husband is dead." Wasn't there something else she might have said, something gentler that would have cushioned the blow? Couldn't she have found some softer words that would have blunted the impact of that starkly life-changing reality?

"Dead?" Terry repeated, as though in a daze and not quite capable of grasping the word. "You're saying Bucky is dead?"

Joanna nodded. "The firefighters found him in the back of the barn when they went inside to douse the flames."

Terry Buckwalter leaned back against the headrest of the seat, momentarily closing her eyes. Joanna expected that any moment a torrent of tears would start, but that didn't happen.

"How can that be?" Terry murmured. "He was fine when I left at noon. What happened?"

"We won't know for sure about that until after the autopsy."

The word "autopsy" seemed to be a catalyst. Terry grasped the steering wheel with both hands and pulled herself up straight. Since she still hadn't taken the keys out of the ignition, a hollow bell-like tone was bonging out some infernal warning signal. The racket was driving Joanna crazy, but Terry Buckwalter seemed oblivious to it.

"Why an autopsy?" she asked.

Reaching across Terry, Joanna tried to extricate the key, but it wouldn't pull free from the ignition. The gesture was enough to let Terry know what Joanna was trying to do. She silenced the ringing bell herself by removing the key with the aid of some hidden steering-column-mounted release.

"Who ordered it?" Terry asked again. "Don't I have any say in that?"

"No, you don't," Joanna explained. "The autopsy was authorized by Ernie Carpenter. He's the homicide investigator on the case."

"Homicide. You're saying Bucky was murdered?"

Joanna nodded. "Yes," she said. "That's tentative, of course, but that's the direction the investigation is taking at this time."

Joanna was still waiting for Terry's shock to wear off and for the tears to start. For a moment or two it seemed as though they might, but then Terry turned away from Joanna. She pointed a shaking and accusing finger at Hal Morgan's six-year-old maroon-colored Buick Century.

"It was him, then, wasn't it," she said softly. "It has to be him."

"Hal Morgan?" Joanna asked.

Terry nodded.

"It could be," Joanna allowed, "but of course we don't know that for sure. Not yet. The investigation is just now getting underway."

Without a word, Terry Buckwalter reached into the pocket of her leather bomber jacket and pulled out a scrap of paper, which she handed out the open door to Joanna.

"What's this?" Joanna asked.

"Read it," Terry answered. "Hal Morgan said he would kill Bucky, and now he has."

"Hal Morgan threatened Bucky? Where? When? Nobody told me that this morning."

"It wasn't today," Terry said. "It was last year. In Phoenix. At the courthouse. I saw him once in the hallway outside the courtroom."

"What did he say?"

"He didn't *say* anything," Terry answered. "He gave me that note. Read it."

Carefully Joanna began opening a tiny piece of paper that had been folded and refolded until it was smaller than an ordinary shirt button. Once unfolded, the scrap of paper was little more than an inch square.

The message itself, written in tiny script and in fading lead pencil, contained what amounted to two words. "Exodus 21:12."

Joanna studied the note for a moment and then looked back at Terry Buckwalter's pale face. "Hal Morgan threatened Bucky with a Bible verse?"

Terry nodded. "Yes."

"What does it say? Offhand, I don't remember which verse this one is."

"I didn't know it either," Terry said. "Not at first. I looked it up that night in the Gideon Bible in my hotel room." Closing her eyes, she recited the words from memory. "He that smiteth a man, so that he die, shall be surely put to death."

"And you kept it?" Joanna asked. "The note, I mean?"

"Yes," Terry said. "I put it in my makeup case and then I forgot about it. Until this morning. When I was putting on my makeup, I saw it again and I remembered. With Hal Morgan stationed right outside the clinic gates and carrying his picket sign, I could hardly forget."

"Why did you put it in your pocket today?" Joanna asked.

"What?" Terry asked. She seemed to have traveled far away.

"You said you've had the note in your makeup kit for months, but today you're carrying it around in your pocket," Joanna said. "Why is that?"

Terry shrugged. "I meant to talk to Bucky about it."

"You meant to, but you didn't?"

Terry shook her head. "I never had a chance. By the time I came over to the clinic from the house, Bucky was already out in the parking lot raising hell. You were there, so you know what that was like. And when we went inside, we got so busy that I never had another opportunity."

"I'll need to keep this," Joanna said, nodding toward the note. "I'll have to give it to Detective Carpenter."

"I understand," Terry said. "It's all right."

Carefully refolding the scrap of paper, Joanna dropped it into her own pocket. When she looked down at Terry, the woman was still sitting there with both hands on the steering wheel, staring dry-eyed out through the T-Bird's bug-spattered windshield.

"Are you all right, Terry?" Joanna asked, concerned that the other woman was going into shock. "Is there someone I can call to come stay here with you?"

Stony-eyed, Terry shook her head and climbed out of the car, shutting the door firmly behind her. "No," she said. "I don't need anyone right now. In fact, I should go in and check on the animals, especially on the post-ops. And Tigger, too," she added. "If Bucky didn't get around to pulling out those quills, I'll have to call Dr. Wade down in Douglas and see if he can come help out."

With that, Terry Buckwalter hurried into the parking lot. A thunderstruck Joanna Brady watched her go. Nothing could have prepared her for Terry's reaction, or rather, the lack thereof, to news of her husband's death. It was almost as though Joanna had told her that Bucky had been called out of town for a few days on some reasonably urgent but non-life-threatening emergency.

Just then Ernie Carpenter, once again wearing his natty suit, emerged from the rest room, lugging his suitcase. "What's going on?" he asked, examining Joanna's face. "Has something happened?"

Joanna nodded. "Terry Buckwalter came home a few minutes ago. Someone called the golf course and told her about the fire. I just now informed her that Bucky's dead."

"Oh," Ernie said. "If she's here, maybe I can talk to her for a few minutes right now. It'll save me having to make another trip later."

"Do you mind if I tag along?" Joanna asked.

Carpenter's steel-gray beetle brows knitted themselves into a frown. "Look, Sheriff Brady, I gave you my word. When I interview Mrs. Buckwalter, if it doesn't look like it's necessary, I won't say a word about the condoms. You don't need to come along and check up on me."

"It's not that," Joanna said.

Still looking at the clinic door through which Terry Buckwalter had disappeared, Joanna reached into her pocket and pulled out the folded note. "Before you talk to her, there are two things you need to know. Number one, this note is one that Hal Morgan gave Terry Buckwalter in the hallway of the Maricopa County Courthouse last year. She considers it to be a death threat, and so do I."

Unfolding the note, Ernie Carpenter held it at arm's length. "What's it say? I confess I'm not up on my Bible verses this afternoon."

"The gist of it is pretty much an eye for an eye and all that jazz."

"I see." Ernie dropped the note into his pocket. "I believe you said two things."

"Forget what I said about not telling Terry Buckwalter

about the condoms," Joanna answered. "My guess is she already knows."

"What makes you say that?"

"Women's intuition," Joanna answered.

"In a homicide investigation, women's intuition doesn't count for much," Carpenter observed. "You'll have to do better than that."

"When I told her, she didn't cry," Joanna said.

"Didn't cry?" Carpenter asked.

Joanna shook her head. "Not at all. Not a single tear. It was almost as though she already knew she had lost him. After that, finding out he was dead didn't really matter."

A look of intense interest washed across Detective Carpenter's face. "Did she say anything?" he asked.

"No," Joanna answered. "It's more what she *didn't* say. At first she looked stunned. I *thought* she was going to cry, but she didn't. Instead, a minute or so later, she walked into the clinic to go look after the animals."

Ernie considered Joanna's answer for a moment. "Different strokes for different folks," he said. "Not everybody reacts to this kind of news in exactly the same way."

"Maybe so," Joanna agreed. "I can tell you this, though, from personal experience. Within five minutes of hearing Andy was dead, the last thing in the world I thought of was doing my job."

"What did you think about?" Ernie Carpenter asked.

Joanna's eyes filled with tears. Four and a half months after the fact, tears could still sneak up on her and catch her unawares. "That I would never see him again," she managed. "That I'd never be able to talk with him or laugh with him. That we would never eat another meal together or sleep in the same bed."

Ernie Carpenter listened gravely and then he nodded. "Maybe Terry Buckwalter isn't quite as sad to lose Bucky as you were to lose Andy, Sheriff Brady. Andy was a quality type of guy. Bucky was..." The detective paused and shrugged. "Well, Bucky was Bucky," he finished at last. "From what I hear, that wasn't all good."

He waited long enough for Joanna to dry her own tears. "Do you still want to come with me while I talk to her?"

Joanna nodded.

"Come on then. I really meant what I said a little while ago. I'm hoping we'll be able to make a respectable homicide investigator out of you yet. Women's intuition and all."

5

IT was so late by the time Joanna finally escaped the office that Eva Lou and Jim Bob Brady, Jenny's paternal grandparents, insisted that they both stay in town for dinner. Joanna was only too happy to accept what was offered. Eva Lou's winter evening fare included a hearty bowl of navy bean soup and a thick slab of her prizewinning, skillet-baked corn bread.

Naturally, Bucky Buckwalter's death was one of the major topics of conversation, although Joanna tried to keep the discussion as low-key as possible. Joanna avoided the use of the word "murder," saying only that Doc Buckwalter had died in a fire in the animal clinic's small barn.

"But Kiddo's all right?" Jenny asked in a subdued voice. "He didn't get hurt or anything, did he?"

One of the reasons Jenny had always liked going to the clinic was that Bucky had often let her go out to the corral to give the vet's rangy gelding a carrot or two.

"No," Joanna assured her. "Kiddo's fine."

Jenny turned her fathomless blue eyes on her grandfather.

"Kiddo's a nice horse," she said. "Dr. Buckwalter promised me once that he'd let me ride him someday. I guess now that'll never happen."

"No," Jim Bob agreed. "I don't suppose it will."

"What about Tigger?" Jenny asked. "Will he be able to come home tomorrow?"

Joanna knew from talking to Bebe Noonan that Bucky hadn't managed to pull out Tigger's porcupine quills prior to his death. Terry Buckwalter had been in the process of getting Dr. Reginald Wade, the vet from Douglas, to come look after whatever animals were still in need of treatment—Tigger included. But Jenny seemed to be on a fairly even keel this evening, and Joanna didn't want to say or do anything that would upset her.

"Most likely he'll be home tomorrow, although I'm not sure when."

"Before I go to school?"

"We'll see," Joanna told her. If there was going to be another blowup on the subject, Joanna wanted it to take place after they left Jim Bob and Eva Lou's cozy duplex rather than before.

Jenny finished the last of her soup, put down her spoon, and pushed her chair away from the table. "Can I be excused then?" she asked, addressing her grandmother.

"May I," Joanna corrected automatically.

Eva Lou smiled. "Sure, sweetie," she said. "You run along and play for a while. It'll give your mom a chance to relax a little."

Jenny darted out of the dining room, heading for the bedroom/playroom her grandparents had declared her private domain in a house that was often Jennifer Brady's home away from home. Jim Bob Brady waited until she was out of earshot. "So old Bucko bit it," he said solemnly. "He couldn't've been very old."

"Fifty-three," Joanna answered, sipping the cup of after-dinner decaf Eva Lou had placed in front of her.

"He was always a great one with horses, even when he was little," Jim Bob continued. "I'll never forget that deal with the second-story horse up Brewery Gulch. You ever hear about that?"

Eva Lou nodded. It was a story they had all heard many times, but Joanna obligingly shook her head. "Second-story horse?" she asked.

"Bucky wasn't no more'an eleven or twelve when he pulled that one off. A couple of drunken rodeo riders raised so much trouble in Tombstone during Heldorado that they got run out of town. They ended up in a rented room up over the old Plugged Nickel. That was back before the place burned down. The next day they went right back to Tombstone, got in a card game, and won themselves a horse. I don't know if they cheated or what, but that night, because they were afraid the former owner would come try to steal the horse back, they took the critter upstairs with them when they went to bed."

"Upstairs?" Joanna asked, egging him on. "You mean over the bar?"

"That's right. The bartender heard the horse moving around up there and called the cops. None of the city cops had any idea what to do. When they first got there, they could barely open the door to the room because that horse's butt was right in the way. He was standin' there tied to the bedpost, just as pretty as could be, with both the drunks passed out cold on the bed.

"The one cop had a camera with him. He was gonna take

a picture to prove it was real, that it wasn't something he and his partner had just made up. Fortunately, the other cop had the good sense to talk him out of it. If a flash had gone off behind him like that, the horse most likely would've gone straight out the window and ended up splattered all over the street.

"Anyways, the police were still millin' around out front and scratchin' their heads when Bucky Buckwalter came down the Gulch to pick up the papers for his paper route. Except for him, his whole family was a shiftless bunch of do-nothin's, but that Bucky was a worker. He was out making his own way long before he shoulda.

"So Bucky showed up and found out what was goin' on. He convinced the cops to give him a chance to bring the horse out. And he did it, too. Covered the horse's eyes with his jacket and then led him right down them wooden stairs, one step at a time, talkin' to him a mile a minute like those so-called horse whisperers you hear so much about these days.

"Li'l Bucky got his picture in the paper afterward, too. Everybody said he was a hero. Once they sobered up, those cowboys sure as heck thought so, too. Get thinkin' about it, I do believe they even gave him a reward."

"Nobody ever said he wasn't good with animals," Joanna said quietly, thinking of Terry Buckwalter and Hal Morgan. "But when it came to people..." Deciding against saying anything more, Joanna let the unfinished statement linger in the air.

"So the killer's that fellow from Wickenburg then?" Eva Lou said, changing the subject. "The one whose wife died up in Phoenix? That's what it sounded like on the news tonight."

"Hal Morgan is under investigation in the case," Joanna told them. "But that's all. Under investigation. It's still too early to say. Ernie Carpenter talked to some of the people who used to work with Morgan when he was a police officer in southern California. They all said he was a great cop who would never take the law into his own hands."

"But who knows what a fella will do if he's pushed too far?" Jim Bob Brady asked. "I, for one, can see that the poor guy's got a point. After all, his wife is dead. Gone for good. All Bucky gets hit with for doin' it is nothin' more than a little ol' slap on the wrist. What's a man supposed to do?"

"Let justice take its course," Joanna said. "Bucky was given a legal sentence for vehicular manslaughter. He was also sentenced to undergo drug- and alcohol-treatment. He did both those things. According to our judicial system, he paid his debt to society. That should have been the end of it."

"Guess that's pretty much Arlee Campbell's position, too," Jim Bob said.

Arlee Campbell ran the county attorney's office, and Jim Bob's assessment was right on the money. One of the reasons Joanna had been late leaving the office was due to the fact that she had been tied up talking on the phone with the county attorney himself. She had listened to old Windbag Campbell go on and on, at tedious length, telling her all about how murder is murder, no matter what. About how vigilante justice amounts to no justice at all.

"You're right," Joanna said. "Arlee told me this evening that if we end up charging Hal Morgan with Bucky's murder, the county attorney's office will prosecute him to the full extent of the law."

"How's Terry taking all this?" Eva Lou asked. "She's always seemed like such a down-to-earth person and just as pleasant as she could be."

"All right," Joanna said, choosing not to mention that throughout the hour long, late-afternoon interview with Ernie Carpenter, Bucky Buckwalter's widow had never shown the slightest sign of any emotion other than her initial surprise.

"I suppose it's too early to know about funeral arrangements," Jim Bob ventured as he stood up to begin clearing the table.

"As a matter of fact it isn't," Joanna told them. "By the time Ernie Carpenter and I got around to talking to Terry, she had already contacted Norm Higgins. The funeral home will be picking up the body from Dr. Winfield's office as soon as he finishes the autopsy. According to Terry, the funeral will be at the mortuary up in Bisbee on Friday morning."

"We should go by all means," Eva Lou said. "Put it on the calendar, Jim Bob." Eva Lou turned back to Joanna. "Do you have any idea what time?"

"It'll be ten o'clock," Jim Bob said. "That's when ol' Norm likes to schedule them things. Any earlier, he says, and you have to rush breakfast. Any later, and you end up missing lunch."

"Norm Higgins could afford to miss a few breakfasts and lunches," Eva Lou observed.

Jim Bob held up a hand. "Now, Eva Lou," he told his wife. "Don't you go being so hard on the man. Norm Higgins is an old buddy of mine."

"An *overweight* old buddy of yours," Eva Lou added.

Listening to her in-laws' gentle bickering only underscored the loving humor that was a hallmark of their long-term marriage. Their constant sparring back and forth was part of what made their relationship work. Their companionable squabble somehow made Joanna feel better.

She watched as Jim Bob Brady carefully made a penciled notation of the memorial service on the Davis Insurance Agency calendar that graced the Bradys' kitchen wall. Looking at him, she realized fondly that here was a man—the genuine article. She'd bet her life that her father-in-law had never once been reduced to carrying a packet of condoms around in his wallet. If Jim Bob Brady died first, Eva Lou wouldn't be in for any unpleasant surprises in that regard.

Joanna put down her empty cup, pushed back her own chair, and made for the kitchen sink. "Oh, no, you don't," Eva Lou told her. "You go on home and attend to your chores. Jim Bob and I will do the dishes. It's his turn to wash, mine to wipe."

"You're sure?"

"Of course I'm sure." Eva Lou smiled. "I wouldn't want Jimmy here to have a chance to stop complaining about his dishpan hands." She paused then, and looked her daughter-in-law in the eye. "How are you doing?"

Joanna gave her mother-in-law a wan smile. "You read me like a book, don't you? I'm doing medium. I guess this is all hitting just a little too close to home. Once upon a time, in the good old days, murder was something that happened somewhere else, to people we didn't know."

"Well," said Eva Lou kindly. "You go on home and try not to think about it."

Leaving her stack of dishes on the counter, Joanna was only too happy to oblige. "Come on, Jenny," she called down the short hallway.

It took several minutes to gather Jenny's gear—schoolbooks, jacket, and lunch box—as well as Joanna's own purse. It was only eight-thirty or so by the time they reached High

Lonesome Ranch, but Joanna was so tired that it felt like much later.

A single bulb burning outside the garage told Joanna that Clayton Rhodes, her eighty-something neighbor and hired hand, had come by and fed all the animals. Paying Clayton to do the outdoor chores on a regular basis had been Joanna's first big concession to being a single mother with a young child and a demanding career. There simply wasn't enough of her to go around when it came to taking care of Jenny, doing the housework, and looking after two dogs and ten head of cattle as well.

When she reached the back door, Joanna found a scrawled note from Clayton stuck on the door frame with a pushpin. "Fed Sadie," the note said. "Couldn't find no Tigger. He maybe run off."

Guiltily, Joanna crumpled the note and stuck it in her pocket. It had been thoughtless of her not to have left word about Tigger for Clayton so he wouldn't have worried or wasted any time looking for an animal that was safely stowed in a kennel at the Buckwalter Animal Clinic. Meantime, Sadie, lonely after a day on her own, was ecstatically licking Jenny's face.

"Don't let her do that," Joanna admonished.

"She's just kissing me because she missed me," Jenny said. "It doesn't hurt anything."

Joanna managed to stifle an urge to deliver an Eleanor Lathrop–like lecture on the subject of dogs and germs. Instead, she sent Jenny off to take her bath and settled down at the telephone desk in the living room to take messages off the machine. There were several.

"I'm home," Eleanor Lathrop said through the recording machine's speaker. She sounded chipper as ever, as though, for her, cross-country plane flights were mere everyday occurrences. "Give me a call as soon as you get home. We need to get organized about tomorrow. Have you made any arrangements for Eva Lou and me to get out to Palominas to the women's club luncheon?"

Eleanor had been back in town only a matter of hours. Minutes, maybe. Already she was dishing out orders. Joanna, seeing her mother through the prism of her own difficulties with Jenny, was determined not to let it affect her. She made a note to call her mother.

The next message came on. "Hello, Joanna," said *Bisbee Bee* reporter Marliss Shackleford. "Do give me a call at home this evening."

Joanna gritted her teeth. Marliss, who took a good deal of pride in her self-styled position as gossip columnist for the local paper, had been a thorn in Joanna Brady's side for far longer than she had been writing "Bisbee Buzzings." Naturally Marliss was far too important to do anything as courteous or convenient as leaving her telephone number on the message.

"I guess I'm supposed to know it by heart," Joanna muttered to herself, as she made a note on the pad.

The third call was from Joanna's most unlikely friend— Angie Kellogg, a former L.A. hooker who, with Joanna's and Marianne Maculyea's help, had managed to escape "the life." Angie now lived in her own little two-bedroom house and worked as a bartender up in Brewery Gulch. The Blue Moon Saloon and Lounge was right next door to the empty lot that had once held the Plugged Nickel. Because Angie was still relatively new to town and reveling in what she saw as the "Wild West" atmosphere, Joanna made a note to remind herself to tell Angie the story about Bucky Buckwalter and the second-story horse.

"You're not going to believe this," Angie's message said breathlessly. "They've called me for jury duty. That's never happened to me before. It says I have to go to the courthouse three weeks from now. Is this for real? Do I have to do it? Call me."

Joanna laughed as she made another note and erased that one. Angie had only recently succeeded in passing her driver's-license exam for the very first time. No doubt, that had landed her in the motor-voter rolls, and on the jury-selection list as well. Given the context of Angie's previous life, her consternation was easy to understand. And if this was a first for Angie, Joanna thought, there was a good possibility that the reverse was also true. It was distinctly possible that having an ex-hooker on a jury would be breaking new legal ground in Cochise County.

The next two calls were both hang-ups with no message. "If you don't leave a message, I can't call you back," Joanna informed her anonymous callers.

The last message was from Bebe Noonan. "Mrs. Brady, I'm sorry to call so late, but I wanted you to know that Dr. Wade just finished treating Tigger. He'll be ready to come home tomorrow. Dr. Wade will be at the clinic early tomorrow morning to make arrangements either to send all remaining animals home or to transfer them to his facility down in Douglas. If you could come pick Tigger up sometime between seven and nine in the morning, we'd really appreciate it."

"Mom," Jenny called from the bathroom. "What are you doing?"

"Taking messages and returning telephone calls," Joanna said, pressing the erase button. "What do you need?"

"Nothing."

Shaking her head, Joanna dialed her mother. "Hi, Mom. How are you?"

"Bushed," Eleanor said. "If you hadn't called me back within the next ten minutes, I was going to take the phone off the hook and go to bed. They don't call it jet lag for nothing. My body is still on East Coast time. I feel like it's the middle of the night instead of just a little past nine."

"Go to bed then," Joanna said. "What's stopping you?"

But Eleanor was already off on her own tangent. "It's such a shame they've had to close the hotel kitchen for the time being. It's makes it terribly inconvenient that they've moved the luncheon so far out of town."

A grease fire the week before had put the Copper Queen Hotel's kitchen facility out of commission. The establishment was now on a month-long enforced sabbatical while workmen cleaned up the mess and spruced the place back up. One of the previously scheduled functions that had been forced to move to an alternate facility was the Cochise County Women's Club midwinter luncheon.

"Palominas isn't that far," Joanna said. "And I'm sure the dining room at the Rob Roy will be more than adequate. People claim the food there is great."

"Be that as it may," Eleanor returned severely. "It's still a real hardship for some people. Take Eva Lou, for example. The Bradys have only the one car. Since it's a 'ladies only' event, Jim Bob isn't invited. You can hardly expect him to drive Eva Lou all that way out to the golf course and then just hang around in the parking lot waiting for the luncheon to get over."

It occurred to Joanna that Jim Bob Brady was entirely capable of fending for himself, including walking into the restaurant and ordering his own lunch. Unfortunately, Eleanor Lathrop had her own particular take on the situation, and she wasn't letting up.

"Couldn't you give Eva Lou a ride?" Joanna asked.

"Me!" Eleanor echoed. "Do you mean to say that I'm not riding to the luncheon with you? After all, you're the honored guest, and I *am* your mother."

"But—"

"It never occurred to me that I wouldn't be riding with you. I've already made arrangements to have a tune-up on the Volare tomorrow morning. I'm supposed to drop it off at the shop tomorrow morning at eight."

Joanna had started the conversation with the best of intentions. She had been determined to give Eleanor the same benefit of the doubt that Joanna wanted from Jenny. Within seconds, however, she could feel herself being sucked back into all the old games.

"Mother," Joanna cautioned. "With everything that went on at the office today, the department is going to be a zoo. I'm not sure what time I'll be able to get away."

"Well then," Eleanor sniffed. "If you can't take me, I guess I won't be able to go at all."

"What about Margaret Turnbull? She's going, isn't she? Couldn't you ride out with her?"

"For goodness' sake," Eleanor said. "She drove all the way up to Tucson today, just to pick me up. Haven't we already inconvenienced her enough? Just forget it. It won't kill me to miss it."

Joanna sighed. It was the same old story. *Checkmate,* she thought. Why couldn't she get along with Eleanor the way she did with Eva Lou? Was it Eleanor's fault or Joanna's?

"All right," Joanna said, knuckling under the same way she always did. "Call Eva Lou and have Jim Bob drop her off at your house. The luncheon doesn't start until noon. I'll pick you both up at your house around eleven-thirty."

"Is that soon enough?" Eleanor asked. "I'd hate to be late. Wouldn't eleven-fifteen be better?"

Joanna closed her eyes. *Give the woman an inch* . . . she thought.

"Eleven-thirty will be plenty of time, Mother," Joanna said, striving mightily to keep her tone civil. "Since I'm supposedly the guest of honor, I'm sure they won't start without us."

"I certainly hope not," Eleanor said.

"Good night, Mother."

But Eleanor Lathrop was just hitting her stride. She wasn't nearly ready to punch the "off" switch. "Remind me to give you your presents tomorrow when I see you. I brought a wonderful little coat home for Jenny, and you'll never believe what I got you. Guess."

"I can't. Tell me."

"Egg cups."

"Egg cups?" Joanna asked.

"Marcie is such a wonderful housekeeper," Eleanor gushed. "And on Sundays, she makes these wonderful breakfasts with that expensive microwave bacon and fresh-squeezed orange juice and soft-boiled eggs in these marvelous little egg cups, with tiny spoons and everything. Eating those breakfasts made me feel so spoiled, like I was living in a book, an English novel with rashers of bacon and all that. You'll love them, by the way. The egg cups, I mean."

"I'm sure I will, Mother," Joanna said, feeling virtuous

for not pointing out that neither she nor Jenny was particularly fond of soft-boiled eggs. "And I'll remind you to give them to me. In the meantime, I'm going to have to go. I have several other calls to return."

"Isn't it after nine?" Eleanor asked. "Are you sure it's all right to call people back this late?"

"I'm sure it's all right, but the longer we talk, the later it gets," Joanna returned. "Welcome back and good night, Mother. See you tomorrow."

"Good night, Joanna," Eleanor said. "See you at eleven-thirty sharp, but make it earlier if you possibly can."

"Right," Joanna said, returning the handset to its cradle. "Will do."

She reached into the top drawer and pulled out the phone book. Marliss Shackleford's number was listed under the initial M. Marliss herself answered after only one ring.

"Sheriff Brady here," Joanna said. "Returning your call."

One of the things Joanna disliked about Marliss was the way the woman purred into the phone. "Oh, Joanna," she breathed. "I'm so glad you were able to get back to me tonight. With all those goings-on about Dr. Buckwalter, I wasn't sure you'd manage it."

Wanting to keep the call on a strictly businesslike basis, Joanna tried to pass the buck. "If you're calling about that, Marliss, you'll have to go through Chief Deputy Montoya. He's the department's official public information officer. It's best if all media inquiries are channeled through him. He'll be back in the office at eight o'clock in the morning . . ."

"Don't worry," Marliss said. "This has nothing whatever to do with the Buckwalter case. I was calling you about something else entirely."

"What?" Joanna's question sounded blunt, but she let it stand. She was too tired to do anything else.

"I was calling about Marianne Maculyea," Marliss said.

"Marianne," Joanna echoed. "What about her?"

"I'm worried about her, is all," Marliss said. "Several other people are as well. Is everything all right between her and Jeff?"

"Is everything all right? What kind of a question is that?"

"Well." Marliss hesitated. "Jeff Daniels has been gone for almost a month now. I heard late this afternoon that the Canyon Methodist Board of Directors met earlier today. They had to advance Marianne quite a big chunk of money. You don't suppose Jeff has gotten himself in some kind of trouble, do you?"

Joanna bristled. "Marliss, I'm sure whatever action the board took was supposed to be confidential."

"Oh, of course."

"Are you on the board of directors?" Joanna demanded.

"No," Marliss countered, "but one of my friends is. She said—"

"If it's supposed to be confidential, then I don't want to know what anyone said," Joanna interrupted. "It's none of my business, and it's none of yours either, Marliss. Good night."

"But wait," the other woman said hurriedly. "Don't hang up. What I'm afraid is that Jeff Daniels has gotten himself in some kind of trouble with the Chinese authorities and that Marianne needs the extra money to bail him out. He's always struck me as sort of a hippie type. And I just saw a *National Geographic* program on TV, on *public* televison, of course, that talked about all the drugs and hippies in Goa, India, which happens to be right next to China, you know. I thought that if anyone would be aware of what was really going on, it would be you."

The word "hippie" might have gone out of favor in the rest of the world, but among old-time Bisbeeites it still accounted for anyone who veered ever so slightly out of the norm. With a mighty effort, a seething Joanna Brady attempted to keep from saying everything that was on her mind. The end result left her voice quivering like a serving of underdone church potluck Jell-O.

"Jeff Daniels went to China to bring home a baby," Joanna said. "He's in a place called Chengdu, which, as I understand it, is far better known for its coal dust than it is for drug trafficking. If there has been any delay in Jeff's return, I'm sure it has absolutely nothing to do with what you regard as Jeff Daniels' *hippie* tendencies."

"Joanna, I'm only doing my job," Marliss objected. "If there's something going on, the public has a right—"

"No, you're wrong, Marliss," Joanna shot back. "This has nothing to do with your job. It has nothing to do with being a reporter and everything to do with being a gossip. Let me give you a word of advice, Marliss Shackleford. If one word of this shows up in that column of yours—one single word—I'll come up to your office and make you eat the damn thing."

"Joanna . . ."

"Marianne Maculyea may be a good enough Christian that she can turn the other cheek to people like you. But I'm not. I'm nothing but a poor, miserable sinner. My cheeks don't turn."

"That sounded like a threat."

"As a matter of fact, it was," Joanna growled into the phone. "You can count on it."

She flung down the receiver and stood there glaring at it

with as much loathing as if it were a coiled snake, one that might strike at any moment. Seconds later she was stabbed by an attack of remorse. How much of that blast of steam had Marliss actually deserved and how much should have gone to Eleanor Lathrop? One thing was sure, however. Joanna wasn't about to call Marliss back and apologize.

"Mom?" Jenny emerged from the bathroom, wearing nothing but a sodden bath towel wrapped around her still-wet body. Her blond hair dripped water onto the carpet. "What's the matter?" she asked, looking up at Joanna in big-eyed concern. "I heard you yelling. I was afraid something was wrong."

Ignoring the wet towel, Joanna pulled Jenny to her, holding the child close. "I'm fine now," Joanna said.

"But who was that on the phone?"

"It doesn't matter," Joanna said. "It wasn't important."

"It wasn't Grandma Lathrop, was it?"

"No, it was somebody else—someone who made me mad. You don't need to worry. It has nothing to do with you."

"But you hardly ever yell," Jenny said, her eyes misting over with a veil of tears. "Usually, when you get mad at me, you get quiet, not loud."

Moving Jenny to arm's length, Joanna smiled down at her. "You know me pretty well, don't you."

Biting her lip, Jenny nodded.

"Well," Joanna continued. "The person on the phone wasn't very nice. Sometimes that's contagious. I ended up yelling, and that makes me almost as bad as she is."

Jenny considered that for a moment. "Back before Daddy died, I used to think that everyone was nice."

Joanna shook her head, then gathered her daughter into

her arms once more. "So did I," she said. "But, Jenny, we have to remember that most people still are. There are just a few bad apples. And you know what they do, don't you?"

Jenny nodded gravely. "Grandpa Brady says they spoil the whole barrel."

"Right," Joanna said. "Now off you go to bed. It's getting late. We have to get up early in the morning to go pick up Tigger. Bebe Noonan left a message that we can come get him anytime after seven."

"You mean I can go, too?"

"If you're ready."

Motivated, Jenny started for her bedroom. "Good night," she said from the doorway.

"Good night, Jenny."

She went into her bedroom and closed the door. A moment later it opened again. "Mom?"

"What now?" Joanna asked.

"How many apples are in a barrel?"

Joanna couldn't help laughing. "I have no idea," she said. "That's a question only Grandpa Jim Bob can answer. You'll have to ask him. Good night now. Go."

When the door closed for the second time and stayed closed, Joanna breathed a sigh of relief. For that one evening at least, Jenny had seemed like her old self. That was something to be grateful for, something to appreciate. It made her hassles with both Eleanor Lathrop and Marliss Shackleford pale in significance.

Smiling to herself, Joanna picked up the phone once more. This time she dialed Angie Kellogg to let her know that being selected for jury duty wasn't the end of the world. At least this time when Angie showed up in a courtroom, it would be with the prospect of someone else going to jail. That ought to be some small consolation.

6

"THERE you go, Sheriff Brady," Dr. Reginald Wade said the next morning as a red-eyed Bebe Noonan led Tigger out into the reception area on a lead. As soon as he saw Jenny, the dog went crazy. Reggie, a long, tall drink of water with a crooked grin and an easygoing manner, leaned back against the counter and watched the dog's joyous reunion with his tiny mistress.

"You'd think he'd been locked up here forever," he said.

"At home the two of them are inseparable," Joanna said, "except, of course, when Tigger takes it into his head to go chasing after porcupines."

The vet nodded. "Speaking of which," he said. "It must have been close to twenty-four hours from the time that dog of yours and the porcupine started mixing it up before I was able to get after those quills. Fortunately, Bucky had Tigger under sedation and on an IV, so he came through it like a champ. By the way, I noticed that his chart called for a rabies vaccination. I gave him one while we were at it."

Looking from Dr. Wade to Bebe Noonan, Joanna reached

into her purse to retrieve her checkbook. "Who do I pay, then?"

"Pay Terry, by all means," Reggie Wade said. "I'm just helping out. Filling in until Terry has a chance to sort things out. Had our situations been reversed, I'm sure Bucky would have done the same for me and my furry patients. Putting Terry's mind at ease about the animals is the least I can do."

"That's very kind of you," Joanna said. "Thanks." She turned to Jenny. "Go ahead and get Tigger in the car. If you want to have breakfast before I drop you off at school, we're going to have to get a move on."

Jenny reached into her coat pocket and pulled out a carrot. "I brought this along for Kiddo. Do I have time to take it to him?"

"Sure," Joanna said. "But hurry."

Jenny raced out the door, taking Tigger with her. Meantime, Bebe came hurrying into the reception area along with yet another client, a young mother who had come to collect her family's newly neutered basset-hound pup.

While Joanna paid Tigger's bill, Reggie Wade helped discharge the basset. His kindness in doing so made a real impression on Joanna. It seemed to her that was what small-town America was all about—neighbors helping neighbors even when, under normal circumstances, they might have been considered natural competitors rather than allies.

As Joanna made to leave, Reggie met her at the door, pulling a business card out of his pocket. "If Tigger tangles with that porcupine again, here's my address down in Douglas. I'm just north of the fairgrounds."

"Thanks," Joanna said, taking the card. "You think he'll do it again, then?"

Dr. Wade shrugged. "Who knows?" he said. "You never can tell. How many times is it now?"

"Three so far."

"It sounds to me as if Tigger and that porcupine have a grudge match going. There's always a chance the porcupine will decide to move along. Barring that, I don't think anything short of a baseball bat is going to get Tigger to leave him alone. He's convinced he's going to win."

Joanna put the card in her pocket. "In that case," she said, "I'd best keep your address handy. You'll probably be hearing from us again real soon."

On the way back out to the ranch, Jenny sat in the back seat with Tigger's head cradled in her lap. "What's going to happen to Kiddo?" she asked.

"What do you mean?"

"You should have seen him when I gave him his carrot. He seemed so sad."

Joanna bit back the urge to explain to Jenny that horses don't get sad, but Jenny was already hurrying on with her own agenda. "Couldn't we buy him, Mom? Please? We've got plenty of room. I'd help take care of him. Honest, I would."

"Buy a horse?" Joanna choked. Another animal to care for was the last thing she needed.

"Don't you remember?" Jenny wheedled. "Daddy told me I could have a horse someday."

"Someday maybe," Joanna said. "But not right now."

After that, Jenny drifted into a morose silence that lasted all the way out to the ranch and back into town. Unfortunately, the mood was catching. As Joanna looked out at miles of winter-blackened mesquite it seemed to her as though the whole hundred-mile-long expanse of the Sulphur Springs

Valley was dead; as though the landscape would remain bar-
ren and forlorn forever.

Just like the two of us, Joanna thought.

By eight, Jenny had picked her dispirited way through an
order of French toast at Daisy's, and Joanna had dropped her
off at school. With the morning's somber mood still hanging
over her, Joanna arrived at her office in the Cochise County
Justice Center.

Joanna's secretary, Kristin Marsten, wearing her signature
short skirt, had just presented Joanna with a stack containing
two days' worth of untended correspondence when Deputies
Voland and Montoya came into her office for their early
morning briefing.

The two of them could have been Mutt and Jeff. Voland
was big and burly and loud—prone to throwing his considerable weight around. Frank was slight and quiet, tending
more to negotiation than to barking orders. Their only common physical trait came from seriously receding hairlines.

From day one, relations between the two chief deputies
had been as much at odds as their physical characteristics.
"Oil and water" was the best way to describe it. Voland's
long history with the department made him the consummate
insider. It usually meant he stood firmly behind doing things
the way they had always been done. Montoya, a former Willcox City Marshal, had been one of the two men who had run
against Joanna in the contest for sheriff. People had been surprised when one of her first acts upon assuming office had
been to draft a former opponent, appointing him to be one
of her two chief deputies. Most longtime sheriff's department
employees, Dick Voland included, regarded Montoya as a
rank outsider.

At the time of the appointment, Joanna had made it clear

to Frank that she wanted him aboard so she could be assured of having at least one sure ally in the department. In the months since, Frank had served her in that regard both cheerfully and adeptly. Outside the department, he acted as a public lightning rod. Inside, he functioned as a behind-the-scenes departmental barometer.

On this particular morning, as Voland and Montoya took their usual places at the conference table in Joanna's office, she was dismayed to see that the usually upbeat Frank seemed downright glum.

"So what's been happening?" Joanna asked, opening the session with the customary question. Dick Voland complied, quickly delivering the department's unvarnished overnight statistics.

"Five U.D.A.'s (undocumented aliens) picked up between Douglas and Bisbee along Border Road and two more just outside Tombstone on Highway 80. Turned them over to the Border Patrol. Two drunk drivers. One domestic. A single-vehicle, alcohol-related rollover just south of Elfrida. That's about it. Pretty quiet, even for a Tuesday."

"Anything on the Buckwalter case?" Joanna asked.

"According to Ernie, Hal Morgan's still in the Copper Queen Hospital. They're treating him for smoke inhalation and a skull fracture. I've posted round-the-clock guards outside his room."

"Why?" Joanna asked. "He doesn't sound like a flight risk. He's a retired cop with a home and a job in Wickenburg. All the people Ernie talked to in California yesterday, guys who knew him when he was still a police officer, said Hal Morgan was a great guy, one who wouldn't hurt a fly."

"Try telling that to Bucky Buckwalter," Dick said, leaning back and drumming his fingers impatiently on the arm of his chair. "Once a cop goes haywire, there's no telling what he might do."

Joanna looked to Frank. "What do you think?" she asked.

"I've been trying to tell Mr. Voland what I think all morning. I've been attempting to explain to him the grim realities of our budget meeting with the board of supervisors yesterday. Any overtime we pay in January is going to have a direct bearing on our ability to cover shifts come the end of the year."

"Budgets, smudgets," Voland sneered. "I know those guys. They're always dishing out this belt-tightening crap, but when push comes to shove—when public safety is on the line—they always cave. One way or another, they manage to find the money."

"Let's not get off on the budget problems right this minute," Joanna said, holding up her hand to stifle the debate. "First let's deal with the Hal Morgan issue. What does Ernie say? Why don't we have him come in and give us his take on the situation?"

"Because he's already up at the coroner's office," Voland answered. "Winfield has another autopsy scheduled for today—the stiff from Sunizona that we found yesterday." Voland paused long enough to consult his notes. "The dead guy's name is Reed Carruthers, by the way. According to Ernie, unless Winfield finds something unforeseen in the autopsy, it's not a case to concern us. Natural causes rather than a homicide. But at ninety-three, when a guy takes off walking in the middle of a January night with no coat or jacket, you've gotta say it's old age plain and simple."

Voland looked up. When no comments were forthcoming from either Joanna or Frank, he continued. "According to Ernie's report, Carruthers' daughter, Hannah Green, has been looking after him for years. She claims he's been sleeping so little of late that she's all worn out. Two nights ago, he evidently waited until she was asleep and then took off."

"Wait a minute," Joanna said. "Isn't this the same guy who had a bloody wound on his head? Wasn't that why Ernie was called out to Sunizona in the first place?"

"That's right. The initial police report said that Carruthers fell off a fence and hit his head on a rock. According to Ernie, that's pretty much what happened. I'm sure once Dr. Winfield finishes the autopsy, he'll be able to give us a more definitive answer. As soon as he's done with Carruthers, he'll be moving right on to Bucky Buckwalter."

"Which brings us right back to the Hal Morgan problem," Joanna put in. "Has Ernie talked to the man?"

"To Morgan? Not that I know of," Voland replied. "At least he hadn't the last time I heard from him. My understanding is that Morgan's doctor still won't let anyone in the room."

"If the man's physical condition is that serious," Frank Montoya offered, "then it strikes me he's in no shape to take off under his own steam."

"In other words," Joanna said, addressing Frank, "you don't think the guard is necessary."

"Not at this time. At least not until he's either well enough to be released or until we've made a decision to charge him. On the other hand, if Dick here insists on having a guard, then he needs to pull someone in off patrol to do that duty. This morning I took a look at Deputy Pakin's time sheet from yesterday. He pulled an eighteen-hour shift. That's ridiculous. I hate to think how much we paid per hour to have somebody guarding a bedridden patient who was too sick to move."

Joanna looked to Dick Voland. "You still have a guard on duty there this morning?"

Voland nodded.

"And it's someone who was off duty rather than pulling a deputy off patrol?"

The chief deputy squirmed. "Well, yes, but—"

"No buts, Mr. Voland," Joanna snapped, cutting him off in mid-excuse. "Enough of this. I'm going to go track down Ernie Carpenter. Once I talk to him, I'll make the call on whether or not the guard is necessary. From now on, whoever stands guard duty comes from the regular patrol-duty roster. Overtime is out. Is that understood?"

"Yes, ma'am," Voland responded with just a trace too much emphasis on the "ma'am" part. "You're the boss," he added, standing up. "Is that all?"

Joanna glanced at Frank. "I don't have anything else," he said.

"That's all then," Joanna answered.

A steamed Richard Voland marched out of the office. "He's not a very good loser, is he," Frank Montoya observed as the door swung shut.

"It's not a matter of winning or losing, Frank," Joanna said, a little dismayed to find herself defending Dick Voland. "Since you're still here, there must be something on your mind. Tell me."

"I've been hearing some grousing out there among the troops."

"That's hardly news. What kind of grousing?"

"Some of the deputies are saying that if you hadn't sent Deputy Pakin on his way early yesterday morning, Bucky Buckwalter wouldn't be dead."

Joanna felt the hot blood rush to her cheeks, but there was

no point in denying the charge. She herself had reached much the same conclusion. "Maybe it's true," she ventured quietly.

Frank shook his head. "No way. If killing Bucky was Morgan's whole purpose in coming to town, he would have waited until Pakin left regardless of how long it took. Your ordering Pakin to leave had nothing to do with it."

"Thanks, Frank," Joanna said. "I appreciate your saying that, but if it turns out that the investigation shows I'm partially responsible for what happened, then I'm prepared to live with the consequences. In the meantime, my deputies are entitled to their opinions."

"If they're looking to lay blame," Frank said, "there's more than enough to go around." With that, he opened a file folder and dropped a sheaf of papers onto Joanna's already cluttered desk.

"What's this?" she asked.

"Just for the hell of it, I went surfing the net last night. I called up all the press coverage I could find on the Bonnie Morgan case from last year. I also talked to some of the Phoenix P.D. guys who handled the case. You might want to take a look at all this *before* you make a final decision about stationing a guard at the hospital. Rather than taking a hike, I think it's far more likely that Morgan is going to use this whole thing as a forum for focusing attention on what happened to him and his wife."

"All this time I thought you were lobbying against posting the guard because you thought Hal Morgan was innocent."

Frank Montoya shook his head. "I'm a good Catholic boy," he said. "Anybody who's been raised Catholic knows that martyrs always get the best press. So why should we spend money to guard him when he's going to make far more of a splash by going to jail than he will if we just let him go?"

Joanna smiled. "I'll try to bear that in mind, but I'll read through this all the same." She glanced down at the top article, the headline of which said: "Wrong-Way Driver Kills Pedestrian." Joanna looked back over at Frank. "Thanks for gathering all this together. Is that all?"

"Pretty much."

"What's your game plan for the day?"

Frank checked his watch. "I've got a press conference in half an hour. After that I'll most likely spend the rest of the day working on those budget figures. I'll probably still be working on them when hell freezes over. What about you?"

Joanna looked at the several separate stacks that covered most of the surface of her desk. "First I have to deal with a mountain of paper. That'll probably eat up most of the morning. At noon there's the annual women's club luncheon. This is the meeting when they present the department with the framed photo of yours truly for our little photo display out in the lobby. I'm expected to give a speech."

"That should be fun," Frank said. "Especially with all this Buckwalter business just hitting the fan."

"It's not that. Mother made it a point of coming back from D.C. in time so she could be in attendance at the luncheon. I adore those kinds of events where I get to do double duty— daughter and sheriff at one and the same time."

Frank chuckled and headed for the door. "Good luck with that," he said. "I wouldn't want to be in your shoes."

Joanna was determined to infuse a little bit of humor into an otherwise grim morning. "It's just as well," she said. "You'd look pretty funny in two-and-a-quarter-inch heels."

Once she was alone, Joanna dutifully turned to the stack

of correspondence Kristin had indicated was most urgent. Even as she filled out the registration form for the Arizona Sheriff's Association meeting in Lake Havasu City in two weeks' time, her eyes kept being drawn to the plain manila folder Frank Montoya had dropped on her desk. Finally, with the form half completed, she pushed it aside and opened the folder.

The first article was a straightforward fatality accident account—who, where, when:

A pedestrian struck by a speeding pickup in a downtown crosswalk has become Phoenix's fifth traffic fatality of the new year.

Bonnie Genevieve Morgan, fifty-two, a Wickenburg resident, was run down and killed last night at nine-thirty when a pickup crashed into a pair of pedestrians at the intersection of Third Street and Van Buren. Ms. Morgan and her husband, Halford William Morgan, also of Wickenburg, were returning to their hotel room after attending a movie. Ms. Morgan was pronounced dead at the scene while her husband was uninjured.

The driver of the vehicle, Dr. Amos Buckwalter of Bisbee, was treated for cuts and bruises at Good Samaritan Hospital before being booked into the Maricopa County Jail on suspicion of vehicular homicide. Buckwalter was reportedly in Phoenix to attend the annual meeting of Arizona State Veterinarians' Association being held at the Phoenix Convention Center.

Investigators at the scene say that the incident is most likely alcohol-related.

Shaking her head, Joanna put down that page and picked up the next one. Here there was very little text, only a picture of a street sign with a bunch of balloons on strings tied to it. "Balloons, a bouquet of roses, and a single candle mark the corner of the intersection where Wickenburg resident Bonnie Genevieve Morgan died last night in the Phoenix area's fifth fatality traffic accident of the year."

The third page contained the text of the article that accompanied the picture:

In honor of their nineteenth wedding anniversary, fifty-six-year-old Hal Morgan of Wickenburg presented his wife, Bonnie, with a bouquet of nineteen balloons, a dozen long-stemmed yellow roses, and a weeknight's stay in the honeymoon suite of the Hyatt Regency Hotel.

Morgan spent his anniversary night alone. His wife, Bonnie Genevieve Morgan, the victim of an allegedly drunk driver, died in a crosswalk less than two blocks from their hotel.

Today, balloons and roses as well as a number of candles form part of an impromptu memorial gracing the corner of Third and Van Buren where Bonnie Morgan became the fifth traffic fatality on Phoenix area streets so far this year.

Joanna could stand to read no further. Her eyes blurring with tears, she looked again at the picture. Bonnie Morgan had died on the night of her wedding anniversary. Andrew Roy Brady had died on his wedding anniversary, too. Joanna had been sitting at home—waiting for him and steamed that he was late for their tenth anniversary getaway—when he was gunned down by the drug dealer's hired hit man. Andy hadn't died that very night. In fact, he hadn't died until the afternoon of the next day, but as far as Joanna was concerned, he had died on their anniversary, when he spoke to her for the last time.

"JoJo," he had whispered, calling her by the pet name only he had used. "JoJo. Help me." That was before the ambulance arrived, before the helicopter ride to Tucson and before the killer paid one final visit to finish his deadly work. But for Joanna Andy's life had ended in the bloodied sand of the wash, and the date that had once marked one of the happiest days of her life now commemorated her worst nightmare rather than her wedding.

For the space of several minutes Joanna stared at the picture with unseeing eyes, letting the events surrounding Andy's death play themselves out one more time. What if she had gone looking for him earlier? What if she hadn't left the hospital waiting room when she did? What if? What if? These were questions that still haunted her months later. The only difference was, usually they assailed her in the middle of the night when she was alone in her bed and attempting to fall into some kind of fitful sleep. This time, thrown into an emotional relapse by the eerie similarity between Bonnie Morgan's death and Andy's, Joanna found herself sitting at her desk with unchecked tears streaming down her face.

"Sheriff Brady . . ." Unannounced, Joanna's secretary burst into the room. Kristin stopped short when she caught a glimpse of Joanna's face. "Excuse me," she said in confusion. "I didn't know . . . Is something the matter?"

"It's all right," Joanna said, quickly wiping at her eyes. "Every once in a while, things just get to me. I end up all weepy with no real warning or reason. Just ignore it. Eventually it goes away."

Kristin was already backing out of the room. "I'll come back later," she said. "When you're feeling better."

"No," Joanna insisted. "Come back now. What's up?"

"Detective Carpenter just came in. He's on his way to Sunizona again, but he wanted to talk to you for a few minutes before he leaves."

"Sunizona," Joanna repeated. "Why's he going back there?"

Kristin shrugged. "He didn't say."

Joanna sighed. "Give me a minute to fix my face," she said. "Then send him in."

Reaching for her purse, she dug inside until she located her compact and lipstick. She had pretty well repaired the damages by the time Ernie let himself into her office.

"Sunizona again?" Joanna asked. "Did somebody else fall off a fence up there?"

She had thought a wry comment might help them both, but a somber Detective Carpenter seemed unmoved. "That's the whole problem," he grunted, sinking into a chair. "Nobody fell off a fence—not even Reed Carruthers."

"But I thought . . ."

"So did I," Ernie answered. "But I've just come from Dr. Winfield's office. Reed Carruthers didn't die of a single blow to the head from falling on a rock. According to the doc, he suffered from blunt-instrument head trauma—multiples of same. In other words, somebody literally beat his fucking brains in, if you'll pardon the expression."

It was the first time Ernie Carpenter had ever used the F-word in Joanna's presence. It was an indication of how distressed he was over missing something he now thought should have been obvious.

"No need to apologize, Ernie," she said.

"Thanks. At any rate, I'm going to head back up there in a few minutes and try talking again to his daughter, Hannah."

"You think maybe she had something to do with his death?"

"We'll see. According to Carruthers' doctor up in Willcox, Hannah Green has been her father's sole caregiver for a number of years now. His condition has kept her virtually homebound. Who else would have had an opportunity? Maybe taking care of him got to be too much for her and she just lost it—lost control. That happens sometimes. What gripes me is that I didn't see it to begin with."

Joanna nodded. "All right," she said. "But if you're off to see Hannah Green, what about Hal Morgan?"

Carpenter gave Joanna one of his beetle-browed frowns. "What about him?" he asked. "The guy's still in the hospital, isn't he?"

"As far as I know. Have you talked to him yet?"

Ernie shook his head. "Not so far. His doctor wouldn't let me near the guy last night. I may be able to see him later on this afternoon, when I get back to town. I wanted to wait until I had autopsy results, and they won't be ready until later today. I just left the coroner's office a few minutes ago. Dr. Winfield is up to his ass in alligators this morning. As I walked out the door, he was completing the paperwork on one autopsy and had yet to start the next one."

"Autopsy results or not," Joanna interrupted, "you're still convinced that Hal Morgan's our man? That he's responsible for Bucky Buckwalter's death?"

"No question." Ernie Carpenter answered without the slightest hesitation. "We've got him dead to rights on this one. You can count on it, Sheriff Brady."

"All right," Joanna said. "Keep me posted."

Moments later, with Ernie off and running, Joanna turned back to the various stacks of paper littering her desk. Determinedly, she shoved the material concerning Bonnie Morgan's death back into its file folder, then she refocused her attention on the half-completed conference registration form. With that finished, she tackled the backed up correspondence.

Concentrating on clearing her desk, Joanna totally lost track of time. She was reading over an incomprehensible set of new federally mandated guidelines regarding jail-inmate rights when Kristin tapped on her door once again.

"What is it now?" Joanna asked.

"Your mother's on the line," Kristin answered. "She's wondering where you are and aren't you going to be late for the luncheon?"

It took a second or two for realization to dawn. "Damn!" Joanna muttered, leaping out of her chair and grabbing her purse. "What time is it, anyway?"

"Twenty to twelve," Kristin answered.

"I'm late," Joanna said as she bolted toward the private entrance in the corner of her office, one that opened directly onto her reserved parking place. "Tell her I'm on my way."

She started the Blazer and rammed the gear shift into reverse. If eleven-thirty was too late to pick up Eleanor Lathrop and Eva Lou Brady to take them to the women's club luncheon, then eleven forty-five would be that much worse.

Nice going, Joanna told herself as she headed for her mother's house. *What do you do for an encore?*

7

EXPECTING to be raked over the coals because of her late arrival, Joanna was surprised to find that her mother was in an expansive mood. While Joanna pushed the Blazer well beyond the posted speed limits, Eleanor regaled Eva Lou Brady with stories about her trip to Washington. It seemed that everything Bob and Marcie Brundage had done to entertain her had been perfectly wonderful, with the minor exception of finding a suitable beautician.

"I was so happy to get back to Helen Barco this morning and have a *real* shampoo for a change," she announced. "All those places I tried in D.C. believe in using blow-dryers and curling irons. That's just not the same thing as rollers and a real hair dryer."

Only half listening as she drove, Joanna marveled at how easy it seemed for Bob and Marcie to get along with Eleanor. Having grown up in an adoptive family, he and Eleanor were evidently able to relate to one another as adults, without all the complications and conflicts of childhood and adolescence getting between them. In a way, Joanna felt almost jealous.

Maybe, if she and Eleanor had met on an adult basis as well, in some kind of social setting, perhaps they, too, would have been able to like each other. As it was . . .

Joanna came back into the conversation in time to hear her mother declare, "People like that are an absolute menace." Eleanor was half-turned in the passenger seat and speaking over her shoulder to Eva Lou, who was seated in back. "They take the law into their own hands, without giving a thought to anyone else."

For a moment, Joanna thought the discussion had something to do with her driving. Carefully, she eased her foot off the accelerator and watched the speedometer fall from eighty back down to a more responsible sixty-five. Eva Lou's reply, though, was proof enough that the Bucky Buckwalter murder was actually the subject under discussion.

"I suppose Terry will have to close the place up," she said.

Eleanor nodded. "That's what she said when I saw her this morning. That she's already making arrangements to sell out. It has something to do with the fact that she can't keep the clinic open without a licensed vet on the premises."

"What will people in Bisbee do about their pets in the meantime?" Eva Lou asked.

"Drive sixty miles roundtrip, I suppose," Eleanor answered. "They'll either have to go all the way out to Sierra Vista, or down to Douglas."

Eva Lou clicked her tongue. "That could be a real hardship. Think about poor old Mr. Holloway. He just loves that cute little dog of his. He calls her Princess, and treats her like one, too. They go everywhere together, but Jed Holloway's eyes are getting so bad now that he only drives in town anymore. He'd never dare go as far as Douglas. What's he going to do the next time Princess needs a shot?"

"I can't imagine," Eleanor sighed. "That's exactly what I was saying a moment ago," she added. "I feel sorry for the man, losing his wife and all. But still, he might have given some thought about how his actions would affect the rest of us."

Joanna felt like saying that Hal Morgan's grief-fueled fixation on Bucky Buckwalter had most likely left no room for thinking about the consequences of depriving the citizens of Bisbee of their only vet. She thought about it, but let it go. Instead, she focused in on one part of her mother's conversation—that Terry Buckwalter would be closing the Buckwalter Animal Clinic.

"You saw Terry Buckwalter in town this morning?" Joanna asked.

Eleanor nodded. "That's right. At Helene's," she replied. "She was having her hair and makeup done. I have to say, she looked great—better than I've ever seen her." Eleanor turned to Joanna and gave her daughter's hairdo a critically appraising once-over.

"Speaking of hair, isn't it about time you had yours cut again? It's getting a little long. You probably should have had it done before today's luncheon. Aren't there going to be newspaper photographers?"

This was part of what Joanna had dreaded about accompanying Eleanor to the luncheon. It was inevitable that she would end up on a tightrope, caught between the two widely divergent roles of dutiful daughter and sheriff honoree. In the past, she might have been pulled into one of Eleanor's endless debates on the subject of beauty and grooming, but for once, she wasn't. She was too preoccupied with something else, something Eleanor had said. The words had hit far too close home.

Soon after Andy's death, almost within days, any number of unscrupulous real estate vultures had shown up on her doorstep. All of them had been eager to buy her out—to take High Lonesome Ranch off her hands—at bargain-basement prices. She had felt as though they all thought the words "widow" and "sucker" were one and the same. Now she found herself wondering if some of those same kinds of low-life scum were busily targeting Terry Buckwalter for the same reason—to cheat her—without even having the good grace to wait for Bucky to be properly buried.

"You're sure Terry Buckwalter said she's selling the practice?" Joanna asked.

Eleanor hesitated. "She didn't tell me exactly," Eleanor said. "Not in so many words. She was leaving Helene's at the same time I was going in. I only saw her on her way out the door, but that *is* what she told Helen Barco. And she's not just unloading the clinic, either. She's going to sell out completely—the house, the practice, everything.

"Now then," Eleanor added, blithely changing the subject. "Would you like me to make an appointment for you? At Helene's, I mean. You should have seen what Helen did for that frumpy Terry Buckwalter. You'd be amazed. The haircut and makeup made all the difference in the world. In fact, I almost didn't recognize her."

All the old conditioning was there and all the old patterns. Eleanor's offer of help, which was actually nothing but art-fully disguised criticism, was an old, old ploy. Joanna was within a heartbeat of rising to the bait when she caught sight of Eva Lou's face in the rearview mirror. Eva Lou's quick wink, accompanied by a sympathetic smile, were enough to bring Joanna up short. *Let it go,* the wink seemed to say. *Don't let her do this.*

It was enough of an assist so Joanna was able to stop the rising retort before it ever made it out of her mouth. Instead, to her surprise, she discovered it was possible to shrug off her mother's none-too-subtle attack while at the same time saluting Eleanor's unwavering single-mindedness.

"Thanks all the same, Mother," Joanna said with a smile. "I'll have to see when I can work a haircut into my schedule and set the appointment on my own."

To Joanna's amazement, that was all it took. Once she let it go, so did Eleanor. By the time they reached the Rob Roy parking lot a few minutes later, Eleanor was happily telling Eva Lou all about Bob and Marcie's bone-china egg cups.

It was ten after twelve. Between golfers and luncheon attendees, the parking lot was fairly crowded. Joanna dropped Eleanor and Eva Lou at the door and then drove to the nearest available parking place at the far end of the lot. As she stepped out of the Blazer, she realized that the car next to hers was a familiar-looking aging white T-Bird that looked very much like Terry Buckwalter's.

Sure enough, when she went around to the back and looked at the vehicle license, the license surround was printed with the words, "Have you hugged your vet today?"

Joanna was stunned. She had been surprised by Terry Buckwalter's matter-of-fact acceptance of what had happened to her husband, but was the woman out playing golf the very next day? That was astonishing. Unheard of. And if Joanna was shocked by the idea, Terry Buckwalter was making a social faux pas that would set tongues wagging all over Cochise County for years to come.

Shaking her head, Joanna headed for the dining room,

where a man met her at the door with a charming proprietary smile. "You must be Sheriff Brady," he said. "Your lovely mother said you'd be along any minute. I'm Myron Thomas, the manager."

Myron was short and round. He had penetratingly blue eyes, a courtly manner, and a slightly foreign but entirely unrecognizable accent.

"How late am I?" Joanna asked.

"Not at all," Myron said easily. "The ladies were so enjoying their pre-lunch cocktails that they're only just now settling into the dining room. If you'll come this way, Sheriff Brady, I can take you directly to your place."

As soon as Myron led the way into the dining room, Marianne Maculyea came hurrying to meet them. "Thank goodness you're here," she said. "Until your mother and Eva Lou showed up, I was afraid you weren't going to make it. I've just been drafted into introducing you. Come on. You're seated right next to me."

"What happened to Marliss Shackleford? I thought doing the introduction was her job."

"So did I," Marianne answered. "Maybe she's sick. All I know is, she isn't here. Linda Kimball, the women's club president, asked me to pinch-hit."

After their telephoned confrontation the night before, Joanna couldn't help being grateful that Marliss wasn't doing the introductory honors. With no love lost between the two women, there was no telling what Marliss might have said.

A waitress bearing two loaded salad plates stood waiting for Joanna and Marianne to slip into their places. As she sat, Joanna was pleasantly surprised to see her mother smiling in Joanna's direction from two tables away. Eleanor Lathrop's glass of "house" white wine was raised in a salute. Using her water glass, Joanna returned the favor.

Linda Kimball leaned her stout frame in Joanna's direction. "I hope you don't mind that there wasn't room at the table for both your mother and your mother-in-law. I did find a place where they could be together."

"That's fine," Joanna said. "I'm sure they appreciate it."

"And how are things out at the sheriff's department this morning?" Linda asked. "Hopping, I presume."

"You could say that," Joanna said with a nod. "That's why we're so late, as a matter of fact."

"Don't worry about it," Linda said. "Most of the ladies have never been here before. The social hour gave them all a chance to explore. I think even nondrinkers like me were getting a kick out of prowling around. Makes me feel like somebody dropped me somewhere smack in the middle of the Cotswolds."

When Linda turned away to speak to the person seated on her left, Joanna had an opportunity to study her surroundings. The room was lovely, and spacious enough to hold the ten or so tables of twelve without seeming the least bit crowded. Dark walls and wood, as well as indirect lighting concealed behind deep-profiled cove molding near the ceiling gave the place an elegant ambience. If the food came close to matching the atmosphere, it was little wonder that the Rob Roy had emerged as the dining place of choice in Cochise County.

Linda stood up and tapped her water glass with a spoon, calling them to attention. "Good afternoon, ladies," she said with a smile. "Please stand for the invocation. Reverand Maculyea?"

With the invocation and flag salute over, the luncheon

began in earnest. In years past, Joanna would have been almost sick at the prospect of standing up later and giving a speech. Fortunately, running for sheriff had cured her of all fear of public speaking. She was able to enjoy the food and to chat with her table companions without succumbing to a case of nerves.

"Have you heard anything more from Jeff?" Joanna asked during a moment of relative privacy.

A cloud seemed to pass over Marianne's face. "Nothing," she said. "Not a word. The board advanced the money he said he needed. I wired it to him yesterday afternoon, but at this point I have no way of knowing whether or not he received it."

"Don't worry," Joanna said. "It probably arrived there right on time. If it didn't and he really needed the money, he would have called by now."

Marianne nodded, but still she looked troubled. "The problem is, spending that money now is going to leave us strapped later on. I can't imagine what Jeff was thinking when he asked me to come up with that much more. When he gets back, he may have to go to work just to help keep us afloat. Who'll take care of the baby?"

"You'll work it out," Joanna told her. "It's not the end of the world. Lots of kids grow up with two working parents."

"But that's not how we *planned* it," Marianne argued.

Marianne Maculyea always appeared to be so calm and poised and completely all-knowing. It startled Joanna to realize that she already possessed intimate knowledge of something her friend and pastor was just beginning to learn.

"Welcome to parenthood, Mari," Joanna said with a reassuring smile. "It's *always* full of surprises. Now when can I schedule the baby shower?"

"Not until they're home," Marianne insisted. "I keep worrying that if we do anything beforehand, something will go wrong and the whole thing will fall apart."

Just then Linda Kimball rose to her feet and once again called the group to attention. "Ladies today we have as our guest the newly elected Sheriff of Cochise County, Joanna Brady. I believe Sheriff Brady will be honoring us with a few remarks—a state-of-the-county talk, if you will, rather like the President's state of the union.

"Unfortunately our first vice president, Marliss Shackleford, is ill today. Substituting for her and making both the introduction and the official presentation will be our second vice president, the Reverend Marianne Maculyea."

Before Marianne stood up, she reached down beside her chair and picked up a paper-wrapped parcel. "As you may suspect, I was asked to do this introduction just a few minutes ago. It's a pleasure, however, since Joanna Brady and I have been friends for years. We met in seventh grade at Lowell School, longer ago than either one of us wants to remember. Not only is Joanna a good friend, she's also one of the most resilient people I know.

"Most of you know the series of tragedies that, by force of circumstance, vaulted Joanna Brady into the position she holds today. As Arizona's first and only female sheriff, we've all heard and read a good deal about how *different* she is, as though, by virtue of being sheriff, she's somehow grown two left feet. I can assure you that, although she may be very different from our previous sheriffs, she's still very much the same old Joanna Lathrop Brady I've always known and loved.

"I've heard it said on occasion that she became a sheriff without really meaning to. In a way, that's true. She set out on the very ordinary path of becoming a wife and mother, but when she reached a fork in that road, she knew which path to follow.

"Those of you who haven't yet seen the women's club's display at the Cochise County Justice Center may not know that it consists of a series of framed pictures—formal portraits, if you will—of all Joanna Brady's male predecessors in the office of Cochise County Sheriff. If you were to study the pictures as a group, I believe you'd find the officers featured there to be a pretty tough-looking bunch of customers—every man of them. Some of them look more like desperadoes than they do like upholders of law and order.

"When Sheriff Brady gave us the snapshot she wanted us to frame and use, her chosen pose sparked some controversy. And so, before I make the official presentation, I'd like to ask Joanna herself to please stand and give us a little background as to why she selected this particular photo. Please help me welcome Sheriff Joanna Brady."

To a roomful of warmly welcoming applause, Joanna stood up and made her way to the podium. "Thank you, Marianne. You're absolutely right, I never thought I would be elected sheriff, but now here I am. You're right, too, about all the emphasis on how 'different' I am. Bearing that in mind, maybe I would have been better off sticking to a more formal portrait. The one I chose, though, is of me when I was seven or eight years old and setting off—Brownie uniform and all—to sell my first batch of Girl Scout cookies.

"Some people may laugh to hear this, but selling those cookies marked a real watershed for me. I was scared to death. I didn't think I'd ever have nerve enough to talk to people and to ask them to buy something from me, but I did. Some of the boxes of cookies went to people I knew, but most of them went to strangers—to people I met at the post office and the grocery store. Over the years I got better at it. The year I was in the seventh grade, I sold five hundred boxes—enough cookies to be awarded the prize of two weeks of summer camp at Whispering Pines up on Mount Lemmon. Believe me, that's a lot of Thin Mints."

Joanna paused while the room filled with laughter. "Was that important?" she continued. "It must have been. Years later, I applied for a job with Milo Davis at the Davis Insurance Agency here in town. Milo asked me if I'd ever had any selling experience. I told him yes, Girl Scout cookies. I got the job. Last fall, when it came time to talk to strangers again, the voters of Cochise County gave me this job as well.

"I suspect that there are lots of women out there who are just like me, women who, as little girls, made their first forays into the world of work by selling Girl Scout cookies. Marketing those boxes of cookies is a very real job. It consists of deciding to do something, of setting a goal, and then making it happen.

"So when you look at this picture of a little girl with her Radio Flyer full of cookies, remember, that little red wagon is the vehicle that led to one I drive now—to the one that's parked outside, at the far end of the parking lot. You'll know it when you see it. It's the big white Blazer with the light bar on top and with the insignia of the Cochise County Sheriff's Department painted on the door. I see selling that wagonload of cookies as the beginning of the path that led me, inevitably, to this one. And remember, too, the next time you buy a box of Thin Mints, you may be buying those cookies from a future President of the United States."

As Joanna sat down, the women in the room rose to their feet, cheering and applauding. Gratified but feeling self-conscious, Joanna waited for the applause to die down. It was then she caught sight of Terry Buckwalter.

A wall of smoky glass separated the dining room from the lounge area and the bar beyond it. Eleanor was right. Terry's hair was different, but not that different. Joanna watched as Terry Buckwalter, accompanied by a man, sauntered across the room. The two of them took seats at the bar. From the hand gestures and movements that accompanied the conversation, Joanna could see that Terry was evidently enjoying her part of the animated conversation. In one short day, Terry Buckwalter had undergone a total transformation.

When the applause ended and Marianne made the official presentation, Joanna managed to stand and string together a few words of acceptance, but she did so without ever letting the two people in the other room totally out of her sight.

Once the ceremony was over, Joanna leaned over to Marianne. "Could you do me a big favor?"

"Sure," Marianne answered. "What?"

"There's something I have to do. Could you please give Eva Lou and my mother a ride back to town?"

"I'm in the Bug," Marianne replied, referring to her venerable late-sixties, sea-foam-green V.W. "But since there's only the two of them, I'm sure there'll be plenty of room. Do you want to tell them, or should I?"

"I will," Joanna told her. "Eva Lou probably won't mind, but you know Eleanor."

Marianne nodded. "What kind of car did you say your brother drives?"

"A BMW," Joanna answered. "A five-forty-i."

"The Bug will be a big comedown if she's used to that, but she'll get over it."

Which turned out to be not entirely true. "You want me to do what?" Eleanor demanded.

"Shhh," Joanna said. "Don't make a fuss, please. I want you to ride home with Marianne. There's someone here I need to talk to."

"So talk," Eleanor said. "What's the big problem?"

"It's police business."

"Come on, Eleanor," Eva Lou said. "If Joanna has something to do, it won't hurt us to ride back home with Marianne."

"We'll wait," Eleanor insisted.

"It's confidential, Mother," Joanna said. "And I have no idea how long it will take."

"We'll wait in the car."

"No, you won't," Joanna said, keeping her tone level but firm. "I'm sorry, but I have a job to do here. I expect you to go home with Marianne and let me do it."

What had worked in regard to the hair appointment didn't work when it came to the ride back home. The corners of Eleanor's mouth turned down.

"Well!" she exclaimed in a voice that bristled with indignation. "I never!"

It took time for the women to drain out of the dining room, especially since most of them wanted to pause for a word or two with the guest of honor and to admire the photo. To Joanna's relief, Terry and her male friend were still seated at the bar when Joanna's last well-wisher headed for the parking lot. As Joanna walked toward them, she realized that, close up, the change in Terry Buckwalter was even more remarkable.

"Terry?" Joanna asked tentatively, easing herself up on an empty stool on Terry Buckwalter's far side.

"Joanna!" Terry exclaimed, swinging around to face her. "What are you doing here?"

Joanna held up the framed picture. "I was here for the women's club luncheon," she answered. "I saw you come in and thought I'd stop by to see how you're doing."

Terry didn't look particularly thrilled. Her tone of voice implied that Joanna's interest in her well-being wasn't much appreciated. "I'm doing fine," she said. "I just want to be left alone."

The man seated with Terry hurried off his barstool and came around to meet Joanna, one hand extended. Looking at him from behind, Joanna had assumed from the plentiful mop of reddish hair on his head that he was someone in his thirties or forties. Now that he stood in front of her, though, she realized he was far older than that. He was strikingly handsome—tan and fit, with aquiline good looks and an infectious grin that was both boyish and friendly. Still, he had to be pushing sixty if he was a day.

"Come on now, Terry," the man urged. "Don't be so standoffish. Who's your friend? Why don't you introduce us?"

"This is Peter," Terry said without enthusiasm. "Peter Wilkes, my golf pro. And this is Joanna Brady."

"Joanna Brady." Frowning, the man repeated the name, then he snapped his fingers as if a light had been switched on in his head. "As in Sheriff Joanna Brady?"

Joanna nodded. "One and the same."

"I remember now. Esther and Myron—Myron is my partner—mentioned something about a special luncheon today. If I'm not mistaken, you were the guest of honor. I hope everything measured up to your expectations."

As soon as she heard Peter Wilkes's name, Joanna recognized it as the other half of the pair of men who were responsible for the Rob Roy in the first place. The problem was, Joanna had understood that the two men were a gay couple rather than simply partners. If that was the case, what was going on between Peter Wilkes and Terry Buckwalter?

Peter politely backed away. "If you two will excuse me, I have another lesson coming up in just a few minutes. You shot a great game today, Terry. That back nine was terrific. Keep up the good work."

"Thanks," Terry said with a smile. "It was pretty good, wasn't it?"

Peter Wilkes nodded. "It was a lot better than pretty good."

"You'll check for me then on the other?" Terry asked.

Peter looked down at his watch. "I don't know if I'll be able to reach him today. But yes, I will check. You can count on it. As soon as I know anything, I'll let you know."

Peter Wilkes hurried off in the direction that led out to the pro shop. Joanna waited for a moment, wondering what exactly Wilkes was checking on. Then the bartender appeared. "What can I get for you?" he asked, addressing Joanna.

Joanna shook her head. "Nothing for me," she said. "I just finished lunch."

Terry Buckwalter, however, pushed her empty glass across the bar. "I'll take another," she said.

The bartender disappeared, returning a moment later with a tall drink that looked like nothing more serious than a glass of iced tea. Without a word, Terry tore open two packets of artificial sweetener and stirred them into the glass. Only then, as she stirred the dark brown liquid, did Joanna notice the other thing that was different about Terry Buckwalter—

her wedding ring was missing. There was a pale circle on the tanned skin of her finger that showed plainly enough that a ring had once been there. Now it wasn't.

Glancing at her own left hand, Joanna caught sight of the two rings she still wore. One was the plain gold band she had worn from her wedding day on. The other was the diamond solitaire engagement ring, an anniversary present from Andy that she hadn't actually received until after he was already in the hospital, dying. She had gone from the middle of September to almost the end of January without finding the strength to remove either one of them. Terry Buckwalter had removed hers within the first twenty-four hours.

"So what do you want?" Terry asked, as her eyes met Joanna's in the reflection of the mirrored bar. Distractedly, she ran the ringless hand through her hair. When she took her hand away, the precision-cut hair fell flawlessly back into place. For a change, Helen Barco had outdone herself.

"I just wanted to talk to you," Joanna said.

"To talk or to lecture?" Terry Buckwalter demanded. "You disapprove, don't you—of my new haircut, of my playing golf, of everything about me."

"Terry, I certainly didn't mean—"

"Didn't you?" Terry Buckwalter interjected, her whole body radiating hostility. "That's why you didn't leave when all those other women did. You wanted to have a private word with me. You wanted the opportunity to give me the benefit of all your vast experience as a recent widow. You wanted to let me know what's appropriate and what isn't. Well, Sheriff Brady, here's some news from the front. I'm not nearly as good as you are at playing that role. The part suits you to a T. On me, it sucks."

As Terry's voice rose, heads turned in their direction as

other people in the bar—mostly male foursomes—glanced their way.

"Please, Terry," Joanna began. "You don't understand. All I—"

"Yes, I do understand," Terry returned. "I understand perfectly. So you and Andy had a fairy-tale marriage. Lucky for you. Bucky and I didn't. I made the best of a bad bargain, and maybe so did he. But all that's over now. Your Andy's dead, Joanna. Here you are getting to play sheriff and to do things maybe you've always wanted to do. It's time for me to do the same thing—time for me to do what *I* want for a change. Do you understand?"

"Yes," Joanna murmured, hoping to calm the woman down. If nothing else, to get her to lower her voice. "Yes, I'm sure I do."

"No, you don't," Terry Buckwalter returned coldly. "I don't think you do at all."

With that, she slammed a five-dollar bill down on the counter. "Keep the change, Nate," she called to the bartender, then she stood up and stalked out the room.

Left behind with the men in the room still staring at her, Joanna wondered what she had done wrong and why her asking to talk to Terry had unleashed such a powerful reaction. Half a minute later, a speeding white T-Bird flashed by the glassed-in front entryway on its way out of the parking lot.

Maybe she's right, Joanna found herself thinking. *Maybe I don't understand.*

8

FEELING frustrated, Joanna left the Rob Roy for the fifteen-mile drive back to Bisbee. Along the way, she mulled over what had happened with Terry. Joanna had been curious about whoever was with Terry on the day after Bucky Buckwalter's death, but that hadn't been her primary concern. More than anything, she had wanted to speak to Terry, widow-to-widow, long enough to mention the inadvisability of making any momentous financial decisions in too much of a hurry.

That heartfelt warning had gone unsaid in the face of Terry's seemingly unprovoked anger. What was going on? Prior to Joanna's arrival in the bar, she had observed Terry Buckwalter and Peter Wilkes from a distance for the better part of half an hour. During that time the two of them had been chatting away as though neither of them had a care in the world.

Maybe that was it in a nutshell. Maybe, with Bucky Buckwalter dead, that was absolutely true. If Peter Wilkes and Terry Buckwalter had something going, then Joanna's seeing them together might well have precipitated Terry's angry reaction.

Small towns have certain expectations of what's appropriate and what isn't after the death of one of their own. Bisbee, Arizona was no different. Joanna wondered how many other luncheon attendees had witnessed and been shocked by Terry's carefree attitude the day after her husband's murder. The difference between police officers and ordinary citizens, however, was that the former's opinions could lead to questions of an official nature—to questions and, sometimes, to convictions.

Other people might disapprove—quietly or otherwise—of Terry's actions: of her peeling off her wedding ring less than twenty-four hours after her husband's death or of her possibly carrying on with Peter Wilkes. As for Joanna, personal reservations aside, she had a moral obligation—a duty—to learn whether or not cause and effect were involved. Was it possible that Terry Buckwalter and/or Peter Wilkes had something to do with Bucky's death? If so, that would go a long way toward explaining the sudden chill in the air when Joanna had interrupted Terry's lighthearted performance as the merry widow.

Joanna couldn't recite the exact statistics, but she knew full well that people were far more likely to be murdered by those nearest and dearest to them than they were by complete strangers, mere acquaintances, or business associates. In some troubled marriages, homicides became a permanent substitute for divorce, although, once again, statistically speaking, violence-prone husbands used that escape hatch far more often than did vengeful wives. Still, women weren't immune. They resorted to such a method of dissolving a relationship, too, on occasion, especially when the murderous wife had a possible alternative to the troublesome husband already lined up and waiting in the wings.

Is that what's going on here? Joanna wondered.

It was generally assumed that Peter Wilkes was involved in a devoted, long-term relationship with his partner—the guy named Myron who ran the restaurant. But just because that was common gossip around town didn't necessarily make it true. Maybe Peter Wilkes was a switch-hitter—AC/DC, as Andy used to say.

Clearly Peter Wilkes and Terry Buckwalter were up to something that went beyond a simple above-the-board pro/golfer relationship. Whatever it was, neither of them had been willing to discuss specific details in front of Joanna.

Suppose, Joanna told herself, *Bucky was an insurmountable roadblock to whatever Wilkes and Terry had in mind. What might the two of them have done then when someone from out of town, someone with a perfectly believable motive for Bucky's murder, had shown up on the scene?* Slowly, the idea began to coalesce in Joanna's mind. *If Terry wanted to ditch Bucky Buckwalter, wasn't Hal Morgan the perfect fall guy?*

Unbidden, Joanna's mind wandered back to the previous afternoon. She remembered how Terry Buckwalter had casually reached into her pocket and pulled out that damning scrap of paper—the one containing Hal Morgan's purportedly handwritten note. If, as Terry maintained, the note had been hidden in her makeup case for months, why did she suddenly and conveniently have it in her possession, to pass along to investigators on the very day of her husband's death?

That's easy, Joanna thought. *To point a finger at someone else. At Hal Morgan.*

One terrible injustice had already been visited on the man.

He had lost his wife to a senseless, tragic death. Now another blow was about to fall if he ended up being charged with murder in the death of Bonnie Morgan's killer.

That hadn't happened yet, not officially, but only because Ernie Carpenter had so far been too busy to get around to crossing the t's and dotting the i's. At this point, Morgan was still only a suspect—some would have said *prime* suspect— in the case.

With her heart quickening in her breast, Joanna realized that Bucky Buckwalter's killer had counted on that. Whoever the perpetrator or perpetrators were, they had killed the man with some confidence that the homicide investigation would go no deeper than the obvious: Hal Morgan had come to Bisbee with a clear motive for wanting to harm his wife's killer. If that man was now dead, it naturally followed that Hal Morgan had killed him.

What came over Joanna then wasn't exactly a chill. It was more like a vibration—a telling, steady thrum that came to her from the inside out, letting her know that she had stumbled onto something—something important. She had never experienced any sensation quite like it, but she knew at once what it was. Without understanding how, she knew—beyond a doubt—that Hal Morgan was innocent. He hadn't killed Bucky Buckwalter. Somebody else had, someone who had cynically exploited Hal Morgan's lingering grief and had used it to further his or her own deadly purposes.

The moment of realization rang so true that Joanna felt almost giddy. She was suddenly so excited—so energized and focused—that she had to concentrate on lifting her foot off the accelerator to keep from mashing it all the way to the floor.

And then, in that peculiar way minds work, a long-buried

memory surfaced in her head. She was twelve years old again and sitting at the breakfast table in her parents' home on Campbell Avenue. Eleanor had been cooking breakfast and was just then slamming the frying pan into the sink, when Big Hank Lathrop came into the room and poured himself a cup of coffee.

Sheriff D. H. Lathrop had been out all night investigating a homicide crime scene. He had come home at sunup to shower, change clothes, and eat breakfast before heading back to the office.

"I don't know why you had to be out there all night like that," Eleanor complained as she slid a loaded plate in front of him. "You're not as young as you used to be, Hank. You can't expect to work around the clock without having it affect you."

"But Ellie . . ." he objected. Big Hank Lathrop was the only person in the world Eleanor Lathrop ever allowed to call her by a nickname. "You just don't understand how great it feels. I knew from the beginning, from the moment we got there, that George Hammond was lying through his teeth when he said that him and his buddy—"

"He and his buddy." Eleanor's habitual corrections of her husband's grammar were so much business as usual that Big Hank barely missed the beat of his story. ". . . he and his good buddy, Lionel Dexter, were out hunting. Hammond claimed that he stumbled and that his thirty-ought-six went off by accident. All of a sudden, right while he's in the middle of telling this long, complicated story, I realize it's a crock. Ol' George is making it up as he goes along. I can't tell you how I knew; I just did. As soon as I caught on to him, I couldn't stand to walk away without managing to trip him up."

The whole time Big Hank had been speaking, ostensibly

he had been telling the story to his wife. But ever so often, as he spoke, his eyes would stray to Joanna, including her in the conversation, saying to her—in that quiet, unspoken way of his—that she, too, was included in the storytelling. The message behind his words came through to his daughter loud and clear. He was letting her know that it was all right to love something—to care passionately about it—even if someone else in your life, someone you loved, didn't necessarily share your enthusiasm.

Sitting down across from him, Eleanor's disapproval was as plain as the permanently etched frown that furrowed her forehead. "Did you?" she asked. "Trip him up, I mean."

Big Hank's face had lit up like a Christmas tree as he continued. "You bet. All night long Georgie had been telling us about tripping over something—a rock, or maybe even a branch or a root. He claimed that's how come the gun discharged. So come sunup, I tell him, 'Okay, Mr. Hammond, all's we need now is to have you show us whatever it was you tripped over.' So he leads us to this big ol' rock and tries to pass that one off as being it, except anybody who knows a thing about guns and trajectories and all that can see it isn't true. From where the rock is and where and how we found the body, you can tell those two things just don't add up.

" 'Look here, Georgie,' I said. 'This whole thing's a bunch of B.S. It couldn't have happened this way, and you know it. How about if you just haul off and tell us the truth?' And you know what happened? He did. Just like that. Broke down in tears and started spilling his guts. The thing is, if I hadn't called him on it, George Hammond might have gotten away with murder."

Eleanor, listening in silence, refused to be swayed by either her husband's story or by his enthusiasm in telling it.

"You still shouldn't have stayed out all night," she responded at last when he finished. "You'll be paying for this foolishness the whole rest of the week."

It was amazing to Joanna how everything about that whole scene had lingered in her memory. It was all there, in full living color and sense-around sound. She could hear and smell the frying bacon. She cringed at the enamel-chipping clatter when her mother pitched the frying pan into the sink and avoided the soul-shriveling frown that etched her mother's forehead.

Even at age twelve, Joanna had known there was more at stake in that small kitchen than the loss of one night's sleep. Although she was years away from being able to sort it out, she understood there were other, more weighty issues hidden in the dark undercurrents of the words being bandied back and forth across that kitchen table. And now, some seventeen years later, Joanna finally did see.

After years of enduring her mother's unremitting criticism, she realized that D. H. Lathrop had been Eleanor's target long before his daughter was. When he was no longer there to bear the brunt of it, Joanna had been forced to take his place. The constant arguments between mother and daughter—disagreements that lingered to this day—were and had always been nothing more than extensions of that original conflict. It was a natural outgrowth of who Joanna's parents were and what made them tick.

Big Hank Lathrop had thrown himself into living without reservation. He had grabbed hold of everything life had to offer. Eleanor had clung to the sidelines. Unable to compete with her husband out in the world, she had cut away at him at home, constantly trying to whittle him down to her size. She was smart enough not to reveal her hand by directly belittling his triumph in the Hammond case. That would have exposed her own jealousy of his devotion to duty. Instead, she cloaked her rebuke in the socially acceptable guise of wifely concern—of Big Hank's needing his rest—rather than saying what she really meant. Never once did she admit that anything that took her husband's attention away from her— Big Hank's job included—was a rival to be attacked on all possible fronts.

Suddenly, as clearly as Joanna sensed Hal Morgan's innocence, she could see that her mother had spent her whole lifetime claiming the high moral ground, all the while cutting everyone else down to size. In negating other people's accomplishments, she magnified her own.

The things that had driven Big Hank—the same needs and desires that had sent him out on a nightlong mission to match wits with a killer—were the ones that motivated Joanna as well. Those were the very ingredients lacking in Eleanor's own makeup. She had lived her life vicariously, first through her husband's work, and later through Joanna's work and her happiness with Andy as well. No wonder Eleanor Lathrop was angry and drowning in self-pity. Only by diminishing others could she maintain her own fragile self-worth.

Those insights all washed over Joanna in a series of crushing waves. When the flood ebbed, it left behind, like debris deposited on a sandy shore, an adult understanding not only of both of Joanna's parents but of herself as well.

There could be no doubt that, in spite of it all, D. H. Lathrop had continued to love his wife. The reverse—Eleanor's love for Big Hank—wasn't as easy to discern. Big Hank had managed to maintain the relationship by learning to disregard the hurtful things that came out of Eleanor's mouth.

Unfortunately, that simple survival trick was one his daughter had yet to master.

Joanna realized now, though, that he had demonstrated it back then. With Joanna sitting at the breakfast table, watching and hanging on his every word, he had simply set Eleanor's biting criticisms aside. He had let them flow over him and then he shook them off as a dog sheds a coatful of water. Instead of internalizing his wife's carping, he had simply deflected it. But first, he had winked at his daughter.

"That's funny, Ellie," he had said. "I must be younger than you think, because I don't feel the least bit tired. Fact of the matter is, I think I could go out right this minute and lick my weight in wildcats."

Seventeen years later, Joanna felt exactly the same way— ready to take on all comers. She had left the Rob Roy feeling drained. The hassle with her mother over the ride home, as well as the confrontation with Terry Buckwalter, had taken their toll. But now, convinced she had made a vital connection in the Buckwalter case, she felt miraculously recovered. Rather than driving directly back to the department, she headed for the Copper Queen Hospital.

On the way, she radioed to the department to see if Ernie Carpenter could meet her there. Unfortunately, Dispatch reported that he was still up in Sunizona. Putting the radio mike back in its clip, Joanna made up her mind.

That's all right, she told herself. *I'll make like the Little Red Hen, and I'll do it myself.*

Once inside the hospital, she saw Deputy Debbie Howell stationed in the hallway outside the door of Hal Morgan's private room. Instead of going directly to the room, Joanna headed for the nurses' station. Mavis Embry, the heavyset woman issuing orders at the nerve center of the hospital, had been a recent nursing school graduate working in the delivery room on the night Joanna Lathrop was born. Now she was the Copper Queen's head nurse.

"What can I do for you, Joanna?" Mavis asked.

"I'm here to see Hal Morgan."

Mavis shook her head. "Dr. Lee says no visitors. He's over in the clinic, if you want to talk to him about it. Until I get the okay from him, nobody goes in the room."

Nodding, Joanna headed toward the clinic wing of the hospital. Dr. Thomas Lee was standing out in the hall, perusing someone's chart. "Dr. Lee?"

Lee, a Taiwanese immigrant and a recent medical school graduate, was only an inch or two taller than Joanna's five-foot-four. He peered at her through the tiny round lenses of his wire-rimmed glasses.

"Yes?" he answered.

Joanna opened her leather wallet that displayed her badge. He frowned. "The officer who was here earlier disturbed my patient. He needs rest."

"Another officer was here?" Joanna asked in surprise. "Who?"

"A big man," Dr. Lee told her. "Voland, I believe was his name. He, too, carried a badge."

"Dick Voland is one of my deputies," Joanna said.

Dr. Lee drew himself up to his full height. "I do not care for his bedside manner," he declared. "You can tell him from me that he is not to enter the rooms of any of my patients without my permission in advance. Is that clear?"

Joanna nodded. "Perfectly," she replied. "But would it be possible for me to speak to Mr. Morgan? It's a matter of some urgency."

"Mr. Morgan has had a severe blow to the back of his head," Dr. Lee replied. "He needs his rest. You promise not to take too long?"

"I promise," Joanna said.

"Very well," Dr. Lee returned. "I will call Mrs. Embry and let her know."

When Joanna returned to the nurses' station, Mavis Embry waved her on by. "I guess you know which door," she said.

Deputy Debbie Howell, stationed directly outside the door to Hal Morgan's room, was a single mom and a relatively new hire in the department. As a consequence, she was low-man on Dick Voland's patrol roster. She greeted Joanna with a pleasant smile. "Good afternoon, Sheriff Brady."

"Good afternoon, deputy," Joanna returned. "How's it going?"

Deputy Howell shrugged. "B-o-r-i-n-g," she answered. "The only people who've been in or out so far are doctors and nurses. No other visitors at all."

In fact, a printed "No Visitors" sign had been affixed to the door frame. "I've spoken to Dr. Lee," Joanna said, pushing the door open. "I won't be long."

Hal Morgan lay on his back on the bed. His head was swathed in bandages. At first Joanna thought he was asleep. He lay with his face turned toward the window, and he didn't move when the door opened. Walking quietly to the far side of the bed, Joanna was surprised to see that his eyes were open. He was staring out the window. Following his gaze, she looked out through the slight distortion of the green mesh screen that covered the window. Half a mile away, the rusty-red tailings dump reared abruptly into the air, reaching heavenward toward an intensely blue canopy of sky.

"Mr. Morgan?" Joanna asked.

Frowning, he turned to look at her. For a moment Joanna wasn't sure whether or not he recognized her. With head injuries, she knew there was always the possibility of loss of memory. Short term memory, especially of events that occur within hours of the injury incident, can disappear forever.

"Sheriff . . . Sheriff . . ." Morgan struggled.

"Brady," Joanna supplied. "Sheriff Joanna Brady."

He nodded and then grimaced, as though even that small movement had pained him. But when he spoke, his voice emerged with surprisingly clarity and force.

"I don't care what that Voland character says," Hal Morgan told her. "I didn't kill Amos Buckwalter."

There was a single chair next to the window. Joanna sank down onto it. "What's the last thing you remember?" she asked.

"Wait a minute, Sheriff Brady," Morgan said with sudden wariness. "I put in my twenty years. Voland already told me I'm a suspect. There's an armed deputy stationed outside my door. I'm not talking to anyone—you included—without having an attorney present."

"Do you have one?" Joanna asked.

Morgan frowned. "Do I have one what?"

"An attorney," Joanna answered. "By the way, the best defense attorney in town is a guy by the name Burton Kimball."

Reaching into her pocket, Joanna pulled out one of her business cards—one of the shiny new ones with the words "Joanna Lee Brady, Sheriff of Cochise County," printed on the front. Turning the card over, she scrawled Burton Kimball's name on the back and then handed the card to Hal

Morgan. He squinted at it for a moment as though his eyes weren't quite working properly. "What's this?" he asked.

"The name of that defense attorney," Joanna replied. "You'll have to call him, though. He's good, but he's not likely to show up unless you call him. Ernie Carpenter, my homicide investigator, is bound to be in touch before long. You'll want to have Burton on tap when that happens."

Morgan lowered the card and stared at Joanna. "Why are you telling me this?" he asked.

Joanna looked down at her hands. "Maybe because I believe you when you say you didn't do it?"

Momentary anger flickered in Hal Morgan's deep-set eyes. "Look," he said, "if this is one of those good cop/bad cop deals, forget it. It's not going to work. I've played that game myself a time or two. No matter what you say or do, I still didn't kill Amos Buckwalter."

"I didn't say you did," Joanna replied. "In fact, I believe I said the exact opposite."

Looking away, Hal Morgan tossed the card onto his bedside table. "What are you here for, then?" he demanded.

"To ask a few questions."

"Like what?"

"Like what do you remember about yesterday?"

"Very little from noon on," he said.

"But before that?"

"Pretty much the whole thing," he replied. "I remember meeting you. I remember standing outside the fence at the animal clinic all morning long. Up until noon."

"And then?" Joanna urged.

"It must have been right around then when Buckwalter's wife came outside, got in her car, and drove off. I assumed that Buckwalter was alone in the clinic, but a few minutes later he came outside with somebody else—another man. The two of them walked toward the barn."

Joanna sat forward on her chair. "What did this other man look like?"

Morgan looked at her quizzically. "You believe me, then?"

"Why shouldn't I?"

"When I told Voland the same thing, he made me out to be a liar. He said I made the other guy up in hopes you'd go looking for someone else to pin it on."

"Did you?" Joanna asked.

Morgan shook his head. "No," he said. "He was there. I saw him."

"What did he look like?"

"That I can't tell you," Morgan answered. "Not really. I was on the far side of the cattle guard, outside the fence. From that distance, I couldn't see either one of them very well, but I'm fairly certain one of them was Buckwalter. I recognized his shirt. The other one, I never saw before. I do remember wondering how he could have gotten inside the clinic without my seeing him. One thing for sure, he didn't come in through the gate."

"He probably came through the house then," Joanna supplied. "The Buckwalter house faces another street, but there's a path that leads back and forth between the house and the back of the clinic."

"I see," Morgan said.

"So what happened next?" Joanna asked.

"Both of them, Buckwalter and the other guy, walked into a metal building, a shed that looked like a barn."

"And then?"

Without answering, Hal gave Joanna a shrewdly appraising look. They were both aware that, over his objections, they had slipped into a mode where she was asking questions, and he was answering them. For a time, Joanna thought he was going to clam up completely, but after a moment he continued.

"Pretty soon I heard someone yelling. It sounded like somebody calling for help from inside the barn, so I left the gate and went running that way. The last thing I remember was going in through the door—going from bright sunlight into a sort of dusky gloom. Then something hit me on the back of the head. The next thing I knew, I woke up here with my lungs on fire and with a killer headache that just won't stop."

Joanna nodded. "I see," she said.

"Why is that?" he asked. "If Deputy Voland doesn't believe me, why do you?"

"It occurred to me this afternoon that maybe someone else—somebody with his or her own reasons for wanting Bucky Buckwalter dead—is using your motivation as camouflage. Whoever the killer is, he's expecting us to take things at face value—to charge you and let him off the hook."

As a sudden expression of comprehension flashed across his face, Hal Morgan raised himself on his elbow. A few minutes earlier, the mere act of nodding his head had pained him. This time, if the pain was there, it didn't seem to register or show. Suddenly Hal Morgan was transformed into a cop again—a cop on the trail of a killer.

"Do you know who it is?" he demanded.

Joanna shook her head. "Not yet," Joanna said. "But I have a few ideas. Talking to you has given me a few more."

Morgan studied her for a minute, then he eased himself back down on the pillow. "You know, I did want to kill him once," he admitted. "The night Bonnie died, I could have done it with my bare hands. I think I would have, if somebody hadn't stopped me. And I still felt the same way when I saw that smug little bastard in Phoenix last summer. I went there thinking there was going to be a trial, that I'd have a chance to testify. But Buckwalter's lawyer had already worked out a plea bargain. When I found out about that deal, I might still have done something drastic if it hadn't been for Father Mike."

"Father Mike?" Joanna put in. "Who's he?"

"A friend of mine. Father Michael McCrady. I met him through M.A.D.D."

"Is he a counselor for them, or a chaplain maybe?"

Morgan shook his head. "No. He's a member, just like everybody else. His sister was a nun in Milwaukee. A drunk ran her down in a crosswalk as she walked from her school back to the convent after a school Christmas pageant. Of all the people I talked to after Bonnie's death, Father Mike was the first one who got to me, the first one who made sense. Talking to him finally made me see beyond my own hurt, made me see the big picture. He helped me understand that we were all in the same boat and that it's useless to take your hurt and anger out on a single individual. It's far more important to get people in general to see that drunk driving is a menace to everyone. Father Mike is the one who convinced me that by working with M.A.D.D., by raising people's awareness, maybe I can keep what happened to Bonnie and me from happening to someone else."

"In other words," Joanna said, "you're saying that you didn't come to Bisbee to kill Bucky Buckwalter?"

Hal Morgan's gaze met and held Joanna's. "That's right," he said. "I came to pass out leaflets."

Joanna thought for a moment before she spoke again. "Yesterday afternoon, Terry Buckwalter gave me a note, one she claims you gave her up in Phoenix. It was written in pencil and had a reference on it to a Bible verse."

Morgan nodded and closed his eyes. "Exodus 21:12," he said. " *'He that smiteth a man, so that he die, shall be surely put to death.'* "

"You did give it to her then?"

"Yes," Hal Morgan said. "And at the time, I meant every word of it, but, like I said, that was before I met Father Mike."

Another long silence followed. "Am I under arrest then?" Morgan asked at last.

"No," Joanna told him. "Not yet."

"What's the point of the deputy, then?"

"Some people seem to think you're a flight risk," Joanna answered.

"Some people," Morgan repeated. "Like your friend Voland, for instance? What about you, Sheriff Brady? What do you think?"

For a moment, Joanna considered how she should answer. What she thought was complicated by what she felt, and what she felt was directly related to her own experience. On one side of the scale there was the far-too-blithe, wedding-ring- and grief-free Terry Buckwalter. On the other was Hal Morgan, a seemingly honorable ex-cop who, almost a year later, was still grieving over the loss of his beloved wife. Terry's reaction to Bucky's murder was totally foreign to Joanna Brady, while Hal Morgan's continuing anguish was achingly familiar. Based on those stark contrasts, it wasn't too difficult to see where Joanna Brady's sympathies might fall.

"Have you ever been in Bisbee before, Mr. Morgan?" she asked.

He shook his head. "Never," he told her.

"Even so," Joanna said quietly, "you may have heard something about me and my husband." She paused and had to swallow before she could continue. "His name was Andy—Andrew Roy Brady. He was murdered last September seventeenth. He was shot and died the next day—the day after our tenth anniversary."

The look on Hal Morgan's face registered both surprise and pain. "I'm sorry," he murmured. "I had no idea."

Joanna acknowledged his condolence with a nod and then continued. "His killer was a hired gun—a hit man working for a Columbian drug lord. The killer's name was Tony Vargas."

"Why are you telling me this?" Morgan asked.

The room became deathly silent as Joanna sought the courage to finish her story. "Vargas didn't go to prison," she finished at last. "He died. I killed him. I shot him."

"You shot him yourself?"

Joanna nodded. "It was ruled self-defense, so there was never any trial, but if I had needed a defense attorney, Burton Kimball is the one I would have called."

Morgan's eyes narrowed. "Wait a minute; a little while ago you said you believed me."

"I do," Joanna answered. "But just because I do doesn't mean everyone else will."

Hal Morgan reached out and retrieved Joanna's business card. It was only when he was holding it in his hand, examining it, that she noticed his fingers and saw that Hal Morgan was still wearing his wedding ring. Three weeks under a year after his wife's death, he had yet to take his off. Terry Buckwalter's was already history. The contrast was telling.

Morgan was still looking at the card when he spoke again.

"I'm sorry about your husband," he said. "I didn't know."

"Thank you," she returned.

"Is that why you're helping me?" Hal Morgan asked.

Joanna shrugged. "Maybe," she said, standing up. "If nothing else, I know how you feel."

"Won't it cause trouble for you?" he asked. "With your people, I mean?"

She smiled. "It could. On the face of it, there's certainly potential for a conflict of interest. That's why I'm not pulling the deputy, even though I personally don't believe you need an armed guard."

"It's okay," Morgan said. "I understand." Then, after a moment, he added, "Your homicide dick isn't going to like it when he finds out you've referred me to a local defense attorney."

"Who's going to tell him?"

For the first time there was the slightest hint of a smile lurking under Hal Morgan's gray-flecked moustache. "Not me," he said, holding out his hand. "Thanks for everything."

Joanna shook hands with him, then walked as far as the door, where she stopped, pausing with one hand on the lever. From a law-enforcement standpoint what she had done made no sense. On a personal level she was incapable of doing anything else.

"You're welcome," she told him. "And good luck with Burton. He's a good man."

9

ONCE back in the Blazer, Joanna radioed the department and asked to be patched through to Dick Voland. "I've just come from the hospital," she told him.

"You went to see Morgan?"

"That's right," Joanna said. "And I talked to Deputy Howell, too. She's due to get off at three. Do you have an officer scheduled to relieve her?"

"Not yet," the chief deputy returned. "I was waiting for marching orders from you. Now that I know you're not pulling the guard, I'll definitely have someone there by three."

"Still no overtime, though, Dick," Joanna cautioned. "I want you to utilize people from the regular patrol roster."

"Right," Voland agreed. "No overtime." He paused. "I'm really glad you've come around to my way of thinking on this one, Joanna. I was afraid Morgan would stage some kind of miraculous recovery and just walk out of the hospital. Ex-cop or not, I don't want to lose this guy. Neither does the county attorney."

Dick Voland's voice on the radio was surprisingly cordial.

No doubt that had something to do with his mistaken belief that Joanna, too, had now joined the others in their conviction that Hal Morgan had murdered Bucky Buckwalter, that the case was as good as closed. It seemed a shame to let him know otherwise.

"Where's Ernie?" Joanna asked.

"He and Jaime Carbajal are still up at Sunizona. Things are hopping up there. Doc Winfield called a few minutes ago wanting to talk to him as well, but Ernie's come up with some kind of hot lead in the Carruthers case. I just sent Dave Hollicker hightailing it up to Sunizona with a search warrant. It sounds like Ernie's convinced that the daughter, Hannah Green, did her old man in. The problem is, right this minute no one can find her."

Since Ernie already had the Carruthers autopsy results in hand before he left town, Joanna knew that whatever the coroner was calling about had to have something to do with Bucky Buckwalter.

"Doctor Winfield is done with the Buckwalter autopsy then?" Joanna asked.

"Sounds like. It's not typed up or anything. That won't happen until tomorrow, but Winfield was willing to brief Ernie on the results in the meantime."

"What time will Ernie be getting back to town?" Joanna asked.

"No idea whatsoever," Voland answered. "But most likely it'll be late. You know what Ernie's like once he gets his nose to the ground. I told the Doc that he probably won't turn up any before tomorrow morning."

That news disappointed Joanna on two fronts. For one, without Ernie talking to Winfield, the department wouldn't have access to even the most preliminary autopsy results until noon the next day at the earliest. Not only that, if Hal Morgan's version of the events leading up to Bucky's murder was correct, someone besides Morgan had visited the crime scene.

Joanna needed someone to check that out, to go canvassing the Buckwalters' Saginaw-area neighbors searching for any kind of corroboration. She had hoped that job would fall to Ernie. But there were time constraints. The questions had to be asked while details were still fresh in people's minds, before they forgot something they had seen without any comprehension of its potential importance. If Detective Carpenter was otherwise occupied, someone else would have to pick up the slack and do the shoe-leather work—someone from Dick Voland's Patrol Division. That was bound to blow Joanna's cover with her chief deputy. But that was what she'd been elected for—to take the flak.

"Tell you what," she said. "I'm almost at the traffic circle. Instead of coming straight back to the department, I'll stop by Doc Winfield's office and see what he has to say. In the meantime, when you start passing out today's assignments, I want you to send at least one deputy over to Saginaw to talk to Bucky Buckwalter's neighbors. I want to know whether or not anyone saw a strange vehicle parked near the house or clinic around noon yesterday."

There was a moment of dead air over the radio. When Dick Voland spoke again, all trace of cordiality was gone from his voice.

"Why on earth would we want to do that?" he demanded.

"Because we need to," Joanna replied. "And we need to do it A.S.A.P."

"Wait a minute," he said. "Don't tell me. I'll bet Hal Morgan passed along his 'second man' pile of crap. He fed me that same line of bull. Don't fall for it, Joanna. It's nothing but a sucker ploy designed to throw us off track."

We're off track, all right, Joanna thought, *but somebody else put us there.* When she spoke, though, she made sure her voice stayed calm and even.

"Whether or not I *fell* for something is immaterial, Dick," she said. "I want Hal Morgan's story checked out."

"But I thought . . ." Voland sputtered. ". . . with your leaving him under guard . . ."

"We're keeping a guard on the suspect because you seem to feel it's necessary," Joanna said. "But just because you and the county attorney happen to be convinced of Hal Morgan's guilt doesn't necessarily make it so. Our department has an obligation to check out all the evidence, to bring it to a court of law, and then let a judge and jury decide. For today, I want one officer from the day shift and one from the night shift working the problem right up until nine o'clock, or until the ends of their respective shifts, whichever comes first."

"But, Patrol is already spread so thin—"

Joanna didn't give Voland time to finish voicing his objection. "Just do it, Dick," she interrupted. "That's an order. I'll see you as soon as I finish up with Doc Winfield."

The Cochise County Coroner's office was in Old Bisbee, halfway up Tombstone Canyon, beyond the courthouse in what had once been a grocery store. During the mid-eighties and long out of the milk-and-bread business, the derelict but still serviceable old building briefly had been brought back to life to house what was purported to be a low-cost, prepaid funeral service—Dearest Departures.

Its arrival in town had caused quite a stir. Popular opinion at the time held that the Dearest Departures plan for "discount dying" spelled the end of the line for people like Norm Higgins and other longtime members of family-owned funeral and mortuary businesses. Dearest Departures was supposed to do for the mom-and-pop mortuary business what McDonald's had done for hamburgers—standardize things and lower costs over all. People predicted that Higgins Funeral Chapel and Mortuary would soon disappear off the face of the earth.

It turned out, however, that Dearest Departures was far more of a marketing concept than it was a going concern. It was actually a get-rich-quick pyramid scheme couched in terms that sounded far better than the principals were prepared to deliver.

Franchisees were promised a complete business plan—building, state-of-the-art equipment, and in-depth training for one set fee. A slippery company-hired contractor had come to town with an itinerant crew and a motor-home-based workshop. Almost overnight the crew successfully remodeled the aging storefront into a reasonable facsimile of a mortuary. Unfortunately, corporate training of franchisees and their employees didn't measure up to the contractor's ability to transform space. The Dearest Departures "store" in Bisbee, one of the first in the country, had opened with a cadre of people who had barely managed to pass the state licensing requirements and who really didn't know what they were doing.

In the Bisbee franchise, trouble showed up almost as soon as the doors opened in the form of several public relations disasters. The first Dearest Departures funeral was that of longtime Bisbeeite Ralph Calloway. Due to an unfortunate employee screw-up during in the embalming procedure, Ralph's send off had a distinctly unpleasant odor. Days later, two bodies were misfiled, with unfortunate and irrevocable results. Miss Maybelle Cashman was mistakenly cremated while Doris Bellweather's body showed up in the coffin at what was supposed to be the Cashman viewing.

Dearest Departures had been open for less than two weeks, but the Cashman/Bellweather episode proved to be the local franchise's undoing. The well-organized business plan called for a considerable cash flow based on relatively low-cost but prepaid services. Once people stopped prepaying and took their business back to Norm Higgins, it was only a matter of time. Norm's costs may have sounded like the high-priced spread, but at least people had some confidence that Norm and his boys would stick the right body in the right box.

One month later, Dearest Departures was dead in the water. The owners locked the place up and abandoned town in the middle of the night, leaving behind a bunch of bad debts and a few very unhappy prepaid and unburied customers. Less than a year later, the parent company was out of business as well. When the building in Bisbee, along with all existing equipment, was about to be auctioned off for back taxes, some bright-eyed public servant came up with a better idea. The Dearest Departures facility in Tombstone Canyon was transformed, with a modest capital outlay, to house the offices of the newly appointed Cochise County Coroner, Dr. George Winfield.

Doc Winfield had come to Bisbee by almost as circuitous a path as the building he now occupied. A trained pathologist specializing in oncology with a practice in Minneapolis, he had lost heart when first his wife and, soon after, his only daughter had succumbed to cervical cancer. No longer willing to fight the good fight, he had given up on cancer and returned to school to study forensic pathology. Winfield had graduated with that speciality at a time when most of his original medical school class was thinking of retirement. Two months later, he had answered a blind ad in the *Wall Street Journal*. He arrived in Bisbee as a permanent snowbird in time to oversee the remodeling of the new facility.

As careful with public money as he was with his own, George Winfield had changed only that which was necessary. The walls of his office were still draped with lush burgundy velvet curtains that, as he said, still had several good years of use left in them. That explained why, when Joanna Brady pulled up to his office, she parked her Blazer in a spot once reserved for Dearest Departures hearses.

"Why, Sheriff Brady," Winfield said easily, rising in true gentlemanly fashion when Joanna knocked, unannounced, at his open door. "What can I do for you?"

"Ernie Carpenter's been called out of town because of . . ." she began.

George Winfield nodded knowingly. "Dick Voland already told me. Because of the Reed Carruthers case," he finished.

"Right. I was in the neighborhood, though," Joanna said. "I thought I'd come by and see if there was anything important enough for me to pass along to Ernie tonight."

"Like I told Dick, I don't have anything in writing yet," George answered. "At this point I'm limited to one half-time clerk-typist. She only works mornings, regardless of how many bodies turn up in the morgue. I can verbal you some preliminary results, but that's about it. You can't have it in black and white officialese until around noon tomorrow."

"I'd appreciate anything you could tell us. So would my public information officer," Joanna told him.

Winfield leaned back in his chair. "Amos Buckwalter was

dead before the fire ever started," he replied without further preamble. "The lung damage I saw would be consistent with what one would expect from a long term smoker, but not from someone dying of smoke inhalation."

"If the fire and smoke didn't kill him, what did?" Joanna asked.

"He died of a single puncture wound."

"A puncture wound? Where?"

"Right here," Winfield said. He turned slightly in his chair and pointed to a spot just over the top of his stiffly starched shirt collar. "It's in this little indentation. There were also two matching abrasions on the outside of his neck—one on either side. If you're wondering about a murder weapon, I'd say you'd do well to go looking for a pitchfork."

"A pitchfork!" Joanna exclaimed, remembering what Bebe Noonan had said about stumbling over a pitchfork when she found Hal Morgan lying in the burning barn. "You're sure that's what it was?"

Winfield nodded. "My older brother and I spent lots of summers working on our uncle's farm back in Minnesota," he said. "We hated each other's guts. Still do, as a matter of fact. Believe me, I know the receiving end of a pitchfork when I see one. Incidentally, I have the scars to prove it, right here on my upper thigh. I could demonstrate same, if you'd like."

George Winfield was sixty if he was a day, and Joanna recognized the remark as nothing more than gentle teasing. "No, thanks," she said. "If you don't mind, I think I'll just take your word for it. Now, if you could give me something a little more official-sounding than that, I'd appreciate it. I need the kind of verbiage I can pass along to Frank Montoya. He's the guy the reporters are calling for details on this case. In dealing with the media I'm sure he'd benefit from having something more concrete and more anatomically correct than pointing to the back of his head or giving the newsies a lecture on the inherent dangers of pitchforks."

"Happy to oblige," George said.

A few minutes later, armed with the needed information, Joanna stood up to leave. "By the way," George said as she started for the doorway. "What do you hear from Ellie?"

Ellie?

Joanna stopped in mid-stride. It had been years since she had heard anyone refer to her mother by the pet name only her father had used.

"Ellie?" she repeated stupidly. "You mean my mother?"

Winfield looked confused. "I hope I'm not mistaken," he said. "I understood Ellie to say that you were her daughter."

"Eleanor Lathrop is my mother," Joanna managed.

Nodding and looking relieved, George Winfield smiled. "And she was going to D.C. to see her son."

"Right," Joanna said.

"I believe she expected to be home by now."

"She is," Joanna answered stiffly. "She came home last night."

George Winfield smiled again. "Good," he said. "Ellie's a lovely lady. We met at the Arts and Humanities Council. Mel Torme is doing a show in Vegas over the next three weeks. I told Ellie that as soon as she got back from D.C., I'd try to get us tickets. Now that she's back in town, I'll have to give her a call."

Joanna attempted a weak smile. "You do that," she said. *And so will I!*

Stunned, Joanna headed back to the department. *Mother is dating? Eleanor had a boyfriend?* All that seemed unthinkable, yet Winfield's use of the name "Ellie" confirmed it.

So what are you so upset about? Joanna chided herself. *Why shouldn't she?*

After all, Big Hank Lathrop had been gone for years. What startled Joanna—what bothered her—was that she was on the outside looking in. Obviously Eleanor had a life of her own, one her daughter knew very little about.

Once back at the Justice Center, Joanna quickly became so embroiled in what was going on there that her personal concerns were temporarily pushed aside. First she briefed both Frank Montoya and Dick Voland on the Buckwalter autopsy preliminaries. Then, after being briefed herself on how the Sunizona investigation was proceeding, Joanna shut herself away in her corner office to try to retake control of her day.

There were more than a dozen telephone calls waiting to be returned. As she made her way through them, one by one, she sat with her phone to her ear, staring out the window of her corner office at the employee parking lot and at the desert landscape beyond it.

She knew the desert was anything but empty. Occasionally jackrabbits and coyotes would show up outside her window. Quail and roadrunners were commonplace. Once she had glimpsed a small herd of foraging javalenas. They had dodged between the cars and trucks on their way to make a scavenging raid on the garbage outside the jail kitchen.

Today, though, there was nothing visible in the animal kingdom to lighten Joanna's mood. Even the majestic landscape itself failed to move her.

To the north stood a jagged wall of rugged gray hills. Each steep hillside wore a jaunty crown of perpendicular limestone cliffs. To the west were the shale-covered foothills of the Mule Mountains. Their deep-reddish flanks hinted that perhaps unmined copper still lingered beneath their rocky, scrub-oak-dotted surfaces.

Usually, this particular view comforted Joanna. Not today. As the sun went down, sending long grotesque shadows of spiny ocotillo dancing across the gradually emptying parking lot, Joanna felt even more bereft. More wronged.

How dare Eleanor do that!

For as long as Joanna could remember, Eleanor had extracted information from her daughter with all the finesse and expertise of a trained inquisitor. She had expected—no, demanded—that her daughter have no secrets. But the reverse wasn't true—not even close. And why was that? If Joanna was expected to share everything about her own life, why wasn't Eleanor?

He called her Ellie! Joanna thought, hurt anew that George Winfield could so casually call her mother by that private and, to Joanna, very precious name. The man had been in town only a matter of months. How was it possible that he and Eleanor had grown so close without Joanna knowing anything about it?

Lost in reverie, Joanna was shocked when Kristin popped her head in the door. "It's five o'clock," she announced. "I'm leaving."

When the door closed behind her, Joanna looked down at the untouched mounds of correspondence that still littered her desk. In contemplating a run for the office of sheriff, it had never occurred to her that her days would be devoured by paper. She hadn't anticipated having to sort through stacks of junk mail in order to find and deal with those few pieces of correspondence that actually contained something of consequence.

Disgusted as much with the process as with herself, she

was stuffing the piles into a briefcase when Dick Voland tapped on her door. When he stepped into her office, he was smiling. "I just picked up a little something I thought you'd like to know about," he said.

Joanna finished filling her bulging briefcase and forced it shut. Voland looked so smug, so pleased with himself, that she knew it had to be bad news—for someone.

"What's that?" she asked.

"I got to thinking about what you told Frank and me earlier, about Doc Winfield saying the murder weapon might possibly be a pitchfork."

"Yes," Joanna said.

"A little later I remembered Ernie saying something about a pitchfork being found at the crime scene, so I checked in the evidence room. Sure enough, the pitchfork was there, all right, although no one had gotten around to doing anything with it. I took it on myself to order a set of prints. Guess what?"

"I hate to think."

"Hal Morgan's prints were on it. How do you like them apples?"

Voland's gleeful grin reminded Joanna of an obnoxious, sharpshooting kid from Greenway School who had wiped out everyone else's collections of marbles without ever learning the art of graceful winning.

The withering look Joanna leveled at Voland wiped the smile off his face. Had someone held a mirror in front of her right then, Joanna would have been shocked to see a much younger version of the unsmiling, soul-searing gaze that was Eleanor Lathrop's stock-in-trade. "So what's the point?" Joanna asked.

Voland's face fell. "Isn't it obvious?" he returned. "Morgan's prints are on the murder weapon. He's lying about all of it, including this 'second-man' stuff that sounds like it's straight out of the old 'Fugitive' reruns on TV. I'm in favor of turning my deputies loose from the wild-goose chase you've got them on."

"What other prints were on the pitchfork?" Joanna asked.

Voland look dismayed. "There weren't any others."

"Why not?" Joanna asked. "Doesn't that strike you as odd? I happen to have a pitchfork in the barn at my place right now," she added. "I can assure you that if anyone dusted the handle, there'd be all kinds of prints—ones from every person who's ever used it. Most people aren't in the habit of wiping pitchfork handles before they go to work on the business end of it."

"What are you saying?" Voland asked.

"That if there aren't any other prints on that handle, then the ones that are there were put there deliberately. Planted."

"You mean, as in put there to frame Hal Morgan?"

"Exactly."

Dick Voland's head began to shake. "No way," he said. "You're reaching,"

"That may be," Joanna conceded, "but I'm telling you this, Mr. Voland. The search for Hal Morgan's 'second man' isn't a wild-goose chase until I say it's a wild-goose chase. Is that clear?"

He looked at her for a moment as if he was prepared to argue. Dick Voland wasn't any better at losing than he was at winning. "Yes, ma'am," he said. "You're the boss."

"Thank you," she said. "And now, if you don't mind, I think I'll go home. It's been a long day."

She drove straight to her in-laws' house, picked up Jenny, and then headed out to the Safeway in Don Luis for an abbreviated grocery-shopping trip. Bread, milk, eggs, juice, fruit, luncheon meat. "What are we having for dinner?" Jenny asked as they hurried up and down aisles, stacking items into the cart.

"How about chorizo, eggs, and flour tortillas?" Joanna suggested. Jenny made a face.

"What's the matter?" Joanna asked. "The last time we had it, you told me you loved chorizo."

"It's okay," Jenny said. "But eggs are for breakfast. Why couldn't we eat with the G's? Grandma was making stew. She said there was plenty."

"We can't eat with Grandma and Grandpa every night, even if they invite us," Joanna told her daughter. "I know they don't mind, and Grandma is a wonderful cook. But still, it's an imposition. We don't want to wear out our welcome."

"But we hardly ever have real meals anymore," Jenny complained. "Not like we used to when Daddy was alive."

Jenny's quiet comment flew straight to her mother's heart. It was true. When Andy was alive, mealtimes had been important occasions—a time and a place to reaffirm that they were a family all by themselves, separate and apart from his parents and from Joanna's mother as well. In a two-career home, breakfast and lunch had been catch-as-catch-can in the breakfast nook and the same had held true when Andy was working graveyard or night shifts. But when all three of them had been home for dinner together, the meal had automatically turned into an occasion. Much of the time, they would set the dining room table with the good dishes and with cloth napkins—for just the three of them.

In the months since Andy died, eating at the dining room table by themselves was something Joanna and Jenny had never done. There it was too painfully clear that Andy's place was empty. Quick meals of scrambled eggs or grilled cheese sandwiches eaten in the breakfast nook didn't carry quite the same emotional wallop. Until right then, however, Joanna hadn't known Jenny was feeling deprived. Maybe it was time to reconsider the chorizo option.

Mentally calculating what staples she still had at home, Joanna dropped a package of pork chops into the basket, along with a container of deli-made coleslaw and a bottle of sparkling cider.

As Jenny and Joanna headed for the checkout line, their cart almost collided in the freezer aisle with a cart pushed by a man named Larry Matkin. Larry, a Phelps Dodge mining engineer, was fairly new to town, although Joanna had seen him several times at various civic meetings around town. Matkin was a member of the Rotary Club, but he had visited Joanna's Kiwanis club to give a talk on the prospects and economic implications of P.D.'s reopening mining operations in the Bisbee area. He was a tall, lanky guy with reddish-brown hair, glasses, and a prominent Adam's apple. His speech had been dry as dust.

"Sorry," Joanna said with a laugh. "You know how it is with women drivers."

Matkin, stacking typical bachelor fare of frozen TV dinners into his cart, seemed to see no humor in her comment. He didn't smile in return. "It's okay," he mumbled. "No harm done." For a moment it looked as though he was going to say something more, then he changed his mind. With his face flushing beet-red, he turned his attention back to the frozen-food case.

"What was the matter with that man?" Jenny asked, as they reached the check stand. "It was only a little bump. Why'd he get so mad?"

"What makes you think he was mad?" Joanna asked.

Jenny wasn't a child to be easily thrown off track. "Didn't you see how his face turned all red?"

"That doesn't necessarily mean he was mad," Joanna explained. "It could be he's shy."

"Maybe it means he likes you then," Jenny theorized.

Joanna looked down at her daughter in shock. "I don't think so," she said.

"But it could happen, couldn't it?" Jenny insisted. "He might ask you out. What then? Would you go?"

Unsure how to answer or even *if* she should answer this unforeseen dating question, Joanna was saved by the timely intervention of the check-out clerk. "Paper or plastic?" she asked.

Joanna wanted to leap across the check stand and hug the woman. "Paper," she replied gratefully. "Definitely paper."

10

HALFWAY home, with the groceries safely stowed in the back, Joanna was still mulling over the implications behind Jenny's disturbing question when the child lobbed yet another one in her direction.

"Did you catch him?" Jenny asked.

"Catch who?" Joanna asked, mystified by a question that was so far from what she'd been thinking.

"The guy who killed Dr. Buckwalter."

"No." Joanna answered truthfully. "We're working on it, but I'm afraid Detective Carpenter didn't make all that much progress today. He's been up in Sunizona working on another case."

She realized as she said the words that she wasn't giving Jenny a very comprehensive or detailed answer. As such Jenny probably didn't find it very satisfactory, but it was the best Joanna could do. When Andy had been a deputy, Jenny had always shown a precocious interest in his work and in everything that went on in the department. When she had asked those kinds of questions of him, Andy had been only too happy to respond. He had always answered with a no-holds-barred candor that Joanna found disquieting even then. In the present circumstances—with the scars from Andy's death still so near the surface—such questions and their accompanying answers bothered her even more. Joanna always worried that something she might say would bring up topics that would be painful to Jenny and hurtful to her as well.

Driving through the last glimmers of twilight, Joanna clung to the steering wheel and worried where Jenny's inquisitive mind would take them next.

"It's my birthday pretty soon," Jenny said.

Mistakenly assuming this was nothing but another one of Jenny's mind-bending changes of subject, Joanna let her guard down. "Not for another three months yet," she returned.

"What are you going to get me?" Jenny asked.

Joanna shrugged. "Three months is a long time," she said. "I haven't given it all that much thought."

"Well," Jenny said, sitting up straight and folding her short arms across her chest. "I already know what I want for my birthday."

"What?"

"What I told you before—Dr. Buckwalter's horse. Kiddo. Daddy said I could have a horse someday. He *promised*. Besides, Kiddo will be lonely without someone to love him. What if he gets sold for dog food or something?"

"Jenny," Joanna said firmly. "Nobody's going to sell Kiddo for dog food. But you have to understand what's going on here. I'm all alone now—alone and overloaded. Between work and home, I can't take on one more thing without falling apart. There's a whole lot more to taking care of a horse than scratching him on the nose when you feel like it and giving him a carrot once in a while."

"That's not true!" Jenny spat back at her.

"It *is* true," Joanna insisted. "Horses require a lot of hard work."

"Not that," Jenny said. "What you said before. About being alone. You are *not* alone. You have me, don't you?"

Moving as far away from her mother as possible, Jenny scrunched up against the passenger's door and stared wordlessly out the window. Joanna sighed. Another night; another firefight.

Parenting, Joanna thought to herself, *sure as hell isn't all it's cracked up to be.* Aloud she said to her daughter, "I didn't mean that—the alone part. All I'm saying is that there are already too many chores . . ."

"I want a horse," Jenny said. "You're just being mean. If Daddy were alive, he'd let me have Kiddo. I know he would."

By then they were coming down High Lonesome Road and slowing for the turnoff that led off into the ranch itself. There was nothing Joanna could say. She had already learned, just as Eleanor Lathrop had before her, that it's impossible to win an argument with a dead parent. From Jenny's perspective, Andrew Roy Brady was perfection itself. By comparison, Joanna was drab, ordinary, and desperately flawed by the responsibility of sometimes having to say no.

Joanna slowed to a stop. "Just go get the mail, Jenny," she said wearily. "We'll talk about this again in the morning when we're both not so tired."

Without a word, Jenny shoved open the door, leaped down to the ground, and then darted back across High Lonesome to the wagon-wheel mounted mailbox Andy had been so proud of. Joanna sat waiting in the idling Blazer. She could have been watching Jenny in the rearview mirror. Instead, she was looking up the road and waiting to see if the dogs would come galloping out of the darkness into the glow of her headlights and wondering whether or not they'd be sidetracked by the lanky jackrabbit that usually set the pace for an evening race through the valley.

Joanna was just beginning to notice how long Jenny was taking when the car door opened. "Mom?" Jenny said. Her voice was so tentative, so unlike her, that Joanna realized at once something was wrong.

"Jenny!" she demanded. "What's the matter? Are you all right?"

"Somebody's here," Jenny said, her voice still strangely uncertain. "She's got me by the arm, Mom. She's hurting me."

Alarmed, Joanna spun in her seat. Across from her, outside the car door and just beyond the dim orange glow cast by the overhead light, stood Jenny. Beside her was the huge hulk of an oversized human being. Had Jenny not used the word "she," Joanna would have had no way of knowing whether or not the apparition was male or female.

"Get in the car, Jenny," Joanna ordered.

"I can't." Jenny whispered back. "She's got me by the arm."

"Who are you?" Joanna demanded of the stranger. "What do you want?"

"I don't mean you nor your little girl no harm," a woman's voice said. Her words had the slow, soft cadence of someone who, at some time in her life, had lived in the hill country of east Texas. "I got to talk to you, Sheriff Brady," the woman continued. "I *got* to talk to somebody."

Despite the curiously soft-spoken speech, Joanna sensed a very real menace lurking in the barely whispered words. There was a peculiar intensity—a hopeless urgency—in the voice that came from that ghastly mound of flesh. It was the voice of someone with nothing left to lose. That realization caused the skin to prickle on the backs of Joanna's arms. The hairs on the back of her neck stood on end. Everything about the woman screamed, "Danger! Danger! Danger!"

Twisting and turning, Jenny tried ineffectively to escape the woman's grasp, but she held on tight.

"Who are you?" Joanna asked again, knowing even before the woman spoke exactly what her answer would be—what it had to be.

"My name's Hannah Green," she said. "I believe some of your people are looking for me, Sheriff Brady. They all think I kilt my daddy."

"And did you?" Joanna asked.

That instinctive question shot out of Joanna's mouth long before she considered the consequences of the question or the implications of any possible answers. Hannah Green was, after all, a homicide suspect. She was a person who should have been read her rights before there was any exchange of information. But Hannah Green also posed a very real threat to both Joanna and Jenny. In those circumstances, the Miranda ruling went straight out the window.

Still squirming, Jenny started to whimper. "Let go. You're hurting me."

If she heard her, Hannah Green gave no sign. Her whole being was focused on Joanna. "Of course I kilt him," she said. "I kilt him because he deserved it. And you woulda done the same thing if'n he'd treated you the way he treated me. Daddy was mean, you know. Just as mean as he could be."

Joanna's heart fluttered in her throat. In those first few moments of rising panic, dozens of conflicting thoughts whirled through her brain. This was exactly what had happened to Andy. He, too, had been accosted on this same road, less than a mile from home. For some unknown reason, he had let down his guard long enough to give his killer a fatal opening. Now it looked as though Joanna had made the same mistake. She, too, had fallen prey to that false sense of security—a kind of phony King's X—that comes from being "almost home."

What would all those textbooks she had read up at the Arizona Police Officers' Academy have to say about this kind of situation? Call for backup? Of course, but how? And who? What backup would she find, way out here, five miles from town? Joanna's closest neighbor was Clayton Rhodes, her handyman. But he would already have come to the High Lonesome, done his evening chores, and gone back to his own place a mile farther up the road.

Joanna was unable to tell whether or not the woman was armed or what, if any, harm she intended to do Jenny. Trying to grapple with how to respond, Joanna found herself in an impossible situation—one with no clear-cut choices, no absolute right or wrong.

She was still fighting panic and searching for direction when Hannah Green spoke again.

"Me an' the little girl here is gonna catch our deaths if we don't get inside real soon, ma'am."

The woman sounded calm enough. Afraid of doing something that would provoke her, Joanna swallowed her fear and tried to brazen it out.

"Get in, then," she ordered. "Both of you."

Without having to be urged a second time, Jenny scrambled into the middle of the front seat while Hannah Green heaved herself up onto the steep running board. For a moment, Joanna considered floor-boarding the accelerator, but with the woman's iron grip still fastened to Jenny's upper arm, that wasn't an option. A jackrabbit start would have thrown the woman to the ground, but she might have pulled Jenny out of the truck with her.

The pungent stench of body odor filled the Blazer as Hannah Green sank heavily onto the seat. She was a wide load of a woman, wearing a lightweight quilted flannel jacket that didn't quite fasten around her expansive middle. Under that was a dress—the gored skirt of a housedress of some kind. Her feet were clad in worn loafers and sagging white anklets. Her right hand—the one that wasn't inexorably attached to Jenny's arm—was buried deep in the pocket of her jacket. Joanna wondered whether there was a weapon concealed in the folds of that enormous jacket. In the end, she simply assumed there was one. There had to be.

That assumption didn't change when Hannah let go of Jenny's arm with the left hand and reached across her own body to pull the door shut. Between them on the seat, Jenny whimpered again and rubbed her arm.

The thought of a gun in the hands of a suspected killer terrified Joanna Brady. Not for herself. After all, she was wearing a set of soft, custom-made body armor. In a gunfight, she would have the benefit of whatever protection the bullet-resistant material had to offer. On the other hand, Jenny, the little blond-haired person sitting directly between Hannah Green and Joanna, had nothing at all—no protection whatsoever.

In the limited confines of the Blazer's front seat, in a confrontation where Jenny was bound to be caught in the crossfire, Joanna's own weapons were worse than useless. Neither the sturdy Colt 2000 in its underarm holster nor the palm-sized Glock 19 she wore in a discreet small-of-back holster—would do the least bit of good.

Sick with her own impotent terror, Joanna bit her lip so hard she tasted blood. Shoving the Blazer into gear, she sent it surging forward. The truck rattled over the uneven iron rails of the cattle guard with tooth-loosening force as they started toward the ranch house. The car door had been open long enough that a sudden chill had settled into the Blazer's interior. Even so, as the heater geared up to reheat the inside of the vehicle, Joanna noticed the palms of her hands were so sweaty she could barely control the slick surface of the bucking steering wheel.

Make her talk, Joanna coached herself. That was the prime directive when it came to hostage negotiations—getting the perpetrator to talk. "How did you get here, Mrs. Green?" Joanna asked, forcing her voice to sound as normal as she could make it under the circumstances.

"Hitchhiked some." Hannah's terse answer was little more than a grunt. "Walked the rest of the way."

"But why did you come here?" Joanna asked. "Why come to my home instead of my office?"

"Didn't plan on comin' here at all," Hannah said. "Not at first. When I left the house, to my way of thinkin', I was lightin' out for Old Mexico. Changed my mind, though. Got halfway there and decided crossin' the border was a bad idea. That's just like me, though. Changin' my mind. Daddy always said that was one of the reasons I'd never amount to nothin'. He said I never stuck to any one thing long enough to make it work." There was a slight pause before she added, "Not till now."

"Why were you going to Mexico?" Joanna asked.

"Come on, Sheriff. I may be dumb, but I'm not stupid," Hannah said. "I thought I could run away. Go down there and hide. Like they do in the movies sometimes—they go to another country and lie low for a while. The cops are lookin' for me, aren't they? That Detective Carpenter?"

Joanna didn't answer. Just then Sadie and Tigger appeared in the middle of the road, racing toward the Blazer. Two pairs of bouncing, glowing eyes caught in the beam of the headlights. When the dogs finally reached the vehicle, they gamboled around it, barking in a joyous ritual of greeting before once again racing off toward the house.

"Heard them dogs earlier," Hannah Green said. "They was raisin' a ruckus. I didn't want to have nothin' to do with 'em. That's how come I waited back there, back by your mailbox."

"Mom," Jenny began, but Joanna shushed her.

"Why are you here, Mrs. Green?" Joanna asked, returning to her original line of questioning. "What do you want?"

"To talk, I guess," the woman answered sadly. "To tell somebody my side of the story for a change. I thought, you bein' a woman and all, that maybe you'd understand why I done it. Why I had to go an' kill him. I sure enough did. He deserved it, though. That man was meaner 'an a snake. Some folks get nicer when they get old, sorta sweet and quiet-like. Not him, not my daddy. He just got meaner 'n' meaner, only he was real mean to begin with."

Saying that, Hannah Green subsided into a brooding silence Joanna found even more unnerving than her self-incriminating words. Jenny, eyes wide, shot her mother a questioning look. Grimly Joanna shook her head, hoping that single, unspoken warning would be enough to stifle any further questions or comments from her daughter.

As the Blazer rounded the last curve in the road and pulled into the yard, Joanna's newly installed motion detector snapped on, bathing the whole area in light. Looking at Hannah Green over the top of Jenny's frizzy blond head, Joanna saw a weary, grim-faced woman. She had to be in her late sixties at least. Her lank, shoulder-length iron-gray hair wriggled with natural curls as though from a recent, unset permanent. What must have been several missing molars gave her left cheek a hollow, crushed-in look. Her eyes stared straight ahead with the eerie stillness of someone under the influence of a hypnotist. Or of drugs.

Joanna looked out at the yard and at the dogs cavorting in happy circles around the Blazer, waiting for it to stop and for the passengers to climb down. Their ecstatic welcome did nothing to lighten Joanna's growing sense of foreboding. Never had the High Lonesome seemed so isolated. Never had her neighbors seemed so distant. For all the good it did her, town could just as well have been light-years away.

Shutting off the ignition, Joanna removed the key. In the process, she gave Jenny's knee what she hoped was a reassuring pat. In the passenger seat, Hannah Green sat still as death. Finally Joanna reached for the door handle.

"It's cold out here," she said, forcing into her voice a composure she didn't feel. "We'd better go on inside."

"Don't mind if I do," Hannah said, heaving herself out the other side of the truck.

Joanna had hoped the process of opening the car door would force Hannah to remove her right hand from her jacket pocket, revealing once and for all whether or not she was armed. Instead, she once again let go of Jenny long enough to reach across her own body to manipulate the door. Then, after shoving it open, Hannah once again locked her puffy fingers around Jenny's arm, dragging the unprotesting child with her across the seat. As the two of them exited through the right-hand side of the Blazer, Joanna was grateful that Jenny had sense enough not to struggle.

Knowing she had to keep herself focused and absolutely clearheaded, Joanna let her breath out slowly. She stepped down onto the ground only to be subjected to Tigger's and Sadie's ecstatic greetings. Wildly wagging and whining in welcome, neither of the dogs seemed to pay any attention to the stranger in their midst. Joanna could see the dogs' primitive logic. Joanna and Jenny had brought the stranger home. Therefore, she must not pose any danger.

Thanks, guys, Joanna thought. *Some watchdogs you turned out to be.*

Joanna moved toward the tailgate. "We have groceries in the back," she announced. "I have to get them out."

"You go right ahead and do that," Hannah Green said. "I come this far. I'm not in no hurry."

With Jenny walking between them, the two women made their way from the Blazer to the fenced yard and up the walkway. It was cold enough for Joanna to see her breath. Both she and Jenny had been wearing warm clothing, even in the heated vehicle. Hannah Green had been outside in the terrible chill with bare legs and only that thin jacket.

She must be frozen, Joanna thought. *How long had she been waiting there, I wonder?*

Once on the back porch, Joanna had to put down the two bags of groceries. Mustering every bit of courage she possessed, she stepped forward, keys in hand, to unlock the door. That process meant turning her back on Hannah Green, and Joanna did it with an almost sickening sense of dread. It took three tries before she finally managed to fit the key in the lock. At last the door swung open. Joanna breathed a sigh of relief.

"Come in," she said, picking up the groceries and stepping over the threshold. Hannah and Jenny followed her inside, bringing the cavorting dogs with them.

"You must be freezing," Joanna said as she switched on the overhead light.

"I am just a little cold," Hannah Green replied. "Not too bad, though." She stopped in the middle of the floor and stared down at the dogs, who were still milling around the room. Jenny dropped to the floor with them, threw both arms around Tigger, and buried her face in the flowing golden fur on the back of his neck.

"Daddy wouldn't never let me have a dog," Hannah was saying, as Joanna placed the bags of groceries on the counter. "He hated having animals inside the house. Said they was filthy." For a space she stood there watching Jenny and the dogs. "What do you call 'em?" she asked at last.

When Jenny didn't answer, Joanna did. "The bluetick hound is called Sadie. The funny looking one with the white patch around his eye is Tigger."

"And they won't hurt me?" Hannah asked.

"No," Joanna said reassuringly. "They're fine."

The two women stood facing each other across the kitchen over the heads of Jenny and the dogs. Hannah's hair hadn't been washed in a very long time. Neither had the rest of her.

"You sure them dogs won't bite?" Hannah asked.

"I'm sure," Joanna said.

Tentatively, Hannah reached out her hand. "Come here, doggy," she said. "Nice doggy."

Sadie was the first to notice Hannah's outstretched hand.

With her head cocked to one side and with her nose quivering an inspection, she stood up and came over to where Hannah was standing. As Hannah ran her hand down the dog's smooth, blue-black coat, a strange look passed over her bedraggled, wrinkle-scored face. It was a look of almost childlike wonder.

"I never knew a dog would be this soft!" she exclaimed.

Jenny pulled away from Tigger's neck and looked over at Hannah with a disbelieving blue-eyed stare. "You mean you've never even *touched* a dog before?" Joanna cringed at the arch skepticism in Jenny's voice. Joanna was afraid the very tone of it would upset the woman.

"Jenny," Joanna hissed. "Mind your manners."

Hannah, however, was so preoccupied with petting the dog that she didn't seem to notice. Tigger, always eager to receive his share of attention, stood up and came to collect some petting for himself. While Joanna watched breathlessly, Hannah Green's other hand emerged from the concealing pocket and came to rest on the second dog's raised forehead. Only then did Joanna realize that Hannah Green wasn't armed.

Her right hand didn't hold a weapon—could not have held a weapon. The whole hand was horribly maimed. Useless, mangled fingers bent crookedly across a partially missing thumb.

"What kind of a dog is this?" Hannah Green asked distractedly as her crippled hand ran back and forth across Tigger's silky blond head.

"Half golden retriever, half pitbull," Jenny answered. "His owner died, and we adopted him. He's real smart, except for porcupines. He keeps coming home with his face covered with porcupine quills. When that happens, we have to take him to the vet."

Jenny faltered then. In talking about her dog it seemed as though she had forgotten the strained circumstances that surrounded the question. Remembering, she fell silent.

For Joanna, the realization that Hannah Green's right hand didn't contain a gun completely changed the dynamics of the situation. At first she wasn't sure how to react. It was still possible that Hannah might be concealing another weapon somewhere else on her body, but somehow, watching her pet the dogs, Joanna doubted that.

Maybe what Hannah Green had told them in the beginning was true. Maybe all she really wanted to do was talk. To that end, the best thing Joanna could do was try to establish a sense of rapport, a sense of normalcy. She dropped her purse on the counter beside the grocery bags. "Are you hungry?" she asked. "Would you like something to eat?"

"Just a piece of bread or two would be fine," Hannah answered. "And maybe a little bit of jam if you have some."

"I was going to bake a couple of pork chops," Joanna said. "If you don't mind waiting until they cook, I'm sure we'll have plenty to go around." She looked at Jenny. "While the food's cooking, Jenny, you get busy with your homework. You told me you have a whole bunch of math to do for Mrs. Voland's class."

Jenny shot her mother a surprised look. "But Mom . . ."

"No argument, young lady." Joanna abruptly stifled Jenny's objection before the child could reveal that her teacher's name was really Mrs. Harper, not Mrs. Voland. All Joanna could do was hope Jenny was smart enough to take the hint. Take it and act on it.

"No argument at all," Joanna finished. "Get now. And

take the dogs with you. They'll just be in the way. Mrs. Green and I need to talk."

Without further discussion, Jenny took the dogs and her school backpack and retreated to her bedroom. Relieved that, for the time being at least, Jenny was out of any immediate danger, Joanna turned to the everyday task of putting away groceries. After the unnerving terror of the preceding minutes, the little kitchen seemed impossibly warm and homey. Despite Hannah Green's still ominous presence, folding the empty paper bags and putting them in the bottom drawer gave an air of mind-bending domesticity to the proceedings.

Hannah Green slid onto the bench in the breakfast nook and slouched there. The despair emanating from her was almost as powerful as the stink of her great unwashed body. Her flat, vacant features could never have been considered remotely attractive, but she seemed at home in her placid ugliness.

"Before you and I say anything more, Mrs. Green," Joanna cautioned, "you must understand that I'm a police officer. Since you're a suspect in the death of your father, you probably shouldn't be talking to anyone—me included—without first consulting an attorney and without being read your rights."

"Don't care none about my rights and can't afford no fancy attorney," Hannah returned morosely. "All's I've got with me is just what I had laid by in my underwear drawer. Five hundred fifty dollars and some change. I don't reckon that'd go any too far in hirin' me one of them there lawyers."

"If you can't afford an attorney—"

"Besides," Hannah continued, seemingly unperturbed. "Don't much want one anyways. I already tol' you I kilt him.

And if'n they send me to jail, leastways I'll have food to eat and a roof over my head. It serves him right, my daddy. He allus said I wasn't smart enough to rub two sticks together. He allus said that without him I'd just up and starve to death. Well, I reckon I won't. Nobody'll let me starve in jail, will they?"

Joanna had pried the plastic wrap off the pork chops and begun to season them, dropping them into a cast-iron skillet and browning them before placing the skillet in the oven. "No," she agreed. "I don't suppose they will."

"See there?" Hannah said. "I'll be fine. Just fine."

Joanna could think of nothing to say in reply.

"Aren't you going to ask me why I did it?" Hannah asked a moment later. Joanna shook her head. "I'm gonna tell you anyways. You see, I just wanted to change the damn channel. That's all. Daddy wouldn't never let me watch what I wanted. It was just pure meanness on his part. That's what made me so mad. He didn't want to watch nothin' else. Didn't care about no other channel so long as I couldn't watch what I wanted. He just got up and went outside and took that clicker with him. I coulda changed it on the set, but I wanted to use the clicker like a regular person.

"He went out and I went chasin' after him, tellin' him to bring it back—to bring it back right now. But he wouldn't. Wouldn't no way. Jus' kept right on walkin'—didn't even have no coat on—and I kept right after him, yellin' my fool head off, tellin' him to give it back. And then somethin' happened. He musta tripped and fell and didn't get up. The next thing I knowed, I was standin' over him with a rock in my hand, bashin' the back of his head in, all the while screamin' at him at the top of my lungs. 'Give it to me. Give it back!' "

Hannah Green told her story with a minimum of emotion, delivering the details with a chilling dispassion that seemed to imply she was still more upset about the loss of the remote control than she was about her father's death.

Maybe she is crazy, Joanna decided.

Sitting there hunched in the breakfast nook, with her multiple chins resting in her good hand and with the ruined one once again back in its concealing pocket, Hannah Green didn't appear to be a danger to anyone. Still, Joanna recognized that she would need help in dealing with this woman. She could go through all the motions of playing hostess, of feeding her unwelcome guest and warming her. But somewhere along the line, the charade would come to an end. Joanna knew that when that moment arrived, she would need back up. Had Jenny understood or not?

As Joanna continued with dinner preparations, she wondered if it would be possible for her to find some plausible excuse to slip into her bedroom. There, in a matter of seconds, she could dial 9-1-1 and call for help. What Joanna feared, though, was that once Hannah's suspicions were aroused, she might fly into the same kind of murderous rage that had overtaken her when she killed her father.

"And then," Hannah went on, taking up her story again after a long, thoughtful pause, "when I knew he wasn't movin' no more, I turned him over on his back and left him there. Left him starin' up at the sky. Even if he was dead, I wanted him to see my face afore I left. I wanted him to know it was me and nobody else 'at kilt him. Then I pulled 'at there remote right out of his pocket and went back home. But my program was over by then. It was a special about Judy Garland, and I missed the whole thing. Course, it could be on the reruns later. Maybe I'll have a chance to see it then. Do they have TVs in jail?"

With the meat in the oven, Joanna started peeling potatoes.

"They do," she answered without conviction. Even if television sets were available to inmates, it didn't seem likely that Hannah Green's fellow prisoners would be any more interested in a Judy Garland retrospective than Reed Carruthers had been.

How is it possible, Joanna wondered, *that this whole thing started over a stupid television remote control? How can that be? Was that all there was to it? Was a simple argument over a television channel enough to send a murderous Hannah Green hurtling through the cold desert night?*

What Hannah said next chilled Joanna to the bone. It seemed almost as though the woman had peered into her skull and heard those unasked questions.

"It wasn't just the TV, neither," Hannah Green continued doggedly.

"It wasn't?"

Hannah shook her head. Removing her damaged hand from her pocket, she held it up to the light, examining the bent and useless fingers. "I did it because of this here, too."

"Because of your hand? Are you saying your father did that to you?"

"I was gonna to leave oncet, but he didn't want me to," Hannah recalled. "Mama was real sick, you see. Daddy needed someone to stay there and take care of her. He slammed my hand in the car door so as I couldn't go."

"When did that happen?"

Hannah shrugged. "A while back," she said.

"How recently?"

"Not recent. It was after my husband divorced me and I came home to Daddy and Mama's place."

"When?" Joanna urged, thinking as she asked the question that if Reed Carruthers had attacked his daughter, Hannah might be able to enter a plea of self-defense.

"Nineteen sixty-five or so, I guess," Hannah Green answered after a period of frowning consideration. "That musta been about when it was."

"More than thirty years ago?"

Hannah shrugged. "That's right. Like I said, it's been a while."

Somewhere at the far end of the house, the dogs began barking. The chorus was stifled almost immediately. Daring to hope that help was at hand, Joanna carefully rinsed the potatoes, put them in the pressure cooker, added water and salt. As she placed the potatoes on the burner, someone began pounding on the seldom-used front door.

Concerned that any intrusion might upset the woman, Joanna glanced at her warily. "Someone's at the door," Joanna said.

The woman nodded but didn't move.

"I'll have to answer it."

Hannah nodded. "You go ahead," she said.

By the time Joanna had crossed the kitchen to the doorway into the dining room, Jenny had already opened the front door. Detective Ernie Carpenter burst into the living room, followed closely by Dick Voland.

"We've got the house surrounded," Ernie barked. "Where is she?"

"In the kitchen," Joanna said, motioning in that direction. While Ernie pushed past her into the kitchen, Dick Voland slid to a stop beside Joanna.

"Are you and Jenny all right?"

"Yes," Joanna said.

From out of nowhere, Jenny suddenly squeezed between them and grabbed Joanna around the waist. She clung there, saying nothing.

"Is she armed?" Dick asked.

"I don't think so," Joanna managed.

The flood of relief that washed over her then took her by surprise. One moment she was laughing. The next, laughter unaccountably changed to tears.

"Mommy, why are you crying?" Jenny asked, peering up into her face. "I called Mr. Voland. Isn't that what you wanted me to do?"

That was the precise instant when Joanna's knees buckled and would no longer support her weight. If Dick Voland hadn't been right there to catch her, she might have fallen all the way to the floor. She was still sobbing as he took her gently by the shoulders and steered her to one of the dining room chairs.

"Shhhh now," he said, awkwardly patting her shoulder. "It's okay, Joanna. Everything's under control."

11

T H E next half hour or so was a blur of frantic activity. The whole house buzzed with cops while Joanna fielded a concerned call from Marianne Maculyea, whom Jenny had also called, reassuring her that everything was fine, that help had arrived, and that Hannah Green was being taken into custody. When it was time for Ernie Carpenter to lead a handcuffed Hannah Green out to the waiting patrol car, they came through the living room, where Joanna and Jenny were sitting on the couch.

Hannah stopped in front of them. "Them dogs of yours is real nice," she said to Jenny.

Jenny nodded. "Thank you," she murmured.

Then Hannah looked at Joanna. For a few seconds their eyes met. There was such an air of hopelessness about her—such beaten-down defeat—that Joanna couldn't help feeling sorry for the woman. Even at Joanna's worst, in those bleak days right after Andy's death, she hadn't been nearly as lost as Hannah Green. One important difference was that Joanna

Brady had been blessed with something to live for—she'd had Jenny. Hannah Green had nothing.

"Thanks for lettin' me get that load off my chest," Hannah said. "Needed to tell somebody. Guess I been needin' to for years."

"You're welcome," Joanna said.

"Come on now," Ernie Carpenter urged, taking Hannah by the elbow and propelling her forward. "We've got to get moving."

Joanna walked them outside. When she came back into the house, she could smell something burning. Out in the kitchen, the pot with the potatoes in it had burned dry. "Damn!" she exclaimed, dashing for the kitchen. "There goes dinner."

Dick Voland followed her into the kitchen and then stood leaning against the kitchen counter as she rinsed what was left of the scorched potatoes and rescued the pork chops from being burned to a crisp.

"This is a nice place you've got here," Voland observed, looking around the efficient but spacious kitchen.

"Thank you," Joanna said. "You've never been here before, have you?" Voland shook his head. "Well," Joanna said, "I can't take any credit for it. My in-laws are the ones who did the kitchen remodel."

Voland nodded. "It is a long way out of town."

Joanna stopped stirring the gravy and stared up at her chief deputy. She didn't have to be psychic to know where he was going on this one. "It's not that far," she said.

"But what if Jenny hadn't been smart enough to call me and let me know what was happening? What would you have done then?"

Joanna went back to the gravy. "I would have thought of

something," she said. "Actually, I don't think we were ever in any real danger. It may have been scary at the time, but Hannah Green wasn't armed. She didn't try to do either Jenny or me any harm."

"But she could have," Voland countered. "And so could any other crazy who might choose to show up here."

"What are you saying?"

Voland shrugged. "With a house like this, on some acreage with your own well, you could probably sell it in a minute. Maybe buy something in town. A place where Jenny could walk back and forth to school and where you wouldn't be out here all by yourselves."

Joanna and Dick Voland were so at odds most of the time that Joanna found it oddly touching for him to be concerned about her safety. The fact that he would actually come right out and say something about it was downright disconcerting.

Joanna shook her head. "I appreciate the suggestion, Dick," she said. "But the High Lonesome is Jenny's and my home. It's the one Andy and I planned and worked for together. I'm not letting someone scare me out of living here."

"No," Dick Voland said a moment later. "I suppose not."

The afternoon had stretched so long after the luncheon that her trip out to the Rob Roy with her mother and mother-in-law seemed eons ago. Still, Dick Voland's suggestion about Joanna's selling the High Lonesome had reminded her of something else, something Eleanor had said. Joanna knew that even raising the issue would put an end to this amicable but highly unlikely truce between Dick Voland and her. She decided to go ahead and risk it.

"Speaking of selling," she said. "Did you know Terry Buckwalter is making arrangements to sell out Bucky's practice?"

Voland looked surprised. "So soon?" he asked. "With a business like that, especially one with a professional involved, I would have thought it would take months, if not years, to unload it. Where'd you hear about that?"

"At the luncheon today," Joanna replied. "Actually, that little nugget of intelligence came straight from my mother, who got it from Helen Barco at Helene's Salon of Hair and Beauty."

"Who's buying the place?" Dick asked. "Most likely someone from out of town."

"Mother didn't say," Joanna told him. "I meant to mention it to Ernie, but we didn't have time to talk about anything but Hannah Green."

"It's probably not that important," Voland said. "But I'm going by the department on my way home. If Ernie's still there, I'll let him know."

"While you're at it, there's something else I forgot to mention," Joanna continued. "I ran into Terry Buckwalter out at the Rob Roy today, too. When I saw her, she was just coming back from a game of golf. She looked like a million dollars, her wedding ring was among the missing, and it looked to me like she might have something going with her golf pro. The guy's name is Peter Wilkes. Tell Ernie to check him out, too."

"Peter Wilkes!" Dick scoffed. "Isn't he one of the"—he paused, searching for some kind of acceptable phraseology—"gay blades," he said finally, "who started the Rob Roy in the first place?"

Joanna nodded. "He and his partner."

"What would he have going with Terry Buckwalter, then?" Voland asked.

"I don't know," Joanna said. "That's what I want Ernie

to check out. He might want to start by talking with Helen Barco."

"Wait a minute," Voland said. "Aren't you reaching on this one?"

Joanna had been right. Word by word, sentence by sentence, the truce between Joanna and her chief deputy was disintegrating.

"What do you mean, reaching?" she asked.

"Look, Joanna," Dick Voland said reasonably. "I can see where you're coming from. What happened to Hal Morgan's wife is more or less the same thing that happened to Andy. They're not exactly the same, mind you. But they're close enough for you to have lost perspective—to be viewing things through some misguided sense of sympathy."

"Sympathy!" Joanna began, but Voland went right on talking.

"You shot Tony Vargas dead, but it wasn't a premeditated thing. Hal Morgan came here to Bisbee with every intention of doing exactly what he did—of taking the law into his own hands. This afternoon and tonight, I sent those two deputies over to Saginaw, just like you wanted me to. They didn't find anything, Joanna—not one blessed thing—to support Hal Morgan's lame story. Now here you come with this fruitcake business about Terry Buckwalter and Wilkes. It's just . . . just ridiculous."

The heat Joanna felt rising up her neck had nothing to do with either the bubbling gravy on the stove or with the potatoes she had just mashed.

"Leaving no stone unturned isn't ridiculous," she said curtly. "It's called doing a thorough investigation, Dick. And before you start casting aspersions about who has and who hasn't lost perspective, you might consider that, if nothing

else, I'm looking at Hal Morgan with a presumption of innocence. You and Arlee Campbell keep acting like the man's
already been tried and convicted. I want Peter Wilkes
checked out, and Terry Buckwalter as well."

"Right," Dick Voland said. "I'll make sure to pass the
word along."

The food was ready to be put on the table. "Would you
like something to eat?" Joanna asked in the awkward pause
that followed.

"No, thanks," Voland said. "In fact, maybe I'd better head
out and get on this right now. After all, I wouldn't want any
of these valuable leads to slip through our fingers."

The sarcasm in Voland's last sentence wasn't lost on
Joanna. She had heard it before on other occasions. She was
learning to live with it, and most of the time it didn't bother
her. Tonight it did. For a while it had seemed she might be
gaining ground in Dick Voland's opinion. Earning her stripes.
But his parting remark proved otherwise.

Even so, she didn't want him to go away angry. She followed him as far as the back porch. "Thanks, Dick. Especially
for dropping everything and coming as soon as Jenny called."

He looked back at her. "You don't have to thank me," he
said. "Of course I came. It's my job."

Shaking her head, Joanna went back inside and called
Jenny to dinner. The child came at once and attacked her food
with more enthusiasm than she had shown in months. She
had polished off her very well-done pork chop and was
working her way through a mound of peas before she slowed
down enough to talk.

"I was watching out the window when Detective Carpenter took Mrs. Green out of the house and put her in his car,"
Jenny said thoughtfully. "I felt sorry for her. She seemed

more sad than crazy, and she didn't do anything to hurt us. What's going to happen to her?"

"I don't have any idea, Jenny, and that's the truth."

"Will she have to go to prison?"

"Maybe. That'll be up to the judge to decide," Joanna said.

"Will she have to go to court?"

"Most likely."

"But she's poor, isn't she?" Jenny asked. "She looked poor."

"I think you're right," Joanna said. "She looked poor to me, too."

"So how will she pay for a lawyer then?" Jenny asked. "Don't they cost a lot of money?"

"If she can't pay for a lawyer, the judge will give her one. That's called a court-appointed attorney."

"And she doesn't have to pay then?"

"No."

All of Jenny's peas had disappeared. The only thing remaining on her plate was a single helping of coleslaw. Before Jenny started on that, she shot her mother a subtly appraising glance. "Was Mr. Voland mad that I called him?"

"Mad?" Joanna returned. "Not at all. Why do you ask?"

"I heard him just before he left. It sounded like he was yelling at the top of his lungs."

"We were having a discussion," Joanna said. "A disagreement."

"About what?"

"About how to do things," Joanna answered after a moment's consideration. "He thinks the department should do things one way, and I think we should do them another."

"Well," Jenny said. "You're the boss, aren't you? Isn't he supposed to do things the way you want?"

Joanna had to smile at Jenny's uncomplicated view of the world. Things either were or they weren't. Politics hadn't yet intruded on Jenny's consciousness. As far as Joanna could tell, neither had the battle of the sexes.

"Do you remember all those old Calvin and Hobbes books that your dad loved so much? Remember how Calvin never wanted to let Susie in his club?"

Jenny nodded.

"Dick Voland reminds me a little of Calvin. He liked the department a lot better when it was a private club with no girls allowed."

"If he doesn't like you, why doesn't he quit and go work somewhere else?" Jenny asked.

"It isn't quite that easy, Jenny," Joanna told her daughter. "Not for either one of us. Dick Voland has been in law enforcement a long time. I haven't. There are all kinds of things I can learn from him that will make me a better sheriff. The only problem is, sometimes it isn't easy for the two of us to work together."

"Still," Jenny insisted firmly, "he shouldn't yell. It isn't nice."

Joanna smiled. "No, it isn't, but fortunately I'm pretty tough. I can handle whatever he says."

"Sort of like sticks and stones can break my bones?"

"Exactly," Joanna said. With a laugh she picked up the two empty plates and carried them to the sink. "It's exactly like that. Now hurry off to bed, Jenny. It's late. We'll leave the dishes until morning."

Ignoring her overloaded briefcase, Joanna headed for her own bedroom. Setting her alarm for five, she fell into bed and was asleep within minutes. The dream came later.

She and Andy were together once again. The two of them, hand in hand, were strolling through the dusty midway of the Cochise County Fair while Jenny, carrying an enormous cloud of cotton candy, darted on ahead. The sun shone, and Joanna felt warm and happy. Even in her sleep, she savored the sense of well-being that surrounded her.

The two of them had stopped beside the carousel when Jenny came racing back toward them. "There's a great big Ferris wheel. Can we ride on it, please?"

Andy reached into his pocket, pulled out his billfold, extracted some money, and handed it over to Jenny. "You go get the tickets, Jen," he said. "Mommy and I will be right there. We'll all ride it together."

Once again, Jenny raced off. Soon, without any intervening walking, they were stepping up the slanted wooden ramp and the attendant was fastening the wooden pole across the front of the car. "No swinging now, you hear?" he warned.

The Bradys—Andy, Joanna, and Jenny—were the last passengers to board. Once they were locked in place, the Ferris wheel started its upward climb. Jenny, her whole body alight with excitement, sat in the middle. Andy leaned back in the seat, smiling. With one arm he reached across behind Jenny until his wrist and hand were resting reassuringly on Joanna's shoulder.

Joanna didn't much care for Ferris wheels—didn't like the way they went up and up and up until you were at the very top with nothing at all beneath you. Nor did she enjoy the stomach-lurching way in which the world dropped out from under you. Suddenly, as they fell, she realized that the comforting weight of Andy's hand had disappeared from her shoulder.

Concerned, she looked across the seat. Jenny had scrambled over to the far side of the car—to the place where Andy had been sitting—and was frantically peering out over the armrest.

"Daddy, Daddy," she screamed. "Come back. Don't go. Please don't leave us."

But Andy was already gone. He had disappeared into thin air. When their car hit the bottom of the arc, Joanna could see no sign of him.

"Stop this thing," Joanna shouted at the attendant. "Let us out. My husband fell. We've got to find him."

The attendant pointed to his ears, shook his head, suggesting that he couldn't hear, and then touched the control panel. Instead of stopping, the wheel sped up to twice its previous speed, racing up and then plummeting down into the void, with Joanna floating helplessly in her seat. Jenny inched over until she managed to grab on to her mother. As the wheel went round and round she clung there, sobbing in terror. Then, suddenly, everything stopped. The car Jenny and Joanna were in was at the very pinnacle of the Ferris wheel. From there they could see for miles—off across the fairgrounds and the racetrack, to Douglas and Agua Prieta and to the parched desert landscape beyond.

They stayed there for the longest time, with Joanna searching in every direction for some sign of Andy, for some hint of where he might have gone. At last the wheel moved again—down, down, down—until it stopped at the bottom. The attendant, grinning, leaned forward to unlatch the wooden bar. It wasn't until she stood up to walk down the ramp that Joanna realized she was naked. And all around her, watching, were people from the department. Dick Voland and Ernie Carpenter. Kristin and the clerks from records. The deputies from Patrol and the guards from the county jail.

Surprisingly, she wasn't the least bit embarrassed. Instead of shrinking away and trying to cover herself, Joanna was angry. Furious! How could Andy have done this to her? How could he have gone off and left her alone like this? He should have stayed with her—stayed with them both.

She heard a bell then. Andy had always liked the sledgehammer concessions. In those games, a strong enough blow from a hammer would ring the bell at the top of a metal pole. The resulting prize was usually nothing more exotic than a shoddily made teddy bear or an awful cigar. Still, Andy loved to try his hand at it. Joanna looked toward the bell, hoping that whoever was ringing it would turn out to be Andy. She could see the pole, the bell, but there was no one in sight. Still, the bell continued to ring, over and over, until it finally penetrated her consciousness. The insistently ringing bell was coming from a telephone—the one on Joanna's bedside table.

As she raised herself on one elbow to grope for the receiver, she glanced at the glowing green numbers on the clock radio. Twelve forty-seven. Who the hell was calling her in the middle of the night?

"Sheriff Brady," she answered, her voice still thick with sleep.

"Sorry to wake you," said Larry Kendrick from Dispatch. "We've got a problem here. The jail commander asked me to call you."

Sitting up, Joanna fumbled for the switch on the bedside lamp. "What is it?"

"We just found Hannah Green dead in her cell," Kendrick said.

"Dead!" Joanna echoed. "How can that be? What happened?"

"She hung herself from her bunk," Larry said. "Or, more accurately, strangled herself. With her bra."

"Has somebody called Dick Voland and Ernie Carpenter?"

"Dick's already here. Ernie's next on the list."

"I'll be right there, too," Joanna said, scrabbling out of bed. In a turmoil, she slammed down the telephone receiver and tore off her nightgown. She was half-dressed when she stopped cold.

What about Jenny?

Jenny was in bed and sound asleep. It was nearly one o'clock in the morning. With this kind of emergency, Joanna might be gone for several hours. She couldn't very well go off and leave Jenny alone, asleep in a house a mile from the nearest neighbor. But waking her up and taking her along was equally impossible. What should she do? Bed her down on the couch in Kristin's office and expect her to sleep while all hell broke loose around her?

Sinking back down on the bed, Joanna realized she'd have to call someone. Whom? Her mother? Eva Lou or Jim Bob Brady? They would have been asleep for hours. It wasn't fair to wake them up. The same held true for Marianne Maculyea. She'd be asleep, too. Despairing, Joanna glanced at the clock once more—five to one.

And that's when she realized that there was one friend who would still be awake. One A.M. would be closing time at the Blue Moon Saloon and Lounge up in Brewery Gulch. Angie Kellogg would just be getting off work. In Angie's previous life, and in this one as well, she lived what was essentially a night shift existence. Other people might think it was the middle of the night. For Angie, it was late afternoon.

Seconds later, worrying that she might already be too late, Joanna dialed the number. "Blue Moon," a voice said. "Angie speaking."

"Thank God you're still there. It's Joanna."

"Of course I'm still here," Angie replied. "It's not quite one yet. I'm just washing up the last of those god-awful ash-trays. What's the matter?"

"I've got to go into work, and I don't know what to do about Jenny. I need someone to look after her while I go back to the office."

"Now?" Angie asked.

"There's been a problem over at the jail. Once I go in, no telling how long I'll be there. I don't want to wake Jenny up—tomorrow's a school day—but I don't want to leave her here by herself, either."

Angie Kellogg still couldn't quite fathom how she had become friends first with Joanna and then with Joanna's friends, the Reverend Marianne Maculyea and Jeff Daniels. What she did know, however, was that those three people were the ones who had made her new life possible. Faced with an opportunity to repay some of what she regarded as an overwhelming debt of kindness, Angie was eager to help.

"Do you want me to come there, or would you like to bring her to my place?" Angie asked.

"If it wouldn't be too much trouble, I'd appreciate your coming here," Joanna answered.

"Sure," Angie answered. "No problem. I'll be there just as soon as I can. I'll lock up right now, but I'll leave Bobo a note so he'll know why I didn't finish cleaning up."

"You're sure he won't mind?"

"No. Not at all, but it'll still take the better part of twenty minutes for me to get there."

Joanna looked at the clock once more. It was one straight up. Still, after what had happened earlier that evening, Joanna wasn't willing to leave Jenny alone, not even for a minute. "Don't rush, I can wait that long," she said. "The woman's dead. My getting there a few minutes earlier or later isn't going to make a bit of difference."

As Joanna hurried into her clothing, she was over-whelmed with guilt. Hannah Green had come to Joanna, come specifically to the sheriff, for help. Joanna had done what she could for the unfortunate woman—handled the situation to the best of her ability. She had been terribly moved, as much by Hannah's broken spirit as by the woman's mangled hand and crippled fingers. Joanna had listened and had been kind to her even while using Jenny to engineer the woman's capture. There was nothing bad or dishonorable in that. It was Joanna's job.

Still, she felt guilty. In the first days and weeks after Andy's death, she, too, had lived with the same kind of abject hopelessness that she had recognized in Hannah Green. Joanna, too, had seen a future empty of all promise and possibility. Even now, the future still didn't look all that bright, but at least Joanna could see that she *had* a future. Hannah Green did not.

Joanna Brady had Jenny to live for, but she had something else as well—something beyond simply being needed. As an upholder of law and order, she still possessed a good deal of faith in the justice system. Just as Joanna had told Jenny, she would have expected Hannah Green to have her day in court. A court-appointed attorney would have been at her side. She would have had the opportunity to tell her story to a jury.

Having heard it all—the years of casual and debilitating meanness Reed Carruthers had inflicted on his daughter—surely no jury would have convicted Hannah Green of first degree murder. Maybe not even of manslaughter.

Had Hannah Green only lived long enough to hear that verdict read in court! But she had not. Instead, she had short-circuited the justice system by taking her own life. She had come to Joanna and willingly confessed to the crime of murder because she had already made up her mind. Long before she climbed into Joanna's Blazer she had known that whatever confession she made to Sheriff Brady was all the unburdening she would ever have a chance to do.

So why didn't I order a suicide watch for her? Joanna demanded of her reflection in the mirror. *Why didn't I see it coming?*

Did that mean it was her fault? Was it a natural outgrowth of her own lack of experience? There had been other, far more experienced, officers involved in what had happened, but Hannah Green had died on Joanna's watch. So, although Joanna might not be directly to blame, responsibility for what had happened rested squarely upon her shoulders.

She was just finishing combing her hair when Angie Kellogg drove into the yard. It should have taken a full twenty minutes for her to drive from the Blue Moon in Brewery Gulch to High Lonesome Ranch, but her Oldsmobile Omega stopped outside Joanna's gate in just under fifteen. Joanna stifled the barking dogs and then rushed into the yard to meet her.

"What's going on?" Angie asked. "You sounded upset."

"One of the inmates committed suicide at the jail," Joanna answered. "I'll probably be gone the rest of the night, so when you get tired, go ahead and bed down in my room. If

I get home before you're up and out, I can always sack out on the couch."

"Are you sure?" Angie asked.

"Yes, I'm sure," Joanna said. "After all, you're the one who's doing me the favor. Thank you."

"Go and don't worry," Angie said. "I'm glad to help out,"

A few minutes later when Joanna pulled into the Cochise County Justice Center, the place was alive with people moving around in the clear, chill night. The driveway was thick with a clot of vehicles. She recognized most of the emergency equipment. Picking her way up the drive, she came around to the back of the building. There, she pulled into her reserved parking place.

When she opened the car door, she was momentarily blinded by the flash of a camera. "Who the hell is that?" she demanded as spots of light continued to dance in her eyes.

"Kevin Dawson with the *Bisbee Bee*," a voice said out of the darkness. "Any reason you're sneaking in the back door, Sheriff Brady?"

"This happens to be my parking place," Joanna snapped back at him.

"Do you have any comments about what happened in the jail tonight?"

"My comment, Mr. Dawson, has to do with the fact that this parking lot is off limits to the public. I suggest that you get back around to the front of the building where you belong."

"Come on, Sheriff Brady. I'm just doing my job."

"So am I," she told him. "Now get moving."

She stood and watched until he disappeared around the corner of the building. To steady herself, she paused long enough to take several deep breaths. She gazed up at the canopy of stars and tried to prepare herself for what was coming. This would be an ordeal for all concerned. Kevin Dawson was only the beginning of it.

Using her combination on the push-button lock, Joanna let herself into the building through the private door that led directly into her office. When she switched on the lights, she found to her surprise that the room was already occupied. Ernie Carpenter was sitting in one of the captain's chairs opposite her desk. He looked up at her. His face was bleak, his skin ashen.

"I blew it," he said.

"You had no way of knowing," Joanna told him, dropping her purse on the corner of the desk and then coming around to stand leaning against it. "Don't blame yourself, Ernie. I've been thinking about it all the way here. It's not my fault, and it's not yours, either."

"But it is," Ernie insisted. "Don't you understand? Nothing like this has ever happened to me before. I'm usually a better judge of people than that—better at reading what's going on with them. I've always prided myself at being able to tell in advance if someone's going to turn violent on me or go gunny-bags. I didn't see this one coming, not at all."

"How long had Hannah Green been in her cell before it happened?" Joanna asked.

Ernie shook his head. "Not long. No more than half an hour or so. She waived her right to a lawyer, so Jaime and I stayed long enough to get the whole interview down on tape. I'd just managed to drag my ass home and crawl into bed when the call came in saying she was dead."

"Did she leave a note?"

"No. Nothing."

"Not nothing, Ernie. Her confession to you and Jaime, her confession to me was a note of sorts."

"I realize that now," Ernie agreed. "I should have picked up on it at the time. But I didn't. That's why I'm quitting."

Reaching into his pocket, he pulled out the leather wallet with his badge in it and tossed it on Joanna's desk. Joanna could barely believe her eyes or her ears. "Quitting?" she echoed.

"That's right."

"Over this? Over Hannah Green?"

Ernie nodded. "If you want me to, I'll go write my letter of resignation right now. That's why I was waiting for you here in your office. I wanted to talk to you alone. Without Dick Voland hanging around. He'll try to talk me out of it."

"You don't think I will?"

"Why should you? Look, there are other, younger, guys coming along. I've put in my twenty-plus years. This wasn't a fatal error for me, but it sure as hell was for Hannah Green. By the time we had finished talking to her, I could see that if she was telling us the truth about her father, we'd have a problem when it came to charging her with murder one. Maybe we could get voluntary manslaughter. Maybe even second-degree homicide. Whatever the charges might have ended up being, they wouldn't have amounted to a capital offense. She may have committed a crime, but she shouldn't have died for it. The fact that she did is my fault plain and simple. Who's to say that the next time I won't screw up worse and somebody else will die? Jaime Carbajal, for example."

"You're overreacting," Joanna said.

"The hell I am."

Joanna picked up the wallet. The leather was still warm

to the touch from being in Ernie's pocket. She flipped it open and studied the badge. The picture was of a somewhat younger man. A man with a less florid, less careworn face. "Detective Ernest W. Carpenter," the card said. "Cochise County Sheriff's Department."

"You've been here a long time," Joanna said softly. "Since my father's time."

Ernie nodded. "That's right. Your dad is the one who hired me. That's so long ago it seems like ancient history."

"How many times, in all the years you've been here, have you had two homicides and a suicide in three days?" Joanna asked.

Ernie looked up at her quizzically. "Never," he said.

"Is there a chance that you're spread too thin right now? That you've been doing too much? Could that account for your not reading Hannah Green the way you might have under ordinary circumstances?"

"I suppose it could," Ernie allowed grudgingly. "Jamie and I have both been working our tails off."

"What about Jaime?" Joanna asked. "Do you think he's ready to step into your shoes? Is he capable of doing this job without you?"

Folding his arms, Ernie stuck his feet out in front of him and examined his shoes. For the first time ever, Joanna noticed that his usually immaculate wing tips were in need of a shine. "Jaime's young," Ernie said. "But he's getting there."

"But he's not all the way up to speed yet, is he?"

"No."

"If you drop the ball now, Ernie, you'll leave us all in the lurch. Jaime will be in over his head, so will I. So will my department."

"But what about . . ." He stopped.

"Hannah Green?"

Ernie nodded.

"I've been thinking about that all the way here," Joanna said. "We gave Hannah Green what she wanted and needed, Ernie. You and Deputy Carbajal and I not only listened to her, we believed her. It may have been the first time ever in her poor unfortunate life that anyone really listened to her. If Reed Carruthers was the kind of man we both suspect, he never paid any attention to a word she said—including what television channels she wanted to watch."

Holding out the wallet, Joanna handed it back to Ernie. He studied it. "So what are you saying?" he asked. "What do you want me to do?"

"Stay," she said simply. "Go over to the jail and take charge of our part of the investigation. Hannah Green's death will have to be investigated by an outside agency, of course. Dispatch has already called in the State Department of Public Safety, haven't they?"

Ernie nodded. "But you're to handle our end of it," Joanna said.

When Ernie Carpenter looked up at her, his eyes were grave. "You're sure?"

"Absolutely," Joanna said with conviction.

Slowly, Ernie pulled himself up and out of the chair. He stood there with the leather wallet still open in his hand, staring down at his badge. "All right, then," he said. "I'll get on it. You're sure you don't mind having old duffers like me hanging around?"

Joanna shook her head and smiled. "It's the old guys, as you call them, who keep the rest of us from having to reinvent the wheel. Not only that, if I were dumb enough to let you quit over Hannah Green, then I'd have to quit myself.

After all, I didn't see it coming any more than you did. As of right now, we'd both be out of a job."

Closing the wallet, Ernie stuffed it back in his pocket. "I guess I'd better get cracking," he said. "Are you coming along over to the jail?"

"In a minute," Joanna told him.

Ernie headed for the door. "All I can say is, Sheriff Brady, you're a hell of a salesman. I'll bet Milo Davis is still kicking himself over losing you."

At the time Joanna left the insurance agency, she had not yet quite completed the transition from office manager to sales, but there was no reason to explain that to Ernie—not right then.

"I hope so," Joanna said. "I certainly do."

12

IT was almost seven by the time Joanna stumbled home. She walked into a house that was alive with the fragrance of frying bacon and brewing coffee. Jenny and Angie Kellogg were already eating breakfast in the kitchen nook. Because she planned on trying to grab another few hours of sleep, Joanna passed on Angie's offer of coffee. Instead, she opted for a glass of orange juice. Dragging the kitchen stool to the end of the breakfast counter, she sat down, kicked off her shoes, and began rubbing the soles of her aching feet.

"Where were you, Mom?" Jenny asked. "Angie said you had to go to work."

All the way home, Joanna had dreaded having to answer that question. She was already so mind-numbingly weary, she had hoped to dodge the subject of Hannah Green entirely, but now Jenny's questioning stare made avoiding the issue impossible.

"Mrs. Green died last night," Joanna said carefully, mincing around the word "suicide." "She died at the jail after the guards put her in her cell."

Jenny's eyes widened momentarily, then she turned to Angie. "Mrs. Green is the one I was telling you about," Jenny explained. "She was waiting by the mailbox when we came home last night." The child turned back to her mother. "What happened? Was she sick?"

Maybe Andy would have been brutally honest at that point, but Joanna simply wasn't up to it. "Yes," she answered. "She was very sick." *Which isn't a complete lie,* she thought. *But it's a long way from the truth.*

"Couldn't a doctor have saved her?" Jenny asked.

"I don't think so," Joanna said. "A doctor did come to the jail afterward, but he was too late."

Jenny seemed to consider that for a moment. Then, abruptly and with childlike unconcern, she simply changed the subject. "The quail were here just a little while ago," she said. "We used to have roadrunners out here, too," she added in an aside to Angie. "But that was before we got Tigger."

Angie Kellogg, newly come to the wonders of birding, both feeding and watching, looked horrified. "You mean your dog chases them?" she asked.

"Of course," Jenny said with a shrug. "He chases everything, but the only thing he ever catches is porcupines."

"Can't you make him stop?" Angie asked.

"Not so far," Jenny said.

The jarring juxtaposition of Hannah Green's death and Tigger's senseless antics cast Joanna adrift from the spoken words. Looking around the kitchen, she realized that the place was spotless. When she had left the house, dirty dishes and pots and pans from last night's long delayed dinner had still been stacked on the counter and in the sink. Between then and now, someone—Angie, no doubt—had rinsed them, loaded and run the dishwasher, and emptied it as well. The unspoken kindness and concern behind that simple act made Joanna's eyes fill with tears of gratitude.

"I love roadrunners," Angie Kellogg was saying when Joanna tuned back into the conversation. "Growing up back in Michigan, I used to think they weren't real, that the people who made the Roadrunner/Coyote cartoons had just made them up."

"I like those cartoons, too," Jenny said, scrambling out of the breakfast nook. "But I always feel sorry for the coyote."

Without having to be told, she took her dishes as far as the sink, rinsed them, and loaded them into the dishwasher. Then she headed for the bathroom to brush her teeth.

"Thanks for doing the dishes," Joanna said. "You didn't have to do that."

"I didn't mind," Angie answered with a laugh. "It was fun—almost like playing house. And it's so peaceful here. I never knew there were homes like this."

Over the months, Joanna had heard bits and pieces about Angie Kellogg's past, about the sexually abusive father who had driven his daughter out of the house. For Angie, life on the streets in the harsh world of teenaged prostitution had been preferable to living at home. Only now, living in her own little house, was she beginning to learn about how the rest of the world lived. Joanna looked around her clean but familiar kitchen and tried to see it through Angie's eyes. The place didn't seem peaceful to her. There was still a hole in it, a void that Andy's presence used to fill.

"I didn't know where all the dishes went," Angie continued. "I told Jenny that if she'd put them away for me, I'd give her a ride to school."

"You don't have to do that," Joanna said.

"Why not?" Angie returned. "Greenway School is just a

little out of the way. It won't take more than a couple of minutes for me to drop her off. That way you can go to bed. You look like you need it."

Unable to argue, Joanna stood up. "If anything," she said, "I feel worse than I look."

She staggered into the bedroom and dropped fully clothed onto the bedspread. Jenny stopped by on her way to her own room. "Aren't you going to get undressed?" she asked.

"I don't think so," Joanna said, pulling the bedspread up and over her. "I'm too tired."

Sound asleep, she didn't stir when Jenny and Angie left the house a few minutes later. The phone awakened her at eleven. "Sheriff Brady?" Kristin Marsten asked uncertainly.

Joanna cleared her throat. Her voice was still thick with sleep. "It's me, Kristin," she said. "What's up?"

"Dick Voland asked me to call you. There's going to be a telephone conference call with someone from the governor's office at eleven-thirty. Can you make it?"

"I'll be there," Joanna mumbled as she staggered out of bed. Showering and dressing in record time, she headed for the office. *The governor's office,* she thought along the way. *Why would Governor Wallace Hickman be calling me?*

As Joanna drove into the Justice Center compound, she saw that the front parking lot was once again littered with media vehicles, including at least one mobile television van from a station in Tucson. Fortunately, out-of-town reporters, unlike Kevin Dawson of the *Bisbee Bee,* had no idea about the sheriff's private backdoor entrance. Joanna took full advantage of that lack of knowledge. Without having had the benefit of a single cup of coffee, she wasn't ready to face shouted questions from a ravening horde of reporters. For them, Hannah Green's life and death meant nothing more than a day's headline or lead story. For the police officers involved, Joanna Brady included, Hannah Green's death meant failure.

Climbing out of the Blazer, Joanna heaved out her briefcase as well. She had dragged it back and forth from the office without ever unloading it or touching what was inside. No doubt today's batch of correspondence was already waiting for her. Any other day, the thought of all that paperwork would have been overwhelming. Today, Joanna welcomed it. By burying herself in it, perhaps she'd be able to forget the sight of a massive, lifeless Hannah Green slumped at the end of her jailhouse bunk, the air choked out of her by the tautly stretched elastic of a grimy bra that had been wrapped around and around her neck and finally around the foot rail of her upper bunk.

As soon as Joanna was inside, Kristin Marsten brought her both the mail and a much-needed cup of coffee.

"What's happening?" Joanna asked. "And who all is here?"

"Mr. Voland, of course," Kristin answered. "He was here when I arrived. Detective Carpenter showed up a few minutes ago, along with Tom Hadlock." Tom Hadlock was the jail commander. "Deputy Montoya is here, but he probably won't be included in the conference call. He's out front dealing with the reporters."

"Better him than me," Joanna said grimly.

Cup in hand, feigning a briskness she didn't feel, Joanna marched into the conference room with five minutes to spare. Ernie Carpenter, Dick Voland, and Tom Hadlock were already there. Grim-faced and red-eyed, none of them seemed any better off than Joanna felt.

Joanna looked questioningly at Dick Voland. "What's this all about?"

Voland shrugged. "Politics as usual," he said. "It's no big thing. Whenever something off the wall happens, Governor Hickman wants to be in on it. He probably wants to be reassured that this isn't something that's going to come back and bite him in the butt during the next election."

"What's going to bite him?"

"Hannah Green's death."

"How could what happened to Hannah Green hurt Governor Hickman?"

Voland shrugged. "You know. Allegations of possible police brutality. Violations of constitutional rights. That sort of thing."

Joanna could feel her temperature rising. "Are you saying Hickman may try to turn that poor woman's death into a political football?"

"It wouldn't be the first time," Ernie said. "And it sure as hell won't be the last."

When the phone rang, Joanna punched the speaker button. "Yes," she said.

"Lydia Morales with the governor's office is on the phone," Kristin said.

"Put her through."

Lydia Morales sounded young—about Joanna's age, perhaps—and businesslike. "Governor Hickman wanted me to get some information on the incident down there last night," Lydia said. "He'll have access to the Department of Public Safety's files, of course, but he did want me to ask a question or two. For instance, the victim, this Hannah Green, she wasn't black by any chance, or Hispanic, was she?"

"Black or Hispanic?" Joanna repeated. "What does that have to do with it?"

Lydia paused. "Well, certainly you understand how, when a prisoner dies in custody, there can always be questions of racism or police brutality or . . ."

"Or violation of constitutional rights," Joanna finished.

"Right," Lydia Morales confirmed brightly.

Hearing Lydia's response, Joanna knew Dick Voland was right. This really was politics as usual. Lydia Morales and Governor Hickman had no real interest in Hannah Green's tragic life and death. They were looking for votes, plain and simple. They were checking to see if there were any political liabilities involved or gains to be made in the aftermath of what had happened the night before in the Cochise County Jail. How many constituents would be adversely affected, and could the governor be held accountable?

"You never answered my question about Hannah Green," Lydia persisted.

Joanna tumbled then. In the minds of the governor's political strategists there were, presumably, both a black voting block and an Hispanic one as well. Unfortunately for her, Hannah Green fit in neither category.

"Hannah Green was an Anglo," Joanna said tersely

"Good," Lydia returned. "That will probably help."

"Help what?" Joanna asked.

"How this thing is handled," Lydia returned. "The kind of press it's given. Believe me, trying to fight a racism charge is tough. Definitely lose/lose all the way around."

Joanna was stunned at being told that having an Anglo woman die in her jail was somehow less politically damaging than having a black or Hispanic prisoner die under similar circumstances. Joanna was still reeling under the awful burden of her own part in Hannah Green's death. So were the other weary, grim-faced police officers gathered around the conference table.

All her life, Joanna had been teased about her red hair and her matching fiery temper. Something about Lydia's glib response set off an explosion in Joanna's heart, one she made no effort to contain.

"What you're saying, then," Joanna said, "is that violations of constitutional rights are more important if the person being so violated happens to fall in one or another of the politically approved minority categories?"

The question stopped Lydia cold. "I'm sure I . . ." she began.

"Perhaps you could give Governor Hickman a message for me," Joanna continued. Her voice had dropped to a dangerously low level. "You can tell him that Hannah Green's constitutional rights *were* violated."

"Were?" Lydia Morales repeated. "Don't you mean *weren't?*"

"No," Joanna corrected. "I mean *were*. I believe that our investigation will find that her civil rights were violated for years. Every day, in fact, starting with the moment thirty years ago when her father slammed her hand in a car door and then refused to take her for proper medical treatment. From that time on, and maybe even earlier, Hannah Green was denied life, liberty, and the pursuit of happiness."

"By her family, you mean," Lydia said, sounding relieved once more. "Not by a police officer. That would make her death unfortunate, of course, but it shouldn't be a problem from the governor's point of view."

From the governor's point of view!

"It should be," Joanna shot back. "Hannah Green may not

have a natural base of constituents, but let me remind you, Ms. Morales, two people are dead down here. Most likely those two deaths are attributable to the rising tide of domestic violence. An abuser is dead, and so is his victim. If Governor Hickman isn't worried about that, he sure as hell ought to be. Good day, Ms. Morales."

Reaching out, Joanna jabbed at the speaker button, depressing it and disconnecting the call. Then she looked at the three men gathered around the conference table. Tom Hadlock said nothing, but Dick Voland was grinning from ear to ear. Ernie Carpenter was actually applauding.

"Way to go," Dick Voland told her. "It's not exactly how to go about winning friends and influencing people, but I couldn't have said it better myself."

Tom Hadlock pushed his chair back and stood up. "Glad that little coming to God is over. Now, if you don't mind, Sheriff Brady, I think I'll go home and try to get some sleep."

As Hadlock shuffled out of the room, Joanna turned back to the others. "What about you?"

Ernie leaned back in his chair and rubbed his eyes. He looked as though he was barely awake. "I'm here now," he said. "I could just as well go to work on something. God knows there's enough for me to do." Joanna had hoped he would go home to get some sleep, but she decided not to argue the point.

Turning to Voland, she realized that the sudden spurt of anger toward Governor Hickman's deputy had helped clear her own head. "Anything from Patrol I should know about?" she asked.

"Dr. Lee dismissed Hal Morgan from the hospital a little while ago," Voland answered. "According to Deputy Howell, he's gone back to his motel room, to the place he rented when he first came to town several days ago."

After the intervening crisis with Hannah Green, Hal Morgan seemed worlds away. It took a few seconds for Joanna to switch gears. News that Hal Morgan had been turned loose meant that soon the heat would be turned back up on the Buckwalter murder investigation.

"What motel?" Joanna asked.

"The Rest Inn, out in the Terraces."

"There's still a deputy with him?"

"So far. Deputy Howell again."

Joanna turned to Ernie. "Have you made arrangements to talk to Helen Barco yet?" she asked.

Ernie had been sitting there with his bloodshot eyes half-closed. Now they came open. "Why on earth would I want to talk to Helen Barco?"

Joanna turned back to Dick Voland. "Didn't you tell him what I told you?"

Voland shook his head. "Sorry about that," he said. "Things got so hectic around here that it must have slipped my mind."

"What slipped your mind?" Ernie asked.

"Sheriff Brady is under the impression that Terry Buckwalter may have something going with Peter Wilkes, the golf pro out at the Rob Roy," Voland said.

There was no sense in Joanna's making a fuss about Dick Voland's neglecting to pass along her lead to Ernie Carpenter. They were all so tired and so overworked right then that it was to be expected that some things would drop through the cracks. Still, she wasn't going to sit there quietly and let Voland discount her suggestions.

"I *know* they're up to something," Joanna said. "Ernie, the reason I want you to go see Helen is that Terry Buckwalter had a complete makeover at Helene's yesterday morning. She did it early enough so she could go out and play a round of golf afterwards—the day after Bucky's death. I'm under the impression that Terry told Helen something of her plans for the future. Those plans need to be checked out."

Joanna returned to Dick Voland. "Is there anything more happening in the Buckwalter case? Anything else Ernie should know about?"

Eager to make his escape, Voland stood up. "Not that I can think of," he said, heading for the door. "That should just about cover it."

Once the chief deputy was gone, however, Ernie Carpenter made no move to get up. "I need to talk to you about this," he said.

"About what?" Joanna asked.

Ernie sighed. "Look," he said, "I'll be happy to run out to the Rest Inn and interview Hal Morgan. And I'm more than happy to drive out to the Rob Roy and talk to this Peter Wilkes. No problem. But I can't go talk to Helen Barco. I won't."

"Why not?" Joanna asked.

There was a long pause. "Because she won't speak to me," Ernie Carpenter answered.

"She won't speak to you? Of course she will. You're a detective. Talking to people is your job."

Ernie considered for some time before he answered. "Years ago, I dated Helen's daughter Molly. Did you ever hear anything about that?"

"No," Joanna answered. "I didn't even know Helen has a daughter."

"Had, not has," Ernie corrected. "And not many people

do. Molly Barco and I went to high school together. We dated for a while. I was older than she was by a good three years. After graduation, I went away to college. That's where I met Rose. It was love at first sight. The real thing, not just some kind of puppy love. When I came back to Bisbee at home-coming to break the news to Molly that Rose and I were go-ing to get married, she more or less went haywire. She had always been a little on the wild side. She took off. Went to San Diego to live with her cousin. She died two months later, three months shy of her seventeenth birthday. A sailor on leave stabbed her to death just outside Balboa Park. He claimed she was a prostitute and that when she pulled a knife on him, he stabbed her in self-defense. He was tried, but he got off."

"That's why Helen Barco doesn't speak to you?" Joanna asked. "She blames you for what happened to her daughter?"

"Helen has every right to blame me. I blame myself," Er-nie said. "Molly was an only child. She was young and sweet and vulnerable, and far more in love with me than I was with her."

Joanna thought of the many times she had been in Helen Barco's beauty shop and the countless times Eleanor Lathrop had gone. Yet Joanna did not remember ever hearing any mention of the Barcos' murdered daughter.

"That's one of the reasons I became a cop," Ernie contin-ued. "And a detective, too. I always felt as though I owed Molly that much—to do what I could to help others, even though I couldn't help her. I've run into Slim around town on occasion. He's always civil, if not pleasant. Helen cuts me dead whenever she sees me. It would be useless for me to try to talk to her about Terry Buckwalter."

The room grew still. "Should I go see her?" Joanna suggested at last.

Ernie nodded. "That's probably a good idea," he said. "If you don't mind, that is. Otherwise, I could ask Jaime Carbajal to do it, but I just sent the poor guy home to get some shut-eye himself."

"I don't mind," Joanna said. And then, because Ernie looked so beaten up, she tried to lighten his load. "I've been needing a haircut for weeks anyway. This would be a good excuse, and subtle, too, don't you think? Sort of like going in undercover?"

Ernie Carpenter stood up and gave Joanna the ghost of a grin. "You may be able to get away with that line," he said, "but it wouldn't work for me. Not in a million years."

Once back in her office, Joanna picked up the phone and dialed Helene's Salon of Hair and Beauty. The first time she dialed the number, the line was busy. While waiting to dial again, she thumbed through her newest stack of correspondence. Halfway down, she found that morning's issue of the *Bisbee Bee*.

Curious, Joanna picked it up. There staring back at her, was her own picture. The photographer had caught her in the flash of the camera as she exited her Blazer. Next to that was a very uncomplimentary mug shot of Hannah Green.

The caption under Joanna's picture said, "Sheriff Joanna Brady returns to her office by a back entrance following the suicide of a Cochise County Jail inmate."

"That wormy little son of a bitch!" Joanna said.

Tossing the paper aside, Joanna dialed Helen's number once again. This time it rang. Helen Barco herself answered the phone.

"Joanna Brady here," Joanna said. "There isn't a chance

you could work me in for a haircut sometime today, is there?"

"How soon can you be here?" Helen returned. "Lonnie Taylor canceled just a few minutes ago because she has to take her mother out to Sierra Vista to see the doctor. If you can be here in the next twenty minutes or so, I can work you in with no problem. Otherwise, you're out of luck."

"I'm on my way," Joanna said. "Hold the chair for me."

She drove into town feeling as though she were privy to something she didn't want to know—to a part of Ernie's history as well as of Helen Barco's that shouldn't have been any of Joanna Brady's business. But it was. She felt as though, with her newfound knowledge, she owed Helen Barco the courtesy of a condolence. And yet, since Helen herself hadn't mentioned her daughter, Joanna realized that her saying anything at all about Molly Barco would be a rude intrusion.

When Joanna walked into the beauty shop that day, she felt weighted down by all that secret knowledge. The eye-watering smells of permanent-wave solution and chemicals made her want to run for cover. A woman Joanna didn't recognize sat enthroned under a beehive-shaped dryer with a dog-eared *People* magazine thrust in front of her face. She looked up and nodded in greeting when Joanna opened the door.

"How's Jenny's hair doing these days?" Helen asked as she flipped a plastic cape over Joanna's shoulders.

Two months after Jenny's ill-fated permanent, the solution-damaged hair was finally beginning to grow out. "It's much better," Joanna said. It was easy for her to be gracious at that point. After all, she had a good deal to be thankful for. Jenny was alive and well. Her hair would eventually outgrow the effects of that bad permanent. Helen Barco's daughter was dead.

Helen shook her head sadly. "I don't know what got into me," she said. "I haven't had a disaster like that since back when I was first going to beauty school. Your mother and I just got carried away talking and I plumb forgot to set the timer."

"We all make mistakes," Joanna said.

It wasn't until after her hair was shampooed and Helen Barco was snipping away that Joanna finally got down to business. "I saw Terry Buckwalter yesterday," she said. "She looked great."

"Doesn't she though!" Helen Barco agreed with a smile. "She was my first appointment yesterday morning. She had a complete makeover, including letting me do her colors. I fixed her up with new lipstick and nail enamel as well. Those new spring lines do a lot for her. They'd be fine for you, too, Joanna. You should try them."

"I'll think about it," Joanna said. "But I'm still not ready. Getting back to Terry, though, I barely recognized her. People will be surprised when they see her at the funeral tomorrow."

"That's what she said, too," Helen said. "That people will be surprised. They'll have plenty to talk about when Little Miss Mousie shows up at the funeral looking like a fashion plate." Helen clicked her tongue. "It does make such a difference. It's a crying shame she didn't have it done years ago. But I don't think that's why she did it now—the funeral, I mean. It sounded to me like she had some kind of important appointment coming up this weekend. She wanted to look her best for that."

"Did she say what kind of appointment?" Joanna asked.

"Not exactly," Helen said. "Whatever it is, it isn't here in town. I believe it's up in Phoenix. Or maybe Tucson. I forget which."

"A meeting, or a date?" Joanna asked, thinking once again of Terry Buckwalter's missing wedding ring.

"Oh, I'm certain it wasn't a date," Helen said quickly. "I believe it had something to do with golf. Something with a whole bunch of letters. L-something and some kind of school—a V-school or a T-school, I forget."

Over the years, Joanna had picked up a little golfing lingo just from having Jim Bob and Andy Brady watch weekend golf tournaments. "Q-school?" she asked. "Is Terry trying to get into a qualifying school?"

"That's it," Helen said. "Those are the exact words she used. Qualifying school. And she wants to go on a tour of some kind."

"The L.P.G.A.?" Joanna asked incredulously. "Terry Buckwalter thinks she's going to go off on the Ladies Professional Golf Association tour?"

"How did you put that together?" Helen said. "You really are a detective, aren't you. Your mother is always telling me how smart you are. This is amazing."

Joanna thought about Terry Buckwalter. She didn't know exactly how old Terry was, although she had to be somewhere in her mid- to late thirties. For years, Terry had served as an unpaid assistant tennis coach at the high school, but as far as Joanna could remember, that had come to an end several years earlier. It was a hell of a long way from playing small-town tennis to hopping on the L.P.G.A. circuit as a professional golfer.

"She's that good?" Joanna asked.

"Evidently," Helen Barco said. "She seems to think so, and so does that guy out at the Rob Roy."

"Terry spoke to you about Peter Wilkes?" Joanna asked.

"You bet she did. To hear her talk, you'd think he's the greatest thing since sliced bread."

That stumped Joanna. If Terry Buckwalter and Peter Wilkes had something going, wouldn't they be a little more discreet about it than that?

"It sounds expensive as all heck," Helen continued. "She did say that with the insurance and all that she'd come out all right, although she is selling, you know."

"Selling what?"

"The practice," Helen answered. "Since she isn't a veterinarian, she can't operate it herself. The same thing would happen to Slim if he was left holding this shop. He wouldn't be able to do a thing."

"Bucky's been dead for two days and she's already sold the practice? How can that be?"

"She said it was something Doc Buckwalter set up himself a long time ago. It's not final yet, by any means, but it sounded like it was pretty much a done deal. According to her, that nice Dr. Wade from down in Douglas is the one who'll be buying it. The practice and the house both. Once she has the money, she'll be free to do whatever she wants."

Joanna couldn't help wondering exactly what kind of "deal" Terry Buckwalter was getting. Dr. Wade might be just as kind as could be when it came to pulling out porcupine needles, but how nice would he be when it came to taking advantage of a widow?

"If he's moving in this fast," Joanna said, "he's probably buying the place at fire sale prices."

"Could be," Helen Barco said, "but Terry seemed happy enough about it. Like she was getting just what she wanted. According to her, Dr. Wade is planning on bringing in some young vet fresh out of school to help him run both places. Terry says Dr. Wade was such a help to her last year when Bucky was out of town that she knows people can trust him to do a good job."

That was all that was said. Helen's next client showed up right then. Still, Joanna was filled with misgivings. Outside in the Blazer, she sat for some time with the engine running but without putting the truck in gear, puzzling about this latest batch of information.

By Bisbee standards, Terry Buckwalter's behavior was nothing short of outrageous. And suspicious as well. With Bucky not yet in his grave, Terry was cashing in all the jointly held marital assets to go on the pro-golf circuit? What kind of a harebrained scheme was that?

Joanna wasn't a golfer, but she knew enough about how sports tournaments in general worked to understand that only the very few top players actually made a living at it. The people farther down the line followed the play from one course to the next, but they did so on their own, sometimes barely covering expenses, to say nothing of eking out a living.

For years Joanna had been privy to the entire Davis Insurance Agency book of business. Milo Davis handled all kinds of insurance—property/casualty, life, health, disability, and group. The Buckwalters as well as the Buckwalter Animal Clinic had been full-service customers.

Closing her eyes, Joanna tried to remember the Buckwalters' several bulging files. One of them—the one with the orange tag on it—had dealt with nothing but life insurance. It seemed to Joanna that there had been several policies, whole-life and term insurance both. There had been some insurance on Terry, but since Bucky had been the professional and the major source of income, the bulk of the coverage had been on him.

But what kinds of face amounts? Joanna wondered. Probably no more than two hundred thousand or so. Maybe three hundred on the outside. Combined with whatever pittance Reggie Wade was paying for the veterinary practice, that would give Terry Buckwalter a fairly nice piece of change to go out into the world as a single woman. It wasn't a huge amount, but it would have provided years of security if she didn't blow the whole wad on something or someone stupid.

And then Joanna thought of Peter Wilkes. Was this really about Terry Buckwalter trying to break into the pro tour circuit, or was it something far more sinister? In her mind's eye, Joanna saw it as one of the old story problems from arithmetic.

Life-insurance proceeds plus sale of property equal cash equals motive for murder. *That's it,* she thought. *It has to be. Bucky Buckwalter was killed for the money. The question is, was it Terry, was it Peter Wilkes, or was it both of them acting together?*

Shoving the gearshift into drive, Joanna pulled out of her parking place and headed for the Buckwalter Animal Clinic. In a way, solving a murder case was very much like playing a complicated game of tag.

And the cops are always it.

13

I T wasn't until Joanna pulled up to the entrance to the Buck-walter Animal Clinic that she realized she didn't know what she was doing there. Posted on the upright at the end of the cattle guard was a hand-lettered sign that announced: "Closed Until Further Notice."

Joanna hesitated. She had already turned on her turn signal to go back onto the highway when she noticed there were four vehicles parked beside the building: Terry Buckwalter's T-Bird, Bebe Noonan's Honda, Bucky's van, and a U-Haul truck.

Helen Barco's right, Joanna told herself. *Terry's already sold the place, and she's moving out.*

Rumbling across the iron rails of the cattle guard, Joanna drove into the lot and parked in an empty space between the truck and the two cars. Her tires had raised a cloud of rust colored dust on the graveled lot. She waited long enough for the cloud to settle before opening her door.

As soon as she stepped up to the building entrance, she heard the sound of raised voices. The front door had been propped open, most likely to allow for carrying things in and out. Even had the door been closed, Joanna probably could have heard what was being said inside. Terry Buckwalter was literally screaming at Bebe Noonan. With one hand poised and ready to knock, Joanna stood listening.

"But what am I supposed to do?" Bebe Noonan was saying.

"Do!" Terry Buckwalter exploded. "Get rid of it and act like it never happened."

"But it did. You don't mean—"

"That's exactly what I mean," Terry shot back. "And if you don't, you can't expect me to be responsible. You've got no right. It isn't mine, now is it! I made that decision a long time ago. If you had a brain in that head of yours, you'd do the same damned thing."

"But I want it." Bebe's response was a wail of anguish. "I want it!"

"Have it then!" Terry stormed. "Keep the damned thing. Do whatever the hell you want. But don't come crying to me for financial support, because I'm not paying. Do you understand me? Not one thin dime. Now get the hell out of here. Go on. Get! Before I do something we'll both regret!"

Joanna stepped aside as a tearful Bebe Noonan burst out through the open door. Looking neither right nor left, she raced to the Honda. Falling into it, she turned on the engine, wound the car into a gravel-spattering reverse, and then tore out of the lot. Not knowing what to do next, Joanna stood there and watched, replaying the words she had just heard.

Have it then, Terry had said. *Keep the damned thing*. Joanna knew at once that it wasn't a *thing* the two women had been discussing—it was a baby. Bebe Noonan's baby.

Moving into the doorway, Joanna stepped into the clinic's

reception area and pulled the door shut behind her. A stony-eyed Terry Buckwalter was sitting behind the counter.

"Bebe's pregnant then?" Joanna asked. Wordlessly, Terry Buckwalter nodded. "And Bucky's the father?"

Terry shrugged. "That's what Bebe says. I've got no reason to call her a liar. She says she's going to sue me for child support. Like hell she is. He wouldn't let me have a baby, why should she?"

The bitterness, anger, and betrayal in Terry Buckwalter's voice were enough to take Joanna's breath away. "What do you mean, wouldn't *let* you?" she repeated.

"When I got pregnant, Bucky told me that if I went through with having the baby, I'd be on my own," Terry replied. "That raising it would be my responsibility, not his."

"He couldn't have done that."

"Yes, he could, and he would have, too," Terry said. "So I did what he wanted. I had an abortion."

"You were already married?" Joanna asked.

"Yes."

"And he still made you do that—abort the baby?"

"Yes."

Behind the counter, Terry Buckwalter opened a desk drawer and began sorting through the items she found there—tossing some into a box and some into the trash while leaving the rest. For a space of almost half a minute, Joanna could think of nothing to say. She was too busy remembering Andy's delighted grin when she had told him she was pregnant. Pregnant and unmarried. *Roe versus Wade* was ancient history by then. Joanna could have opted for an abortion, but there had never been any question of what to do. They had married and lived, reasonably happily, for as long an ever after as had been granted to them.

"That shocks you, doesn't it," Terry Buckwalter said quietly.

Across the distance of the counter, their eyes met briefly. In the space that followed, Joanna noticed that Helen Barco's day-old haircut still looked terrific, although the makeup job didn't quite measure up. No doubt Terry had used all the same products Helen had applied, but Terry's inexpert hand hadn't achieved the same results. Still, she had tried, Joanna realized. She had put on makeup just to come across the backyard footpath to start packing up the clinic.

"I guess it does shock me," Joanna admitted. "I didn't think . . ."

"Husbands were like that?" Terry asked. "It depends on the raw material, doesn't it," she added with a derisive snort. "Some people marry Eagle Scouts. Others don't."

Sheriff Joanna Brady had come to the clinic on an investigative mission, thinking that she would catch Terry Buckwalter in the act of doing something wrong, something incriminating. Instead, they were talking together in a nakedly unguarded way that had everything to do with hurt and loss and grief and nothing at all with murder. In that room, littered with half filled packing boxes, they were simply two women comparing the jagged pieces of their broken hearts.

"How long has Andy been gone?" Terry asked.

"A little over four months," Joanna said.

"I'm sorry," Terry said. "Sorry for you. But you have to understand, my marriage has been over a lot longer than that. I did my grieving a long time ago."

"You knew about them then?" Joanna asked. "About Bucky and Bebe?"

"Knew they were screwing around? Of course I knew.

You've probably already figured out that she wasn't the first. She is the last, though. I'm just surprised he let her get pregnant. He usually insisted on using protection."

"How long has it been going on?" Joanna asked.

Terry shrugged. "Bebe's worked here for the better part of two years, so I suppose it's been about that long. When it came to assistants, Bucky never could keep his pants up."

"Why didn't you put a stop to it?" Joanna asked. "Why didn't you throw him out, or else fire her?"

"What good would it do? He'd just find another one," Terry answered. "He always did."

"Why didn't you leave then?"

"You mean why did I put up with it? You have to understand that what I had with Bucky was a hell of a lot better than what I came from."

"How could this be better?" The words were out of her mouth before Joanna could stop them.

"For one thing, for the first time in my life, I had a real home. And a certain amount of respect, from other people, if not necessarily from Bucky. Later on, when I realized I'd traded one set of problems for another, I couldn't see any alternative. With no formal education beyond my sophomore year in high school, I was afraid I wouldn't be able to make it on my own. So that's what I did—put up with things. Ignored them.

"The last couple years, though, I stayed because I wanted to—because it was convenient. After all, I was finally getting a chance to do something for me. I used to play tennis, but the first time I held a golf club in my hand, I knew it was something I could do—something I'd be good at. I also knew that what I wanted to accomplish would take time. Time and money. Without Bucky I wouldn't have had access to either

one. I would have had to have a job that didn't include afternoons off. I wouldn't have had time to play, to say nothing
of money for greens fees."

Joanna was stunned. "You're saying you stayed married
for the sake of golf?" she demanded.

"Damned right. And it's been worth it, too," Terry Buckwalter declared. "I'm going to make it, Joanna. Just you wait
and see. I'm going to go all the way to the top, and nobody's
going to stop me. Not Bucky and not Bucky's little bastard,
either."

For Joanna, grief had manifested itself with tears that
came and went, washing in and out without warning, periodically overwhelming her. For Terry Buckwalter, it seemed
to be anger.

Abruptly, Terry pushed the chair back from the desk. "I
just made some coffee. Do you want some?"

Detouring around a collection of packing boxes, Terry led
Joanna into a backroom that was lined with lab equipment.
On the far end of a Formica counter top sat an aged glass
coffeemaker filled with newly brewed coffee. Terry filled a
stained china mug with strong, lethal-looking coffee.

"No, thanks," Joanna said. "I'll pass."

Terry opened a drawer beneath the counter and pawed
through the contents. She plucked out a set of keys, a pocket
knife, several matchbooks, and a selection of refrigerator
magnets. After tossing those into one of the boxes, she
slammed that drawer shut and went on to examine the next
one.

"You're moving, then?" Joanna asked.

"As soon as I can," Terry returned. "All I'm doing today,
though, is clearing out a few personal things—pictures,

knickknacks, personal junk. The kinds of things the new vet won't have any use for."

"A new vet. It sounds as though you've sold the practice."

"Pretty much," Terry said. "It's not all finalized yet, but it will be before long."

"Aren't you worried about moving too fast?" Joanna asked. "If you make important decisions like that too soon, there's always a chance someone will take advantage of you."

Terry smiled for the first time. "I've been taken advantage of by an expert," she said. "Compared to that, this is fine. Besides, it was all set up long ago. Bucky and Reggie made all the arrangements late last fall, shortly after Bucky got out of treatment. The valuations were all set then. Nobody's cheating. Reggie Wade is buying the practice under that pre-set formula, less the money we already owe him. If something had happened to Reggie, Bucky would have done the same thing—bought him out. Actually, setting that whole process up in advance is probably the nicest thing Bucky Buckwalter ever did for me."

"Less what money?" Joanna asked.

"Reggie Wade lent Bucky and me money last year when things went so sour. After the accident, we had to post a bond, pay for lawyers and all kinds of other expenses that weren't exactly expected. We tried the bank first, but I guess they figured if Bucky went to jail, there'd be no way for us to pay it off. We were right up against it when Reggie came to the rescue. He and Bucky worked out a deal. Reggie lent us what we needed, using the practice as collateral."

"Sounds like a nice guy."

"You don't know the half of it," Terry said. "If it hadn't been for him, I don't know what I would have done. By the time we'd paid off the defense attorneys and it was time for Bucky to go for treatment, we were tapped out completely. I knew I needed a substitute vet while Bucky was gone, but there wasn't a dime to pay for it. Reggie came to the rescue again. Reggie and Bucky had covered calls for one another on occasion. This time, he subbed for Bucky on top of keeping up with his own practice. When I told him about the money situation, he told me not to worry. He was nice enough to add his bill for professional services rendered to the other loan. That's the only reason we made it through."

"What you're saying is that Dr. Wade has what amounts to a mortgage on the practice."

Terry nodded. "For right now. When the sale closes, he'll give me the difference between the valuation formula and what he's already paid. And as for moving fast, we pretty much have to. The valuation formula is based on selling the practice as a going concern. If there's too much of a break, then customers end up going elsewhere."

"And this is a regular buy/sell arrangement?"

"Maybe not regular," Terry allowed. "When Milo Davis set it up, he said it was a little unusual. Still, though, it worked."

"Milo set it up?"

"It wasn't all finalized until Bucky got out of treatment in mid-December."

That was why Joanna had known nothing about it. The buy/sell arrangements had happened after she left the insurance agency.

"You're saying that Reggie Wade is paying full value without any haggling?"

"No haggling at all. He's following the buy/sell agreement right down to the letter."

Joanna nodded. The idea that moving too fast would leave Terry Buckwalter open to being cheated had been one of Joanna's concerns. Judging from what Terry had said, however, that evidently wasn't the case. In addition, Joanna liked knowing that Milo Davis, her ex-boss, had been involved in drafting the agreement. Milo was scrupulously fair.

"That reminds me," Terry said. "What about the insurance?"

"What about it?"

"How long will it take to pay off? I know I'll have to sign claim forms and all that, but I'm trying to get some idea of how long it will take to pull all of this together so I can leave town."

Somehow, Terry Buckwalter's desire to put Bisbee behind her no longer seemed nearly as sinister as it had earlier. Considering the situation with Bebe Noonan, Terry's wanting to leave town was entirely understandable. Nonetheless, when it came to insurance proceeds, desire and reality were on a collision course.

"With a death like this," Joanna told her, "a homicide, investigations are automatic. Those take time. Months, in fact."

"Months!" Terry echoed. "But why an investigation? Bucky's dead, isn't he? We owned the policies, we paid all the premiums, and I'm the beneficiary. What's there to investigate?"

Lots, Joanna thought. "For one thing," she said aloud, "insurance companies generally don't want to pay out benefits until they're reasonably assured that a killer isn't reaping some kind of financial reward. They frown on beneficiaries who murder in hopes of collecting."

"They can do that?" Terry asked.

"They *do* do that," Joanna told her.

"But I don't want to wait," Terry said. "The next qualifying school starts in a matter of weeks. If they let me in, I
don't want to miss the opportunity. Peter's worked so hard
on getting me this chance to prove myself. I can't blow it
now."

"What chance are you talking about?" Joanna asked.

"Remember Peter Wilkes, my golf pro? You met him the
other day. He has an old friend, a grade school buddy, who
owns golf courses and golf equipment stores all over the
country. According to Peter, he also has enough pull so that,
if I'm good enough, he can maybe get me a spot in the next
Q-school strictly on his say-so. If I do well there, I'll be able
to get a provisional card. It's the chance of a lifetime, Joanna.
A chance to finally get to do something."

"What would have happened if Bucky hadn't died?"
Joanna asked.

"I would have gone anyway," Terry said determinedly.

"Did Bucky have any idea all this was going on? That
you were making these kinds of arrangements?"

Terry looked at Joanna and shook her head. "You really
don't understand. Bucky had his life and I had mine. We
lived in the same house, but that was more a matter of con-
venience than anything else. It beat paying two sets of house
payments."

Terry Buckwalter was describing a kind of empty marriage that was totally outside the realm of Joanna Brady's
experience. She glanced first at her own wedding ring and
then at the pale white imprint left behind where Terry had
removed hers.

"Would you have divorced him?" Joanna asked.

"I don't know," Terry said. "I was building up to it.

Thanks to Peter, I was finally coming to a point where I had enough confidence to think I could make it on my own."

"Without having to kill him?"

Terry looked sharply at Joanna. "Yes," she said. "Without having to do a thing. I may be relieved he's gone—glad that I don't have to do anything or jump through any legal hoops to resolve the situation. But that doesn't mean I killed him."

Joanna nodded. "No," she said, "I don't suppose it does."

For the better part of half an hour, the two women had been speaking together in a totally candid fashion. Terry's answer was delivered with such blunt, unblinking openness, that Joanna didn't doubt it. The problem was, if Hal Morgan wasn't responsible for Bucky's murder and if Terry wasn't either, then who was?

"You didn't mention any of this the other afternoon when Detective Carpenter and I were here."

"Believe it or not," Terry said, "I have some pride. With Bucky gone, I didn't see any reason to dig up all this crap. That was before I knew about Bebe's being pregnant. That's going to be tough to keep under the rug."

"I remember your telling us that Bucky was home the whole evening the night before he died. Is that true?"

"No."

"Where was he?"

"You guess," Terry said.

"With Bebe?"

"Probably," Terry replied. "Obviously I don't know for sure. It isn't the kind of thing someone would tell his wife, not even a worm like Bucky. 'Hey, I think I'll dash out to Double Adobe and knock off a piece of tail.' "

Joanna heard once again the hard edge of anger in Terry's biting words. This time she recognized them for what they were. A different form of grief perhaps than dissolving into tears, but grief nonetheless. In Terry Buckwalter's case, it wasn't a matter of mourning something that had ended so much as something that had never been.

"That's where Bebe Noonan lives?" Joanna asked gently.

Terry nodded. "On her folks' place. It's three or four miles east of Double Adobe."

"Someone will have to talk to her."

"I know. Do you think—?" Terry stopped abruptly.

"Do I think what?"

"No," Terry said, shaking her head. "Never mind. She wouldn't have."

"Wouldn't have what?"

"Bebe was there at the time Bucky died, wasn't she?" Terry asked. "Maybe he told her the same thing he told me— the same thing I told Bebe just a little while ago. To get rid of it. Maybe he gave her a choice of the baby or him and she was smart enough to choose the baby."

"Was she here the day before, when Hal Morgan first showed up?" Joanna asked.

"Yes."

"So she would have known about the whole thing— would have known that Hal Morgan had plenty of reason to see Bucky dead?"

"Yes."

"Is there anyone else?" Joanna asked. "Anyone besides you and Hal Morgan and Bebe who might have wanted to see your husband dead?"

"I can't think of anybody," Terry said with a rueful smile. "But isn't that enough? They say three's a charm."

"Yes," Joanna said. Checking the time, Joanna started for the door. "They do."

Terry followed her. "I'm still under suspicion, aren't I?" she asked.

Joanna nodded. "For the time being, everybody's still under suspicion. It's probably better if you don't leave town."

"But what about the golf game with Peter's friend?"

"When and where is that scheduled?"

"Sunday," Terry answered. "In Tucson. He wanted to do it tomorrow, but I told him I couldn't on account of the funeral. That would look bad even for me."

"Where in Tucson?"

"Peter and I are supposed to meet him out at the Westin La Paloma at noon. You're not planning on having someone follow me up there, are you? It might screw up my game."

"I don't know," Joanna said. "We'll have to see. Once I give Ernie Carpenter this information, I'm sure he'll want to talk to you again."

"I won't be hard to find," Terry said resignedly. "I'll be around."

Joanna got as far as the front door of the clinic before she remembered to ask one last set of questions. "On the morning Bucky died, what time did you leave the clinic?"

"Eleven thirty. Peter and I had a twelve-seven tee-time. I was almost late."

"I talked to Hal Morgan yesterday," Joanna said. "He claims that there was someone else in the barn with Bucky before he died. Some man. Did Bucky have any appointments scheduled for that time?"

Without a word, Terry slipped into Bucky Buckwalter's private office. Joanna followed behind. It was a plain, minimally adorned place with an oak-laminate desk and a bank of metal file cases. One wall held a series of diplomas. The most expensive item in the room was a two-by-three-foot oil painting of Kiddo, Bucky Buckwalter's quarter horse gelding.

Terry picked up a desktop calendar, opened it, and handed it over to Joanna. A metal clip held the calendar open to the current week. "That's Bucky's personal calendar," Terry explained. "Take a look. The clinic appointment book is out at the reception desk. I can get that one for you as well."

While Joanna examined the first calendar, Terry returned with the other one. From eleven o'clock through two o'clock on the day in question, nothing at all had been scheduled. Without comment, Joanna handed both books back to Terry. "I guess I'd better be going," she said.

Still holding the calendars, Terry Buckwalter followed Joanna to the clinic door. "I don't know if you want my opinion or not," she said, "but I still think Hal Morgan did it. What's more, I hope he gets away with it."

Joanna's jaw dropped. "You do?"

"Think about it," Terry said. "It's almost like one of those old romantic stories of the knights of the Round Table. Hal Morgan really loved his wife. He loved her enough that he was prepared to kill for her. Bucky never felt that way about anybody, except maybe for that damned horse of his. Which reminds me. You don't happen to know of anyone who'd be interested in buying Kiddo, do you?"

Joanna thought of Jenny and her approaching birthday. "How much?" she asked.

"Two hundred bucks," Terry replied. "He's worth more than that, but he was Bucky's horse, not mine. I don't even like him much, and I've got no way to ride him. All the saddles and bridles and currying equipment got burned up in the barn. The feed, too. The sooner I unload him, the better."

Kiddo was no longer young enough for the racing circuit,

but he was a good, fine-looking horse. Joanna knew enough about horses to realize Terry's selling price was far lower than it should have been. Fire-sale prices. One step above dog-food prices. If Joanna offered to buy Kiddo for that, she'd be doing exactly what she'd worried about others doing to Terry—taking advantage of her misfortune.

"Jenny's interested in having a horse," Joanna said.

"I thought she might be," Terry said. "Whenever she came here, she always seemed to have either a carrot or an apple in her pocket. That's why I mentioned it."

"Thanks," Joanna said. "I'll think about it and let you know."

Out in the Blazer, Joanna was eager to tell someone what she had learned, but the long night had evidently taken its toll. No one she asked for was in or available—not Ernie Carpenter, not Jaime Carbajal, not even Dick Voland. Her original plan had been to drop by the department and pass along her latest tips. Now, though, she changed her mind.

Joanna's interview with Terry Buckwalter had worked far better than she would have expected. The dynamics of two women talking had made it possible for her to emerge with more information than Ernie had been able to elicit in a full-court press of an interview. It was possible that the same thing would happen with Bianca "Bebe" Noonan.

Half an hour later, three and a half miles east of Double Adobe, Joanna turned right just beyond a battered, bullet-sprayed mailbox marked "R. Noonan." The moment she drove in through the gate, she felt as though she had landed in a slum. The hundred yards or so of dirt road between the fence line and the collection of buildings were strewn with trash. Shards of broken beer bottles glittered, marking the edge of the road. Windblown papers clung to the bottom strand of barbed wire. Hulks of several wrecked vehicles in various stages of deterioration dotted the desert on either side of the road. When she reached the buildings, the cars she found parked there weren't in much better shape than the junked ones she had passed earlier. Several of the tumble-down buildings seemed barely capable of remaining upright. In fact, the remains of what may once have been a barn had blown over on its side, leaving behind a knee-high stack of gray, tinder-dry wood.

The house itself was a ramshackle clapboard affair seemingly held together by little more than multiple layers of peeling paint. A sagging front porch teetered drunkenly to one side. The remains of a screen door, permanently stuck open, sagged on a single hinge. A long-legged mongrel dog lay in front of the closed front door. He sat up, scratched himself deliberately, then came to the edge of the porch, barking without much enthusiasm or threat. That changed, though, once the faded front door opened and a middle-aged woman in worn jeans and a man's flannel shirt stepped outside. The trashy house, the weed-choked yard, the woman herself conveyed the same air of uncaring hopelessness and disrepair.

As soon as the woman appeared, the dog went through a sudden ominous transformation. His hackles came up. Now each deep-throated bark was accompanied by a threatening show of teeth.

Wary of the dog's sudden change in personality, Joanna rolled down the window. "I'm looking for Bebe," she said. "Does she live here?"

"Out back," the woman answered. "Take this driveway and go on around to the back of the house. Her place is the trailer, not the bus. You go on ahead. I'll keep Buddy here with me."

Buddy. Of course. That was exactly the name people like that would give to a vicious dog.

Following the directions, Joanna drove around the house. The Blazer's passing sent a flock of chickens scurrying in all directions. Out back, positioned at either end of a no longer functional clothesline in a yard randomly punctuated by any number of dead appliances, sat a small camper/trailer and a converted school bus. Halfway down the side of the bus a stovepipe, belching smoke, stuck up out of the roof. From the looks of the moldering rubber tires, both formerly mobile vehicles had been marooned in place for a very long time.

Bebe Noonan's Honda was parked beside the door to the camper. Taking a deep breath, Joanna crawled out of the Blazer and walked up to the door.

Bebe answered her knock. "What do you want?" she demanded, standing in the open door and barring Joanna's way.

"I need to talk to you," Joanna said.

Bebe shook her head. "I don't want to talk to anyone. Leave me alone."

"Do your parents know about the baby?" Joanna asked, ignoring Bebe's attempted dismissal. "Or are you still trying to keep it a secret?"

Bebe's face registered shock, then dissolved into a torrent of anguished tears. "Oh, please. You didn't tell my mom, did you?"

"No," Joanna said. "I didn't tell anybody. Not yet. Let me in."

Wordlessly Bebe complied. Moving away from the door, she allowed Joanna to step inside. The room was impossibly hot. The windows were covered with a thick layer of steam.

"Please don't tell my parents," the young woman begged,

pulling the door shut and following Joanna to a tiny table with two bench seats. "Please."

Uninvited, Joanna sat down. Bianca Noonan sank down opposite her. "How did you find out about it?" she continued. "Did Terry tell you?"

"You didn't see me at the clinic a little while ago?"

Bebe shook her head.

"I'm not surprised," Joanna said. "I was just outside the door when you came rushing out. You and Terry were arguing when I got there. I couldn't help overhearing what was said. It's true then? You are pregnant?"

Bebe nodded.

"And Bucky Buckwalter is the father?"

Instinctively, as if to protect her unborn child from Joanna's prying question, Bebe's hand went to her belly. "What if he is?" she asked. "Terry can't take it away from me, and neither can you."

"You're planning on keeping the baby?"

"Yes," Bebe whispered. "Of course. I want this baby. So did Bucky."

"He knew about it then?"

Bebe hesitated. "He was happy about it. Glad."

"Wasn't that awkward for him, having you turn up pregnant with his baby while he was still married to Terry?"

Bebe's chin jutted out determinedly. "They were married, but he didn't love her anymore. And she didn't care about him, either. Ask her. She'll tell you. She was always busy with other stuff, like golf every afternoon. Even when she was there at the clinic, she was mean to him. Sometimes she said such ugly things to him, I was surprised he didn't hit her. And she wouldn't have kids. He wanted to, but she wouldn't. Did you know that?"

And there it was. As simple as that. Bucky Buckwalter had lied to this young woman, betraying her as well. "Terry Buckwalter couldn't have children," Joanna said softly. "She had a complete hysterectomy several years ago. I know because I helped handle the insurance claim."

Dismay washed across Bebe's face. "But . . ."

"That's not what he told you, is it," Joanna said.

Bebe considered for a moment, then seemed to gather her resources. "It doesn't matter what he said. Bucky wanted a baby, and now he's going to have one."

Expecting contrition, Joanna wasn't quite sure how to proceed. "Maybe," she suggested. "Are you sure?"

"You mean, am I sure I'm pregnant? Yes. I haven't been to a doctor, but I know."

"No," Joanna said. "Are you sure he wanted it?"

Bebe's tough facade crumpled. "No, I don't know," she wailed. "I was going to tell him, but I never got a chance. My appointment to see the doctor isn't until next week. I was sure, but I wanted it to be official. But I *know* Bucky would have wanted it."

"And you thought he'd divorce Terry to marry you?"

"Yes. He would have, too."

"How many other people know about this?" Joanna asked.

"Other people? Terry and you, I guess."

"No one else?" Joanna asked. "No old boyfriends who might be jealous? No male relatives who might take exception to Bucky Buckwalter for taking advantage of you?"

Joanna waited a moment to let those words register. Bebe's lower lip trembled. Her eyes filled with tears once more. "I never had any other boyfriends," she said. "Bucky was it.

For me, he was the only one. I loved him, and I'm sure he loved me, too."

No, he didn't, Joanna thought. But she didn't say it. Didn't contradict. Instead she sat back on the chair. "Tell me about him," she said.

And Bebe Noonan did.

14

I N the course of the next hour and a half, as Joanna talked to Bebe Noonan, she learned something else about the stark realities of being a police officer. Yes, she had signed up to catch bad guys and do paperwork and do battle with the board of supervisors. But she had also signed up to share other people's pain. Bebe Noonan was in pain.

Her tidy little camper was totally at odds with the rest of the Noonan place. The trailer may have been small and cramped and hot, but it was also spotlessly clean. The chrome faucet gleamed. Covers on the neatly made bed were absolutely straight. No hint of dust or dirt marred the cracked linoleum floor. The room's sole decoration was a hand-painted ceramic wall plaque that announced, "Jesus loves you."

Bebe's trailer constituted a small, pitiful piece of order bravely wrested from the utter chaos around her. Listening to Bebe talk, Joanna realized that Bebe's sense of desolation went far beyond the physical ugliness and apparent poverty of her surroundings. Her isolation was emotional as well as physical.

Bianca Noonan lived on her parents' place, but she lived separate from them as well. As she told her story, it was plain to see that she lived there out of necessity rather than choice or out of some sense of warmth and family togetherness. As Joanna listened to Bebe talk, she was surprised to notice, for the first time, that this plain young woman—with a wiry frame, dishwater-blond hair, and almost total lack of self-confidence—bore an eerie resemblance to a much younger Terry Buckwalter. A pre–Helen-Barco Terry Buckwalter.

No wonder Bucky had hired Bebe to work for him. No wonder she had been so susceptible to his charms and empty promises. No wonder, either, that she so desperately wanted to keep Bucky Buckwalter's baby. With or without the presence of a father, Bebe wanted this child. A baby would give her someone to love. Someone who, unlike her own family, might love her in return.

The more Joanna heard, the more she realized how sad the whole situation was. She knew, too, that it would continue to be so far into the future. It was difficult for her to keep from saying some of the things that were on her mind—lessons she had already learned the hard way—about how demanding it was to be left to raise a child alone. Finally, exhausted by the telling of it, Bebe Noonan simply ran out of steam.

"How old are you?" Joanna asked after a long pause.

"Twenty-three," Bebe sniffed.

"What are you going to do?"

"I don't know."

"Tell your parents?"

"I can't," Bebe whispered.

"You'll have to tell them sooner or later," Joanna insisted.

"My dad'll kill me when he finds out."

Joanna shook her head. "He won't be happy, but he'll cope," she interjected. "That's what parents do."

"But he'll say I'm no good," Bebe continued. "He'll throw me out. I'll have to find someplace else to live."

"Then you'll find an apartment of your own," Joanna told her.

Bebe's eyes filled with tears once more. "How? I've been living here for free. Even so, I can barely afford my car payments. That's why I went to see Terry. I wanted to ask her for help with the baby. And she told me to . . . to . . ."

"I heard what she told you," Joanna said. "And you can't very well blame her."

"No," Bebe said. "I suppose not, but I thought maybe . . ."

"You thought what?"

Bebe shrugged. "That since it's Bucky's baby, that maybe she'd give me something. You know, that she'd offer to help out with money. She'll have insurance and stuff. She'll be able to afford it."

Joanna thought of Terry Buckwalter, suddenly unencumbered and liquidating assets as fast as she could so she could get on with her own life. In the meantime, here was Bebe expecting to put a very compelling, living and breathing wrench in the works. Joanna felt sorry for both women. She felt even sorrier for the baby.

"Have you seen a lawyer?" she asked.

"No," Bebe said. "I haven't even seen the doctor yet. Why would I need a lawyer?"

"Because if you're expecting to collect money from Bucky's estate or from his Social Security account, you'll have to file a paternity suit. You'll have to prove Bucky is the baby's father. In order to do that, you'll need a lawyer. It's not all that hard to establish paternity these days, but you'll need to collect some DNA evidence. The only way to do that is with a court order. You'll be better off doing it *before* Bucky is buried rather than afterward."

"But do I have to?" Bebe asked miserably. "Do I have to go through all that—get a lawyer and go to court and all like that? If I do, my parents will know, and so will everybody else."

"I told you before, Bebe. People—your parents in-cluded—are bound to find out eventually," Joanna pointed out. "And if what you say is true, if your parents really are going to throw you out, then you'd better start acting like a grown-up right now and making some arrangements to pro-tect not only yourself but also the baby. Social Security isn't going to pay survivors' benefits to a child based on your un-substantiated claim as to who the father might be. You're going to have to prove the baby is Bucky's. If I were you, I'd get on the telephone right now."

"Is that why you came to see me?" Bebe asked. "To tell me that?"

"No," Joanna said. "I came to ask you if you were with Bucky the night before he died. Terry told me he wasn't home that night. I thought maybe he might have been with you."

"He wasn't with me," Bebe said. "I only wish he had been. The last time I saw him was that afternoon. The day before he died. At work."

"Do you have any idea where he might have been that evening, then?"

Bebe shrugged. "Probably playing poker. He did that a lot."

"With whom?" Joanna asked.

"I don't know. He never really told me. And I didn't ask.

I didn't think it was any of my business. That's what love is all about," she added. "Learning to trust."

Joanna was so astonished by that statement that she wanted to scream. *He was married to another woman, screwing around with you, and you* trusted *him? How stupid can you get?*

Exasperated beyond bearing, Joanna glanced at her watch. "I have to go now," she said, getting to her feet. "I have plenty to do, and so do you."

Bebe followed her out the door to the car. "Do you know which lawyer I should talk to?" Bebe was asking. "About the DNA thing, I mean."

Joanna realized that she had already said far too much. If she said anything more, she would simply be helping to pit two bereaved women against one another. "No," Joanna said. "I don't have any idea who to suggest. You'll have to figure it out for yourself."

It's part of being a grown-up, she wanted to say. *Part of being a parent.* But Joanna Brady had reached the limit on her ability to give advice. "If I were you," she said. "I'd check in the phone book—the Yellow Pages."

Bebe's face dissolved into a watery smile. "Thank you," she said. "I'll go to work on that right away."

Feeling a little like King Solomon offering to carve up the baby, Joanna headed back toward the Cochise County Justice Center. Considering all that had happened in the past two days, that name had an ironic, almost cynical, ring to it. Was there any such thing as justice to be found in a case like this one? Or for people like Hannah Green? For two cents, right about then, Joanna Brady would have been happy to turn in her badge and go back to being the office manager of an insurance agency.

By the time Joanna pulled into her parking place, it was

well into late afternoon. She felt as though she had been dragged through a wringer. Lack of sleep from the night before gnawed at her whole body. Once again she was grateful for the privilege of that reserved parking space and for the private entrance that allowed her to come and go without having to face whatever crisis was currently in process in the main lobby.

The door between Joanna's office and Kristin's was closed, and Joanna didn't rush to open it. Stuck to the middle of her desk was a stack of messages. Thumbing through them, Joanna found the usual assortment. Two calls from Eleanor Lathrop, one each from Frank Montoya and Dick Voland. The last one came from Marianne Maculyea. That was the first message Joanna attempted to return. There was no answer. The moment Joanna depressed the switch hook to try making another call, Kristin appeared at the door, closing it behind her as she entered.

"Until I saw your line light up, I didn't know you'd come in," she said. "There are some people outside waiting to see you."

"Who?" Joanna asked.

"One's a priest. He said his name is Father Michael McCrady. The other is a really scary-looking guy in leathers. He says his name is Frederick Dixon. He claims he's a friend of yours. I checked your calendar and didn't see any appointments, so . . ."

"Frederick Dixon . . ." Joanna mused. "That doesn't ring any bells. What does he look like?"

"Thirties or forties maybe," Kristin answered. "I can't really tell. But he's bald. Not a hair on his head."

"Butch Dixon!" Joanna exclaimed. "I always forget his name is Fred."

"Who's Butch Dixon?"

"He is a friend of mine. From up in Peoria. He runs a café that's close to the Arizona Police Officers' Academy. I met him in November and again this month when I was up there. What's he doing here?"

"I have no idea," Kristin said sourly. "He showed up over an hour ago. I told him you were out and I didn't know when you'd be back. He said it was all right, that he'd wait."

"And who's the other one again?"

"Father McCrady. Father Michael McCrady."

Joanna nodded. "Hal Morgan's friend."

"By the way," Kristin added, almost as an afterthought, "we had a call from the Highway Patrol a little while ago. There's been a bad accident off Highway 80, east of Tombstone. A speeding van full of U.D.A.s lost control and flipped. It sounds like a real mess. We've got cars en route, but nobody from our department is on the scene yet."

The fact that people were waiting for her in the front office faded into insignificance. Traffic incidents involving vans packed to the gills with undocumented aliens, most of whom were never properly belted in, often resulted in terrible carnage.

"If the Department of Public Safety is investigating, how come they're calling us?" Joanna asked.

"It was a pursuit. The officer tried to pull the van over for faulty equipment. Instead of stopping, the driver turned off onto a county road. That's where the accident happened."

"Who all's going?" Joanna asked.

"All three deputies from that sector, and Ernie Carpenter as well."

"It's a fatality?"

Kristin nodded. "I guess," she said. "At least one. There could be more."

"What about Dick Voland?"

"He's going, too. He's still in his office right now, but he'll be leaving in a minute."

It would have been easy for Joanna to sit back and let her deputies handle what was bound to turn into a major incident. But Sheriff Brady was working very hard at earning the reputation of being a hands-on sheriff. "So will I," she said.

"What should I tell the two guys out front, then?" Kristin asked.

"Nothing," Joanna said. "I'll handle them myself."

Pulling herself together, she walked out into the reception area. Up in Phoenix, Joanna had heard Butch mention his Goldwing on occasion, but this was the first time she had seen him clad in full-leather motorcycle regalia. He was stretched out comfortably on the couch, feet on the glass-topped coffee table, reading a book. Appropriately enough, the book was none other than *Zen and the Art of Motorcycle Maintenance*. Meantime, an elderly gentleman in white-collared priests' attire paced back and forth in front of Kristin's desk.

The moment Joanna came into the room, Butch closed the book, smiled broadly, and hurried to his feet. "Joanna," he said. "There you are."

At only five feet seven or so, Butch Dixon was relatively short, but powerfully built. As Kristin had noted, Butch's shaved head was absolutely bald, but the pencil-thin mustache he had sported several months earlier was gone. Its absence made him look younger.

"What are you doing here?" Joanna asked, walking forward to shake his hand.

"Decided to take a few days R and R," he said. "A couple of years ago a guy showed up at the Roundhouse claiming that he could get drunk in any mining town in Arizona and wake up in any other mining town and never know the difference. I decided to put that to the test."

"You came here to get drunk?"

Butch grinned. "No. I came to see if there's any difference. I've been to Globe and Miami and Superior. I've even been to Ajo and Morenci before, but I've never been to Bisbee. If you and Jenny don't have plans for the evening, I thought maybe I could take my favorite lady cop and her daughter out for pizza or something."

Joanna shook her head. "Sorry, Butch," she said. "Not tonight. A call just came in. I've got to go to Tombstone right away. It's a traffic incident that will probably take most of the evening."

Disappointment washed briefly across Butch's face, but that was followed by a good-natured grin. "Maybe tomorrow, then," he said cheerfully. "I'm staying at the Grand Hotel from now through Monday. Give me a call and let me know."

Joanna was disappointed, too. Butch Dixon had been an interesting, fun person to be around. An evening of lighthearted conversation and pizza would have been just what the doctor ordered after this impossibly grueling week.

She smiled. "It sounds good," she said. "I'm sorry about tonight, but . . ."

"I know," Butch said. "Don't worry about it. When duty calls, you've gotta go. I'll talk to you tomorrow."

With that, Butch grabbed his helmet and book and left, leaving Joanna both relieved and sorry he was gone. She turned, then, to the priest: a white-haired, gaunt figure of a man. Behind thick steel-rimmed glasses his gray-blue eyes were at once piercing and kind.

"I'm Sheriff Brady," she said, offering her hand. "What can I do for you, Father McCrady?"

"I'm a friend of Hal Morgan's."

Joanna nodded. "I know," she said. "From M.A.D.D. Mr. Morgan told me about you. I'd be happy to speak to you, but as you heard, there's been an emergency . . ."

"Yes," he said, "I understand. But what I have to say won't take long. I just wanted to thank you for putting Hal Morgan in touch with Burton Kimball. Hopefully it won't be necessary for Hal to utilize Mr. Kimball's services. Still, it was very kind of you to make that connection for him."

"I'll say it was," Dick Voland growled. The chief deputy, hat in hand, had entered the reception area just in time to hear what Father McCrady had to say. "Sheriff Brady seems to be celebrating Random Acts of Kindness Week a little early this year," he said.

Joanna turned on him. "I believe that's enough, Dick."

"I'm on my way to Tombstone, Kristin," he said with a glower. "I don't know when I'll be back." He headed for the door.

Joanna stopped him. "Wait a minute, Dick," she said. "I'm going there, too. Maybe we should ride over together. It'll give us a chance to talk. You and I seem to have more than one topic to discuss."

"But I was leaving right now," Voland objected.

"So am I," Joanna returned.

Voland sighed. "Which car?" he asked. "Mine or yours?"

Joanna realized that if she and her chief deputy were about to have a battle royal, it was important that Joanna Brady be the one in the driver's seat. "Mine," she said, then she turned back to Father McCrady. "If you'll excuse us, we have to go now."

"One more thing, Sheriff Brady," the priest said. "Hal isn't actually charged with anything at the moment, is he?"

"Not yet," Joanna replied. "My chief detective has been occupied with a number of other cases, but that could change. The Buckwalter incident is still being actively investigated."

"That being the case, is it really necessary to have a police officer following him around everywhere he goes? Hal is finding that very disturbing."

Joanna glanced in Dick Voland's direction. He nodded back at her. Urgently. "Homicide is also disturbing," Joanna said evenly. "At this time we still believe a police presence is necessary."

"But why?"

"Because he's a flight risk," Voland put in, answering Father McCrady's question in Joanna's stead.

Father McCrady peered around Joanna and let his eyes settle on her chief deputy. "I can assure you that Hal Morgan didn't kill that man. Nevertheless, he has given me his word of honor that he'll make no effort to leave Bisbee until the investigation is complete and he has been fully exonerated."

"Hal Morgan's word may be good enough for you," Dick Voland said. "But it doesn't mean much to anyone else. We're working on physical evidence."

"What physical evidence?" Father McCrady asked.

"Obviously we can't reveal that," Joanna said. "What Mr. Voland and I are both saying, Father McCrady, is that the guard stays for the time being."

Hurrying back into her office, Joanna called Jenny at her grandmother's house. "I've got to go to Tombstone," she said. "It's a serious car accident. I may be very late. Would you please ask Grandma and Grandpa Brady if you can spend the night?"

Any other night, Jenny would have been thrilled at the prospect of sleeping over. Tonight was a different story.

"Oh, Mom," she whined. "Do I *have* to?"

"Yes," Joanna said. "Now hurry and ask."

Minutes later, Joanna and Dick Voland were in the Blazer. With siren wailing and lights flashing, they headed for Tombstone. Voland sat on the rider's side, with his arms crossed tightly across his chest. Maneuvering through town, Joanna concentrated on her driving. As they started up the Divide, however, before Joanna had a chance to say a word, Voland surprised her with an unexpected apology.

"Sorry about that Random Acts of Kindness comment," he said. "I don't know what gets into me sometimes. And thanks for backing me up on the Morgan surveillance, too. I've just got a feeling about this Morgan guy. I can't explain it."

"You've been checking him out?"

Voland nodded. "I have. That's what worries me. Nobody has a bad word to say about him. Nicest guy you'll ever meet. Trust him with my life. Honest as the day is long."

Joanna thought of her own meeting with Hal Morgan. That was how he had struck her, too. Honest.

"Maybe the people who are telling you those nice things about him are right. Maybe he didn't do it."

"And maybe he did," Voland insisted glumly.

Joanna spent the rest of the trip to the accident scene recounting to her chief deputy what she had learned in the course of the day. She told him about Terry Buckwalter's plan to sell her husband's practice and leave town as soon as possible. She also told him about Bebe Noonan's pregnancy. Voland whistled when he heard that.

"I know Ernie was out talking to the Rob Roy guy this afternoon," Voland said. "So he may have found out about the golf stuff, but the pregnancy bit is something else. How'd you find that out if Ernie didn't?"

There was a certain grudging respect in Dick Voland's voice, something Joanna had never heard there before. "Just lucky, I guess," she said.

Several miles passed before Dick Voland spoke again. "The last time I remember seeing Terry and Bucky together was at a football game last fall. They seemed just fine—as normal as apple pie. There was no way to tell all this other stuff was going on, but that's the way life works. You think people are fine, and then one day they blow up in your face." He paused. "It makes you wonder, doesn't it?" he added.

"Yes," Joanna agreed. "It certainly does."

In the course of the next four hours, Joanna learned far more than she had ever wanted to know about triage. Nothing she had read in textbooks could have prepared her for the carnage waiting in a gully off a narrow dirt track east of the Tombstone Municipal Airport. Eighteen adults had been locked in the back of the speeding van when it flipped. Two were dead at the scene. Two more were in critical condition and had been airlifted to trauma centers in Tucson. Neither of those two victims was expected to make it. Others, less seriously injured, had been stashed, under guard, in three different hospitals in Cochise County, and two in Tucson. The remaining five, people with injuries no more serious than cuts and bruises, had been booked into the Cochise County Jail.

Just dealing with the prisoners proved to be a logistical nightmare. Most of the time, Border Patrol policy dictates that undocumented aliens simply be returned to Mexico. This time, however, with authorities wanting to file vehicular homicide charges against the driver, it had been deemed necessary to hold all the U.D.A.s in what, for now, was being billed as "protective custody."

The smuggler/driver—who had been wearing a seat belt and wasn't injured in the wreck—had left the scene on foot. After three hours of searching, a canine unit finally found him hiding under a mesquite tree in a wash.

It was almost ten by the time Joanna and Dick Voland returned to the county jail. Not wanting to leave until all the prisoners had been properly booked, Joanna settled down at her desk. There were more messages—two more from her mother and one from Larry Matkin, but Joanna simply put them aside with the others. She would return her calls—all of them—in the morning and not before.

Shortly after eleven Tom Hadlock, the jail commander, stopped by Joanna's office to report that all the prisoners had been booked into the jail.

"I've got the coyote in an isolation cell," Hadlock told her. "I was afraid some of his victims might try to do him in."

"I wouldn't be too surprised if they did," Joanna said. "Any idea who he is?"

At the time of his arrest, the smuggler had been carrying no driver's license and had given what everyone had assumed to be a phony name.

"You bet," Tom replied proudly. "When we ran his prints through that new Automated Fingerprint Identification System, they rang bells from here to Texas. The guy's real name is Jesus Rojas Gonzales. He has three outstanding warrants on non-related drug-running charges—two in New Mexico and one in Texas. Those warrants plus the three kilos of black gold heroin hidden under the floorboards are most likely what triggered his attempt to elude the Highway Patrol officer who was stopping him for nothing more serious than a busted taillight. By the way, how's the officer doing?" Hadlock asked.

"About how you'd think," Joanna replied. "He's in shock. He doesn't think he did anything wrong, but there are plenty of people who are ready to string him up right along with the coyote."

The jail commander grinned. "The Highway Patrol is the state's baby," he said. "It'll be interesting to see what the governor's Ms. Morales makes of this."

After Hadlock left her office, Joanna gathered her purse and coat. She was preparing to leave herself when she realized the light was still on in the reception area outside her door. Stepping across the room, she had just switched off the light and was about to return to her own office when she heard a strange rumbling sound. It took a moment for her to place the noise—someone snoring.

Three offices and the conference room opened off the reception area—hers, Dick Voland's, and Frank Montoya's. Frank's office was empty, as was Joanna's. In Dick Voland's office she found her chief deputy lying stretched out full-length on his couch. Except for his shoes, he was fully clothed. His sock-clad feet stuck out beyond a length of plaid wool blanket. He was sound asleep.

Joanna went over to him and shook him gently by the shoulder. "Wake up, Dick," she said.

His eyes blinked open. Glazed with weariness, he stared at Joanna for a moment without seeming to recognize her.

"Everything here is under control," she continued. "Go

home and get a good night's rest. There's no reason for you to sleep here."

Slowly he swung his feet to the floor and then sat with his hands clasping his forehead. "I can't go home," he muttered.

"Of course you can," Joanna returned. "If you're too tired, I'll get one of the deputies to drive you."

"I said, I *can't* go home!" He drew the blanket around him and sat staring down at the floor. There was something in the way he looked, some quality of abject misery in his voice, that warned Joanna there was more going on here, something over and above his being too tired to drive.

Without waiting for an invitation, she sank down on the couch beside him.

"What is it, Dick?" she asked.

"Ruth kicked me out," he said at last. "She says she wants a divorce, and I haven't had time to go looking for an apartment."

"Ruth kicked you out?" Joanna repeated. "How come? What's going on?"

"She's jealous," he answered.

"Jealous of your job? She's been married to a cop for long enough that she should know how it goes."

There was a long silence. "No," he said finally. "It's not the job. She's jealous of you."

"Of me!" Joanna exclaimed. "You've got to be kidding. That's the most ridiculous thing I've ever heard. You told her there was nothing to it, didn't you?"

"I tried," Dick Voland said miserably. "I don't think she believed me."

Shocked beyond speech, Joanna got up, walked back over

to the doorway and switched on the light. "How long have you been sleeping here?" she asked.

"A week," he said. "I've been keeping my clothes in the car and showering in the deputies' locker room, all the while hoping she'd come to her senses."

"Do you want me to talk to her?" Joanna asked.

"Not on your life!" Dick Voland replied. "That's the *last* thing I want you to do."

15

LATE as it was when Joanna arrived home, she started the washer the moment she walked in the door. She had used the last of her clean underwear that morning. If she didn't stay up late enough to put a load of wash in the dryer, she'd have to wear a damp bra and pair of panties to work the next morning.

Ruth Voland is jealous of me? she thought. *How can that be?*

Once she staggered into bed, sleep came quickly, but so did morning. Feeling guilty about spending so much time away from Jenny, Joanna had set the alarm for six so she could drive into town early and have breakfast with Jenny before she left for school.

She was dressed and close to leaving the house when the phone rang. Hurrying back to answer it, she found her mother on the phone. "You never called me back yesterday," Eleanor complained.

"I didn't get home until almost midnight," Joanna answered. "I didn't think you'd want me to call that late."

"Well, I suppose not," Eleanor agreed. "Were you out

dealing with that awful mess up by Tombstone?"

Joanna sighed. "As a matter of fact, I was."

"What I can't understand is why those people keep on coming here in the first place. Why don't they just stay in Mexico where they belong?"

"Why didn't your great-grandparents stay in England?" Joanna asked.

"That was different," Eleanor told her.

This was a long-standing argument—one that no amount of logic could win. Joanna closed her eyes and prayed for patience. "What is it you want, Mother?"

There was a slight pause before Eleanor answered. "Are you planning on attending the Buckwalter funeral this morning?" she asked finally.

"Yes."

"Well, good," Eleanor said. "You should. Your father always did. Keeping up appearances, you know. In the face of this awful crime wave, it's important that people see you out in public and know you're on the job."

Eleanor hadn't been wildly in favor of her daughter's running for office in the first place. Now that Joanna had won the election, however, Eleanor Lathrop seemed determined to do everything necessary to keep the job of sheriff in the family.

"Right, Mother," Joanna said.

"You know," Eleanor added, "I never remember anything like this number of homicides happening all at once when your father was in office."

No doubt there was a hidden subtext behind that comment. Eleanor was probably building up to letting Joanna know that everything that had happened was all Joanna's fault. It was fine for Joanna to blame herself. It was definitely not okay for her mother to do the same.

"Neither do I," Joanna said. "But times have changed, haven't they?"

"Yes," Eleanor admitted. "I suppose they have. By the way, did you ever talk to Reverend Maculyea? She called here looking for you."

"Marianne called there? That's odd. What's going on?"

"I don't know. You'd better talk to her first thing."

"I will," Joanna agreed. "As soon as I get off the phone with you."

It was only after she clicked the receiver that Joanna remembered that she still hadn't tackled her mother on the subject of her relationship with Cochise County Coroner George Winfield. That conversation was going to come, though, eventually.

Joanna dialed Marianne Maculyea's number without ever dropping the telephone receiver back on the hook. She was worried about calling too early, but when Marianne answered she sounded wide awake, if harried.

"I can't talk long," the pastor said. "I'm on my way out the door to catch a plane."

"A plane. Where to?"

"San Francisco. Jeff sent me a telegram yesterday afternoon. First nothing happens for weeks on end. Then all of a sudden he sends word yesterday that I have to be in San Francisco by noon today. The expectation had always been for him to fly into Tucson and for me to meet him there. He didn't send along any explanation about the change in plan, either. Nothing. Just 'meet us in San Francisco,' and a flight number from Hong Kong. But that's something anyway. At least he said 'us'. It means . . ."

Marianne's voice faltered.

"It means he did get the baby, right?" Joanna finished triumphantly.

"That's right."

"How great! Mari, congratulations. Aren't you excited?"

"Yes, but . . . It's just that . . ."

"It's just what?"

"I've been so worried that there was some kind of hitch and he wouldn't be able to get her out, that I had sort of given up hope. Now I guess I'm a little overwhelmed."

"Do you need a ride to Tucson? Can I come pick you up? God knows, I've put in enough hours at work this week."

"No," Marianne said. "I've asked Billy Matthews from First Baptist to substitute for me at Bucky Buckwalter's funeral. Meantime, I'm driving myself up in the Bug."

Joanna knew her friend well enough to discern the undercurrent of concern beneath her business-as-usual words. "Mari," Joanna said, "what's wrong?"

Marianne laughed. "I'm that transparent?"

"To me you are. Now tell me. What's wrong?"

"I'm scared," Marianne Maculyea said.

"Scared of what?"

"Of becoming a mother. All of a sudden I realized I don't know the first thing about it. What if she gets sick? What if she won't eat or hurts herself? How will I know what to do?"

Joanna laughed at that. "Everybody feels that way in the beginning, but you'll be fine. You and Jeff will be wonderful parents. Just remember, it's all on-the-job training. How soon are you leaving for the airport?"

"Half an hour."

"Promise me you won't go until I get there. Jenny and I have something that we want you to take along."

"All right," Marianne agreed. "I'll wait."

Joanna dropped that call and dialed the Bradys. Jenny answered the phone, sounding sulky. "Guess what?" Joanna announced. "Jeff is on his way to San Francisco with the new baby. Do you want to ride along up to the parsonage with me to give Marianne her present?"

Concerned that something might go wrong, Marianne had absolutely forbidden any presents or baby showers prior to knowing for sure that the adoption would go through. Once Jeff left for China, however, Joanna had bought a diaper bag. In the intervening weeks she and Jenny had added another item or two almost every time they had gone to the store.

The sulkiness went out of Jenny's voice. "But it isn't wrapped yet," she objected.

"It's the thought that counts," Joanna said. "I'm leaving the house right now."

"I'll be ready," Jenny said.

True to her word, Jenny was waiting on the porch when Joanna stopped in front of the Bradys' neat duplex. In her arms she carried a bundle of pink yarn that turned out to be one of Eva Lou Brady's down-soft broomstick-lace afghans.

In the Blazer, Jenny held the afghan against her mother's face. "Isn't it soft? I'll bet the baby's going to love it."

"I'll bet she is, too."

At the parsonage up Tombstone Canyon, Marianne Maculyea was just loading her overnight bag into the VW when Joanna pulled up and stopped behind her. Jenny was out of the car almost before it stopped, carrying the bulging, bunny-covered diaper bag in one arm and the afghan in the other. As soon as Marianne saw them, she burst into tears.

"See?" Jenny said helpfully. "The straps are long enough so you can carry it over your shoulder. Like this."

Laughing through her tears, Marianne slipped the diaper bag on one arm. "I guess this makes it real, doesn't it?"

Crying too, Joanna reached over the beaming Jenny to hold Marianne close.

"Have you named her yet?" Jenny asked.

"Not so far. Sarah's always been my first choice," Marianne replied. "But Jeff and I agreed we wouldn't name her until we both had a chance to get to know her."

"Oh," Jenny said.

"Promise you'll call the minute you get back to town," Joanna urged.

"I will," Marianne said. "And thank you. Thank you for the bag and all the stuff you've put in it. But most of all, thanks for being my friend."

The two women hugged once more. "It takes a friend to have one," Joanna said.

She and Jenny stayed long enough to wave Marianne out of the driveway, then they set off for breakfast at Daisy's. Marianne's good news seemed to have put a golden haze over the whole morning. Jenny was bright and chatty.

"I'm sorry I've been so busy," Joanna said as Jenny plowed through that morning's stack of French toast. "Maybe after I've been doing this job awhile longer, I won't feel like I have to be everywhere and do everything."

"It's all right," Jenny said brightly. "It's not like I'm a baby or anything."

"No," Joanna agreed. "You're not a baby at all."

They were almost at school before Joanna remembered to tell her daughter about Butch Dixon. "By the way," she said, "a friend of mine from up in Phoenix has invited the two of us out for pizza tonight."

"What friend?" Jenny asked.

"Butch Dixon. Remember the man you met up in Peoria?"

"The one with the restaurant with all the toy trains?"

"That's right," Joanna said. "What do you think?"

"I love pizza," Jenny said.

Joanna laughed. "So do I," she agreed.

She walked into her office right on time, only to be greeted by the sound of raised voices. Out in the other room, Dick Voland and Frank Montoya were going at it hot and heavy. She opened her door and walked directly into the melee.

"All right, guys," she said. "What seems to be the problem? And how about if we come into my office to hash this out over three civilized cups of coffee."

Stiff-legged, like squabbling little boys separated by a school principal, the two men came into Joanna's office and took seats at either end of her desk.

"Chief Deputy Voland has deputies stationed in every damned hospital from here to Phoenix," Frank began. "I keep trying to tell him, we can't pay for that kind of staffing without blowing the budget come the end of the year."

"And I keep trying to tell Mr. Montoya that these U.D.A.s are our responsibility. The two that are on life support—one at Tucson Medical Center and the other at University—aren't much of a threat for taking off. But that's not true of most of the others—the ones who weren't so badly injured. The hospital administrators expect some help on this one. They're worried about the safety of their other patients."

Joanna sometimes suspected Voland of empire-building, of playing the old my-department-is-more-important-than-your-department game. "Wait a minute," she said. "These guys are just ordinary wetbacks—field hands mostly, right?"

"Right," Voland agreed.

"Not an ax murderer in the bunch?"

"Probably not," Voland allowed. "At least not as far as we've been able to ascertain up to now."

"So why would they pose a threat to any of the other patients?"

"What if they just walk out?"

"What if?"

"Then we lose whatever case we have against the driver."

"No, we don't," Joanna argued. "The accident was witnessed by an officer from the Arizona Department of Public Safety. He has most of it recorded on video. Even if all the walking wounded were to take off for parts unknown or were deported back to Mexico complements of the I.N.S., we would still have the ones who are physically incapable of leaving."

"You're saying I should pull the guards?" Voland asked.

"Dick, Frank is right," Joanna said. "I don't think the board of supervisors is bluffing on the budget business. If we don't take their threats seriously, if we don't do everything possible to curtail all unnecessary overtime expenditures, come next fall we're going to be in a world of hurt."

"All right," he said. "I'll pull them, every last one of 'em, but I'm going to lodge a formal, written protest. I'm going to say in writing that I disagreed with that decision."

"You go right ahead and do what you have to do," Joanna told him.

"And if one of them disappears, or if there's any other problem, it's on your head."

"I accept full responsibility," Joanna said.

He stood up and stormed off to the door, meeting Kristin Marsten, who was on her way into the room with three cups of coffee. Voland grabbed one of them and huffed off to his own office, leaving Kristin to bring the others inside for Joanna and Frank. Frank waited until Kristin had gone out and shut the door before he said anything.

"What the hell's the matter with that guy?" Frank Montoya demanded. "He's been a complete jerk all week long."

"Give him a break," Joanna said. "I think he's having a tough time of it right now."

"If you ask me," Frank Montoya said, "he's *always* having a tough time of it."

"Let it go, Frank," Joanna said. "Now, besides the disaster up by Tombstone, what else happened overnight?"

Without Dick Voland present, Frank went ahead with the morning briefing. "Nothing much," he said, checking the printed contact sheets himself. "We had so many deputies dragged out of their cars and standing guard duty in hospitals that coverage was a little light county-wide. That's why I was trying to tell Dick . . ."

"Don't beat a dead horse, Frank," Joanna warned. "Go on."

"Naturally the press is waiting for me to make some kind of statement about this latest incident. As of today, Cochise County is two ahead of Pima in terms of homicide victims for the year. That's an unwelcome statistic, especially in view of the difference in population. So far this morning I've had several calls from Tucson and Phoenix stations, radio and television both, asking what's going on down here. Everybody seems to think we're wallowing around in a pool of murder and mayhem."

"Whatever you do," Joanna cautioned, "don't let them talk to my mother. Eleanor Lathrop shares that opinion."

"Are you going to the Buckwalter funeral?" Frank Montoya asked, abruptly switching gears.

"Ernie will be there working, of course," Joanna said. "But I think I'd better put in an appearance as well."

Frank nodded. "By all means," he said.

Just then there was a knock on Joanna's door. Ernie Carpenter opened it a crack and stuck his head inside. "Did you know about this?" he asked, waving a piece of paper in the air.

"What is it?"

"A court order. Bebe Noonan has gotten herself a lawyer and has formally requested a DNA sample from Bucky Buckwalter's body as part of a paternity suit."

"I did know about it," Joanna said. "So did Dick Voland."

"She's pregnant with Bucky's baby?"

"That's right."

"If you knew about it and Dick knew about it, why the hell didn't I?"

"I found out yesterday afternoon. I told Dick on the way over to Tombstone last night, but with all the mess over there, I guess we both forgot about it."

"Thanks a lot," Carpenter muttered. "Thanks a whole hell of a lot." With that he, too, stalked out of the office.

Joanna looked at Frank and grinned. "Well," she said. "I'm two for two. Aren't you going to stomp out and slam the door shut as well?"

"I don't think so," he said. "Whatever the provocation, I think it's bad form to slam doors until after everyone in the office has had a chance to finish at least one cup of coffee."

Frank did leave Joanna's office fairly soon after that. Between then and nine-fifteen, when it was time for her to leave for Bucky Buckwalter's funeral, Joanna at last had some time to make a little progress on the paper debris that covered her desk. As she shuffled through the messages once again, she threw away the ones from her mother and Marianne Macu-lyea. When she rediscovered the one from Larry Matkin, the mining engineer, she tried to return the call. He had left only one number, however, and there was no answer.

At thirty-five years of age and a height of six feet six, Little Norm Higgins was both the youngest and the largest of Norm Higgins' three sons. He collected Joanna Brady at the door of Higgins Funeral Chapel and Mortuary. Taking her arm and speaking in low, respectful tones, he led her to the third row of seats, a place evidently reserved for dignitaries unrelated to the deceased. She was seated between Agnes Pratt and Alvin Bernard, Bisbee's mayor and chief of police, respectively.

Agnes had a tendency to develop skin cancer. On doctor's orders, she always wore hats, although the wide-brimmed, flowered and/or feathered affairs she favored might not have been exactly what her dermatologist had in mind. The one she preferred to wear to funerals was an enormous black straw contrivance with a velvet ribbon and single peacock feather. Over time the feather had become quite bedraggled.

Her Honor inclined her head as Joanna slipped past her into an empty seat. "So sad," Agnes murmured. "So very sad."

Seated as close as she was to the front of the chapel, it was impossible for Joanna to see who all was present. From the noise level it was clear that the place was jammed to the gills. Joanna wondered if the attendance was due to Bucky's prominent position in the community or if, somehow, word had already leaked out that the murdered vet was about to become a posthumous papa.

Shortly before the Reverend Billy Matthews from the First Bible Baptist Church took to the podium, Little Norm was forced to go to the front of the chapel. There, in his whispery, bowling announcers' voice, he urged people to move closer together in order to allow a few more attendees to squeeze in at the end of each cushioned pew.

As the organist droned on and on, playing something mournful but totally unrecognizable, Joanna wondered how Billy, pinch-hitting for Marianne Maculyea, would be able to pull together a meaningful service. If Terry Buckwalter wasn't particularly grief-stricken over her husband's death, would anyone else be?

It turned out that the answer was yes. Any number of people had been touched and saddened by Bucky's passing, and a few of them were willing to come forward and say so. The selection of speakers wasn't exactly standard funeral fare, but they all did well.

First to step forward was an adorable little girl named Winnette Jeffries who also happened to be Agnes Pratt's great-granddaughter. Barely able to see over the podium, a breathless Winnette told how Dr. Buckwalter had saved her puppy after someone had fed the animal poison.

Maggie Dodd, one of Bisbee's most outspoken animal-rights activists, told about how the Buckwalters had saved numerous strays from the fate of lethal injection by offering an adoption service alternative to the local animal shelter.

Last of all was Irene Collins. She tottered up the steps to the podium to give a tearful account of how, on the last day of his life, Bucky Buckwalter had removed a stuck chicken bone from the throat of Irene's poor little kitty, Murphy Brown.

Knowing some of the background, Joanna wasn't surprised that the speakers stressed Bucky's skill as a vet rather than mentioning his interpersonal relationships with human beings. Terry Buckwalter, dressed in a properly conservative navy-blue suit, sat in the first row almost directly in front of Joanna. The widow listened to the various speakers with no show of emotion at all. Bebe Noonan, on the other hand, seated on the far side of the chapel in the same row as Joanna, sobbed uncontrollably from the moment the service started until it was over.

It was only then, when people congregated outside, trying to decide who would be going from the chapel to the Ladies' Aid's luncheon, that Eleanor Lathrop managed to catch up with her daughter.

"What a wonderful service," Eleanor crooned. "Very uplifting, for a funeral. Terry's holding up remarkably well, but did you see how devastated that poor little Bebe Noonan was? Why, the way she carried on, you'd have thought her heart was broken. Bucky must have been a wonderful boss for her to be that torn up over his death."

Joanna looked at Eleanor then, shocked to realize that, for the first time in her life, she knew the whole story behind something while her mother had less than a glimmer. For once Joanna's personal knowledge had outpaced even Helen Barco's incredibly reliable gossip mill. That realization made Joanna feel odd somehow, and old as well. In that instant, it seemed as though their roles were suddenly reversed—as though Joanna were the mother and Eleanor Lathrop the innocent child in need of protection. Not only did Joanna know what was going on, she wasn't at liberty to say.

"You're right, Mother," she said. "Bucky Buckwalter certainly was a boss in a million."

At Evergreen Cemetery, winter had turned the sparse grass yellow. As the vehicles in the funeral cortege emptied, Joanna stayed near the fringes of the group coalescing around

Bucky Buckwalter's open grave. In the funeral chapel Joanna had been so close to the front that it had been difficult to get any kind of an overview of what was going on. Maintaining a little bit of distance in the cemetery allowed for better observation.

Bebe Noonan, dressed all in black, continued to carry on in chief-mourner fashion. Her behavior had already sparked several derogatory comments that, Joanna knew, would only get worse once the real story came out. As it was, her wild abandon of grief stood in marked contrast to Terry Buckwalter's stony reserve. As far as Joanna was concerned, her long talk with Terry at the clinic the previous afternoon had eased some of her concerns about Terry's possible involvement in her husband's death. How Detective Carpenter was viewing the unmoved widow's performance, however, was another question entirely.

Joanna caught sight of Dr. Reggie Wade making his way toward Bebe Noonan. He spoke to her briefly for a few moments. When he finished whatever he had to say, Bebe threw herself into his arms, weeping with renewed vigor. Reggie, looking uncomfortable, held her for a moment before setting her aside and moving on.

Reggie headed toward where Terry Buckwalter was standing, talking to someone else. It took a moment for Joanna to recognize who it was—Larry Matkin. No wonder Matkin had been unavailable to answer his phone. He had already been on his way to the funeral.

Seeing him there, Joanna couldn't help wondering why. Larry Matkin was a relative newcomer to town. What was his connection to Amos and Terry Buckwalter? The thought crossed her mind, but only briefly. It was quickly obscured as Reggie Wade walked up to Matkin and Terry. He moved between them and reached out to pat the widow's shoulder. During the whole ordeal of the day, that simple gesture caused a crack in Terry Buckwalter's unbending self-control. She looked up at Reggie and gave him a wan smile.

Joanna recognized the entire pantomime—the wordless gesture, the answering smile. She herself had been the recipient of the same kind of awkward pats. They had come mostly from Andy's buddies, from men who had found themselves helpless and tongue-tied in the face of Joanna's awful loss. Seeing the whole scene reenacted there in the cemetery brought back far too much of Joanna's own pain. She had to look away.

Eva Lou arrived just then. "What is the matter with that girl?" Eva Lou Brady whispered to her daughter-in-law, nodding in Bebe's direction. "Doesn't she realize that she's making a complete spectacle of herself?"

Still almost strangling on her own flashback of grief, Joanna shook her head. "No," she said. "I don't think she does. And even if she did, I don't think it would make any difference."

Eva Lou abruptly changed the subject. "Are you coming to the luncheon?" she asked.

By then, all Joanna Brady wanted to do was escape the whole thing. "I don't think so," she said. "I'm so far behind that I really shouldn't be away from the office that long."

Eva Lou peered at her closely. "Are you all right?"

"I'm fine."

"You don't look fine," Eva Lou said. "You're so pale that you look as though you might keel right over. You must be working too hard."

"Probably," Joanna agreed.

"Well, cut it out," Eva Lou said severely. "It's tempting

to try to be everything to all people, but you can't keep it up forever. It's too hard on you. You forget to stop and smell the roses. As you know, when those roses are gone, they're gone forever."

It was as close as Eva Lou Brady had ever come to bawling her out. Deservedly so. Joanna took Eva Lou's hand and squeezed it. "That's good advice," she said. "I'll try not to forget it."

Someone else arrived—Don and Louise Watson, bringing Jim Bob with them. After somber greetings all around, the four of them left Joanna where she was, and moved closer to where the other mourners were gathering around the casket-topped grave. There were only a few latecomers still straggling in when Ernie Carpenter sidled up to Joanna.

She had barely glimpsed at Ernie earlier in her office. Now she was shocked by the look of him. His color was bad. There were dark circles under his eyes. The snowballing events of the past few days had put a terrible strain on everyone in the department, but with Ernie as the sole homicide detective, the brunt of the pressure had landed squarely on his broad shoulders.

"The L.P.G.A.?" he muttered. "I still think it's just too damned convenient that Terry Buckwalter happens to have her big-deal golf tryout this weekend. What do you think?"

Joanna looked up at him. Ernie was a good cop, a capable cop. Unlike Joanna, Ernie hadn't recently lost his spouse. Every aspect of Bucky Buckwalter's murder seemed to tug on Joanna Brady's still raw emotional heartstrings. Ernie's judgment may have been impaired by sheer exhaustion, but not by his own prejudices.

As sheriff, Joanna Brady had only one clear option—to step aside and let her investigator do his job. "It's your case,

Ernie," she said. "I don't have an opinion on this one."

"Now that I know about this paternity thing, I need to talk to Terry again. Late this afternoon is probably the first I'll be able to get to it."

"What about sleep?" Joanna asked.

Ernie stopped cold. "Sleep?" he repeated, as though it were a totally foreign word. "Who needs sleep?"

"You do," Joanna answered. "You've been juggling one case after another. How much rest have you had in the past three days?"

"Some," Ernie admitted.

"Five hours? Ten?"

"Something like that," he said.

"That's about what I thought," Joanna said. "I can tell just by looking at you. Don't try to talk to Terry today, Ernie. Let it go. Once the funeral is over, I want you to take the rest of the afternoon off. And the weekend, too. I don't want you near the department any before Monday morning."

"But what about Terry going up to Tucson? What if she takes off and doesn't come back?"

"Then let it be on my head. If she runs away, we'll find her," Joanna said. "But right now, you need some time off. You're off duty from noon today on. That's an order, Detective Carpenter. You've already put in some sixty-odd hours this week. Monday will be time enough to start getting a handle on all of this. If you work yourself into the ground or into the hospital, then where will we be?"

Before Ernie had a chance to reply, the Reverend Billy Matthews launched off into the "dust to dust, ashes to ashes" part of the service. Moving close enough to hear, Joanna watched as Bucky Buckwalter's coffin slowly slid out of sight. As it did so, Joanna was gripped once again by the terrible sense of loss and finality that had assailed her months earlier as Andy's coffin, too, had disappeared from view. The tears that surprised her by suddenly spurting from her eyes had nothing at all to do with Bucky's death.

Glancing over her shoulder, she could see the distant part of the cemetery that held Andy's low-lying granite marker. She and Jenny had been there together only once since the marker was installed. That was on Veterans Day, when they had gone to place a tiny American flag beside the grave.

The service wasn't yet over when Joanna quietly drifted away toward that other part of the cemetery. Almost blinded by her tears, it was all she could do to keep from stumbling headlong over gravestones.

Once there, she stooped to pluck the faded flag out of the ground. Slipping it into the pocket of her coat, she knelt over the plain red granite marker. Chiseled into the smooth red rock was Andy's full name—Andrew Roy Brady—along with the dates of both his birth and his death. At the very bottom of the marker, almost melting into the long yellowed grass, were four simple words: "To serve and protect."

One at a time, she ran her fingers over each of the letters. To serve and protect. That had been Andy's job—his whole mission and purpose in life. It was the reason he had joined the service after high school and it was the reason he had signed on as deputy sheriff once he was discharged from the army. Now those same words constituted Joanna's mission in life as well.

"They can be mighty tough to live by," Jim Bob Brady observed, walking up behind her and laying a steadying hand on her shoulder.

Startled by her father-in-law's voice and touch, Joanna

hurried to wipe the tears from her eyes. She scrambled to her feet.

"They are," she mumbled. "Especially right about now."

"Why? What's wrong?"

Joanna shook her head. "It feels like the bad guys are winning, Jim Bob."

He shook his head. "Aw now," he said. "I wouldn't go so far as to say that. Seems to me you and your people are doin' all right."

Joanna gave him a frail smile. "It's possible you're prejudiced," she said.

"Nope," he declared, "not me. I admit it's been a bad week around here for lots of folks, but I'm sure that before too long you'll sort it all out."

"Sort it all out?" Joanna snorted. "What good will that do? Several people are dead, all of them in my jurisdiction. Five in all, with a couple more lives hanging by a thread. In at least two of those cases my own actions, or inactions on the part of some of my people, are partially responsible for what happened."

"So?" Jim Bob returned. "Most likely those people would be dead regardless of who was sheriff. The only thing you can do is try and see to it that whoever's responsible gets what's comin' to him."

Unable to say anything in return, Joanna turned and looked back toward the mound of flowers next to Bucky Buckwalter's grave. "When people are dead," she said finally, "punishing the killer always seems like too little too late."

"Maybe so, but it's the best you can do. Come along now," Jim Bob added. "It's too chilly for you to be out here very long."

Reaching out, he took Joanna by the hand and pulled her close, then he headed off across the cemetery, leading her back in the direction of the parked cars. "Eva Lou saw you walk off, and she sent me to fetch you. She was concerned."

"I'm sorry to worry you," Joanna said. "That was thoughtless of me."

"That's all right. Problem is, we're in a little bit of a hurry because Eva Lou's due to help serve at the Ladies' Aid's luncheon. I need to drop her by the church before too long. You see, that's Eva Lou's thing, Joanna. Servin' lunch may not seem like much of anything. On the scale of things, it's sort of like you said—too little, too late. But when people are hurtin', fixin' and servin' food is the best Eva Lou can do. You're so busy looking at the murder part of all this that you've plumb forgot it's the lunches and the little things that glue us all together."

Looking up at her father-in-law gratefully, Joanna realized what he was saying was absolutely true. "Thanks, Jim Bob," she said. "I needed that."

16

BACK at the cars, Eva Lou was already waiting in her husband's Honda. "I guess we'll see you later," she said. "Your mother mentioned that you wouldn't be coming to the church."

Joanna smiled in at her through the partially opened window. "What is it Jim Bob always says about a wise man changing his mind?" She took her father-in-law's hand and squeezed it. "He gave me a little pep talk over there. Sort of like the one you gave me earlier. Now that you've both got my attention, I believe I'll come along to the luncheon after all."

Just inside the parish hall of Canyon Methodist Church, Joanna ran into Bebe Noonan. Still dressed in black, she was carrying a plateful of food and looking somewhat restored. She smiled tentatively when she saw Joanna.

"Thank you for your help, Sheriff Brady," she said. "I did just what you said. I asked Dan Storey to represent me—me and the baby."

Joanna nodded. "I heard about the court order, so I knew you must have found someone."

"That's not all, either," Bebe added. "I talked to Reggie Wade a little while ago. Did you know he's taking over Bucky's practice?"

"Yes," Joanna said. "So I heard."

"Well," Bebe went on, "he told me that when the deal goes through, I'll be able to stay on with him. He says it'll be a big help to him if he has someone here in town who already knows Bucky's clients. Since Terry won't be working there anymore, I'll have a full-time job instead of a part-time one. He may even let me stay in the house for a while. That way, he'll have someone to look after things. So we'll be all right, the baby and I, right?"

Joanna had terrible misgivings about what it would be like for Bebe Noonan as a single parent in a small town—particularly an unwed single parent. Joanna had the financial security of some insurance, a reasonably well-paying job, and loving grandparents and friends to backstop her when it came to emergency child care. Bebe Noonan and her baby would have none of those. Bebe seemed to have only the barest grasp of the difficulties ahead. Still, her question pleaded for a simple affirmative answer. Joanna gave her what she wanted.

"Yes, Bebe," Joanna said. "I'm sure you'll be fine."

"Why, Joanna," Marliss Shackleford said, horning her way into the conversation in her customarily pushy fashion. Faced with the columnist's arrival, Bebe Noonan paled and melted into the crowd.

Usually, Joanna would have dreaded running into the reporter in a social setting. Today was different. "We missed you at the luncheon the other day," Joanna said sweetly. "I hope you're feeling better."

Marliss must have had something in mind as she approached Joanna and Bebe Noonan. Now, whatever it was, seemed to disappear in unaccustomed confusion.

"Oh, yes," she stammered uncomfortably. "I was sorry to miss it. I had a little touch of the flu, but I'm fine now."

"Good," Joanna said. "And have you heard Jeff and Marianne's good news?"

"What good news?" Marliss asked.

"Marianne left for San Francisco bright and early this morning. She's going there to meet Jeff and the baby and bring them home."

"Is that right?" Marliss Shackleford's disinterest was unmistakable. She may have been in the *news* business, but *good news* wasn't necessarily her bag.

"I'm planning a shower for them as soon as they get home," Joanna continued cheerfully. "Probably sometime in the next week or so. I'll let you know as soon as I decide when it'll be. Maybe you can put a little announcement about it in your column."

"Oh, no," Marliss objected at once. "I couldn't possibly do that."

"You couldn't?" Joanna asked. "Why not?"

"Marianne Maculyea is a personal friend of mine. I could never use my column in that way. Making a personal plea like that would be a violation of journalistic ethics—a conflict of interest. It just wouldn't do at all. Now, if you'll excuse me . . ."

Joanna felt a certain amount of satisfaction as Marliss Shackleford slipped away from her. Going on the attack was a good way of dealing with some people.

"What was that all about?" Eleanor asked, appearing at Joanna's elbow.

Eleanor Lathrop and Marliss Shackleford were part of the same bridge group and had been known to be thick as thieves on occasion. Here was a golden opportunity to drive a wedge between them. In the end, whether the devil made her do it or not, the temptation was too much for Joanna to resist.

"Actually, Mother," she said confidentially, "Marliss was asking me about you."

Eleanor Lathrop's eyes widened. "About me? Really? Whatever for?"

Keeping her face straight, Joanna leaned closer to Eleanor. "She told me she's heard some rumors about you. I told her she must be mistaken."

"What kind of rumors?" Eleanor asked.

"About you and George Winfield. She said she'd heard that you and the coroner were planning on taking a short jaunt up to Vegas. I told her that was the most ridiculous thing I'd ever heard."

For the first time in Joanna's memory, an aghast Eleanor Lathrop was shocked into absolute silence.

"It is ridiculous, isn't it?" Joanna pressed.

Nodding numbly, Eleanor finally regained the power of speech. "Of course it is," she agreed. "Where do rumors like this start?"

"I can't imagine," Joanna said.

Across the room, she caught sight of Larry Matkin standing near the door. Their eyes met briefly, but then he looked away. His message had said he wanted to talk to her. Thinking now would be a good time. Joanna started moving in that direction. Several people stopped her along the way. By the time she reached the door, he was gone. She even walked out into the parking lot to try to catch him, but he was nowhere in sight.

Oh, well, she told herself. *I'll call him as soon as I get back to the office.* In the meantime, she turned back into the parish hall. By then, the serving line at the buffet had almost disappeared. Taking a plate from the stack, Joanna went to get some food.

Once the luncheon was over, Joanna returned to work with a renewed sense of purpose. She was relieved to find that things seemed to be going fairly well, considering. According to Dick Voland, both of the two critically injured U.D.A.s had been upgraded, one to critical but stable and the other to serious. In addition, none of the hospitalized aliens whose guards had been pulled had made any effort to run away. Jaime Carbajal had spent most of the morning interviewing the jailed crash victims. So far, three of them had expressed a willingness to testify against the driver, as well as against the Mexican national from Agua Prieta whom they all identified as the mastermind behind a very profitable drug and wetback-smuggling operation.

"The Border Patrol is ecstatic to get the goods on this guy," Voland told her. "They've been trying to put him out of business for years. What I can't understand is what's keeping Ernie. He should have been here to oversee the questioning. He was going to the Buckwalter funeral this morning, but I expected him back long before this."

"I sent him home," Joanna said. "And I'd send you home, too, if I could. We've all been working too hard. When I saw Ernie at the funeral, I could tell he was right at the end of his rope."

Voland's eyes bulged. "With all the cases we've got hang-

ing fire? How could you send him home? He's the only detective we have left."

"Why is that?" Joanna countered.

"Why?" Voland shrugged. "The two other guys put in
their twenty years and bailed out."

"I know that," Joanna replied. "What I don't understand
is why Deputy Carbajal hasn't been promoted to detective.
Has he passed the written test?"

"Yes, but I was waiting for Ernie to tell me he was ready."

"What were you really waiting for, Dick? For hell to
freeze over? It just did. We've had five violent deaths in as
many days, and we've only got one detective to cover too
many bases. What's wrong with this picture?"

"But Jaime's not ready yet. He's still too young."

"No, he's not," Joanna stated. "From what you said, it
sounds as though he's doing fine with those guys over at the
jail."

"Yes, but—"

"But nothing, Mr. Voland. Do it."

"Yes, ma'am," Chief Deputy Voland replied. "I'll get right
on it."

"And one more thing. Have you talked to Ruth since last
night?"

Dick Voland flushed. "No."

"Are you going to talk to her?"

"She threw me out," Voland said. "What's the point of
talking? I've made some calls. I think I've lined up an apartment. I'm supposed to go look at it after work."

With that, he turned and stomped out of her office. Joanna
waited for several minutes after he had left before she picked
up the phone and dialed Dick Voland's home number. She
had called it often enough in the past few months that she

knew it by heart. Joanna was still trying to imagine what she would say to Ruth Voland when the answering machine clicked on telling her that no one was home.

Relieved, but sorry, too, Joanna put down the receiver and went to work. Half an hour later Kristin called in on the intercom to announce that someone named Philip Dotson was waiting in the outer office.

"Philip Dotson?" Joanna returned. "Who's he?"

"He's Reed Carruthers' nephew and Hannah Green's cousin," Kristin replied. "He says he came here directly from George Winfield's office. He was supposed to talk to Ernie Carpenter, but since Ernie's not in, Deputy Voland suggested that he talk to you."

Here it comes, Joanna thought, shifting her paperwork to the far side of her desk. *This will probably be my first wrongful-death suit. Do I talk to the guy alone, or do I call for reinforcements?* The problem was, Dick Voland had already passed the problem on to her, and Frank Montoya would be out of the office for the next several hours.

Time to be a grown-up, Joanna thought.

After a moment's reflection, she pressed the intercom talk button. "I'll see him, Kristin," she said. "Go ahead and show him in."

By the time Kristin ushered the visitor into the office, Joanna was standing, waiting to greet him. "Good afternoon," she said, holding out her hand. "I'm Sheriff Brady. I'm sorry we're meeting under such tragic circumstances."

Dotson, a tall, spare man in his late forties or early fifties, bore no family resemblance to his dead cousin. He was carrying a cowboy hat, an old one made of worn gray felt.

"Tragic?" he repeated with a shrug of his narrow shoulders. "I don't know. Couldn't be helped none, I guess. It was bound to happen."

Joanna motioned him into one of the two visitor's chairs. He sat down, carefully balancing his hat on the threadbare knee of a pair of worn Levis'. "What couldn't be helped, Mr. Dotson?" Joanna asked.

"Reed Carruthers was a son of a bitch, if you'll pardon the expression, ma'am. It's a wonder somebody didn't cave his head in a long time ago. His poor wife—my Aunt Ruth— was my mother's sister. For starters, Aunt Ruth is the one who shoulda done it. There may be meaner men on the face of the earth; I just haven't had the misfortune of meeting any of 'em. Leastways not so far. And as for Hannah, she was always a couple tacos short of a combination plate, if you know what I mean."

"You're saying she was mentally disturbed?" Joanna asked.

"Amongst the family, we always said she was just plain crazy—crazy and dumb both. She got away from her old man once when she run off and married that trucker from Dripping Springs, Texas. What nobody could ever figure out was why she come back home once that marriage broke up, or why she stayed, either one. Guess she thought she just didn't have no other choice. The thing is, if she'da left him, she pro'ly coulda made it on her S.S.I. Aunt Franny—Franny Langford, my mother's older sister—woulda taken her in in a minute if need be. Hannah never woulda been left out on the streets."

"Your cousin was receiving Social Security income based on what?" Joanna asked.

"Who knows?" Dotson said. "On account of being crazy, I expect. Disabled, one way or the other. I'm sure my uncle never let her keep none of the money to spend on herself. That wasn't his way."

Joanna thought of the five hundred or so dollars Hannah had said she had hidden away in her underwear drawer. For someone in her straitened circumstances, that must have amounted to a fortune. How long had it taken the poor unfortunate woman to accumulate that much of a hoard?

"So what can I do for you today, Mr. Dotson?" Joanna asked.

"I just come to town to retrieve the bodies and make arrangements. Only havin' one body sent back, really. My uncle's gonna be buried here in Bisbee, and the sooner the better. No service, no nothing. I'm havin' Hannah shipped up to Thatcher. Aunt Franny's makin' arrangements for Hannah to be buried in the Langford family plot, where she belongs. Her mother, too, if we can work it out. She's buried over in Willcox, but we're seein' about movin' her to Thatcher as well."

"Has anyone given you your cousin's personal effects?" Joanna asked.

Dotson shook his head. "Not so far. The lady out in the lobby told me I should come here to talk to Detective Carpenter, exceptin' I guess he's not here, so I ended up with you instead."

Joanna pushed the button on her intercom. "Kristin," she said. "Have someone from the jail bring over Ms. Green's personal effects, would you?"

While they waited, Joanna turned back to Philip Dotson. "You wouldn't happen to know whatever happened to Hannah's right hand, would you?"

"Sure," he said. "Reed slammed it in a door once years back to keep Hannah from leavin' home that second time.

Never carried her to no doctor with it, neither. My Uncle Reed didn't believe in doctors. That's how come Aunt Ruth died so young, too. She caught pneumonia and died. If she'da went to a doctor, she'd pro'ly still be around."

Joanna reached for Ernie's written report on the two linked cases—on Hannah Green and Reed Carruthers. "I've had detectives over there at Sunizona asking questions for two days. How come none of the neighbors mentioned any of this?"

"Pro'ly didn't know nothin' about it. Reed Carruthers never was one to wash his dirty underwear in public. My mother's people—the Langfords—is the same way."

Just then Tom Hadlock, the jail commander, showed up in Joanna's office bearing a thin manila envelope and a plastic bag. He dropped the bag on the floor and then dumped the contents of the envelope out onto Joanna's desk.

"Her clothes are all here in the bag," he said. "You're welcome to them if you want . . ."

"I know all about Hannah's clothes," Philip Dotson said. "You go ahead and get rid of 'em. Like as how burnin's all they're good for."

Leaning forward, he saw the stack of clipped-together bills that had fallen out of the envelope. Picking up the paper money, he thumbed through it. "Where'd all this come from?" he asked. "Looks like a bundle. How'd Hannah lay hands on so much money?"

Joanna glanced at the listing on the outside of the envelope. "It's five hundred fifty-six dollars and eleven cents in all," she said. "Hannah told me she had saved it. She claimed she had more than that set aside, so she must have spent some of it on her way to my house."

"Why'd she do that?" Philip Dotson asked, his eyes narrowing. "That's what my Aunt Franny wants to know. If Hannah was just gonna do herself in anyways, why'd she come all that way down here to see you first, Sheriff Brady? Why not just do it at home and get it over with and save everybody the trouble?"

"She said she wanted to talk to a woman," Joanna answered slowly. "She said she wanted somebody to hear her side of what happened."

"And what did happen?"

"According to what she told me, Hannah wanted to watch a particular program on TV, but your uncle took the remote control and ran off outside with it. Hannah went after him, trying to get it back. When she caught up to him, I think she went over the edge and started hitting him."

"She told you then, didn't she," Dotson said. "About my uncle. About how mean he was."

Joanna nodded.

"And you believed her?"

"Yes, I did," Joanna said. "If her case had gone to trial, I don't think there ever would have been a homicide conviction. Manslaughter, maybe. Considering the extenuating circumstances, maybe not even that."

Without another word, Philip Dotson started scooping the money and the few other loose items back into the envelope.

"Don't you want to count the money first?" Tom Hadlock objected. "I need you to sign for it. You should make sure it's all there before you do."

"It don't matter none," Philip Dotson said. "However much it is, it's not enough to fight over."

With careful concentration he signed the form Tom Hadlock handed him, then Dotson stood up. Holding both the envelope and his hat in one hand, he reached out toward Joanna with the other.

"Thank you, Sheriff Brady," he said. "I thank you, and so does my Aunt Franny. She's been cryin' for twenty-four hours straight now, beratin' herself somethin' fierce on account of no one ever listened to Hannah or done nothin' about her. But it turns out now that somebody did listen, and we're mighty grateful. Can't none of us vote for you, on account of we're up in Graham County instead of in Cochise. But we'll all be prayin' for you. Aunt Franny's especially good at that."

"Thank you," Joanna said. "And tell your Aunt Franny thank you as well. Any and all prayers are greatly appreciated. After all, they're part of the glue that holds us all together."

Isn't that right, Jim Bob? Joanna thought as she watched Philip Dotson amble out of her office. *Lunches and prayers, both.*

Through the remainder of the afternoon she continued to wade through the paperwork jungle. She tried several times to reach Larry Matkin, but to no avail. He evidently hadn't returned to his office after leaving the parish hall. The next time Joanna's phone rang, the caller was Butch Dixon. "Are we all set for dinner?" he asked. "What time and where?"

"There's a place called the Pizza Palace out in Don Luis. How about if we meet there around six?"

"Don Luis?" Butch repeated. "Where's that? I thought we were having dinner here in town."

Joanna laughed. "We are. Don Luis *is* part of town. It was incorporated into Bisbee in the fifties, along with Warren, Bakerville, and Lowell. The thing is, all those individual neighborhoods have retained their original names, even though they're all a part of Bisbee proper."

"The Pizza Palace," Butch repeated.

"Do you need directions?"

"No, thanks. I'm sure someone here at the Grand Hotel will be able to tell me how to find it."

Once Joanna was off the phone, she tried Larry Matkin's number once again for good measure. Still there was no answer. About four, Kristin came in with a stack of typed letters for Joanna to sign. "By the way, Deputy Voland told me to tell you he was taking off early this afternoon."

"Did he say when he'd be back?"

"I'm sure he's gone for the day," Kristin said, a trifle too quickly.

Joanna regarded Kristin Marsten with a penetrating look. "I'm sure he won't be coming back to work," Joanna said. "But did he say whether or not he was coming back to sleep?"

Kristin flushed to the roots of her light blond hair.

"So you did know about that?" Joanna pressed.

Kristin nodded.

"Why didn't you tell me?"

The young secretary shrugged. "I guess I was afraid he'd get in some kind of trouble."

"Kristin," Joanna said. "Police officers are a lot more likely to get into trouble if we *don't* know what's going on in their personal lives. As my secretary, you're my eyes and ears around here. Your job is to let me know things that are going on that may have some bearing on the performance of any member of my department. Is that clear?"

"Yes," Kristin replied. "I see."

"Good."

Kristin went out then. As Joanna sat putting her signature at the bottom of the typed letters, she thought about what she had just told Kristin. What she had said was true. But didn't it go further than that, further than just needing to know what was going on? Now that she was aware of the situation in the Voland household, didn't she have some responsibility to do something about it?

Closing up her desk, she took the signed letters out to Kristin to put in the mail. "I'm heading out early, too," she said.

Except, instead of driving directly to Eva Lou and Jim Bob Brady's to pick up Jenny, Joanna drove out to San Jose Estates. Ruth and Dick Voland lived in a four-bedroom stuccoed rambler with a magnificent view of the stately mountain peak several miles south of the border in Old Mexico from which the development took its name.

It was a long time after Joanna rang the bell before the mahogany door opened. Ruth was a heavyset, jowly woman in her early forties. Wearing sweats, she was panting, as though she'd been interrupted in the middle of a workout. Ruth paled as soon as she saw Joanna standing there. "It's not Dick, is it?" she demanded. "Has something happened to him?"

"No," Joanna said. "I came to talk to you."

"Why?"

"You're making a terrible mistake," Joanna said. "Dick and I work together. That's it. There is absolutely nothing going on between us."

Ruth stood back and opened the door, gesturing Joanna into the house. She shrugged. "It doesn't really matter if there is or if there isn't," she said.

"Of course it matters," Joanna returned. "He's out right

now, looking for an apartment. Catch him before he rents one. Have him come back home. You guys have two kids, don't you?"

Ruth Voland nodded. "One in high school and the other in junior high."

"Those kids need their father. Dick is my chief deputy, but when it comes to romance, you don't have a thing to worry about."

"I already told you," Ruth asserted, "it *is* too late. I got sick and tired of listening to him talk about Joanna Brady this and Joanna Brady that twenty-four hours a day. I've found someone else. Kenneth is the coach of my son's bowling team out in Sierra Vista. Ken's already divorced, and I will be soon."

Joanna was stunned. She had somehow thought all she'd have to do was walk up to the door, talk to Ruth Voland a few minutes, and the whole thing would be set to rights.

"You're filing for a divorce?"

"Sure I am," Ruth Voland replied. "Ken and I want to get married as soon as we can."

"But Ruth," Joanna argued. "You've already got a perfectly good husband."

"If he's so damned perfect, you have him then," Ruth Voland said. "It was bad enough when he was married to the job. I could take that. I knew what to expect. But then, when you turned up, it was too much. I'm just a housewife, Sheriff Brady. I don't know what you are, but to hear Dick tell it, you must be right up there with Wonder Woman. I can't compete with that. Now, if you'll excuse me, I need to get back to my Exercycle."

Still in a daze, Joanna walked back to the Blazer, got in, and drove back to her in-law's place in Warren. Jenny was at a friend's house when Joanna got there, and that was just as well.

"What's going on?" Eva Lou asked. "You look upset."

"Ruth Voland has thrown Dick out of the house. She's filing for a divorce. She thinks there's something going on between us."

"Between you and Dick Voland?"

"That's right."

"There isn't anything, is there?" Eva Lou asked.

"Of course not!" Joanna replied indignantly. "We work together, and that's it. I tried to explain that to Ruth. I'm certainly not interested in the man, but I don't think she believed me."

"Probably not," Eva Lou answered. "You've got to look at it through her point of view."

"Which is?"

"Other than being an Avon Lady for a little while a few years back, I don't think Ruth Voland has ever worked outside the home. All of a sudden you arrive on the scene, not just as a fellow officer, but as her husband's boss. He's bound to talk about you. The more he does, the more threatened she must feel."

"But Eva Lou," Joanna argued, "we never *did* anything. There was never anything out of line. We've just worked together, but here she has me cast as the other woman."

"Whether you meant to be or not, you *are* the other woman," Eva Lou said quietly.

"But what should I do about it?" Joanna asked desperately. "What can I do to fix it?"

"Not a blessed thing," Eva Lou answered. "It's strictly

between the two of them. It has nothing to do with you."

The front door banged open and a breathless Jenny came racing into the kitchen. "Hi, Mom," she said. "When's dinner? I'm starving."

17

W H E N Jenny and Joanna reached the Pizza Palace, Butch Dixon's Goldwing was already parked outside the door. They found the man himself inside, seated at an oilcloth-covered picnic table. He was leaning against the wall, still reading the same book. While Jenny headed straight for the video-game arcade, Joanna slipped onto the bench across from him.

"Must be a good book," Joanna said.

Closing it, Butch looked over at her and grinned. "It is," he said. "This is the fourth or fifth time I've read it. It's like reading the Bible. Depending on where you are and what's going on in your life, you get something different out of it with each reading."

He glanced around the room. "Where's Jenny?"

"Waylaid by the video games," Joanna answered with an exasperated shrug of her shoulders. "I gave her a dollar and told her when that's gone there'll be no more."

"If she's any good, she could be gone a long time," Butch said.

"Believe me," Joanna returned, "she's not that good."

"You look tired," Butch said, examining her face. "Rough day, I suppose, with the funeral and all."

Joanna was still so stricken by her confrontation with Ruth Voland that Bucky Buckwalter's funeral seemed days, not hours, away. "It's been a rough week," she said.

Jenny proved to be far better with the video games than her mother had expected. By the time she finally showed up at the table, Butch had already ordered a pitcher of root beer, a large pepperoni pizza with extra cheese, and green salads all around. Left on their own, the two grown-ups had launched off into conversation.

"Well," Joanna said, "what's the verdict on Bisbee so far?"

"It's nice," he said. "And small. And everybody seems to know you."

"That's how small towns are supposed to work. Everybody knows everybody else."

"No," Butch said. "People know you specifically. Several different people have asked me what I'm doing in Bisbee. When I tell them I'm here visiting a friend and that the friend is you, they all have something to say about you."

"Good, bad, or indifferent?" Joanna asked.

"Mostly good," Butch replied. "The people I've talked to seem to be very proud of you. Small-town girl makes good and all that."

Joanna gave him a rueful grin. "Don't believe everything you hear. And remember, I didn't exactly volunteer for this job. I was drafted."

"So were most of the guys whose names ended up on the Vietnam War Memorial in Washington, D.C.," Butch Dixon answered seriously. "But just because they were drafted doesn't keep them from being heroes or martyrs, depending on your point of view."

A moment or two passed. "Does that bother you?" he asked. "The fact that everybody knows you?"

"I guess I'm getting used to it."

Sensing that the conversation was making her uncomfortable, Butch changed the subject. "It's gorgeous country," he said. "The contrasting reds and grays. The blue sky. The whole place is just incredible."

Relieved of her four quarters, Jenny arrived at the table, sampled her drink, smiled at Butch and said, "What kind of pizza?"

"Jenny," Joanna admonished. "Mind your manners. First you should say hello."

"Hello," Jenny chirped in Butch's direction. "And what kind of pizza?"

"Hello yourself," Butch returned. "And the pizza of the day is pepperoni with extra cheese."

"Did you know that's my favorite?" Jenny asked.

Butch nodded. "A little bird told me."

"It did not," Jenny responded, settling onto the bench beside her mother. "*She* told you."

Butch grinned. "You got me," he said. "Now tell me all about this ranch of yours. Where is it again?"

"The High Lonesome is about ten miles the other side of town. Fifteen miles or so from where we are now."

"And the two of you live out there all by yourselves?" he asked. "Isn't it lonely?"

Jenny shook her head. "It's not lonely," she said. "We've got the dogs. And pretty soon we're going to have a horse, too. Mom's going to buy me one for my birthday."

Joanna glowered at her daughter. "I wouldn't be so certain about that horse, Jenny," she said. Then, to Butch, she added, "It does seem a little lonely at times. And there are days when I get so sick of the long commute that I wonder if it's worth it."

"What do you mean, a long commute?" Butch asked.

Joanna shrugged. "Well," she replied, "it's ten minutes to the end of the road and then another seven or so after that to the office."

Butch Dixon's response was a genuine hoot of laughter. "Back in Chicago, where I grew up, twenty minutes was how long it took my father to get to the train station in Downers Grove. Then there was another hour on the train. *That's* a long commute. He did it every weekday for twenty-five years."

"You're from Chicago?" Jenny asked. Butch nodded.

"So how did you get to Arizona?"

"My grandparents—my mother's parents—were among the original buyers in Sun City," Butch said. "I was in sixth grade—just a few years older than you—when my grandfather got sick. My parents pulled me out of school in January so we could come see him before he died. I'll never forget it. It was bitterly cold in Chicago. The streets were lined with thousands of cars that were frozen to the ground and covered by mounds of snow-plowed ice, while people in Sun City were walking around in shirtsleeves, playing golf, and barbecuing on their outdoor patios. I thought I was in heaven. I decided right then that Arizona was the place for me. I told my mother at the time, but I don't think she believed me. It took a few years, but I finally made it."

Their salads arrived then, followed by a steaming pizza. Talk was lighthearted and fun. Joanna enjoyed watching the way Butch teased and charmed Jenny. The child seemed to bask in the attention of this funny but attentive man who not only asked her questions but seemed genuinely interested in her answers. By the time the spumoni ice cream disappeared, Jenny and Butch Dixon had become friends.

"Can't Mr. Dixon come out to the house so we can show it to him?" Jenny asked.

"Maybe he isn't interested . . ." Joanna objected.

"But I want him to meet the dogs," Jenny continued. "You like dogs, don't you, Mr. Dixon?" she asked, checking Butch's face as he answered.

"I love dogs," he said.

"Still," Joanna said, "it depends on whether or not he wants to."

"Sure," Butch said. "I'd love to meet Tigger and Sadie, but what do you think?" he added with a sidelong look in Joanna's direction.

"I don't mind," she said.

They caravanned out to the ranch, with Jenny riding backward most of the way to make sure Butch didn't get lost in the process. Tigger and Sadie both went properly berserk at the sight of the motorcycle, but they were also fairly well behaved once Jenny had introduced them to Butch. When Jenny took the dogs and went inside, Butch and Joanna stood for a moment on the night-chilled back porch staring up at the velvet-black, star-studded sky.

"It's breathtaking," he said quietly. "Beautiful and peaceful both. When you live in the city, it's hard to believe there's anyplace on earth that's still this empty."

"It's not *that* empty," Joanna returned. "My nearest neighbor is just a little over a mile away."

"Only a mile? That close?" Butch laughed. "Listen," he added. "The next time you start wondering about whether or not your commute is worth it, call me. I'll be glad to tell you it is."

Laughing too, Joanna opened the backdoor. "It's cold out here. Come on in," she said. "We do *have* a front door, but most people come into the house this way—through the laundry room."

Thanks to Angie Kellogg's cleaning efforts the previous morning and due in no small part to the fact that hardly anyone had been home in the meantime, the house was still reasonably straight. They had gone only as far as the kitchen when Jenny returned and grabbed hold of Butch's hand.

"Come on," she said. "I'll give you the tour."

While Jenny guided Butch around the house, Joanna ducked into the bedroom long enough to slip off both her holsters and her body armor. Then she went back out to the living room to take messages off the machine. For a change, there were only two—both from Eleanor. Joanna decided those would have to wait until after Butch left. She was sitting on the couch in the living room when the tour ended and Jenny delivered him back there before heading off for her nightly bath.

Butch paused in front of a bookcase and studied the shelf devoted to family pictures. "Andy and you?" he asked, pointing at their wedding picture.

"Yes."

"You must have been very young."

Joanna nodded. "I had just turned nineteen the month before we got married. Andy died the day after our tenth wedding anniversary."

"You were lucky," he said, collapsing into the chair opposite her—the same worn easy chair that had always been Andy's favorite. Joanna winced at the idea of Butch Dixon sitting there. It seemed wrong somehow—disloyal to Andy.

"At least you had ten years," Butch was saying.

At least? Joanna wondered. *What did he mean by "at least"?*

This was a whole new perspective. She had spent so much time during the last few months missing the years she and Andy *hadn't* spent together that it was difficult for her to see those few years in a different light, with her cup half full instead of half empty.

"Some people never have that many," he finished.

Before Joanna had a chance to reply or to learn what kind of private hurt lay behind those words, the phone rang. She hurried to pick it up. If it turned out to be Eleanor, how would she manage to get her off the phone?

"Hello," she said, picking up the receiver. "Joanna Brady speaking."

"We've got a problem," Dick Voland told her. "Hal Morgan's taken off."

"Taken off?" Joanna echoed. "What do you mean?"

"Just that. He's gone. He assaulted Deputy Howell and headed for the hills. From what we can tell, he used a bottle to knock her colder 'an a wedge, then took off in that Buick of his. I've posted an APB. With any kind of luck, he won't make it out of the county."

"How's Debbie?" Joanna asked.

"She's got a concussion. She's been transported to the hospital."

Joanna felt her temperature rise. "If Deputy Howell's already in the hospital, how long ago did all this happen?"

"Half an hour, I guess," Dick Voland replied. "Maybe forty-five minutes."

"Why wasn't I informed before now?"

"I was still here in the office," Voland said. "I've been

handling it. I didn't see any reason to bother you."

Another time, Joanna might have chewed him out for leaving her out of the loop. This time, however, she understood exactly why he was right there, Johnny-on-the-spot, the moment the call came in. She could still see Dick Voland stretched out and sleeping on the couch in his office. And she could still see Ruth Voland standing there in her sweats, telling Joanna about Ken, the bowling coach. Poor Dick.

"So tell me again what happened," Joanna said.

"According to what we've been able to piece together, Debbie must have been out behind the motel, grabbing a smoke. Someone—I'm betting Morgan himself—whacked her over the head from behind. The doc's still picking slivers of broken beer bottle out of her scalp. Anyway, she was left lying unconscious, right beside the dumpster. One of the busboys from the coffee shop came out later on to empty the trash. He's the one who found her and called nine-one-one. By then Morgan was long gone. He left a note, though."

"A note? What kind of note?"

"A suicide note. Typed it on the screen of a little laptop computer he left in his room."

"What did it say?" Joanna asked.

"That Bucky Buckwalter deserved to die. Morgan said he had no intention of going to prison for something that was no more of a crime than putting a sick dog out of its misery."

Joanna felt her stomach contract. In the hospital Hal Morgan had assured Joanna that he hadn't killed Bucky Buckwalter. She cursed herself for being a naive fool. Obviously Morgan had been lying through his teeth, and she had been stupid enough to believe him.

"I have company right now," Joanna said. "If everything is handled . . ."

"Just a minute," Voland interrupted. "Something's coming in from Dispatch."

As she waited, holding the telephone receiver to her ear, she was aware that Butch Dixon was watching her—watching and listening. "Problems?" he asked.

She nodded, just as Dick Voland came back on the line. "Deputy Long, from the northern sector, just spotted the Buick at the gas station in Elfrida. There are too many civilians around for him to risk doing anything. I told him to hang back and keep Morgan under surveillance."

Joanna was torn. She had been out working every night this week. It sounded as though Dick Voland had things under control. Still, he had called with the expectation that, once notified, the sheriff would do something about the situation. And most sheriffs—most hands-on sheriffs—would have. The problem was, most of them didn't have nine-year-old daughters to worry about.

"Dick," Joanna began. "I can't leave Jenny here . . ."

"I'll watch her for you," Butch offered. "You go. I'll stay right here until you get back."

Covering the mouthpiece, Joanna looked across the room at him. "You don't mind?" she said.

"Not at all."

Joanna hesitated, but only for a second. Then she took her hand away from the mouthpiece. "I'm on my way," she said. "If anybody wants me, I'll be in the Blazer. I'll be in radio contact just as soon as I'm in the car."

Slamming down the phone, Joanna turned toward Butch. "I'm sorry," she said. "You're sure you don't mind?"

"Like I said yesterday. When duty calls, you've got to go. Jenny and I will be fine. We may even watch a little of *My*

Fair Lady before it's her bedtime. She told me it's one of her favorites. I happen to like that one as well."

"Thanks," Joanna said. "I'd better go get ready."

She stopped by the bathroom long enough to let Jenny know what was happening. Then she hurried into the bedroom and put her body armor back on under her clothing—her body armor, her Glock, and her Colt 2000. When she came back out of the bedroom, she found Butch settled on the couch, with the two dogs curled up comfortably at his feet. He was scratching Tigger's ears.

"I think he's adopted me," he said.

"It does look that way," she agreed.

"What are all these scabs all over his face?"

"Tigger's big problem with porcupines is that they can't outrun him. And once he catches one, he thinks he can win."

"I know the feeling," Butch said. "I seem to have the same kind of luck with women."

Not knowing what to say in response, Joanna started toward the door. "Make yourself at home," she said.

He nodded. "I'll wait here and keep the home fires burning," he said. "You go do whatever it is you have to do. But be careful, and come back home in one piece, you hear?"

Joanna started to make some smart-mouthed reply, but she stopped when a lump rose unaccountably in her throat and her eyes suddenly blurred with tears. How many times had she said almost those exact words to Andy when he had been called out to some crime scene or accident in the middle of the night? The words of warning and caution took on a new meaning when someone else said them to you. When someone else cared enough to say them to you.

Nodding, she murmured a quick "I will." Then she turned away before Butch Dixon had a chance to glimpse how his words of concern had affected her. By the time she vaulted into the Blazer and started down the road, she was crying like a baby.

And the thing that made those tears so very puzzling was that she didn't really know why she was crying. She had no idea at all.

By the time Joanna reached High Lonesome Road, she had herself under control enough to stop the tears and switch on the radio. "What's going on?" she asked.

"The situation is under control, Sheriff Brady," the calm voice of Tica Romero, one of the dispatch operators, assured her. "We've got it handled."

Tica's unruffled response was frustratingly low on information. "I'd like to know exactly *how* it's being handled," Joanna responded.

"Deputy Ted Long has the Buick under surveillance. The suspect still hasn't left the gas station. It looks like he's headed northbound on Highway 191."

"What are Deputy Long's orders?" Joanna asked.

"Visual contact only. No hot pursuit. No lights or sirens."

Joanna was relieved. She had visions of civilians caught in an Elfrida shoot-out or maybe some twilight-working farmer on a tractor being creamed by either a fleeing suspect or a speeding patrol car. "Good," she said. "What else?"

"Chief Deputy Voland has authorized establishing a roadblock just beyond the Sunizona curve."

Visualizing the road, Joanna worried about other crossroads that turned off Highway 191 prior to Sunizona—roads that led off into the Chiricahua Mountains on the east or up into the Dragoons on the left. What if Hal Morgan turned off on one of those? In the 1860s, those high desert mountain ranges had been the ones where a canny Apache chieftain named Cochise had led his people in order to elude capture by the U.S. Cavalry. The rugged part of the Dragoons called Cochise Stronghold came by the name honestly. If those steep, rockbound canyons had once been able to afford a safe haven to a whole band of people, Joanna knew it would be all too easy for a single modern-day homicide suspect to disappear into them.

"Can't we put up the roadblock any sooner than that?" Joanna asked. "Why wait so long?"

"Because Deputy Casey can't get there any faster, for one thing. He's on his way down from a domestic over in Dragoon. Chief Deputy Voland figures if Deputy Casey can get as far as Township Butte, he can hide behind the butte to put the roadblock in place. That way the suspect won't be able to see him until he's right there. When he comes around that curve at Sunizona, it'll be too late for him to turn off. The two patrol cars will have him in a squeeze play."

"Where's Chief Deputy Voland right now?"

"He'll be leaving the complex as soon as he finishes gathering the response team. Where are you?"

Joanna's Blazer had just bounced across the last cattle guard on High Lonesome Road. "I'm on my way to the scene, just now turning left on Double Adobe Road at High Lonesome," she responded. "Once I hit Double Adobe, I'll take Central Highway up to Elfrida. Anybody else ahead of me?"

"Nope. Other than Deputy Casey coming south from Dragoon, you're the next one up."

Knowing that, Joanna switched on both flashing lights and siren. The road was relatively straight but narrow and bisected every few miles by washes that made for gut-wrenching dips. She flew through them so fast that more than once the Blazer felt as though it was momentarily airborne.

"He's moving now," Tica announced.

"Which way?"

"North, just like we figured."

Nodding grimly, Joanna kept on driving. It was one thing to know intellectually that Cochise County was comprised of 6,256 square miles. Only now, as Joanna Brady sped first east and then north, did her understanding of the challenging distances in her jurisdiction come fully into focus.

Her departmental patrol division consisted of fifty sworn officers. That sounded like a sizable force but that was *before* it was parceled out—before those fifty officers had to be divided into five separate shifts and spread over seven twenty-four-hour days. Seven days and all those miles. In all, a single patrol officer often was responsible for covering as much as seven hundred square miles.

Considering the fact that a suicidal Hal Morgan had attacked Deputy Howell in making good his escape, he had to be classified as a danger to himself and others. He posed a serious threat to the public welfare regardless of where he was and whether or not he was armed. And across all those vast miles of Cochise County, only two responding deputies and Sheriff Joanna Brady herself were anywhere near striking distance of his damn gas-guzzling Buick.

Several minutes passed before the radio squawked again. "Sheriff Brady?"

"Yes."

"We've got a problem," Tica Romero said. "We've lost him."

"Lost whom?" Joanna demanded.

"Deputy Long. Something's wrong. We've lost radio contact."

Joanna was just coming into Elfrida then, pausing but not

stopping at the junction where Central Highway met 191 and then racing north through town. Highway 191 was a far better road than the one from Double Adobe to Elfrida, but on a better roadway there was always a possibility of more traffic.

No sooner was she clear of the hamlet of Elfrida than she saw the fallacy in Dick Voland's plan. In an otherwise black sky, a pulsating halo of red and blue light threw the silhouetted shadow of Township Butte into sudden sharp relief. The mountain may have hidden Deputy Casey's vehicle, but not the pulsingly eerie glow from his flashing emergency lights. And if, from miles away, Joanna Brady knew the roadblock was there, so did a fleeing Hal Morgan.

"Lost radio contact," Joanna repeated. "How can that be?"

"Hold it," Tica said. "I'm getting something."

During the seemingly endless pause that followed, Joanna held her breath and drove like a maniac. Eventually Tica came back on the air. "Officer down, code three," she said. "Deputy Casey has abandoned the roadblock and is on his way to the scene. So's an emergency medical squad from Douglas."

"What the hell happened?"

"Morgan rammed the patrol car," Tica Romero answered. "Flipped him right over. According to Deputy Long, he's pinned inside his vehicle and needs help."

Even as Tica spoke, the flashing lights of Deputy Casey's patrol car appeared from around the curve and came speeding south. Between Joanna's Blazer and that one there was no sign of any other vehicle.

"And the suspect?"

"Gone," Tica answered.

Except it wasn't possible that he was gone completely. "He didn't come north past Deputy Casey?"

"Not so far."

And no vehicle had come southbound toward Joanna, either. That meant Hal Morgan was out there somewhere, out on the vast plain of the Sulphur Springs Valley, and about to make good his escape. Joanna was north of Rucker Canyon Road by then. That meant he couldn't have turned off there.

Her first urge was to go racing off to the scene, to do what she could to help Deputy Long. But the truth was, help for him was on the way—both in the form of Deputy Casey and the emergency medical technicians from Douglas. Joanna's prime concern had to be capturing Hal Morgan.

Forcing herself to respond logically, Joanna pulled over, stopped on the shoulder of the road, and doused the lights. Groping in the glove box, she located a pair of long-range night-vision binocular goggles. Several pairs had found their way into Joanna's department through participation in the M.J.F., a multi-jurisdiction task force created solely to help local authorities deal with border-focused crime.

As Joanna scanned the horizon, the flashing lights of Deputy Casey's southbound patrol car were even more clearly visible. Between Joanna and the flashing lights was a slowly dissipating cloud of dust. She was sure the dust marked the site of the ramming. Shaking her head, Joanna resolutely turned the goggles away from there and looked out toward the black mound of the Chiricahuas rising out of the desert to the east. Slowly she scanned back and forth between Highway 191 and the mountains along what she thought had to be the approximate location of Highway 181. There were other, smaller, roads the suspect might have taken, but 181 was the main road leading up to the Wonderland of Rocks, a most popular camping and picnicking area known officially as the Chiricahua National Monument. The road was paved and well-maintained, for one thing, and it was the only route that would offer Hal Morgan any real chance of escape. If the suspect stayed on 181, skirting along at the base of the mountains, eventually he would come to a junction with Highway 186. That would take him into Willcox. And beyond that, onto Interstate 10.

Forcing herself to be patient, Joanna continued to scan the horizon. Eventually—after a space of several minutes—it paid off. In a place where, a moment earlier, there had been nothing, there was now a speeding vehicle. Not one that was starting from a dead stop. No, this one was already traveling at full speed when the headlights came on. No, make that headlight. A single lamp. From a vehicle no doubt damaged by running into another.

"Got him!" Joanna yelped triumphantly to the emptiness of the starlit desert sky.

Racing back to the car, she fastened her belt before slamming the car into gear. The tires sprayed rocks and dirt high into the air behind her as she plunged forward onto the highway. As soon as the Blazer was safely back on the pavement, she switched on the radio.

"Suspect vehicle, missing one headlight, is eastbound on 181, probably two to three miles east of 191."

"Copy," Tica replied.

"Contact the Highway Patrol," Joanna continued. "We need them to set up a roadblock south of Willcox where 181 meets 186. If he makes it all the way into Willcox, we may lose him completely."

By then, she had reached the place where Deputy Casey's patrol car was pulled over on the shoulder of the road. Neither Deputy Long nor his wrecked vehicle was visible from the Blazer until Joanna reached a spot where a wash crossed the road. There they were, down in the wash. Barely slowing, Joanna drove straight past.

"I just drove by Deputies Long and Casey," Joanna said. "What's the status?" she asked.

"Deputy Long is conscious and talking," Tica replied. "The ambulance is still a good fifteen minutes out."

Fifteen minutes! In a situation like that, fifteen minutes could mean the difference between life and death for Deputy Casey. And fifteen minutes was a terribly long time for Joanna to go without backup. Still, she couldn't very well expect Deputy Casey to walk away, leaving his fellow officer gravely injured and alone.

"As soon as emergency crews reach the scene, tell Casey to follow me on 181. I'll need him for backup, but not until someone's there to take care of Deputy Long. Got that?"

"Got it," Tica replied.

Gripping the wheel, flying toward the looming darkness of the Chiricahuas, Joanna felt incredibly alone. Once again her hands were so sweaty and slick that it was all she could do to maintain control of the Blazer.

It had been years since she had traveled Highway 181, but she knew it all too well. It led to a place in the mountains where volcanic activity, combined with wind and water erosion, had carved a forest of spindly rhyolite columns and magically balanced boulders. As a child, that part of the Chiricahuas had been Joanna Lathrop's favorite place on earth. Her love affair had ended fifteen years earlier, when Big Hank Lathrop died on that road while bringing home a carload of Girl Scout weekend campers. Since that day, Joanna had never once returned to the Wonderland of Rocks.

Now, for the first time since that fateful Sunday afternoon, Joanna Lathrop Brady was back on that same stretch of highway. Her father had come to his end unwittingly. When he stopped to change a stranded motorist's tire, there had been no way for him to tell in advance that his life was in danger. This was different. Joanna was up against a known killer. Hal Morgan was someone who hadn't hesitated at resorting to violence on more than one occasion.

Joanna knew she was doing the right thing. She had no intention of tackling Morgan on her own. She had called for assistance and fully intended to wait until her backup arrived, but what if help came too late? What if lightning struck twice in the same place? Maybe Highway 181 would take Joanna's life in much the same way it had taken her father's.

Not bloody likely, she muttered under her breath. With that, she reached again for the radio.

18

"**WHAT'S** happening with the Highway Patrol?" Joanna demanded into the radio.

"They're moving," Tica responded. "They have vehicles headed into the area coming from both Bowie and Texas Canyon. It's going to take time for them to get into position. We've also asked the Willcox City Marshal for assistance. The problem is . . ."

"I know. Timing. What about Deputy Casey?"

"The ambulance crew and Chief Deputy Voland both just reached the scene. That means Casey's on his way to you, along with Deputies Voland and Hollicker. The emergency response team is also on its way."

"Good," Joanna said. An intense feeling of relief washed over her. Help was coming. Whatever happened, she wouldn't have to face it alone.

The road was more winding now. Staying on it required all her concentration as she raced through what she knew to be scrub-oak-dotted foothills. Zigging and zagging and bouncing through one wash after another, it was impossible to see any distance ahead. The only consolation was that if she couldn't see very far ahead or behind her, then neither could Hal Morgan. If the Willcox City Marshal was moving into position at the junction, Hal Morgan wouldn't have the same kind of long-term warning he'd had of the roadblock at Township Butte. This time, maybe, they'd catch him.

"Sheriff Brady." The radio squawked again.

"Yes."

"Tom Givens from the city of Willcox is now in place," Tica reported.

"He didn't meet anybody coming northbound?"

"Not so far."

Joanna breathed a sigh of relief. "Good. Then we still have a chance of catching him. Givens knows what we're up against?"

"He's been warned."

So have I, Joanna thought.

The road took a sharp jog to the left and then straightened again. Ahead, Joanna could see the flashing lights of Tom Givens's patrol car. Between Joanna and the lights, there was nothing—no sign of any other vehicle, not on the road nor on either side of it.

"Damn!" Joanna muttered under her breath. "We've lost him again."

When she reached the junction where Highway 181 heads off up into the monument itself, she found that both lanes of the roadway were blocked by a Ford Taurus bearing a city of Willcox insignia.

Recognizing her, Tom Givens stepped out of the vehicle. "Hey, there, Sheriff Brady. Got here just as fast as I could. Didn't see anything along the way," he added. "Not a damned soul. Do you think maybe he might have stopped off at one of the ranches?"

"Douse your lights for a minute," Joanna said. "Just long enough for me to check something out. You can turn them on again if you see anybody coming."

Once again she grabbed up the night-vision goggles. This time she trained them on the part of Highway 181 that climbed up the mountainside.

"There he is," she crowed a minute later when she finally spotted the glow of a single headlight from a moving vehicle. "That's got to be him."

"But why the hell is he going up there?" Tom Givens asked. "There's only one way in and one way out."

"That's right," Joanna said. "We both know that, but maybe this guy doesn't. Hal Morgan is from out of town. Get on the radio and notify the ranger station to be on the lookout. And contact my department, too. My backup's on the way. They'll need to know we've got him cornered."

With that, Joanna headed back for the Blazer. Givens followed her. "The biggest danger is going to come when Morgan figures that out for himself. Do you want me to come along?"

Joanna shook her head. "No. You stay here, just in case he manages to double back and slip by me after all. And get your lights turned back on so somebody doesn't run into you in the dark."

Wrenching the Blazer into a quick U-turn, Joanna started off up the mountain. She was surprised to realize that her hands were no longer sweating. Maybe the bracing chill outside while she talked with Tom Givens had cured the sweat problem. True, she was still scared, but she was also amazingly calm. It was as though the interior of the Blazer had become the eye of a storm. In that sudden stillness Joanna Brady did something she had forgotten to do before. She prayed.

Thank you, God, for bringing us this far. Be with Debbie Howell and Ted Long. And be with me, too. Please.

Just as Tom Givens had pointed out, the biggest danger would come when Hal Morgan finally figured out that he had nowhere else to run. Joanna had no doubt that he'd come tearing back down the mountain then, intent on getting away no matter what the cost. And until her backup arrived, Joanna Brady was all that stood between him and possible freedom.

What had set him off? she found herself wondering. He had seemed so reasonable when she talked to him in the hospital. According to Father Michael McCrady, Morgan had followed her advice and had been in touch with Burton Kimball about retaining him as a defense attorney. What, then, would have provoked him into going on a suicidal rampage in which he had attacked two of her deputies?

None of it made sense, but then it didn't have to. Someone who would take the law into his own hands—someone who would resort to murder in the first place—couldn't be thought to be long on logic. As Joanna steered her way up that twisting mountainous road, she took some small comfort in the realization that she wasn't the only one who had been fooled by Hal Morgan's protestations of innocence. Father Michael McCrady had been, too.

Rounding a particularly sharp curve where one massive five-ton boulder balanced on top of another, she had to jam on the brakes to keep from rear-ending the Buick. Lights out, it was stopped in the middle of the roadway. Too late, she realized this had to be a trap. Hal Morgan was waiting for her, knowing she, too, would have no place to run.

Switching off the engine and dousing the lights, she ducked down on the seat and waited, breathless, for the barrage of gunfire she knew had to come. While Joanna's heart pounded in her throat, the seconds ticked slowly by. There was no sound, no sign of movement from the other vehicle. By then Joanna had her Colt in her hand, ready to return fire if necessary. But none came. Finally, with agonizing slowness, she raised her head. Expecting a bullet to slice into her at any moment, she nonetheless raised herself far enough to peer out over the dash.

As far as she could see, the darkened vehicle was empty. Still expecting a trap, however, she scrambled around until she could reach the switch on her side-mounted spotlight. Turning it on, she sent a blinding beam of light in the direction of the Buick.

With both the inside and outside of the vehicle brilliantly illuminated, there was still no sign of life anywhere around the Buick. Cautiously, Joanna rolled down the driver's window on the Blazer. Immediately her nostrils were assailed by the acrid odor of burned oil. It smelled as though the engine had lost oil and eventually seized up. If so, that would account for why the Buick was stopped in the middle of the road. No doubt the driver had simply bailed out and headed off into the wilderness.

"Mr. Morgan," Joanna called, relieved that there was no audible tremor in her voice. "We know you're here. Come out with your hands up. That way no one else will get hurt. Mr. Morgan?"

Holding her breath, Joanna listened for an answer. None came. Nothing.

"Mr. Morgan," she called again. "Where are you?"

This time there was an answer, but not from a voice. Instead of coming from the surrounding woods, there was a muffled thumping noise that seemed to come from the vehicle itself.

Straining her ears, Joanna cautiously opened the door to the Blazer and set one tentative foot on the grainy pavement.

"Mr. Morgan. We're here to help you. Come out with your hands up."

Once again, she heard the thumping noise. This time she was sure that the sound was coming from the vehicle, from somewhere inside the Buick. Keeping herself half hidden behind the scanty cover of the car door, Joanna wondered what she should do. Walk forward until she was close enough to look in the window? Even as she framed the question, she knew that doing that without proper backup could be fatal.

"Mr. Morgan," she called again, pleading this time. "Give yourself up. Come out with your hands up. We don't want to hurt you."

Now, though, in addition to the thumping, there were muffled cries as well—the grunting, indecipherable groans made by someone desperately trying to communicate but unable to speak. For the first time Joanna considered the possibility that in the process of bolting from the motel, Morgan might have taken someone else prisoner as well. Father McCrady maybe? Someone from the motel—a maid or, perhaps, a fellow guest?

The very thought made Joanna's knees go weak. The thumping came again. More urgently now. Whoever was in the trunk wasn't there of his or her own volition. So where was Morgan? Was he out in the woods somewhere waiting for Joanna to show herself, or was there a possibility that he, too, remained hidden in the Buick? Maybe he had been injured somewhere along the way. Meanwhile, where the hell was her backup?

The pounding came again, but along with the pounding, there was something else as well—a dimly flickering light that hadn't been there a moment before. At the same time she saw the light, she smelled smoke—the pungent odor of burning vinyl. The front seat of the Buick was on fire. Whoever was locked in the trunk was about to be burned alive. There was no time to weigh her own safety against the life of the prisoner in the trunk. Nor could there be any question of waiting for backup.

Racing forward, she flung open the door to the Buick. The whole front seat was aflame by then, from the floorboard back. She punched the trunk release, but nothing happened. With her heart sinking in her chest, she realized that the trunk-release wires that ran under the dash must have already melted.

Spinning around, Joanna holstered the Colt, darted back to the Blazer, and wrenched open the back door. A moment later, her grasping fingers closed around the crowbar she kept on the floorboard under the seat.

It only took a matter of seconds for her to reach for the crowbar, but by then, when she turned back to the Buick, the whole interior of the vehicle was engulfed in flames. There wasn't a second to lose.

Returning to it, she stood for a moment before the closed trunk, trapped in indecision. If she battered the keyhole in, would that release the latch and open the lid? Or would she be better off trying to pry it open?

In the end, that's what she decided. Shoving the business end of the crowbar as far as she could under the trunk lid, she used every bit of strength she possessed to pull on the crowbar. The stiff sheet metal gave a little, but not enough. Not nearly enough. The lock still held firm.

The fire was burning hot enough now that she could feel the heat of it against her face. Another frantic set of pounding, weaker now, came from inside the trunk.

Please, Joanna prayed, leaving God to fill in the blanks. *Please!*

Feeling as though her arms were going to burst with the strain of it, she pulled a second time. And a third. On the fourth, when the lock finally gave way and the lid popped open, she almost plunged headfirst into the trunk herself.

The smoke was in her eyes and nose. She could barely see, but she could feel. Dropping the crowbar, she reached blindly into the trunk. Her hands closed around a pair of trouser-clad legs. Partway up the legs, her fingers encountered a knotted rope. The victim in the trunk was lying on his side, trussed and facing the backseat. He was breathing the hot noxious fumes that were pouring into the trunk.

Still panting with exertion, Joanna tried grasping the man around the waist. He was too big, too heavy. She couldn't budge him. "You've got to help me," she yelled at him. "I can't do it alone."

But there was no response. The fumes had done their work. Bracing her shoulder under him, Joanna finally managed to raise him a few inches off the floor of the trunk when she heard someone behind her.

"What the hell . . . !" Dick Voland exclaimed. "Hollicker, come quick!"

Joanna had never in her life been so glad to see someone.

It took six hands to lift the unconscious man clear of the trunk and carry him back behind the Blazer and far enough

around the curve to be out of harm's way. Next Deputy Hollicker shoved the Blazer into reverse and moved it as well.
And just in time, too. With a terrifying whoosh, the Buick's
gas tank exploded.

Joanna, gasping for breath and coughing her lungs out,
fell to her hands and knees. When the Buick went up, she
heard it go and felt the sudden burst of heat, but she didn't
see it. Then there were hands on her shoulders, pulling her
up.

"Are you all right, Joanna?" Dick Voland asked.

"I'm fine," she choked. "It's just the smoke . . ."

He took her firmly by the arm. "Come on. We've called
for the rangers. They're bringing fire-fighting equipment, so
we'd better get out of the way."

Back at the Blazer, Joanna stood for a moment looking up
at the burning car. "We've loaded Morgan into the rear of
your vehicle," Voland said. "Can you drive, or do you want
me to?"

"Morgan?" Joanna asked, not quite understanding. "Hal
Morgan? You mean you found him, too?"

Voland looked down at her. "Didn't you see him? He was
the guy we pulled out of the trunk."

All Joanna could do was shake her head. And when she
reached for the door handle, there was no strength left in her
hands. Voland opened the door for her. "I'll get in on the
other side," she said. "You'd better drive."

Helping her along as though she were an invalid, Voland
led her around the vehicle and lifted her into the passenger
seat. Then he jogged back and jumped into the driver's seat.

"You realize that if you'd been even thirty seconds later,
Morgan would have bought it. How the hell did you manage
to get that damned trunk open?"

Joanna looked across the seat. Against an orange back-drop, her chief deputy's face stood out in sharp relief. Even through the choking coughs, Joanna could see the concern and compassion written there. She had also heard the pride in his voice. It was easy to see how someone like Ruth Voland might read something into that look that wasn't there.

"I don't know," Joanna returned, then lapsed into yet another fit of shuddering coughs.

She turned around and looked at Hal Morgan. His legs were still tied, but his hands were free. Part of a duct-tape gag was still stuck to his face. He, too, was coughing and choking, trying to clear the bitter, chemical-laced smoke out of his lungs. There were dozens of questions she wanted to ask, but those would have to wait—until they both stopped coughing.

Fortunately, the single tree that had caught fire was far enough from its neighbors that no other trees burned with it. That was partially due to the fact that the fire truck and rang-ers were there within minutes and were able to keep the flames from spreading. Directed by the rangers, a contingent of deputies helped deal with the fire. Once it was out, they settled down to await the arrival of the canine unit. Mean-while, at a turnoff two miles back down the road, Joanna Brady and Dick Voland finally had a chance to interview Hal Morgan. He was bruised and battered from being knocked around in the trunk, but other than that, he seemed fine.

"How did it happen?" she asked.

Morgan shook his head. "I'm not sure. Stupidity, I guess. I spent the afternoon in my room working on my laptop. Ever since Bonnie died, I've been keeping a journal, thinking that someday I might want to try having it published. I was ex-pecting Father McCrady around seven or so. He was seeing friends earlier. We were going to go have a late dinner together, but time got away from me. That happens sometimes when I'm writing. When I realized how late it was, I dashed into the shower. I was in the bathroom just finishing putting on my clothes when someone came bursting into the room."

"Into the bathroom?" Joanna asked.

"That's right," Hal said. "It caught me completely off guard. The door hit me square on the shoulder and pitched me all the way into the tub. Headfirst. It's a wonder I didn't break my neck. Before I had a chance to get my legs back on the floor, something jabbed me in the butt. That's the last I remember."

"Jabbed you. Like a needle, you mean?"

Hal nodded. "That's right," he said. "It felt like a bee sting. Whatever it was, it knocked me for a loop. I don't remember a thing after that until a little while ago, when I woke up in the trunk smelling smoke. You had a guard on me, Sheriff Brady. How did this guy get past the deputy?"

"Cold-cocked her with a beer bottle," Dick Voland said gruffly. "You say guy. Did you see your attacker?"

"No."

"How do you know it was a guy?"

"Because of the way the door hit me. There was real power behind it. Not only that, whoever did it must have lugged me out to the car."

Voland nodded. "I see what you mean," he said. "What about the suicide note?" he added.

Morgan looked puzzled. "Suicide note? What suicide note?"

"The one we found on the computer screen in your room."

Hal Morgan shook his head. "I never wrote anything of the kind," he said.

Joanna turned to Dick Voland. "Who does our composites?"

"We never do composites."

"We're doing one now," Joanna said. "Call up to Tucson and check with both Tucson P.D. and the Pima County Sheriff's Department. Find out who does theirs and see what it would cost to have him or her come down tomorrow. We'll have him go to the hospital and get one from Deputy Long, and then we'll take him out to Elfrida and get one from the clerk in the gas station and from anyone else who may have seen the man."

"You want to do that on Saturday?" Voland objected. "That'll cost a fortune. I thought there was a budget crunch."

"There is," Joanna said. "Since it's a kidnapping, we could always call in the Feds . . ."

"No, no," Voland agreed quickly. "I'll do it."

For a moment, the three people shut inside Joanna's idling Blazer were quiet.

"It's a frame, isn't it," Hal Morgan said at last. "Whoever killed Bucky Buckwalter figured you'd blame me. When it didn't work the first time because that girl dragged me out of the barn, the killer decided to try again. This time with a phony suicide note. The only thing that saved me is the fact that the Buick burned oil like it was going out of style." He looked questioningly at Joanna. "Would you have fallen for it?"

"I'd like to think my people are better investigators than that," she said. "Unfortunately, there's always a chance it might have worked."

"Will he try again?"

Dick Voland was the one who answered that question. "I'd give that one a definite yes. Obviously we can't take you back to the Rest Inn. Does anyone have a better idea?"

After some discussion, they finally decided to call on Father McCrady. One of his friends from seminary was the priest at Saint Dominick's in Old Bisbee. That's where Father McCrady was staying. One phone call was all it took to make arrangements for Hal Morgan to stay there as well. A few minutes after Dick Voland left to deliver Morgan to the church rectory, Ernie Carpenter parked behind Joanna's Blazer.

"So much for my weekend off," he said. "What's happening?"

With that, Joanna launched off into a detailed recitation of the evening's events.

The rest of the night, spent mostly in waiting, passed slowly. For the second time in two days, Joanna Brady found herself stamping around in the cold and the dark while the Cochise County departmental canine unit did its stuff—to no avail. It was almost midnight when the search for the missing driver of Hal Morgan's Buick was finally called off for the night. Rusty, a muscle-bound German shepherd, had led his partner, Mike Cordell, on a trail that went from the charred remains of the Buick to a deserted public campground half a mile back downhill. That was where the scent disappeared.

"Whoever it was must have had a car parked here to begin with," Cordell explained later to Joanna. "Or else there was an accomplice waiting there the whole time."

"But wouldn't Tom Givens have seen them if they came back down the mountain after we were here?"

Cordell shook his head. "Not necessarily. If whoever was driving was familiar enough with the lay of the land, he might have known that there are a couple of private roads—ranch roads—that he could have taken. Following those, he could have made it all the way back to Elfrida without once touching the highway."

"Damn!" Joanna exclaimed. "We had him and I let him get away. Why didn't I think about checking out the picnic area earlier? I must have driven right past it."

Ernie Carpenter was philosophical about the oversight. "I expect you had one or two other things on your mind right about then," he said. "I know I would have."

It was one-thirty when Joanna finally turned onto the road to High Lonesome Ranch. She had been so focused on what was happening with Hal Morgan that, until she drove back into the yard, she hadn't given Butch Dixon's presence there a single thought. She was surprised, though, to drive up and find the whole house ablaze with lights.

When she walked into the house, though, the place was dead quiet. Even the dogs, locked in the bedroom with Jenny, didn't raise a racket. In the living room, Joanna discovered Butch Dixon sound asleep on her couch. His shirt was on the back of the easy chair. His boots and socks were on the floor beside the couch. One of Eva Lou Brady's afghans covered him from chest to toe. There didn't seem to be much point in waking the poor guy up just to send him back to his hotel.

Afraid that turning off the lights might disturb him, Joanna left him as he was while she disappeared into her own room. She set the alarm for seven and then tumbled into bed. Not surprisingly, she was asleep within seconds of putting her head on the pillow.

She awakened minutes before the alarm to the smell of brewing coffee and the sounds of Jenny laughing. For a moment she thought Andy was back. He had always been up early on weekends to make coffee and cook waffles and to share what he called "Daddy time" with his daughter. But then Joanna heard the unfamiliar cadence of a male voice and she remembered that Butch Dixon was there. He had spent the night on the living room couch.

Pulling on a robe and taking a stab at flattening her sleep-bent hair, Joanna hurried out of the bedroom. She found Jenny and Butch in the kitchen, where pieces of her vacuum cleaner were spread all over the breakfast nook. Frowning in concentration, Butch was pulling something out of the guts of the machine while Jenny, fascinated, watched over his shoulder.

"What in the world are you doing?" she asked.

Butch looked up at her and grinned. "Making myself useful," he said. "Unless I'm sadly mistaken, once I get all the pieces put back together, this little hummer is going to work better than it has in years. By the way, I've fixed the broken handle on your silverware drawer and repaired the living room lamp that was falling apart. Later on today, if you'll show me where you keep your washers, I'll tackle that leaky kitchen faucet."

Joanna was stunned. How dare he come in here and start fixing things? "Just what exactly . . . ?" she began indignantly.

"Now, now," he soothed. "What did you expect me to do, sit around and twiddle my thumbs? You don't even have decent TV reception. I was bored. How about breakfast? Jenny tells me that on Saturdays, waffles are the order of the day. I make a mean waffle."

Jenny appeared at Joanna's elbow with a freshly poured cup of coffee in her hand. She passed the mug along to her mother. "I told Butch that if he isn't done with the vacuum cleaner, we can eat in the dining room. I'll even set the table."

"Butch?" Joanna asked.

"I said it was all right for her to call me that," Butch said quickly. "I hope you don't mind."

Shaking her head and knowing she was licked, Joanna took the coffee and sank down onto the bench. "What's wrong with the vacuum?" she asked.

"Part of the problem was all the dog hair hung up on a paper clip in the middle of the hose. I've been tinkering with the motor, though, too. You're going to be amazed when I put it back together."

Butch's high spirits were somehow irresistibly infectious. "I'm sure I will be," she said with a smile. "Have you two made any other plans while my back's been turned?"

"He wants to go on the underground-mine tour," Jenny said. "And to ride over to Tombstone to see Boothill. Can I go along, Mom? Please?"

"You could come, too," Butch offered, looking at Joanna.

Joanna glanced at the clock over the refrigerator. "I'm afraid not. I'll probably have to go into the office today, at least for a while."

The look of disappointment that crossed Jenny's face put a hole in Joanna's heart. "I guess I can't go," Jenny said.

"Wait a minute," Joanna said. "Just because I can't go doesn't mean you can't. You can take the Eagle."

With a sigh of satisfaction, Butch put down the vacuum cleaner motor, stood up, and sauntered over to the kitchen sink to wash his hands. "No Eagle," he said firmly. "Jenny and I'll wing it."

"But . . ." Joanna's tentative objection was immediately overruled.

He grinned at Jenny. "Have helmet and leather jacket. Will travel. But first, you'd better set the table."

19

$ E E I N G$ that the waffle-making was in good hands, Joanna abandoned the kitchen for the shower. She was just starting to towel herself dry when Jenny pounded on the door. "Mom," she said. "Phone. It's Marianne. They're home."

Hastily pulling Andy's old robe over her dripping body, Joanna took the call in her bedroom. "Hello?"

"You're not going to believe this," Marianne Maculyea babbled happily. "There are two of them."

"Two of what?"

"Two babies. Two girls. Ruth and Esther. That's what we're calling them. That was what was going on with Jeff— what he couldn't tell me over the phone or write about, either. And it's why he needed the extra company. He was afraid one of the officials might take offense and change his mind."

Joanna was floored. "You have two?"

"That's right. One of the nurses in the orphanage came to Jeff secretly a little over two weeks ago and told him about Esther. Ruth, her sister, was the baby we were supposed to get originally. Esther would have been left behind. The nurse told Jeff that without Ruth sharing her food, she was sure Esther would die—probably would have died already. Once Jeff knew Ruth and Esther were twins, he couldn't bear to separate them."

"Two. Why, Mari, that's wonderful," Joanna managed as Marianne Maculyea rushed on.

"You should see her, Joanna. She's so tiny—so much smaller than Ruth. It is a wonder she's still alive. They're so different in size that you can hardly tell they're twins. But they are. Ruth is already walking. Esther can't even sit up by herself."

"If they're twins, how can they be so different?" Joanna asked.

There was a slight hiccup in Marianne's happy rush of words. "Esther seems to have some . . . health challenges. She has a heart murmur of some kind. That's why they weren't going to let her go. And that's the other reason Jeff was determined to take her. Left untreated, she'd be dead within months, maybe even weeks."

As she listened, Joanna had dropped into a chair. In all the years she had known Marianne—from junior high on—Joanna had never once heard her friend blither, but that was what Marianne was doing now—blithering. Joanna felt her own eyes brimming with tears of love and concern.

"How serious a heart murmur?" she asked. "And can it be fixed?"

"We don't know yet," Marianne said. "Maybe, with proper medical care and some nourishment. We have an appointment with a cardiologist in Tucson for early next week. In the meantime, she's eating like there's no tomorrow. They both are. As soon as I saw them, I was worried about having only one crib, but Jeff said that's how they sleep—together.

The nurse told him that when they separated them, they were both inconsolable. That the only way they could quiet Esther was by putting Ruth in the crib with her. I think that's why the nurse told him in the first place.

"Jeff kept the whole thing a secret because he wasn't sure he'd be able to pull it off. He was afraid there'd be some kind of last-minute hitch. He could have called once they got to the airport, but he didn't. He decided he wanted to surprise me. Isn't he wonderful?"

"He's wonderful all right," Joanna said.

"When can you come meet them? Do you want to come for coffee later on this morning?"

Joanna laughed. "Are you sure you want company?"

"Absolutely."

"We're about to have breakfast. We'll stop by around ten, but just for a minute. Long enough to say hello. Most likely a friend of mine from out of town will be with us. If you don't mind, that is."

By the time Joanna got off the phone, breakfast was ready. Over breakfast she told Butch about Jeff and Marianne. Joanna and Butch were drinking coffee when the phone rang again.

"It's Sue Espy," Jenny said, holding her hand over the mouthpiece. "She wants to know if I can spend the night tonight."

"Do you want to?" Joanna asked.

"Well?" Jenny said. Surprisingly enough, she was looking at Butch rather than her mother.

Butch looked uncomfortable. "Your mother and I haven't had a chance to discuss it yet."

"Discuss what?"

"I was talking to Jenny earlier about the three of us going

out to dinner again tonight, but to a nice place this time."

Joanna turned back to her daughter. "It's up to you, Jenny. If you want to go to Sue's, that's fine."

Jenny put the phone back to her ear. She listened for a while. Finally she nodded. "Okay," she said. "But I won't come over until sometime later on this afternoon."

Butch sighed and shook his head. "Stood up again," he said. "Just my luck. How about you? Would you consider going to dinner with me anyway?"

"On one condition," Joanna told him.

"What's that?"

"We go in my car. I'm not built for motorcycles."

The phone rang again, almost as soon as Jenny put it down. She answered and, after a moment, handed the receiver to her mother.

"Matt Bly, the composite guy, is due here at ten," Dick Voland announced in his customarily brusque fashion. "We'll go from here to the hospital to interview Deputy Long, and from there out to Elfrida to see the gas-station clerk."

"Who's 'we'?" Joanna asked.

"Jaime Carbajal," Voland answered. "I figured that would give me a chance to check him out and see how he does when he's working solo."

"How about if I meet you at the hospital?" Joanna suggested. "I need to stop by and see how Debbie Howell and Ted Long are doing."

"All right," Voland said, "but be advised. It's just like I said it would be. We're paying through the nose for this guy. I don't want to waste any of his time."

Once the breakfast dishes were loaded into the dishwasher, Jenny gathered up her overnight gear. Then she stood with an impish grin on her face while Butch Dixon zipped her into an oversized jacket and fastened on a helmet. "Ready?" he said.

"Ready," Jenny returned.

To Joanna's ear Jenny's voice sounded strangely hollow and grown up, echoing through the plastic. As she watched Jenny climb onto the motorcycle and settle on behind Butch, Joanna felt her heart constrict. The idea of Jenny's riding off on the thing was terrifying. *What if something happened? What if there was an accident?*

Jenny, on the other hand, was thrilled beyond bearing and waving with delight as Butch Dixon started the smooth-sounding engine.

"See you at Marianne and Jeff's," she crowed. "Bet we'll beat you there."

"No bet," Joanna replied.

Butch grinned at her. "Don't worry," he told her over the drone of the engine. "There are old riders and bold riders, but no old bold riders. I'll be careful."

Shaking her head and stepping out of the way, Joanna couldn't help laughing at that, which was obviously exactly what Butch had intended.

On her way up to the Canyon Methodist parsonage in Old Bisbee, following behind the motorcycle, Joanna gave herself points. After all, she *had* let Jenny go. She had overcome her own objections and let her daughter do something daring, rather than holding Jenny too close and trying to protect her from everything, from life itself.

At the parsonage the three newcomers were part of a stream of well-wishers. They stayed for only a few minutes—long enough for introductions. Ruth was a shy but bright-eyed little one who clung fiercely to Jeff Daniels and didn't want him out of her sight. By comparison, Esther was a pale reflection of her sister. To Joanna's way of thinking, Esther Maculyea Daniels looked very ill indeed. She lay, silent and listless, in Marianne's arms, brightening only when Ruth's face happened to appear in her line of vision.

"I can see why Jeff couldn't bear to leave her," Joanna said quietly.

Marianne nodded while her eyes filled with unshed tears.

"Esther's going to be just fine." Joanna spoke the comforting words with far more conviction than she felt. "Do you have everything you need? Is there anything I can get you?"

"Prayers," Marianne answered. "I think we're going to need a lot of those."

As a new batch of visitors descended on the parsonage, Joanna, Butch, and Jenny headed out. Watching Jenny's halo of golden hair disappear once more into Butch's spare helmet, Joanna found something to be thankful for—two things especially. Not only was Jenny healthy—she was also a long way out of diapers.

She had barely made it to her desk when Ernie Carpenter shambled into her office. There had been dark circles under his eyes on Friday. If anything, now they were worse—almost black rather than merely purple.

"It's Saturday," she pointed out. "I told you to take the weekend off. What are you doing here?"

"These loose ends are killing me," he said. "I can't sleep anyway, so I could just as well be working."

Joanna shook her head. "You look like hell, Detective Carpenter, but we do need you. Next week for sure you're to take some time off. Understood?"

"Right," he said.

"In the meantime, I'm on my way over to the hospital to

watch Mr. Bly, the composite artist, do his stuff. Care to join me?"

"Sure."

They were in Joanna's Blazer, headed for the hospital, when Ernie tapped his head. "I almost forgot to tell you. I spent some time late yesterday afternoon with the guy out at the Rob Roy."

"Peter Wilkes?"

"That's the one. Evidently Terry Buckwalter really is one hell of a golfer. Shoots in the high sixties and low seventies most of the time. As a consequence, there are only a few guys out there, besides the pro, who are willing to golf with her. But he did come up with the name of one guy who has gone out with her several times, even though she's walked all over him. Larry Matkin. Isn't he the young mining engineer who works for P.D.?"

Joanna nodded.

"And wasn't he at the funeral yesterday, too?"

"He was," Joanna said. "Not only that, he called me on Thursday and left a message for me to call him back. I've tried several times, but I've never been able to catch him."

"After this deal at the hospital," Ernie said thoughtfully, "maybe we ought to interview him."

"Sounds great," Joanna said. "Any idea where he lives?"

"No," Ernie said. "But it won't take long to find out."

In Joanna's head, the words "composite-sketch artist" had evoked the picture of an artist—a properly bereted, goateed, and smocked middle-aged man with a sketch pad in one hand and a fistful of charcoal in the other. From that standpoint, Matt Bly hardly measured up. He turned out to be tiny—five feet four, and incredibly young—twenty-four or twenty-five at the outside. He wore thick glasses, had a severely receding chin, and used a laptop computer rather than pad and pencil.

Joanna looked in on a recovering Debbie Howell on her way to Deputy Long's room. When she arrived, the composite creation process was already in full swing. As far as she could see, the whole thing proved to be exceedingly slow, exacting, and eventually disappointing. It had been evening and Deputy Long had been too far away from the suspect to pick up the kinds of painstaking details necessary to put together a successful composite. When Matt Bly pronounced the picture finished, there wasn't anything about it that was the least bit familiar. The artist, however, didn't seem at all discouraged.

"That's all right," he said. "By the time I put this together with the witness we're going to see in Elfrida, it'll be better. Just you wait and see."

While Joanna had been watching the artist in action, Ernie had been out in the corridor using a pay phone to track down Larry Matkin's address. When Joanna came looking for him, the detective was scribbling something in his notebook.

"Got it, Sheriff Brady," he announced. "Matkin lives in a rented trailer out by Gold Gulch."

They took the Rifle Range Road to a trailer parked on the first gentle slopes of Gold Hill. "Why would anyone want to live all the way out here?" Joanna asked, looking up at the steep but knobby mound of rock that Bisbee's school-aged rock climbers knew as Geronimo.

"Beats me," Ernie Carpenter said with a laugh, "but it looks like you don't have much room to talk. The High Lonesome isn't exactly Grand Central Station. Besides, there's nothing wrong with this. He's got phone, electricity, and propane. What more could you want?"

The old-fashioned trailer—a moldering relic from the fifties or sixties—was parked on a concrete slab. Out behind the trailer was a long empty corral. There were no vehicles parked anywhere in sight, and when they pounded on the front door, no one answered. Drawn curtains made seeing inside the place impossible.

Leaving the door, Ernie sauntered over to the edge of the slab and then squatted down to examine the dusty earth. "Looks to me as though this is where he usually parks," Ernie said. "But I'd say he hasn't been home today. These tracks are from yesterday at least, maybe even earlier."

"Do you know his boss?" Joanna asked.

"Skip Lowell, the general manager? Sure," Ernie said, "I know him."

"Why don't we go check with him," Joanna suggested. "Maybe he'll know if Larry's been called out of town. While I drive, maybe you can call in and get Skip Lowell's address."

"Don't have to," Ernie said. "When he and Mindy came back to town, they moved into his mother's old place on the Vista. They're in the process of fixing it up. God knows it needs it. The renters the last owners had in the place really let it go."

After years of working for Phelps Dodge all over the world, Armand "Skip" Lowell had returned to his hometown as general manager of P.D.'s Bisbee operation. Mindy and Skip Lowell had been in town only a matter of weeks and were a long way into rehabbing the early-twentieth-century brick home that had once been one of Bisbee's finest.

Joanna and Ernie found Skip on his front porch. Clad in paint-speckled overalls with a matching sweatshirt, he was carefully using a paint-thinner-saturated cloth to remove several layers of black enamel from the leaded glass panels on either side of the front door.

Skip glanced up at them as they came up the walk. "Howdy, Sheriff Brady, Ernie," he said. "Would you please tell me why someone would use this crap to paint over every goddamned—excuse the expression—window in the place?" he grumbled.

"As I recall," Ernie said, "the last tenants who lived here didn't want any of their neighbors to see the glow of the grow-lights on their marijuana crop."

"I see," Skip said. Shaking his head in disgust, he kept right on cleaning. "What can I do for you?"

"What can you tell us about Larry Matkin?" Joanna asked.

Skip looked at her over the top of his drugstore glasses. "What do you want to know about him?"

"Do you have any idea where he is?"

"Probably out at his house," Skip offered.

Ernie shook his head. "We already checked," he said. "He's not there. Hasn't been all night, from the looks of it. Was he going out of town for the weekend, by any chance?"

"Not as far as I know." Skip put down the paint-blackened cloth and then used a clean towel sticking out of his back pocket to clean his hands. He closed the can of paint thinner. "What's this all about?" he asked. "It doesn't have anything to do with that dead veterinarian, does it?"

Joanna felt her whole body go on point. No doubt, Ernie's did the same. He was the one who fielded the question.

"It could," he said. "What makes you think it might?"

Skip seemed to consider for a moment before he answered. "When you come to a new post like this, it takes time to get the lay of the land. To figure out what's going on and who's responsible for what. All that sort of thing."

Joanna nodded. Taking over as general manager for the

local Phelps Dodge branch didn't sound all that different from taking over as sheriff.

"The guys in corporate up in Phoenix sent me down here to get things moving," he continued. "As you know, we thought we'd be reopening some operations last year, but there have been a few—well, shall we say—unforeseen complications. This has all been very hush-hush, but since the whole story's due to be released publicly sometime in the next few weeks, I'll go ahead and tell you now.

"As you may or may not know, when we decided to return to Bisbee, we had three separate locations we thought might be viable—one north of Don Luis, one just east of Old Bisbee, and one east of Saginaw. The idea was to take core samples from all three, figure out which one had the most potential, and then get that one on a fast track. That's what Larry Matkin's been doing—sampling ore and doing assay reports.

"According to those reports, the site east of Saginaw is far and away the winner. It has a major vein of ore, one that wasn't viable with the old technology. With electrowinning, the new technology, it is."

"If you've got the technology and you've got the ore, what's the problem?" Ernie asked.

Skip Lowell sighed. "When Lavender Pit was opened back in the fifties, homes that were in the way of that operation—places in Johnson's Addition, Jiggerville, and Upper Lowell—were loaded up on axles and trucked to company land elsewhere around town."

Joanna nodded. "Everybody in Bisbee knows about that," she said.

"What everybody doesn't know is that, in the process of moving all those houses, the company ran into a problem.

When they got to one house, a place that belonged to a guy named Melvin Kitteridge, he refused to budge. And the guy had a point. None of the other houses in Jiggerville had mineral rights. His house did. He finally agreed to move but only if the company agreed to give him the mineral rights to whatever other property they moved his house to. And that's exactly what they did. It was a quiet kind of deal. I don't think ten people in all knew about it. In fact, the Buckwalters themselves may not have realized . . .''

"You're saying the Buckwalters own the mineral rights to the property under the clinic?"

"That's right," Skip said. "As I said, most of the houses in Saginaw are located on land the company already owns. We've moved those houses once, and if we have to, we can move them again. The big difficulty is that the main body of ore seems to run directly through the tract we don't own."

"In other words," Joanna said, "when you gave it away forty-odd years ago, you shouldn't have. Now, in order to make the Saginaw site workable, you have to buy it back."

"You've got it," Skip Lowell said. "That's it in a nutshell."

"And you'll be buying it back from Terry Buckwalter?"

"Whoever the owner of record is, that's who we'll buy it from," Skip answered. "The lawyers will be coming down next week to make the offer."

"But what does all this have to do with Larry Matkin?" Ernie asked.

There was a slight hesitation before Skip answered. It could have been evasion, or simply reluctance.

"Obviously, Larry has known exactly what's going on. One day the project is on a fast track. The next, after some company researcher discovers the mineral-rights problem, everything grinds to a halt. Larry had to be told, but he was sworn to secrecy."

"You're worried that he's told someone?" Joanna asked.

Skip shook his head. "No, it's worse than that. In the past few weeks, I've become aware that there have been several unexplained absences on Larry's part. There've been times when I've tried to reach him when he clearly wasn't where he said he would be, where he was *supposed* to be. Late yesterday afternoon, through a fluke, I discovered that he's been golfing at a place out near Palominas. He's been doing it on company time and in the company of Terry Buckwalter. It could be it's all on the up-and-up. But I'm concerned that if they're involved somehow—romantically, I mean—that the company will end up with a conflict-of-interest problem."

Armand "Skip" Lowell was a company man to the bone. His sole worry lay in what kind of corporate repercussions might result from an inappropriate relationship between Terry Buckwalter and Larry Matkin.

Ernie Carpenter and Joanna Brady were cops. Both their minds turned to murder.

"How much is that property worth?" Joanna asked.

"Surely, you don't think . . ." Skip objected.

"How much?"

"Don't quote me on this," Skip cautioned. "The property is probably worth something in the upper six figures. Maybe even more."

Suddenly Joanna was thinking about Terry Buckwalter— about how pleased she had seemed to be at receiving what she considered fair value for her dead husband's defunct veterinary practice. She was hoping to come out of the deal with enough money to pay off her debts and maybe get away clean. She was counting on the insurance proceeds to fund her venture into the L.P.G.A. That didn't add up to an upper-six-figures kind of deal. It sounded to Joanna as though Terry Buckwalter was being shafted. Maybe she knew nothing at all about the mineral rights, and maybe, just maybe, Reggie Wade did.

"Does Terry Buckwalter know any of this?" Joanna asked.

Skip Lowell frowned. "She might," he said. "But she isn't supposed to."

Joanna stood up. "Come on, Ernie. We've got to go."

"But I'm not finished—"

"We're finished for the time being," Joanna told him. "We can come back if we need to. For now, there's something else we have to do."

"What the hell is going on?" Ernie growled as he climbed into Joanna's Blazer. "I don't leave off interviews—"

"I think we've found our killer," she said. "Reggie Wade is pushing through a deal to buy out the clinic at something far less than an upper-six-figure figure," Joanna said. "In fact, I think Terry may have already signed papers on this."

"What are you saying?"

"I'll bet Reggie Wade knows all about this mineral-rights deal. Knew it was coming and knew when it was coming."

"You're saying maybe he and Larry Matkin are in this thing together?"

"It's possible."

"So what are we going to do?" Ernie asked.

"Drive down to Douglas and find out," Joanna told him.

Ernie leaned back in the seat, crossed his arms, and closed his eyes. "Sounds good to me," he said. "Wake me when we get there."

20

As they headed east on Highway 80, Joanna could barely contain her excitement. With Ernie Carpenter snoring softly in the passenger seat beside her, Joanna could see that they were about to crack the case wide open.

They didn't have all the answers yet. So far, there were no proved links between Matkin and Wade. Other than Joanna's having seen them together briefly at the Amos Buckwalter funeral, there were no direct connections. But Joanna was confident those would come. They had to.

Once the deal on the clinic closed, Reggie Wade would have bought himself a fortune for the price of a small-town animal clinic. Joanna's fiction-fueled visions of the kindly, humane vet were fast going the way of the goateed composite-sketch artist. All artists didn't wear beards and mustaches, and all vets weren't James Herriot.

The desultory chatter on the radio told Joanna that nothing much was happening in the county. There was a disabled semi blocking the intersection of I-10 and Highway 90. Dick Voland and Jaime Carbajal were still in Elfrida working on the second composite sketch with Matt Bly. And Sheriff Joanna Brady was driving across the Sulphur Springs Valley on her way to solve Bucky Buckwalter's murder.

On either side of the highway, the winter-blackened mesquite stretched for miles. The trees looked as though they were dead forever, but Joanna knew that within weeks—by the middle of February or early March—they would come alive again. Tender young leaves would cover the whole valley floor with a vivid layer of emerald green.

Speaking into the radio, Joanna let Dispatch know that she and Ernie were on their way to Douglas to interview a possible suspect. "Do you want us to notify the city of Douglas so they can work backup?" asked Larry Kendrick.

Joanna looked across at the slumbering Ernie Carpenter. "Negative," she said, answering quietly so as not to disturb him. "At this time it doesn't look as though that's necessary."

She was just passing the Cochise College campus, halfway to Douglas, when another call came over the radio. Joanna could tell from the urgency in the voices that it was something important, but she couldn't quite make out what was being said.

"What is it, Larry?" she asked.

"We've got a problem," he said. "Up in Pinery Canyon in the Chiricahuas. An explosion of some kind. I've contacted Deputies Voland and Carbajal. They were just leaving Elfrida, which puts them better than halfway there."

Something in the tenor of the words punched through Ernie's drowsing consciousness. He shook his head, rubbed his eyes, and was instantly on full alert. "What's going on?" he asked.

"There's been an explosion of some kind," Joanna told

him. "Up in the Chiricahuas. Details are sketchy yet. Here, you handle the radio."

Taking the mike from her, Carpenter pushed the "talk" button. "Okay, Larry. What have we got?"

"A guy named Dennis Hacker called in the report. He was hysterical. At first all he'd say was something about parrots. I couldn't make it out. Finally he calmed down enough to say that somebody had set off an explosion of some kind. Blew up somebody's cabin. Hacker was afraid it would bother his parrots."

"Parrots!" Ernie exclaimed impatiently. "What do parrots have to do with the price of peanuts?"

"Ed Hacker is a naturalist who works for the Audubon Society. He has something to do with parrots—raising them or setting them free or something."

"I know about that," Joanna said. "There was a feature on him in the paper a month or so ago. He's trying to reintroduce parrots into the Chiricahuas. The problem is, the parrots have evidently forgotten how to open pine cones. Before he can release them, he has to teach them the basics. Otherwise they'll starve to death."

Ernie shook his head. "Enough about parrots," he growled. "What do we know about the explosion? Do we know who owns the cabin?"

"We're working on that," Larry Kendrick returned. "It's one of the places on Forest Road 42, but we're not sure yet which one. There are eight or nine cabins located out that way. Hacker's too focused on his birds to know much about his two-legged neighbors."

"Figures," Ernie said.

"What should I tell Deputy Voland? Will you and Sheriff Brady be heading there?"

Ernie looked to Joanna for an answer. She shook her head. "Not right away," she said. "We'll make one quick stop in Douglas first."

Nodding, Ernie passed that information along to Dispatch, then put the microphone back in its clip.

They drove in silence for a moment or two. "By the way," Joanna asked some time later, "are you wearing your vest?"

Looking uneasy, Ernie Carpenter shook his head. "I left it in my car back at the department," he said. "As far as I knew, we were on the way to the hospital to watch somebody do a composite drawing. Why would I need a bulletproof vest there?"

Most of the younger deputies had responded favorably to Joanna's insistence that officers wear Kevlar vests at all times while on duty. Where she had met resistance was from the old guard—from guys like Voland and Carpenter—the very ones who should have known better.

"Besides," Ernie grumbled, "I seem to have gained a little weight. It doesn't fit me like it used to."

"That extra weight is mostly between your ears," Joanna shot back. "Right now we're on our way to interview a possible homicide suspect. Reach into that plastic container that's right behind my seat. I keep Andy's old vest in there, just in case."

"It'll never work," Ernie objected. "I must outweigh what Andy did by a good forty pounds."

"Too bad," Joanna said with considerable lack of sympathy. "You'll just have to suck it in and make it work."

Without another word, Ernie fished out Andy's old vest. He took off his jacket, buckled the vest on outside his shirt, and then put the jacket back on.

"But I can barely breathe in this thing," he objected. "And it's wrinkling hell out of my clean shirt."

"Let that be a lesson, Ernie," Joanna told him. "Spring for the seven hundred bucks and get yourself a new one. Have it custom-made so it fits."

"Seven hundred bucks? Are you kidding?" Ernie groused. "We'll see. It would have to be pretty damned good to be worth that much."

The bullet-resistant-vest discussion had carried them inside the Douglas city limits. Traveling without emergency lights, Joanna drove through town at the posted limits. After all, since Joanna Brady and Ernie Carpenter weren't calling for local backup, there was no need to advertise their presence in someone else's jurisdiction.

Like the Buckwalter Clinic in Bisbee, Wade Animal Clinic on Leslie Canyon Road was outside the city boundaries. North of the county fairgrounds, Joanna turned into the clinic driveway, only to find the way blocked by a homemade sandwich board sign. Hastily written block letters announced that the clinic was closed. Disregarding the sign, Joanna drove around it.

"Looks like nobody's home," Ernie said.

Wade Animal Clinic, like other small town veterinary practices, was part of an all-purpose compound that included both a residence and clinic facility. The clinic, consisting of two cobbled-together mobile homes, sat near the road. The house, a low-slung brick affair with a deeply shaded front porch, sat farther back, nestled in among a grove of towering cottonwoods.

"Maybe not," Joanna said. "There's a pickup parked over by the house. Let's try there first."

She pulled up and parked beside an empty Dodge Ram

pickup. Both Joanna and Ernie opened their respective doors and started to get out of the truck.

"I wouldn't come any closer if I were you."

As one, both Joanna and Ernie returned to the Blazer, leaving the car doors open. "Who said that?" Joanna demanded. "And where did it come from?"

"The porch," Ernie said. "There's somebody sitting there in the shadow." Shifting his weight in the seat, Ernie managed to tug his 9-mm Beretta from an underarm holster. Joanna did the same with her Colt.

She took a deep breath to steady herself. "It's Sheriff Brady and Detective Carpenter," she called through the open door. "We're here to talk with Dr. Wade."

"You're a little late."

The voice was familiar, but Joanna couldn't place it. Just then, the radio crackled to life.

"Sheriff Brady," Larry Kendrick said. "Aren't you on your way to see Dr. Wade down in Douglas?"

"That's right," Ernie responded. "We've got a problem—"

But Kendrick rushed on. "We've got more info on that explosion. The cabin belongs to the same guy—Reginald Wade. A Mazda Miata registered in his name was found outside. So was Terry Buckwalter's T-Bird."

Earlier, in order to hear the radio over the road noise, Ernie had turned up the volume. Now, in the silence of the clinic yard, the transmission was so loud that not only did Joanna and Ernie hear it, so did the man on the porch.

"See there, Sheriff Brady?" Larry Matkin said. "You should have returned my call right away. If you had, maybe you could have prevented some of this. I wouldn't have found out she was playing me for a sucker. Maybe they'd all still be alive."

"Who would be alive?"

"Terry and Reggie, for starters," Matkin answered. "And me, too."

Ducking behind the dashboard so as not to be visible while he did it, Ernie lowered the volume on the radio and then spoke urgently into the mike, giving their location, calling for backup. Meantime, Joanna knew it was her job to keep the man talking.

"But you *are* alive, Larry," she argued.

"Just barely," he said. "And not for long."

"Are you hurt, then?" Joanna asked. "And are you armed?"

"Hurt? You're damned right, I'm hurt. She really did it to me. Pulled the wool right over my eyes. 'Nobody will ever have to know,' she said. 'Once we have the money, they'll never be able to prove a thing.' I trusted her, for God's sake. I believed every word she said."

With one ear, Joanna was trying to make sense of what Larry Matkin was saying. At the same time, she was trying to keep track of what arrangements Ernie was making over the radio.

"Who are we talking about?" Joanna asked. "Terry Buckwalter?"

"Who else?"

"And what are we talking about proving?"

"I did it for her," he said. "I faked all those assay reports. There's ore there, but not as much as I said. The Don Luis site would be better, but she said as long as she and the doc had their money, they'd make sure I'd get a cut and no one would be the wiser."

"What doc?" Joanna asked. "Dr. Wade or Dr. Buckwalter?"

"Funny you should ask," Matkin said with a derisive laugh. "I never thought she'd kill him to get it, but that only goes to show how wrong a guy can be. As soon as Bucky died, I started wondering about it. Everybody seemed to think that guy Morgan did it, but not me. It was just too damned neat. The company attorney is due in town next week to offer a fortune for the mineral rights, and Bucky up and dies. I figured Terry had to be behind it, but I couldn't figure out how she did it. She had to have had some help. She couldn't have done it all by herself, because she wasn't there when he died. She was with me."

"You're saying Terry and Reggie Wade killed Bucky?"

"If you want, I can have Terry tell you herself. You'd like that, wouldn't you?"

By then Joanna's eyes had adjusted enough to the shadows that she could see him sitting there. He reached down and then hauled something up with one hand. At first Joanna thought it was a lifeless mannequin, but then she realized it was Terry Buckwalter, tottering but upright. Her arms were bound to her body by thick strands of rope. There was a gag around her mouth.

"Tell 'em," Larry Matkin said, shoving the gag aside so she could talk. "Go on. Tell Sheriff Brady what you told me."

"Oh, my God!" Terry Buckwalter pleaded. "You've got to help me. He's already killed poor Reggie. He's crazy. He's got dynamite all over the place. Here on the porch, in the house. Dynamite and blasting caps, both. He's going to blow us all to kingdom come."

"Enough!" Larry ordered. "Tell them the rest of it. About

Bucky." Weeping and shaking her head, Terry dropped to her knees.

"Please," she said. "Please."

Somehow, Joanna found her voice. "Come on, Mr. Matkin," she said. "Give yourself up. There's no point in this."

"I can't," he said. "It's too late."

"No, it's not," Joanna argued. "It's never too late."

On the seat beside her, Ernie Carpenter let out a groan. "Shit!" he said.

"What is it?" Joanna asked, glancing in his direction. "What's wrong?"

Ernie was staring into the rearview mirror. "A car just turned in the driveway."

Behind them, a late-model Chrysler New Yorker had pulled up in front of the clinic. An older silver-haired woman, wearing a bright pink pantsuit, got out of the dark blue four-door sedan. As soon as she opened the door, a small gray dog came tumbling out after her. Ignoring her orders to the contrary, the dog went racing over to the sidewalk, where he lifted his leg and peed on a low-lying manzanita bush.

"Buster," the woman wailed, chasing after him. "You come back here right now."

The dog, enjoying the game, paused just out of reach. He waited until the woman was almost on top of him, then he darted off again—running pell-mell toward the house. Toward Larry Matkin, with the woman chasing after him.

There was no time for discussion, only time to react. "I'll get her," Ernie said, peeling out of the rider's side in a roll. He landed on the ground, crouching and running. The dog, expecting a clear field, ran right into him. Ernie scooped the dog up and then continued forward, grabbing the woman by one arm and spinning her around. Dragging her behind him, he headed for cover on the other side of the sedan.

That took no more than a few seconds. When Joanna looked back to the porch, however, Terry Buckwalter was no longer visible. Neither was Larry Matkin. What was visible, though, chilled Joanna to the very marrow of her bones. In the shadowy gloom of the porch, she saw the single flame of a burning match.

It wasn't a question of heroics. The Blazer was still idling. Slinging the gearshift into reverse, Joanna backed away— backed away and then ducked. Just as she disappeared under the dash, the house exploded. Above her she felt the terrible force of the concussion, heard the awful roar. As the force of the blast reached the Blazer, the windshield blew in with a terrible whoosh. Blew in and then blew out the back as the rear and side windows all shattered. Debris came raining down on her back. When at last she could hear again, the only sound was the steady whooping of the Blazer's car alarm.

Scrambling out onto the ground, Joanna looked back at the house.

It was flattened. Thin wisps of smoke coiled up from the wreckage. She turned around in time to see Ernie hand off the squirming dog to his mistress as though it were some kind of living football, then he started toward the house at a dead run.

Joanna stayed with the Blazer long enough to cut off the alarm and notify Dispatch, then she, too, went racing toward the remains of the house. Ernie was on his hands and knees where the porch had been, lifting a bloodied two-by-four and shoving it out of the way.

"Come on," he said grimly. "Matkin is dead, but Terry's under here. She may still be alive."

He was right. Once they pried the debris off Terry, she was still alive. Barely. It would have been best not to move her, but the tinder-dry wood inside the house was quickly catching fire. When they finally got her loose, they each took her by an arm and pulled her free.

Far enough from the house to be out of danger, they laid her down. While Ernie ran to get blankets, Joanna knelt beside her. "Hold on," she said. "Help's on the way."

Terry's lips moved, but with the sirens coming down Leslie Canyon Road and with the increasing roar of the fire in the background, Joanna couldn't hear a word.

"What did you say?" she asked, leaning closer. "I couldn't hear you."

"Tell Jenny . . ."

"Tell Jenny what?"

"Take good care of Kiddo."

"Of Kiddo. What do you mean? I didn't buy that horse."

Terry Buckwalter shook her head. "No," she managed. "Mr. Brady did."

The E.M.T.'s showed up and took charge then. Joanna moved away and went looking for Ernie Carpenter. He was talking to the hysterical woman, who was still clutching her shivering dog.

As Joanna walked up to them, she heard the woman say, "Buster never bites. He must have been scared to death. You're sure he didn't hurt you?"

"No, ma'am," Ernie said. "I'm fine. Not hurt in the least." He saw Joanna coming. Grinning at her, he gave her a thumbs-up sign. "Thanks to Sheriff Brady here, all Buster got for his trouble was a mouthful of Kevlar vest."

21

TERRY Buckwalter died of her injuries before she ever made it to Cochise County Hospital in Douglas. It took Joanna and Ernie Carpenter the whole remainder of the day just to fill out the requisite reports. By the time seven-thirty rolled around, Joanna was ready to bail out on her dinner engagement with Butch Dixon, but she relented finally and agreed to go after all.

Showered and shampooed and wearing fresh clothes, she picked him up at the Grand Hotel just after eight-thirty.

"Our reservation is for nine," he told her. "Everybody said that the best place around is the Rob Roy. That's where we're going."

"Suits me," she said. "Now that I think about it, I'm close to starving."

They drove in silence for several minutes, long enough for her to maneuver the Eagle out of town and onto the highway. She was driving her personal car. The Blazer, with its shattered windows, glass-shredded upholstery and headliner, was currently out of commission.

"How was your day?" she asked.

"Jenny and I had a great time," Butch answered. "When I dropped her and her gear off at her friend's house, I think we were a real hit. Your daughter is now the envy of the neighborhood."

"Good," Joanna said.

"And how's Jenny's mother? I've heard rumors that it's been a little rough in the law-and-order game today."

The words rushed out then, tumbling over themselves in Joanna's need to unburden herself. Had Jenny been around, she would have had to censor what she said, to tiptoe around some of the uglier implications. It was good to have someone grown-up to talk to, someone who cared enough to listen.

"I'm sorry," she said at last, when she finished. "I shouldn't be running on and on like this, but I'm trying to make sense of it all. I'm glad we finally figured out who did it, but I'm embarrassed, too, that I fell for so much of Terry's story. I shouldn't have."

"Why wouldn't you?" Butch said. "You're a truthful person. You tend to believe what other people tell you. That's a fault in all the liars of this world, not a fault in you."

"Still, you're probably bored to tears."

"Not at all," he replied. "I'm trying to add it all up. It turns out that Joanna Brady is smart but naive. She's also sweet and tough. She's a good mother and a good friend. She's full of raw courage backed up by a certain amount of sheer bluff."

Joanna laughed then. "It sounds as though you think I'm an ordinary schizophrenic."

"No," Butch Dixon said quietly. "Not ordinary in any sense of the word. I think you're downright enchanting."

Embarrassed, Joanna could think of nothing else to say.

They drove on into the parking lot of the Rob Roy in total silence.

Even at nine o'clock, the place was still hopping. Joanna and Butch were shown into the bar to wait for their table to be set. Butch looked around at the golf memorabilia decorating the walls.

"Does the pro out here know what happened to his star golfer?" Butch asked.

Joanna nodded. "As soon as Detective Carbajal and Dick Voland came back from Elfrida, Ernie sent his assistant out here to give Peter Wilkes the bad news. I guess he was pretty broken up about it."

They ordered wine—a bottle of Cabernet Sauvignon. "What are you going to do about the horse?" Butch asked.

Joanna shrugged. "Take him, I guess. What choice to I have? Jim Bob and Eva Lou don't have anyplace to keep Kiddo. I do."

"But don't you resent that? Your father-in-law interfering like that—giving Jenny that kind of birthday present without even consulting you about it beforehand?"

Joanna thought for a minute before she answered. "I guess I do resent it," she admitted. "But I know what's going on. Jim Bob and Eva Lou are just trying to make up for Andy's being gone. I guess we all are," she added.

The barmaid brought the wine and was just in the process of removing the cork when Joanna caught sight of her mother. Eleanor Lathrop and George Winfield emerged from the dining room. While George stopped off to visit with someone in the vestibule, Eleanor headed for the rest room.

"Excuse me for a minute," Joanna said to Butch. "That's my mother. I need to talk to her."

When Eleanor stepped out of the stall in the bathroom a

few minutes later, she was astonished to find her daughter standing there, leaning against one of the washbasins.

"Why, Joanna!" Eleanor exclaimed. "What on earth are you doing here?"

"Waiting for you," Joanna said. "I'm here with a friend and saw you and George Winfield come out of the dining room."

Eleanor was clearly flustered. "I'm sorry, Joanna. I meant to call you and talk to you about this. I'm embarrassed that we didn't have—"

"Mother," Joanna interrupted. "Don't worry about it."

"Don't worry?" Eleanor echoed. "But I should have. It's—"

"What you do or don't do isn't any of my business," Joanna said. "It's your life. Live a little."

"But—"

"No buts, Mother," Joanna said firmly. "Now come on. There's someone waiting for me out in the bar, someone I'd like you to meet."

"Is it a he?" Eleanor asked.

Joanna laughed. "Yes, Mother, a he. His name is Butch Dixon. He's a friend of mine."

George Winfield and Eleanor stayed long enough to be introduced, but they left when the hostess arrived to tell Joanna and Butch that their table was ready.

"Have George and your mother been an item for long?" Butch asked.

"I'm only her daughter," Joanna said with a laugh. "How would I know?"

They had an enjoyable dinner, so nice, in fact, that by the time Joanna dropped Butch off at the Grand Hotel, they had agreed on having a picnic lunch the next afternoon. When

Joanna came home and went to bed, she did so with a sense of completion. She had done her job. She had uncovered things about some of her neighbors and acquaintances that she would rather not have known. She had seen the disastrous results that came when people lied and cheated, but she had also tapped into parts of herself—the courage part Butch had talked about—that she hadn't known existed.

When the phone woke her the next morning, she groaned as she picked it up. "What now?"

"Is it true?" Angie Kellogg asked.

"Is what true?"

"What I read in the paper. I stopped off for breakfast and picked up a newspaper while I was at it."

"I'm not sure what's in the paper," Joanna mumbled, turning to look at the clock. It was five after seven.

"About the guy with the parrots," Angie said. "I think Hacker is his name. Age twenty-seven. Is he for real?"

"As far as I know, yes."

"But I've never seen parrots in the wild, only in cages."

"From what I hear, that seems to be the parrots' problem, too."

"Could I go see them? The parrots, I mean."

Angie Kellogg's enthusiasm made Joanna smile. "Sure," she said. "Mr. Hacker would probably be delighted to meet someone who cares as much about birds as he does."

"But how do I find him?"

"Drive up to Pinery in the Chiricahuas, get on Forest Road 42 and ask for the parrot guy. I'm sure someone will be able to tell you where he is."

"I may just do that," Angie said.

Joanna picked Jenny up from Sue Espy's house in time for Sunday school and church. During the service, Jeff Daniels held the quiet Esther on his lap while it took both Joanna and Jenny to keep Ruth corralled. Marianne's Thanksgiving-in-January sermon left not one dry eye in the congregation. During coffee hour afterward, one whole Sunday-school table was stacked high with baby presents.

Over Jenny's objections, Joanna rushed her out of the social hall before she was able to snag a second helping of cake. "What's the hurry?" Jenny asked.

"We're going on a picnic," Joanna replied. "I've ordered a picnic lunch from the Grub-box uptown. It's supposed to be ready by now."

"Where are we going?" Jenny asked.

"It's a surprise," Joanna told her.

As expected, lunch was packed and ready to go. They drove from there to the Grand Hotel where Butch Dixon sat waiting for them in the lobby reading another book—*Smilla's Sense of Snow.*

Once he was in the car, they headed east on Highway 80. "Where are we going?" Jenny asked again, settling into the backseat.

"The Wonderland of Rocks," Joanna said.

"Where's that?" Butch asked.

"In the Chiricahuas. If you look on the map, it's called the Chiricahua National Monument, but locals call it the Wonderland of Rocks."

"It's where Grandpa Lathrop died, isn't it," Jenny asked quietly.

"Yes," Joanna said. As they drove across and up the long valley, Joanna told Butch the story of Big Hank Lathrop's death, about how he had stopped to change a woman's tire and had been run down by a drunk driver while Joanna and her friends had looked on in horror. "And until Friday night," she finished, "I had never been back."

"Not once?" Butch asked. "Not even with Andy?"

"No," Joanna said. "Not even. But I decided this morning that today is the first day of the rest of my life. This was always one of my favorite places. It was silly to put off coming here for so long."

Driving into the monument, they rode past the greasy oil slick where Hal Morgan's Buick had burned to ashes. Joanna said nothing. That was part of her other life. She was determined not to let work intrude on this gloriously clear, wonderfully warm January day.

The first glimpses of the fantastic rhyolite pillars brought gasps of astonishment from Jenny in the backseat.

"This must have been a sacred place to the Indians who lived here," Butch said. "What did they call it?"

Joanna shook her head. "I don't know," she said. "Whatever it was, they probably kept it a secret, and I don't blame them."

Later in the afternoon, after lunch, while Jenny set off to explore one of the trails, Joanna and Butch sat watching a lizard sun himself. Green-and-gray skin made him almost invisible on the lichen-covered rock.

"So what do you think?" Butch asked. "Will Hal Morgan be able to get his life back now?"

Joanna thought long and hard before she replied. The question had more than one layer of meaning. So did her answer.

"I don't know," she said. "It takes time to get over something like that."

"Yes," Butch Dixon said gently, "I'm sure it does."